ALSO BY JANE SMILEY

FICTION

A Dangerous Business
Perestroika in Paris

The Last Hundred Years Trilogy:
Some Luck, Early Warning, Golden Age

Private Life
Ten Days in the Hills
Good Faith
Horse Heaven
The All-True Travels and Adventures of Lidie Newton
Moo
A Thousand Acres
Ordinary Love and Good Will
The Greenlanders
The Age of Grief
Duplicate Keys
At Paradise Gate
Barn Blind

NONFICTION

The Questions That Matter Most
The Man Who Invented the Computer
Thirteen Ways of Looking at the Novel
A Year at the Races
Charles Dickens
Catskill Crafts

FOR YOUNG ADULTS

The Horses of Oak Valley Ranch Series:
The Georges and the Jewels, A Good Horse, True Blue, Pie in the Sky, Gee Whiz

The Ellen & Ned Trilogy:
Riding Lessons, Saddle and Secrets, Taking the Reins

Lucky

Lucky

JANE SMILEY

ALFRED A. KNOPF
New York
2024

THIS IS A BORZOI BOOK
PUBLISHED BY ALFRED A. KNOPF

www.aaknopf.com

Knopf, Borzoi Books, and the colophon are registered trademarks of Penguin Random House LLC.

Library of Congress Cataloging-in-Publication Data
Names: Smiley, Jane, author.
Title: Lucky / Jane Smiley.
Description: First edition. | New York : Alfred A. Knopf, 2024.
Identifiers: LCCN 2023038153 (print) | LCCN 2023038154 (ebook) |
ISBN 9780593535011 (hardcover) | ISBN 9780593535028 (ebook)
Subjects: LCSH: Women folk musicians—Fiction. |
Self-realization in women—Fiction. | LCGFT: Novels.
Classification: LCC PS3569.M39 L83 2024 (print) |
LCC PS3569.M39 (ebook) | DDC 813/.54—dc23/eng/20230926
LC record available at https://lccn.loc.gov/2023038153
LC ebook record available at https://lccn.loc.gov/2023038154

Front-of-jacket photograph by Andrew Oberstadt
Jacket design by Gabriele Wilson

Manufactured in the United States of America
First Edition

—Facts are in books; if you want to know what people feel, it's in music. All the feelings and all the music of the world can be put down in seven notes: do, re, mi, fa, sol, la, ti.

—GABRIEL BYRNE, *Walking with Ghosts*

Part I

I

WHEN I WAS six and my uncle was twenty-four, he did something that you can't do anymore—he took me to a racetrack across the river called Cahokia Downs. That was where I saw horses for the first time—it was 1955, we didn't have a television yet, so I never watched *Roy Rogers* or *My Friend Flicka*. I had no idea why we were there or what we were supposed to do, but Uncle Drew held my hand, bought me an ice cream cone, walked around when the horses were being mounted, and shouted when they were running. After we had been there awhile, he handed me a piece of paper and a pencil and told me to circle some numbers. I circled 4, then 2, then 8. He then handed the paper to a man behind a window along with six dollars (he later told me it was his last six dollars, but I never believed that). He got another piece of paper back, and we went to our seats. We sat quietly, jumped up and down for the race, and then he grabbed my hand and took me back to the window. He handed in the piece of paper, and the man counted out his winnings—$5,986, all in twenties and two-dollar bills. My uncle was grinning from ear to ear. We walked around for a long time, then we went to the parking lot. Just before we got into his car, he squatted down and put his hands on my shoulders. He said, "Don't tell anyone we've been here, or where you got this money. Hide it, save it, and buy something nice someday." He put a folded green pile in my hand. I stuck it in my pocket, and when we got home just before dinner, I went to my room and shoved it under the mattress. A month later, I remembered it, pulled it out, and counted it. It was forty-three two-dollar bills, the $86 that I later realized would tell everyone where he had been and how he had gotten the money. The reason I waited so long was that the day after we went to the races, on Sunday afternoon, my uncle walked in the front door with a puppy, a cocker spaniel. He said it was a present for me, because he knew I wanted a dog, and I did.

Mom and I had no idea how to bring up a puppy. She was a blond cocker spaniel, and I named her Dizzy, maybe a misspelling of "Disney," since *Lady and the Tramp* was the reason I'd wanted a cocker. Mom only took me to see it one time, but it was as though certain pictures were engraved into my brain: the moon shining over puddles in the road, the spaghetti scene, the shadows, trees looming in the background. Once we had my very own "Lady" in our house, Mom set up a gate that kept her in the kitchen most of the time, and spread paper all over the floor to "paper-train" her. It was my job to feed her—Hill's Horse Meat, which we bought in cans, and which stank so much when I opened the can that I could barely stand it. Fortunately for me, since it was my job to make sure Dizzy went outside and did her business, our house on Skinker had a yard—the four houses between ours and Clayton Road had almost no yards. Dizzy would race out the door and tear around in the grass, often so happy that she would forget to do her business and then come back inside and do it in the kitchen. She wanted to get out of the house and explore the neighborhood. The scariest thing she did was run across Skinker into the park. She never once came back when I was looking for her, though a couple of times, I sat down on the hillside that abutted the park, across from an apartment building called the Wiltshire, and she wandered past and decided to come over to me. I handed her the Milk-Bone and snapped on the leash, but that didn't convince her to like me.

Even when I was six, I knew we were lucky, because I heard my relatives talk about where they had lived before. My grandfather was from Akron and lived there much of his life. Grandmother was born and raised in Galesburg, Illinois. Uncle Hank, who was two years younger than Mom, moved to Houston after the war, but he was the only one, and everyone felt sorry for him. Aunt Louise, who married Uncle Drew about six months after he won the money, grew up in Joplin. Everyone in the family except Uncle Hank had come to live in St. Louis around the time I was born, and every one of them acted like they had been stranded and then rescued and brought to St. Louis to recover. For my grandfather and my uncle Drew, the medicine of choice was the Cardinals, and the miracle-working healer was Stan Musial. For Aunt Louise, it was the houses, the neighborhoods, the lawns, the gardens, the parks, the trees. She loved to have me walk along when she pushed my cousin Allison, who was born when I was eight, up and down the streets. I later found out that she knew about the money Uncle Drew had won, and what she was doing when she was taking walks was thinking about where to live and what to buy. They eventually picked a house, one much more beautiful than the one my grandparents lived in.

My mother, maybe like Uncle Hank, wanted to get out. Before we lived in St. Louis, we lived with my father in New York, in an apartment on East Tenth Street across from Tompkins Square Park. She told me about local markets, about pushing me around the park, about how I learned to walk one day and the next day ran across Tenth Street because I saw a cat on the other side. One car was coming; it screeched to a halt, and the driver yelled at my mother, but I did approach the cat, the cat did lie down, roll over, and allow me to scratch its belly.

The problem was that my father was married to someone else, and his family prevailed upon him to go back to his wife. He lived on the Upper East Side. My mother thought she was going to make it on Broadway; she got bit parts in musicals, with a few lines and a chance to sashay across the stage, but there was something about her voice—perhaps her St. Louis accent or our characteristic family squawking sound—that stood in her way. She once said, laughing, that she got a fairly large part in a successful musical—but when she stood downstage, saying her lines, she saw people in the front rows putting their fingers in their ears. That was her last big part, though for a couple more years, she did dance numbers, kicked up her heels, showed off her stride. Once back in St. Louis, she worked for the Muny Opera, first onstage, then in the office, and later for Kiel Auditorium. She got to the point where she didn't envy the actresses and the musicians, but it took a long time. Even so, that place on East Tenth Street remained her dream house—the paneling, the flooring, the tall windows, the proximity to the Village, to Saks and Bergdorf's, the subway, which she preferred to cars. After she came back to St. Louis, she dated a few men, but in the end they didn't interest her, so we continued to live where *I* wanted to live, in a golden brick house on Skinker, across from the park, walking distance from the zoo and the museums, just down from the Hi-Pointe Theatre.

I knew what my father looked like, because my mother had a small photograph of him that I found in a drawer in her room. He looked like me. When I was in New York in 1969, I saw him on the street, followed him into Zabar's, stood behind him at the counter, bumped elbows with him. He glanced at me, half-frightened, half-angry, and moved away. I ordered the same sandwich he did—pastrami on rye, with a touch of mustard. It was delicious. Perhaps I saw his wife, too. I also discovered (because he had an unusual name, my name—Rattler) where his three children went to school. When yearbooks went online, I managed to look at their yearbook photos. Of all of us, I am the only one who looked like him.

OUR HOUSE WAS fairly large, so Aunt Lily and Cousin Brucie moved in when they "came back from Springfield as quick as she could," and a few friends came and went as their circumstances rose and fell. Did Mom like or dislike having her sister or a friend in the spare bedroom, using the single bathroom, cooking what they liked in the kitchen? There was no way of knowing. She accepted. That's what she did. My grandparents lived on a street in Webster Groves, five doors up from the railroad embankment. There was something interesting in every direction—Deer Creek, the candy cabinet at the grocery store, the school playground, a small park, the railroad tracks themselves, other kids running here, there, and everywhere.

Uncle Drew and Aunt Louise moved into a "plantation style" house with a wraparound front porch, lots of trees, and a sandbox in the backyard, on Argonne, in Kirkwood. It had a bigger lawn, more trees and flowers, and that neighborhood was a wonderful display of different types of houses. Aunt Louise would point at them, say "Colonial," "Mission style," "Craftsman." On Argonne a huge, elegant house with a hedge might be across the street from a tiny one-floor dump. My friend Leslie lived in one of those. Leslie said that the house next door to theirs was haunted, and I believed her, since it was dark brown and surrounded by trees, and the old woman who lived there would shoo us off her lawn even if we weren't actually on her lawn.

Leslie used every visit I made to Uncle Drew and Aunt Louise as an opportunity to come over and play, because she loved their house. She told me that someday she would own this very house, that she would do anything to have it. When I invited her to come to the house that I loved, she would sniff and say, "This is nice." But the main thing I loved about all three houses was the chance to walk walk walk around the neighborhoods, smell the gardens, look at the trees, stare at the other houses.

I was also quite fond of my cousin Brucie. Brucie was older than I was, even though Aunt Lily was younger than Mom. Aunt Lily had a much harder time finding a job when she came to St. Louis than Mom did, because she couldn't help talking back. Eventually, she did manage to hold down a job at a restaurant across from Bettendorf's. She worked as a server, and she developed her habit of talking back into good-natured joking: "I'll have the roast beef and the baked potato." "Really? You might regret that." Big grin. Or, "Pardon me, you forgot to order the Baked Alaska I told them to save for you." Easygoing laugh. Aunt Lily and Brucie eventually moved into a house that was on St. John. Aunt Lily would say, "AT LEAST there are three bedrooms!" Or, "AT LEAST there are a lot of children around." Compared to Uncle Drew's house, or Mom's, or even my grandparents' house, the St. John house was a shack, but, as always in St. Louis, it was surrounded by new houses, old houses, nice houses, wrecks.

DID MOM HAVE a right to Mr. Rattler's name? I am sure not. But in order to move back to St. Louis and avoid scandalizing everyone, she could not share my grandparents' name, Roberts. She made sure that people she didn't know very well called her "Mrs. Rattler" or "May Rattler," even though Grandmother and Grandfather still called her "Martha Roberts," her given name. It was Brucie who told me what a rattler was—at one point when we were staying overnight with my grandparents, he took me down to Deer Creek and led me through the woods, telling me he was going to find one, just to show me. Luckily, he didn't find one (though he said that the rattle would be so loud that we could hear it from ten feet away). "Rattlesnake" was the first thing I looked up in the fall of fourth grade, when the man who sold World Book encyclopedias stopped by and talked Mom into buying a set, just for me. He helped her install them on the lowest shelf of my bookcase, across from my bed. Each volume was so heavy that instead of reading it in bed, as I did the Hardy Boys and the Boxcar Children, I laid it on the rug, crossed my legs, and leaned over it, turning the pages one by one. After rattlesnakes, I looked up horses, cats, dogs, rabbits, parakeets, and each entry led me to others nearby, like hell, Congo, Dostoevsky, railroad, opera.

Every spring, Uncle Drew took me to the Father/Daughter Dinner at school. Mom dressed me up, and of course Uncle Drew was perfectly turned out. Because it was in the spring, the sunlight would be just beginning to fade as we walked to the school, always the long way there and the short way home—over to Clayton, then down Alamo Alley to De Mun, then along the sidewalk past the green grass and under the flowering trees to Northwood. Up Northwood to the school, Uncle Drew telling me about trees or bricks. We ate our dinner, listened to the principal give his talk, then walked home in the dark, past the apartment buildings on Skinker, a walk I was used to, since that's how I went to school in the mornings. No one at the dinner looked at us askance, wondering where Mr. Rattler was. The ones who recognized Uncle Drew nodded to him, and the ones who didn't admired his suit, and also his alligator slip-ons.

When I visited Aunt Lily and Brucie on St. John, Brucie and I always went across the street to a much newer house, where we played with the Johnson boys, Fred and Dan. They had the best trees to climb, and we climbed them over and over—Brucie always got almost to the top and I always stayed two or three limbs from the bottom. Brucie often threatened to launch himself out of the tree, but he never did. Fred, who was my age, maybe eight at the time, did fall out of the tree, breaking his arm. Once it healed, we were all over the tree again. What I learned from the St. John neighborhood was that some people were luckier than others. Some of the kids were Black, some were white, some had fathers, some didn't, some ran faster than others, some read more books, some excelled at slapjack, some never won a penny.

My best friend in that bunch of kids was Diana, the only other girl, an avid reader. I remember asking her lots of questions—why didn't she come to the swimming pool, why was she always reading the same book, why didn't she like ponies, why did she wear mismatched socks? She shrugged. It was Brucie who told me—Negroes weren't allowed in the swimming pool, and maybe not the library, either (he didn't know for sure); she didn't have a television (Mom had finally bought one for us) and so had never seen a pony; and her mom could afford only three pairs of socks at the beginning of the school year (or that was what Aunt Lily said). I began giving Diana books, saying that I'd read them and didn't have room to keep them, but I couldn't figure out how to give her socks. She went to Bristol, I went to De Mun, Leslie went to Keysor. Even then, I thought that the best thing about running around all of these neighborhoods was that when the girls in one neighborhood happened to be mean to me, I always knew that I could beg for a visit to Grandmother, or Aunt Lily, or Uncle Drew, get out of the house, and meet up with an entirely different girl, who would be nice to me, at least for a while.

THE MONTGOMERYS, a family who lived near my grandparents, had eight kids, five boys and three girls. The children all had some chores, but when they'd finished them, they could do as they pleased as long as they were home by dark. If they got into trouble, they were whipped—sometimes the line of the ones to be whipped went down the hall. The boys I played with didn't seem to resent the whippings, but they also did whatever they wanted to pretty much all day long in the summer and whenever they were out of school the rest of the year. Their house had a big side yard. When I was around, I played tag with them, or statues. Once I did walk down to the railroad tracks with Billy Montgomery, who was about Brucie's age. I was afraid to walk up the embankment, for fear that a train would zip by and suck me under (I know now that the trains were only commuter trains, and that at that spot where I was describing what I feared, they had already slowed down for the nearby station). Billy showed me how far I had to stand away from the tracks in order to not be sucked under—it was about eight inches. Billy spent a lot of time down at Deer Creek, fishing for carp and sunfish.

Billy's family was the largest—most of the ones I knew had four children, and so wherever I went to play, there were crying babies and out-of-control toddlers. Mom's house was a quiet refuge of books and music (someone, and let's say it was my father in New York, sent her a record player that played stacks of 45s). Since she worked at the Muny, she especially loved the soundtracks of musicals. Maybe her favorite was *My Fair Lady,* which she got to see in New York when the Muny sent her there to check it out (the Muny was an outdoor theater, so they only operated in the summer). The stack of records was played so often that the tunes and the lyrics were etched into my brain. "What a fool I was, what an addle-pated fool," "Just you wite, 'Enry 'Iggins!," "In America, they haven't used it for years."

Eventually, a traveling company did come to Kiel Auditorium, and Mom took me to see it onstage (dressed in my best dress, the petticoat pricking my waist over and over).

My grandparents' house was small—three bedrooms and a back porch upstairs, a living room, a dining room, and a kitchen downstairs, which was the reason that when Aunt Lily and Brucie had had to find a place to stay, Mom's house was their only choice. But for dinners and parties, my grandparents came first, because my grandmother was a wonderful cook (it seemed like the phrase Mom used most often was "I forgot to go to the store!" followed by "Oh, dear, I didn't get the—") who specialized in fried chicken and beef stew, my grandfather's favorites, followed by sugar cookies and homemade ice cream, my grandmother's favorites. There was a piano, and after the dishes were washed, my grandmother played while my grandfather and any relatives who might be around sang the traditional songs that they loved. My grandfather had a beautiful baritone voice—"baritone" was a word I learned before I understood anything about music. The songs he sang crept into my mind, too—"Oh, Shenandoah," "Tenting Tonight," "The Bonnie Blue Flag," "Red River Valley." My grandmother had a smooth way of playing along, lots of arpeggio. Aunt Lily and Aunt Louise had good voices that melded well, and they liked singing with Grandfather. Pretty much every dinner was followed by a half an hour of singing. After that, my grandfather would take a couple of decks of cards out of one of the drawers in his desk and play a few hands of bridge, which my mother liked. Grandmother never played cards—she would sit down with her knitting. Brucie and I preferred 21 or five-card stud, and Grandfather liked that. He would get out the poker chips, teach us various strategies, and tell us stories about the time he won a hundred bucks on a triple or lost every penny only to win it back the next evening. Across the street and a few doors down, there was a woman who taught piano lessons in her walk-out basement. I took lessons from her for about two years, but I didn't practice much, and so didn't learn much.

On Sundays, grandfather sang in the church choir, and so he

would also walk around the house, singing the hymn he was working on to himself, but loudly enough for us to enjoy it. When he was at work during the day, Grandmother would play the piano for her own pleasure, but the music had no words, so I don't know what she was playing. If I happened to spend the night there on a Friday (Did Mom have a date? No one ever said), we would watch *The Lawrence Welk Show,* and sometimes Grandfather would sing along. When he came to Mom's house to listen to the record player, he would put on Paul Robeson's version of "St. Louis Blues." This convinced me that in St. Louis, music was everywhere, and since I loved music, I believed it. Another Robeson song that he played was "Ol' Man River," and Grandfather liked to sing it as we drove around town, though not in as low a key as Robeson. The windows of the car would be down, and I'm sure everyone we drove past could hear him belt out, "But Ol' Man River, he just keeps rollin' along." He didn't sing the next part, so I never knew that it was a protest song until I was older and saw *Show Boat* on TV. He also didn't have the voice for "Deep River," but he liked playing the recording.

When I walked with Grandmother to the grocery store (not a supermarket), my payment for helping her carry the bags home was a strip of Dots or a few jelly beans from the penny candy cabinet. She loved going to the grocery store and seemed to know everyone we passed on the way. She would wave and smile and call out, "How are you? Lovely day!" or pause, set down the bags, and exchange a few tidbits of gossip. Gossip was rife in our family, too, but it wasn't mean gossip—it was some story about the time Uncle Drew, maybe six, got stuck in the creek and had to wait an hour, or two hours, or all afternoon (probably ten minutes), for Grandfather to find him and pull him out (and Grandfather would imitate the loud sucking sound the boots had made). And then there was the time Mom was four, and Grandmother found her on the roof "waiting for a breeze," as Mom said. The drop at the bottom of that particular roof was eighty feet, since the house was on a cliff. ("Well," said Mom, "it looked like a cliff to me, but it was really just the lean-to. If it had been more than six feet, Daddy wouldn't have had to duck his head every time he went in or out of that door.") Or there was that dog they had, some sort of shepherd. One day, Grandmother was outside behind the house, filling the water bucket at the well, and here came the dog, wagging his tail, carrying Uncle Drew, who was still sleeping. The dog had picked him up by the blanket he was swaddled in. Uncle Drew was maybe a month old. Of all the unlikely stories they told us (with a laugh), this seems the most unlikely to me now, but they swore it was true, and since whenever someone told it, I could picture it, I sort of believed them. Singing songs and telling stories and having a good meal seemed to be what my grandparents did, and had done all their lives. Of course, I later learned everything was more complicated than that—it had to be—but that's what made their house a refuge, while our house remained something like a convenient hotel.

EVERY SO OFTEN, Leslie would say, "Gee, you're so lucky." I assumed that she was talking about Uncle Drew's house, but as soon as she said that word, I would think of the bet at the racetrack, the $86, and the fact that I was never ever supposed to say anything about it. As a rule, whenever anyone said that word, "lucky," I would automatically press my lips together, as if Uncle Drew's secret would pop out in spite of my wishes. Yes, Leslie was obsessed with his house, but usually, she wasn't talking about the house—she might be talking about the brown and white saddle shoes my mother had gotten for me (handsome, but hard to break in), or the fact that my hair was thick and hung below my shoulders (as it required a lot of fed-up brushing by Mom and elicited repeated threats of a "pixie cut," I was not sure that my hair was an example of luck). The time that I remember the most clearly is when we were playing in her sandbox. It was a Saturday afternoon in the spring—as she was saying this, I was looking up at their blossoming dogwood tree, thinking that I liked the fragrance, though some other kids didn't. Her mother came out of the kitchen door with the remains of the baloney sandwich Leslie had left on her plate. Mrs. Curtis stood in front of Leslie with her hands on her hips while Leslie, scowling, ate the rest of the sandwich. She then handed Leslie a napkin, watched while she wiped her mouth, shook her head, took the napkin, and marched back into the house. Leslie asked me what I had had for lunch, and I said a peanut butter and strawberry jam sandwich. She said, "Did you eat all that sandwich?"

I said, "Most of it, I guess."

"You don't have to clean your plate?"

I shook my head. We kept making little mounds in the sand, setting small blocks on the tips, watching to see how they slid off.

"Your mom never talks about the starving Armenians?"

I said, "Who are they?"

She didn't answer.

We went on playing, and I didn't think about this conversation again until the middle of the night, when I woke up and remembered the money. The money was still there, hidden. I got out of bed, down on my hands and knees, reached my arm under the edge of the mattress. I could feel it. I pulled it out, dusty, but still intact, rolled up in a rubber band, green and sturdy. Right then, I knew I was lucky that Mom hated housework and would never bother to sweep under the bed. I put the money back where it was stored, got under the blanket. As I fell asleep, I thought I could feel it beneath me, reassuring and, in a sense, warm.

THAT WINTER, in February, almost everyone talked about luck, because two days before my tenth birthday, a big tornado swept through the county and the city. Brucie, of course, had something to say when I saw him at Grandmother's for dinner the evening before it struck. He told me that the fact that it was so hot was a bad sign. I asked why, and he said the word "tornado." I considered the word "tornado" terrifying—we often had watches and warnings, saw the sky turn green, ran to the basement. All the way home after dinner, I pestered Mom to let us sleep there. The basement of the Skinker house was pretty dank, so Mom was reluctant, but in the end, we took some blankets down the stairs, and she pulled out an old single mattress that one of her friends who had stayed with us brought, and we cuddled up on it as best we could. I would have to say that because the windows of the basement were small, and faced east, we heard a few gusts, but not enough to distract us from my constant waking, and her constant attempts to lull me back to sleep. In the morning, we went upstairs and looked toward the park—some limbs down, one small tree, branches scattered in the road, no cars anywhere, sirens.

What Brucie told me when he and Aunt Lily came over that evening was much stranger—St. John was a dead-end road off Kirkham, just down from Old Orchard, in Webster, where Brucie and I were allowed to go for knickknacks or candy. The tornado had gone straight down Kirkham and into the city. Brucie had actually been awake when it passed—he heard a long gust of wind, and some cracking sounds. He looked out the window, couldn't see anything. He said, "I knew it was a tornado, though." He didn't even think of waking Aunt Lily, and she slept through the whole thing. Brucie told me how narrow a tornado could be—no wider than a car, he said. You could watch it go by and the curtains on your open window might not even be fluttering. Somehow, I was more frightened by his story than ours, though we later found out that the tornado was much stronger by the time it passed us. People were killed, houses were destroyed—one woman, we heard, woke up to the sight and sound of her roof blowing away. Everyone was related to or knew someone who had suffered at least damage, and sometimes destruction. Brucie wanted to look at the pictures in the paper, I did not. Leslie knew all about the tornado, too, and couldn't stop pestering her parents to find another place to live, one with a basement. Like where I lived, lucky me. Mom's office was not far from where the worst destruction happened—some windows were broken, but the roof held on. When she got home from work the first day she went back, she hugged me really hard and said that she was so happy I'd gotten her to sleep in the basement, because according to what everyone said, the path of the tornado had been down past the Hi-Pointe Theatre, then across to the other side of Forest Park. She said, "We were so lucky." After she said that, I went into my room and sat on the floor by the bed with Dizzy in my lap and made a vow never to spend that roll of two-dollar bills—that was where the luck lived, I thought.

Uncle Drew continued to do well, so well that both Grandmother and Grandfather sometimes said, quietly, as if it was a secret, "He was always the smart one." He changed jobs twice, both times for something more lucrative. Eventually, he was in charge of the shoe storage warehouse downtown, and was making enough money to think about moving out of Kirkwood. He and Aunt Louise disagreed, though—she wanted to look around a couple of miles north of their place, in Huntleigh, and he wanted to try the Central West End, which was closer to work. Aunt Louise found a house she loved on Countryside Lane, and I could see why—the road weaved around through the hills and had so many trees that it looked like you could go for a wonderful walk without ever leaving the property. Countryside Lane seemed to me like a vacation when they took me to see it (and the long white fence!). Uncle Drew took us to Westminster Place, and showed us around an "ornate brick mansion" with a circular tower set into the west side of the house. I imagined them giving me my own room, up by the pointed roof of the tower. The funny part was that when they took me to these places, Allison would come along. She walked around and didn't say anything, but she scowled constantly.

In the end, they couldn't decide, and agreed that they did love their place on West Argonne; after all, that was where they began their lives together, and why leave that behind? And Allison said, over and over, "Stay! Stay here!," and then ran to her room and slammed the door. But Uncle Drew was itching to spend his money. He was afraid of something he called a "recession" (Brucie explained to me that a recession was when all the money you thought you had disappeared, and I said, "You mean like, flew out the window?" and he stared at me as if I was an idiot). I said nothing about my $86, but decided to find a rock or a brick and set it on top of the roll of bills.

What Uncle Drew did was go to Mom and ask her, behind my back, where she might like to send me to school.

School, in St. Louis, is a big question, especially high school. Whenever you meet someone else from St. Louis, no matter where you are, the first words out of your mouth are "So where did you go to high school?" My theory about this is not that the person who asks wants to judge you for your socioeconomic position, rather that he or she wants to imagine your neighborhood, since there are so many, and they are all different. When Uncle Drew approached Mom, it was shortly after the tornado (if the tornado had anything to do with it, I don't know). I was in fourth grade. The end of sixth grade seemed to me to be eons away, but Uncle Drew was nothing if not a planner-ahead, and Mom appreciated that. My understanding later was that she considered various options for the next year, until the spring of fifth grade. Then she had to make a decision. One option was Soldan, which was too far away to walk to from our house, but not far from her office at the Muny, straight down Union Boulevard, and because when she was growing up, she had to walk six miles to school, uphill all the way there and back, it wasn't much (she always laughed when she told me this). One reason she loved Soldan was that Agnes Moorehead and Virginia Mayo had gone there, and so had Tennessee Williams, for a year. She pointed Agnes out to me once on TV and later when she took me to see *Pollyanna*. I admit I was unimpressed, because I had my eye on Hayley Mills. She said she wished she had gone there with "Virginia," as she called her, because the two of them were about the same age. We walked past it a few times. It was a beautiful and intimidating building, but the problem was that it was a high school—I had to go somewhere else for two years before I could go there, and she couldn't decide which one. Where we lived was definitely a problem. There would be school buses, but that could be complicated, too. And then she started working for Kiel Auditorium, and walking down Union to the offices at the Muny was no longer an option.

Uncle Drew must have given her the idea, because in the late winter of sixth grade, I found myself taking a test for entrance to a school called John Burroughs that I had never heard of, that no one in my family had gone to, and that was in a neighborhood we never drove around in. I later discovered that it was about this time that Soldan, which had been integrated, apparently with no problems, along with all the other schools in St. Louis in 1954, was becoming predominantly African American. I had no idea what Mom or Uncle Drew said about this. I never heard any of my family using the N-word or being unfriendly toward Black people. When I was at Aunt Lily's with Brucie, Diana and the boys came in and out of the house all the time, and I went to their house, too. Aunt Lily would sit in a chair on Diana's lawn, gossiping and laughing with Diana's mom. Diana, in fact, loved to come on a Saturday morning and watch *My Friend Flicka* with me on TV (she now knew what a pony was and wanted one, just as I did). If it was time for lunch, Aunt Lily served sandwiches to whoever was around because she was afraid that without something to eat, someone would faint and fall out of a tree (no one ever did). At any rate, I took the test. Mom was happy when I got in, and I was relieved—school started a little later in the morning there, and even though it went on till after four every day but Wednesday, I preferred not getting up at six thirty in order to get on the school bus to get there.

I didn't think about it much until sometime in the early summer, when I mentioned it to Leslie, and she said, "You are so lucky."

I said, "Why?"

"That's the best school! All the smart kids go there!"

I said, "You should go there."

She said, "I can't. I have to go to a Catholic school now." Her parents were taking her out of Avery, nearby, and sending her to Mary Queen of Peace, across town. Their goal was Nerinx Hall, or even St. Louis U. High.

I can't say that what she said about John Burroughs and the smart kids made me happy. I assumed that I wouldn't fit in, and so I didn't look forward to it. I let Mom distract me by sending me to summer camp in northern Wisconsin.

Looking back, I'm sure she was glad to get rid of me. Over the years, among our many visitors, there had, of course, been men, single men. Some of them were actors who came to town for a show at the Muny—one of them was Andy Devine, whom I knew from *Andy's Gang,* which I had seen on TV. Another was Bob Hope himself, who was sitting in the living room late at night and smiled at me when I came downstairs for a drink of water. No doubt there were plenty of actors who passed through St. Louis that Mom knew from her days in New York. It took me a long time to realize that some of the men might have been ones she was dating, and I am sure that by the time she sent me to camp, first for two weeks, then, in the following years, for seven weeks, she had decided that even though she wasn't going to marry again, she needed some time to have a decent affair. She was getting close to forty, and maybe she thought that her flirtation clock was running out.

I had been to a few places by that time—down to the Ozarks for two weeks of camp beside the Current River, up to Chicago to visit some of Aunt Louise's relatives, and, of course, according to Mom, New York (though I had no memory of that). It took two long train trips to get to the camp in Wisconsin, by way of Chicago on my own, then to northern Wisconsin with some of the other girls. Though they had been there, they didn't warn me about what I would find: a huge, beautiful lake, vast trees, a wilderness of hills and paths, and, amazingly, cool weather—sweaters and blankets at night rather than throwing off the covers and panting. Some of the cabins were by the shore of the lake, but mine was on a long island that stretched in a curve away from the shore. The cabin was small—four narrow beds jammed into a hut with cracks between the planks—but it was comfortable, and the small size meant that we could whisper to one another as we were falling asleep, the pines overhead tapping the roof of the cabin as the breeze came and went.

What I loved most was that after lunch and dinner, we sat at our assigned tables and sang. One of the counselors played the piano over in the corner, and another one stood up and, in some sense, directed us, or at least waved her hand. We had little books of songs, but it only took about a week to memorize them—most of the songs were rewritten folk songs that promoted loyalty to the camp: "Jack's camp sisters never die, dem bones gonna rise again, bust 'em in the jaw, crack 'em in the eye, dem bones gonna rise again! You tell 'em, sister, you tell 'em, sister, you tell 'em, sister, dem bones gonna rise again." I had no idea it was a spiritual and had never heard it before. We sang it loudly and with determination—and it turned out that the owner of our camp was a single woman and a longtime feminist.

Canoeing in the lake was fun. The stern paddler steered the canoe and the bow paddler was the lucky one—all she had to do was keep paddling and looking ahead. If I looked into the distance, I could see the water shining at the horizon or banks of muddy shore covered by trees. If I looked down, I could see the flicker of a carp or a trout slipping through the water, or flies and moths. Once I saw a fish of some sort, not too far away, rise out of the water and grab something.

The other girls were nice, and I don't remember a single one of them. I think that the counselors kept us so busy that we got into the habit of working together to paddle the canoe or clear the table or clean up our cabins, so that we couldn't ensnare one another in bullying or gossip. By the time I got back to St. Louis, I thought I was ready for the smart kids, come what may.

2

THERE WERE three students at my new school who lived on the other side of the park, in the Central West End, who agreed to let me join their carpool. One of them, I found out when we went to pick them up, lived two houses down from the house with the tower, which was now owned, they said, by a family who had moved from Chicago. The two boys who lived at that house went to Country Day, which, I was told, was Burroughs's big football rival. The drive from our house took about ten minutes, down Clayton Road to Price, then right on Price. I enjoyed the drive—I always looked out the window and listened to the other kids, two girls and a boy, talk about football (our team was called the Bombers) and the Cardinals. The first part of the drive was familiar—tall trees and brick houses, a few walled-in spaces that were schools or convents, I thought, then stores and restaurants and Stix, where my mom loved to shop, then, suddenly, what seemed to me a truly strange and deadly-quiet area where the houses (also brick) hid in the rolling landscape, far from the road. This was Ladue.

The campus of the school was not like any school I'd ever seen before. The driveway ran up along a hill to a sand-colored building with lots of windows and balconies. The perimeter was not marked by fenced-in concrete playgrounds. There were hills, tennis courts, a football field, and hockey fields. I paid more attention to the trees than to the other kids. The two girls I carpooled with were nice enough—they would smile at me, or ask me what I thought of Miss

Fieselman. If they had muffins for the trip to school, they would offer me one.

It took me about two weeks to realize that for some unknown reason, I had been put in the A-section classes in English, arithmetic, and social studies. Mom had never said anything about how I did on the test. When she seemed so happy that I'd gotten in, I had assumed that getting in was the most surprising thing. We had assigned seats. As an "R," alphabetically, I sat toward the rear of the class, so I could see the students in front of me taking copious notes, nodding their heads, apparently following the lecture/discussions that we had. English was okay until we got to *Old Yeller* and I had to imagine rabies. In arithmetic, the teacher's voice seemed to be pounding in my ear. In social studies, I sometimes fell asleep, but I loved to do the homework. I also took French, and in French, I listened to one of the boys, and imitated his accent. As for science, memorizing the periodic table was a little like memorizing the words to a song with many verses. Was I lucky to be going to this school?

Yes, because I loved Junior Chorus. Boys and girls from seventh through ninth grade met four times a week—one time after school on Wednesday—to practice singing for the Fall Recital, the Christmas Program, and the Spring Recital. Our teacher played the piano and directed us from his seat. All of the students took music, but if you wanted to be in the chorus, you had to audition, which meant that Mr. W. asked you what song you would like to sing, and then accompanied you on the piano while you sang it. I chose "Oh, Shenandoah," which Grandfather had engraved in my brain. Mr. W. nodded, put me in the alto section. I saw at once that it was the sopranos who got to sing solo, but I didn't mind. Once again, I was up in the back, lucky to watch and listen. In the chorus, we didn't sing hymns, as my grandfather did, or what I now knew was folk music—we sang Beethoven, Mendelssohn, and Mozart. I knew something about them because of the woman who gave piano lessons in her walk-out basement down the street from my grandparents', but I had been the sort of student who would play the first page of "Für Elise" over and over because I loved the tune but fail to get past the middle of page 2.

Singing was much easier. We held pieces of paper with the words written out, our teacher led the way with his piano, and I was surrounded by older kids who sang melodiously in my ears and knew how to follow instructions. About this time, Aunt Lily bought Brucie a guitar, maybe to keep him out of trouble. Everyone had radios, and we all listened to KMOX. I loved "I Fall to Pieces"; Brucie loved "Runaway"; I loved "Hit the Road Jack"; he loved "Will You Love Me Tomorrow." He spent a lot of time practicing "Johnny B. Goode" but only told me about Chuck Berry in a low voice, because, he said, Chuck Berry had gotten in trouble for doing something that I wouldn't understand. Even though I didn't practice the piano, when I went to Brucie's, I did practice singing along with him as he worked out the versions of the songs he could figure out how to play—he wasn't the sort of guy to take lessons, he always had to do it on his own, "by ear," he said. When we sang for Aunt Lily, she would clap, and when we sang for Mom, she would laugh, but, as she said, "with you, not at you."

Another thing Mr. W. did was form a recorder group for those of us who wanted to play some sort of instrument but didn't have the patience—or the talent—to play something complicated, like a flute or a violin. The good thing about playing recorders was that first you learned to play the soprano one, which was in the key of C. Reading the music was like reading the music of a song. As we got older (and taller), we bought alto recorders, which were in the key of F. Eventually, we might try the tenor, which was back in the key of C and had the most beautiful tone but was the hardest to play. I did practice the recorder—beginning with a high squeal that made the birds fly off the roof, then moving on to something listenable, even by Mom, who was an experienced critic. Mom's specialty in the theater hadn't been music, rather acting and dancing, but she had heard so much music over the years that she had opinions that flickered across her face every time she listened to anyone, even Grandfather.

I kept my eye on her, and saw that she eventually came to enjoy my playing and my singing with Brucie. And it was a passion that got me through the ever-more-complicated things we were supposed to learn about—Manifest Destiny, *Oliver Twist, Three Men in a Boat,* long rows of multiplication and division, as well as ions, gravity, field hockey, soccer, and softball.

Brucie shot up. I was the only person who still called him Brucie. He had lots of friends and was very handsome. He started using some sort of gel on his hair and combing it into a ducktail. He was much handsomer than Steve McQueen or Elvis Presley, slender and supple, but with developing shoulders, still full of information. I could tell that I had the better voice, though—maybe because of our Junior Chorus practice, I didn't go off-key as often as he did.

I made it through seventh grade. In the Christmas recital, I sang the second verse of "Angels We Have Heard on High"—Mary L. sang the first verse in soprano, I sang the second verse ("Shepherds, why this jubilee?") in alto, David sang the third verse in tenor, and John, who had a booming voice that seemed to explode over the heads of the audience, sang the last verse in bass. Then the whole chorus sang the refrain. In the Spring Recital, the quartet was "The Evening," by Brahms. It lasted a little more than three minutes, and took us weeks of practice, but got lots of applause.

I GOT TO BE thirteen. Brucie was fourteen, not a pimple on his face, and fortunately still obsessed with his guitar, but girls would come by his house every few days "just to say hi." They would always be dressed perfectly, and would also be wearing makeup (at least mascara and lipstick). I didn't like the girls, and was jealous of them, too, but one of them did Brucie a big favor—she introduced him to her brother, already in high school (at Webster), who had formed a band and needed a rhythm guitar player. The band called themselves the Big Muddies. The girl (and her brother) lived a few minutes' walk away from St. John, in one of the nice houses on North Gore not far from the one Uncle Drew had considered, that was surrounded by lawns and shacks just like Aunt Lily's on St. John. There were two ways to get there (not including climbing over the back fence)—down to Kirkham, past the church, up Dornell, or another block to North Gore, then up that hill. The girl, whose name was Linda, turned out to be nice, and eventually got a boyfriend, but it wasn't Brucie. It was a guy who had a car ('55 Ford), a driver's license, and an after-school job at a car wash. His name was Joe. Sometimes, he would take Brucie; Linda's brother, Dan; and me to the drive-in for a movie. Brucie, Dan, and I would sit in the front seat, eating popcorn, and Linda and Joe would make out in the back seat. I would occasionally sneak a peek, but if I did, Brucie would elbow me so that I would turn around and watch the movie.

When school ended, I headed off to camp again. What I knew I would miss most at camp was singing with Brucie, and I sincerely hoped that he wouldn't get into trouble while I was gone. There was a boys' camp across the lake from our girls' camp, but Aunt Lily didn't have the money to send Brucie there, and I doubt he would have gone if she had. The forests and the lake and the sunsets and the sky were exactly the same as the previous year. I was put into another cabin deeper into the island. It was larger and had a good view of the lake. Our canoe trips were longer—two nights, three days, now. I was old enough to appreciate the food they served, as well as the singing, and one day, at the end of the after-lunch singing, one of the other girls, who had shot up over the winter and whom the other girls (behind her back) called "the Beanstalk," leaned across the table and said, "Wow! You have a great voice!" That was my first compliment ever, and I cherished it, thinking about it during rest period and after we went to bed. Mr. W. didn't give compliments, and neither did Mom. I now think that they didn't want to encourage me—they wanted me to find my own way.

I got home in mid-August, Mom's busiest time at the Muny. Mom got me two tickets to *The Music Man,* one for the first week of the show, down in the pit, and one for the second week, up toward the balcony. I hadn't seen the movie, because I was at camp when it came out, but plenty of people in the audience had, so I was surrounded by intermittent chitchat about how this production compared to the movie. The Muny had a big stage, so it was a good place to bring on a sizable cast. Like everyone else, I enjoyed the marching scene, and could not prevent myself from mouthing the words to "Seventy-Six Trombones." I recognized the man who played Harold Hill—Mr. Smith. He would come to our house sometimes, and Mom would say, "Mr. Smith has to go to Washington!" at which point they would laugh and I would completely not understand why that was funny. The beat of "Seventy-Six Trombones" was so strong that it was all I could do not to jump out of my seat and march around. When I was in the pit the first time, I kept my eye on the actresses, not exactly on how they acted, but on how they opened their mouths. I would look back and forth from one to the other as they were singing. The one with the deeper voice and better vibrato (I loved that word) would thrust her chin forward, turning her mouth into something of a trombone, or even a saxophone. Her voice seemed to come up under the voices of the others and resonate with theirs. I loved it.

As for Brucie, he had decided to try out for the football team at his school, and had gotten on the team as a substitute end, since he was a fast runner (the year before he had done fall track). Even in the heat and humidity of August, they had to practice every day. He knew better than to complain in front of Grandfather, since Grandfather had played football in college. But he also kept up practicing both with and without the other Big Muddies. He seemed happy.

The Saturday before eighth grade started, Mom got me up early, gave me some oatmeal for breakfast, and took me to the closest department store, Famous-Barr, to get a few new clothes for school. I thought I knew what my size was, but in fact, that size no longer fit. I was not as tall as the Beanstalk, but, as Grandma would have said, "Heavens to Betsy!" My shoe size was as big as Mom's, though I could not have borrowed any of her shoes, because she wore heels every day, including Saturdays and Sundays, unless she was going for a walk in the park, in which case she wore some old oxfords that everyone at school would have sneered at. What I really needed (size 7) was a pair of Weejuns. The only question was, brown or black?

Mom was picky—she said that you couldn't wear brown shoes with anything even semiformal, but that you also couldn't wear black shoes during the day. Finally, she settled on brown—a beautiful deep woody color that I liked—and then she handed me two dimes to put in the slits that crossed the top of the shoes. And it was true, should I have my purse stolen, the two dimes would be enough to get me on the bus. She also bought me a plaid skirt, some knee socks, two white blouses, and two cardigans. It was still warm in St. Louis, so the winter coat, if I needed to replace mine (or if I couldn't use one of hers), could wait.

As with all shoes in those days, it took a while to break in the Weejuns, and I got several blisters, but I was glad to be back on Skinker, and to resume my walks around our neighborhood. I was also glad to see Brucie, who had grown a lot over the summer, now wore a size 10 shoe, and had been practicing like crazy with the Big Muddies. They had played four gigs, and since the only one of them who had a driver's license drove a VW Bug, getting the boys and the instruments, including the drum set, to the gigs took several trips. I was present for the fourth gig, which was on a Friday evening at the restaurant where Aunt Lily worked, and I was impressed with how well the boys sang, and also with Brucie's new fingerpicking skills. He could strum and play a tune, but he could also use one of his finger picks to make a rhythmic "ting" on one of the higher strings in time to the rhythm of the songs. They played two songs I hadn't heard before, "Deportee" and "So Long (It's Been Good to Know Yuh)." The second of these they sang in a very upbeat way, and it perked me up, got me to sing along. "Deportee" they saved for the end of the set. I had never heard it, knew nothing about it, and had tears pouring down my cheeks before the third verse. The audience got silent and stared while Brucie and his partner, Allen, were singing, and I don't think that they noticed, as I did, that the two of them were slightly out of tune, especially on the chorus. As much as I was moved by the song, I was ready to edit their performance—slow down, let the beat be more pronounced, harmonize more evenly. I thought Brucie's guitar playing was wonderful, but not quite loud enough. The next day, Saturday, I got Mom to take me to Aunt Lily's. Brucie was still eating his pancakes. When I walked in the door, Aunt Lily offered me a pancake, too (they were large), and I ate it, but as soon as I was done, I grabbed Brucie's arm and dragged him to his room, where he picked up his guitar, and I began humming the song, since I didn't know the words. He put down the guitar and told me all about the song—written by Woody Someone, an actual plane crash that took place in California about a week after Brucie himself was born, and the article in some newspaper (not the *Post-Dispatch*) named the pilot and the copilot but not any of the ones from Mexico! I kept humming, Brucie picked up his guitar, and we played it seven times. By the third time I knew all the words to the chorus. I leaned toward Brucie and sang with him, gesturing a bit—up, down—with my chin. We slowed it down. I stuck out my chin and gave myself a deeper vibrato, and when he finally put down the guitar, Brucie hugged me and said that I would sing along the next time he played with the Big Muddies.

As often happened with songs I sang, that one stuck in my head all through the afternoon, until I went for a walk in Forest Park and forced it away by singing two or three others. Just before I went to camp, Brucie had played an album for me by a new group named Peter, Paul and Mary. One of the songs got into my memory after two plays—"Lemon Tree." "Lemon tree, very pretty, and the lemon flower is sweet / But the fruit of the poor lemon is impossible to eat." In some ways, the song made no sense to me, since one of my grandmother's favorite drinks was lemonade, and she also made a wonderful pie that used thinly sliced lemons baked with eggs and sugar in a flaky crust. I knew perfectly well that the fruit of the poor lemon was entirely edible if you knew what you were doing in the kitchen, as my grandmother did. But the tune was so lively and melodious that I loved to sing it, and walking in the park, I used it to push out "Deportee." Another song on that album was one my grandfather sang and my grandmother played, though Peter, Paul and Mary called it "This Train" and my grandfather called it "Bound for Glory." They sang it faster than Grandfather did, but I knew all the verses, and when I walked around the park, I sang it to myself in several ways—the tune itself, a harmonizing tune, and a slightly different harmonizing tune. It was interesting to try all the parts, imagine how they could fit together. As I sang one part, I had no problem imagining the others, and so I was hearing the song in my head as a trio. Brucie knew this song, too, but he hadn't suggested it to the Big Muddies because one of the boys was Jewish and they had decided not to sing any gospel songs.

A few days later, I went to a local music store and looked for the Peter, Paul and Mary record as a stack of 45s, so that I could play it on Mom's record player, but evidently 45s had fallen by the wayside, and I saw that I was going to have to talk someone into buying me my own record player, for 33s. I immediately thought of Uncle Drew, then the stash of bills under my mattress. That stash of bills was almost eight years old now. I was sure that Uncle Drew assumed I had spent it. But I hadn't, and I didn't want to. I still thought that it contained my luck. As I was walking in the park, I became concerned about it, cut short my walk, went straight home. It was still there.

I came up with a plan. On the last Sunday before school began, we all gathered at Grandfather's and Grandmother's for some pot roast, mashed potatoes, and the first apple pie of the season. Uncle Hank; his wife, Carol; and his three children were also there. I wormed my way between Uncle Drew and Aunt Louise. When we began to sing after dessert, I sang in my best voice, somewhat more loudly than usual, and I kept my eye on Uncle Drew to see if he noticed. He did—he nodded and smiled, and lifted his eyebrow, especially when I stuck my jaw out. When we were finished and Mom and Aunt Lily were taking the plates off the table, I said, "I wish I knew more songs."

Uncle Drew said, "I wish you did, too."

I said, "I just don't learn them very well off the sheet music. I like to hear them."

We exchanged a glance, and three days later, he dropped by with my very own record player and a stack of nine 33s—*Peter, Paul and*

Mary; West Side Story; Beethoven's Fifth Symphony; *Bo Diddley Is a Gunslinger; Elvis Presley; Joan Baez, Vol. 2; Rachmaninoff: Piano Concerto No. 3;* the Kingston Trio's *Make Way;* and the one that came to be my favorite, Ella Fitzgerald and Louis Armstrong's *Porgy and Bess.* When I listened to it, I didn't realize that Louis Armstrong was the musician that my grandfather referred to as "Satchmo." But I truly couldn't stop listening to it, especially, of course, to "Summertime." And quite often, as the summer faded into fall, I would walk through Forest Park, singing "Summertime."

Mom appreciated my appreciation, and on September 26, she brought a cupcake into my room with a little lit candle stuck in the frosting and said it was George Gershwin's sixty-fourth birthday. She kissed me on the cheek, turned on my record player, and played "It Ain't Necessarily So," which got me right out of bed and into the carpool in a wonderful dancing mood.

At school, things had begun as if they were the same as seventh grade, but a week in, they had changed. I wasn't the only one with bigger feet, and Brucie wasn't the only one who had gotten much taller. One of the boys that I had hardly noticed the year before was now a head taller than most of the others, fairly brawny, and "handsome," a word that we had never used in seventh grade. And many, though not all, of the girls were better dressed, with hips and bosoms and even, perhaps secretly, bits of makeup—pinkish lipstick, a little mascara. Once again, I saw myself as a viewer more than a participant, and the others seemed to see me that way, too. But I did love to sit on the john in the girls' bathroom and listen to the others gossip. The good thing was that they never mentioned me, and the bad thing was that they did mention other girls that I liked, and not in a positive way.

Even though we were only in eighth grade, it was evident who the "handsome" boys liked, and those were the ones who would get raked over the coals in the bathroom—did you see her looking at him? She likes him better than he likes her, no matter what she says. Did you see the way her blouse was unbuttoned? You think that was an accident? What about——? I thought he liked her, but then

I think he noticed that she sits in class with her mouth open all the time. She looks like a dope. So what if he got an F on his test. Grades don't matter for boys.

The girls I liked were the studious ones, especially those who had what my grandfather called "a twinkle in their eye," who seemed to find almost everything that was going on amusing, but who kept their smiles to themselves and never laughed out loud. These girls were often friendly toward me, but they didn't invite me over, confide anything, pass me notes. A couple of them who were in the chorus complimented me on my voice—it was richer now, one of them said. She told me she was "amazed." I had no idea whether this was a compliment or a soft put-down, but I was pleased to at least be noticed. Sometimes, after school, when we were sitting on the steps in front of the main building, waiting for the car to arrive (usually it was Mom who was the late one), the girls I carpooled with would chat with me in an easygoing way. And they still shared their muffins and cookies with me. That was enough. I learned in the girls' restroom to keep to myself.

In the meantime, I got back into the Junior Chorus, and it was a relief, because in English class, history class, and algebra class, I didn't seem to understand a thing. I say "seem" because I thought I did understand, but my teachers didn't agree with me. In English, I sat behind Mary G., who raised her hand often and kept good notes. Whatever she said, I wrote down. The days were long—eight thirty to four o'clock. Since Brucie had decided to play football, there was no going to his place, except on Sunday.

I would do my homework as best as I could right after school, then I would sit down at Mom's piano and play this or that. It helped that she was still at work. Mistakes didn't matter. I would try what I could, listening as closely as I could to what my tunes sounded like. What I wanted was for my ear to be perfect. Mom had plenty of sheet music lying around, since she had to make sure that the singers in the Muny knew what the words were, at least. I made myself try whatever was sitting on the top of one of the stacks (and there were plenty of those). Some songs I knew, or at least had heard, and some

I didn't. But I would play the right-hand part, pay attention to the tune, and then try to sing it.

For the Fall Recital, I was given one solo and one quartet. The recital was to take place in my favorite month, October, which made me happy. In the meantime, on the Friday night after George Gershwin's birthday, the Big Muddies did a repeat performance at Aunt Lily's restaurant, and they did sing "Deportee." Brucie called me up from the audience. I sat down beside him, leaned into the microphone, and did my best. We sang the whole song, and I could feel my cheeks getting wet. When we were finished, there was a long silence. I glanced at Brucie to see if he regretted asking me to sing (though everything sounded all right to me), and then clapping, clapping, and clapping. Smiles burst off our faces, and Brucie gave me a big smooch on the cheek. The clapping was loud, given the fact that there were only twenty-five people in the audience (including Aunt Lily and Mom), and that was enough. When I got to school on Monday, I said nothing about it.

As the autumn went on, I realized that my performance with Brucie was going to be the high point of the year. The Fall Recital went well enough. I mixed up some of the words in the quartet and got a dirty look from the boy who was singing tenor, but I don't know that Mr. W. noticed. We got the regular amount of applause at the end, and Mr. W. seemed satisfied. In the second-to-last game of the fall, Brucie was put in as a substitute for another boy, late in the game. He was looking at the quarterback, or so he said, and an older kid on the other team (Parkway South, I think) knocked him down and broke his right wrist. He didn't even know it was broken until dinnertime that evening. He always said that at first it didn't hurt much, that he was glad that they won the game, and when there was a stab of pain as he was taking off his football jersey after the game, the stab went away so quickly that he didn't think about it. At dinner, he picked up his steak knife to cut the New York strip Aunt Lily had bought just for him, and his wrist hurt so much that he dropped the knife and she jumped out of her chair and pushed him straight out the door and into her car. She took him to the emergency room at Firmin Desloge Hospital.

At about eight p.m., Aunt Lily called Mom from the hospital, told her what happened, and said that the doctors had set his wrist and put him in a cast. Now it was hurting more than it had, but they told him he could take some aspirin. Unusually for Brucie (she whispered to Mom), he was crying. She needed to get him out of there.

They showed up twenty minutes later. Brucie was no longer crying, and he said that it didn't really hurt much. He sat there, looking down. Aunt Lily kissed him on his cheek. She looked as down as he did. Mom, I knew, would take her aside at some point and exclaim, "Why in the world did you let him play football?" but I knew why. Brucie did what he wanted to do, he was athletic and handsome. What else would he do in the fall if not football? My school was crazy for football. The girls played hockey, and I liked it, but the boys who didn't play football just ran around the track or threw things, and it looked as boring as could be. Aunt Lily left after half an hour, because she had forgotten to lock her front door and didn't want to leave the place open with the lights on all night. Mom went to her room to do something, and I sat down on the ottoman in front of the armchair. I said to Brucie, "Come on, tell me how much it really hurts."

He stared at me, then said, "Not much, really, not much. But how am I going to keep playing my guitar? I wish I'd broken my ankle."

I completely sympathized.

It turned out, though, that because he much preferred fingerpicking, he could actually do that even with the cast on. The cast came to the middle of his palm, but his thumb and his fingers, though a little immobilized, were not terribly affected.

MOM SEEMED DOWN. I thought maybe Brucie's injury was the reason, because I couldn't see any other. Grandmother and Grandfather were in good moods, Aunt Lily was making plenty of tips, because her restaurant had hired a better chef, and was charging more, which no one minded because it was good food. She told us that people who were used to going to Schneithorst's, which was very famous and just down Lindbergh Boulevard from their place, were starting to come in, saying, "Well, this is a nice change! Can't have sausage all the time." Their new chef, someone Aunt Lily called Jake, liked variety—some nights he would make pizza, some nights leg of lamb, some nights boeuf bourguignon, some nights my favorite, chicken fricassee. Aunt Lily said that he was new to St. Louis (from Montana or someplace like that) and he loved all the different types of restaurants there were here. Mom liked that, too—one of her favorites was a Chinese restaurant on Brentwood Boulevard.

But dim sum didn't make her happy anymore. It didn't matter where we went, she would sigh, pay the bill, get up without finishing (though I was told to clean my plate, not waste anything). At night, I could hear her footsteps as she wandered around the house, opened the door, went out on the porch (for a smoke), came back in. Something was missing, and, after listening to the girls at school, I guessed it was a boyfriend. The Muny season was over, all of the male actors had gone back to New York or Los Angeles, and maybe I was a problem, too, since she didn't have to watch over me. I did my homework, practiced music, never got into trouble. She knew if she was away, I could be relied upon to leave her a note even if I was only going across the street to watch a movie at the Hi-Pointe, and I could also be relied upon to lock the doors, leave a light on in the kitchen, and take Dizzy, who was now seven, out for a walk. Dizzy could be relied upon to bark if anyone came on the porch, and I could be relied upon to call the police if I saw anyone in the backyard (which I never did). Thanks to her constant contact with actresses and musicians, Mom knew how to present herself, and was fit and attractive, but maybe she had run through the possibilities for a husband, or even a boyfriend, in St. Louis. I didn't know—she didn't tell me—but what happened in the course of that winter showed me.

The first clue happened when I spent a Friday night (with Dizzy) at Grandmother's and Grandfather's house. I had done that fairly often, though not as much as I had before I went to summer camp. However, I had a nightgown in the closet and a few clothes there, too. My grandfather's favorite show on Friday was *Sing Along with Mitch,* which started at seven thirty, and he always sang along. After that we would jump around—sometimes 77 *Sunset Strip,* sometimes something else. I liked *Fair Exchange,* about an American girl who goes to live in London. My grandfather liked cowboys and singing, and my grandmother didn't care. On that Friday night, I got bored with singing along with Mitch and went upstairs to go to the bathroom, and to read while I was in there, which I often did. I came back maybe twenty minutes later, drawn by the fragrance of popcorn, and as I was coming down the stairs, I heard my grandmother say, "Well, she did set her cap for him." I had no idea what that meant, but I remembered the phrase because it was so peculiar. Oddly enough, a few days later, I was lying in bed reading *Sense and Sensibility,* which I liked much better than *Great Expectations,* which we were reading for school, and I came across the sentence "I abhor every commonplace phrase by which wit is intended; and 'setting one's cap at a man,' or 'making a conquest,' are the most odious of all." The sentence was about a girl deciding she was going to get a boy (or a man) to take her as his wife, or at least as his girlfriend. I thought it was odd to think of Mom doing that, but once I understood what it meant, I kept my eye out, but no one came to our house on Skinker.

What Mom was doing on those Friday nights when she left me at Grandmother's was unclear. Whatever it was, she picked me up early enough on Saturday, sometimes earlier than I wanted. If we got home and I meandered around the house, she would say, "Don't you have some homework to do? That school costs plenty, so if you don't get enough out of it, you can go somewhere else." She didn't say where. But I did go to my room, if only to read a book and pet Dizzy, or out into the park, to sing. The real sign that she was in some sort of trouble, internal or external, was that she didn't like me playing the piano in my harum-scarum way, and would say, "Either practice properly, or quit making that noise!" I didn't know what to think, but I didn't talk back, as some of the girls at school said that they did when their mothers got on them—I went out and walked around. When I came back, I can't say that Mom apologized, but she did give me a smile and a pat on the head, as if all was forgiven.

There was another girl at school, in some of my classes, and I might have made friends with her, but she was not a girl to make friends with if you wanted to succeed socially, and she didn't live nearby, so there was no reason to have one of those secret friendships where you spent time at one another's houses over the weekend, or did homework together at night, and gossiped about the other girls for fun. She was tall and gawky; liked reading books, as I did; and was in the Junior Chorus, though up in the back just to the left of the boys because she was so tall. If you asked her where she'd gone to elementary school, she always said, "Avery," which was near my grandparents' house, without even realizing that admitting to having gone to a plain old public school was not the thing to do. I had gone to De Mun, but I never mentioned it, but then, no one ever asked me, either. At any rate, it was known that she was going to our school because her mother, about my mother's age, had met someone wealthy enough to live in Ladue. Mom might have known her, but when she saw her from a distance at any sort of school function, she would look away. It was very much like the girls I overheard in the girls' room wondering aloud how so-and-so had happened to snag such a good-looking junior and claim him as her boyfriend. I had no idea about the man the gawky girl's mom had snagged—was he someone Mom knew?

Well, it turned out he was, and that she had known that his wife had died, that he had very much enjoyed the Muny (the wife had, too), and perhaps Mom was waiting a respectable amount of time to make an attempt to attract him. But it was also evident that however well-dressed Mom was, she did not have the flair that the gawky girl's mother did. And then, the gawky girl's mother had a baby. Whatever Mom's ambitions about the man, I was sure then and I'm sure now that having a baby was not on the menu. He already had two children (the gawky girl sometimes talked about them—one was a junior at a nearby Catholic boys' school and the other one was off to college somewhere). Wouldn't three (including me) be enough? At any rate, that was the man I thought my grandmother was referring to. I subsequently changed my mind.

I changed my mind because we were shopping at Bettendorf's, my mom's favorite place, though the one she preferred was up north, in U. City. We were walking down the vegetable aisle, Mom pushing the cart and me looking at the green beans, when she stopped, turned right, and went down the baking supplies aisle. I didn't see where she was going, but when I looked up, I did see a well-dressed man watching her. He glanced at me, smiled. If he hadn't smiled, I wouldn't have suspected anything, but when he did, I realized that he was the one. I passed him, followed her. Of course there was a wedding ring on his left ring finger—a wide one with some sort of visible engraving. I didn't give him a dirty look. Mom stayed in the baking supplies aisle. At the far end, she kept her eye on the checkout counters, and after a long time, she went to one of them, checked out, even though we hadn't bought everything on the list. She must have missed whatever she had planned for dinner, because on the way home, we went past our place to a Steak 'n Shake. She didn't say why—she just said, "Get what you want." I did—cheeseburger, sauce, fries. She didn't get anything, only ate one of my fries. When we got home, she parked in the garage, we carried the groceries in, and then she said, "You put them away," and ran to her bedroom. Of course I heard her burst into tears within moments—I had seen that she could hardly hold them when she was carrying in the groceries.

It was not ridiculous to suspect that Mom was in love with him—he did look like one of those guys who was both handsome and agreeable, even easygoing, as well as prosperous, and there was no telling what he saw in Mom, but it was evident what she saw in him.

It may be that I got used to Mom being moody and a bit unpredictable, but as school went on, I felt that I had to pay more attention to my homework, the other kids, and Brucie than I did to Mom. There was this sense, even among the popular kids, that dangers were everywhere, and not just in the homework. Our teachers seemed more irritable. My English teacher would write things on the blackboard about grammar and spelling, then suddenly whip around, stare at someone, and then pick up her ruler and slap it on her desk. We all knew why—she didn't like the girls whispering and passing notes during class. But the girls who were whispering and passing notes were also on edge—that was why they were whispering and passing notes. The ones who had been dominant were being replaced by other girls who had gotten prettier or "stolen" someone's boyfriend.

Or did we sense what was about to happen? On a Monday late in October, as everyone knows, it turned out the Soviets were right there in Cuba (only fourteen hundred miles away), basically as far from Miami (where some people we knew went for spring vacation) as we were from Hartford, Illinois. Mom watched President Kennedy on TV, and she told me that everything was going to be all right, but it was evident that she didn't believe it. And after all, why wouldn't they attack St. Louis? McDonald Aircraft was right there, not far from the airport. I didn't say anything, but I wondered what it would be like to see a flash of something in the sky, say, right above the Hi-Pointe movie theater, and then see nothing ever again. I had looked at a book in the public library called *On the Beach,* and just the idea was so scary that I dropped the book on the floor and kicked it under the lowest shelf, and left the library. I'm not sure I was up all night after the president's speech, but the image of an atomic bomb blast went in and out of my mind all night, and I was exhausted the next morning. When we were walking into our first class, I was behind the gawky girl, and she was telling another girl that she had asked her stepfather, the very man I'd thought my mother had set her cap for, if they would flee into the countryside if there was a launch, and he had said no, it wasn't worth it. It was better to die. Evidently, he had read *On the Beach* also.

That evening we did flee to the countryside, in the sense that we went to Uncle Drew and Aunt Louise's for dinner, which was of course delicious—fried chicken and mashed potatoes with what Aunt Louise called a "lava cake" for dessert—and even though Darryl and Allison, who were only kids, were sitting at the table, there was a lengthy conversation about the crisis: what the administration was doing, what they should be doing, whether anyone was in charge. As always at Uncle Drew's, there had been drinks before dinner—whiskey sours or gin and tonics. My grandfather had one; my grandmother drank a Pepsi instead; Aunt Louise, Aunt Lily, and Uncle Drew had two; and Mom had two, then three, then four, which was why, when the discussion got a little heated—not about what the Russians were doing, but about whether Nixon and Lodge would have handled the situation more adeptly than Kennedy and Johnson were—Mom barked out, "Why don't they just get it all over with? What's the point?"

We all knew what she was saying—mutually assured destruction? Nothing wrong with that. She was sagging in her seat, looked sour and depressed. Allison stared at her. Darryl didn't react. Grandmother said, "Good heavens!" and Brucie got up, took me by the hand, and led me to the guest bedroom, picking up his guitar on the way. He still had his cast on, though he was almost finished with it. His fingerpicking wasn't quite as adept as it had been, but he'd made up for it by learning how to use his left hand in a different way—not just holding the chords but using his baby finger and his ring finger to pluck a few strings, which added a kind of variety and resonance to the tunes. I loved it, and was fascinated by it. He started singing. I chimed in, and as always, whatever I had been thinking about, or worrying about, fell away. His voice was getting deeper, or maybe he was just getting more range, because when he sang "Deep River," he went very very deep, and his voice boomed out. It was hard to harmonize with that, but we tried it a few times, until I figured out how to sound, I thought at the time, like a bird flying into the air, flying high over the river, over Jordan. When we finished the song, he kissed me on the cheek, and then we turned away from the window and saw everyone, including Allison and Darryl, standing in the doorway.

Grandfather said, "Come on, you two! Mother just got the piano tuned and we need to sing a few things." That was how our dinner turned around, how we forgot, for the rest of the evening, about the Russian missiles in Cuba, how we brought a few smiles onto Mom's face and got her to sing along on "Stewball."

Back at school, anxiety continued, and we did sometimes discuss whether the missiles would come. I remember sitting in my algebra class, playing with my pencil and staring out the window, wondering if missiles would be sent during the day, or whether they would be saved for a sudden nighttime attack. The weather must have been warm, as it often was in St. Louis in October, thanks to the humidity. At any rate, the window was open, and there was a slight breeze. My algebra teacher, Mr. Yeager, barked my name and startled me. I jerked, and my pencil went flying out the window. Why there wasn't a screen, I have no idea, but there wasn't. Nor did I have another pencil. I had to turn around and get one of the boys to lend me one. The girls all said that they didn't have any extras.

The Cuban Missile Crisis ended, Brucie's cast came off, and he didn't seem to have any residual issues, at least about playing his guitar. The Big Muddies did two gigs, one the day after Thanksgiving and another the next day. There were about fifty people in the audience at the first one, maybe seventy at the second one, and the boys began joking about their upcoming recording contract. I got an A on my algebra test and another A on my paper about *The Pearl*. On the surface, everything seemed to be back to normal, but there was an undertow of fear that I felt almost all the time. We got through Christmas. For the Christmas concert, I sang one short carol—"The Cherry Tree Carol"—solo, as the audience was coming into the auditorium, while Mr. W. softly played the piano. I was standing in the shadow of the curtains, stage right. No one could see me. I thought of the bird flying and did my best to make the song sound as if an angel were singing it. There was not supposed to be applause, since most people were still shuffling in, but the lights were up, and I did see several adults look around. That was praise enough. Mom put a bunch of books under the tree and a tenor recorder, which was made of rosewood and had a beautiful tone. Then we got through New Year's and almost into the spring. Whatever was happening at school, I seemed to be coasting along well enough. A lot of the kids seemed angry or depressed, and I thought, at least I wasn't one of them.

In early March, Grandfather was there when I came out of school one afternoon, and he took me back to his place. I was surprised and glad to see him, especially since the mom who was driving our carpool that day was always late. I waved to the other girls, jumped in the car, and babbled on about this and that, then said, "So, what's for dinner?"

But Grandfather didn't say anything, so I shut up and stared out the window. We got to the intersection of Manchester and Brentwood, and Grandfather said, "Just, please, keep your eye out as we're going down the hill, because your grandmother has something to tell you."

We went down the hill; crossed the bridge over Deer Creek, which was my favorite spot; then turned left and went up the hill, under the tracks. Grandfather dropped me at his house, said he needed to fill up the tank, and I went in.

Grandmother was sitting by the window. She put down her knitting, took a sip of her tea, got up and gave me a hug, then sat on the couch with me and told me that Mom had been driving down that hill on Brentwood Boulevard. She had just passed Manchester—stopped for the red light, waited, went on. And then she crossed the white line, which drivers did, in order to pass someone, but she stayed on the wrong side all the way down the hill. There were plenty of people on the road. Every one of them honked and then pulled over. One man who saw her as she passed him told the police that her face was "either blank or determined"—he couldn't tell. She didn't hit anyone and turned right at Thornton and pulled up in front of a house across from the creek, and waited until the police found her.

I said, "Do you think that the steering wheel was broken? Was there a flat tire?"

Grandmother shook her head, then said, "Honey, she's got to spend the night, um, in jail."

The only thing I knew about jail was from watching *Dragnet* on

TV. I did know where the jail was, in Clayton, not far from Mom's favorite department store, not that far from our house on Skinker. I said, "Why?"

"She's charged with something called 'reckless endangerment.' She has to see a judge tomorrow."

All of Grandmother's words seemed to be hitting me like a hailstorm. The only thing I wanted to do was duck my head and avoid being hit. The only thing I could think of saying was, "Where's Dizzy?"

Grandmother said, "Oh, heavens. I hadn't thought about that. We'll go get her. She can sleep in your room."

It turned out that because Mom had been driving slowly—only about twenty miles per hour, and no one had been injured or struck—they decided to get her a psychiatric evaluation rather than put her on trial, though she did have to pay a fine, for court costs, which Uncle Drew covered. She stayed in jail for two days, not one, then went to a hospital that was south of our house. My grandfather closed up the house (there was talk about selling it that I overheard). I stayed with my grandparents for about a week, and then went to live with Uncle Drew and Aunt Louise, because they had more room. I stayed there for the rest of the school year, got into another carpool. The ride to school was entirely different, and, as always in St. Louis, there were so many things to look at out the window that it seemed like a road trip.

For a long time, I didn't think that I was reacting to what had happened to Mom the way that everyone around me (including the teachers at school, who had been "informed") expected me to react. I did what I was supposed to do, went about my business, was not exactly sad, or even worried. I understood later that I was disoriented, that I had been expecting something ever since the grocery store incident, and that something had happened, and so my sense of reality was confirmed. And we were lucky that the thing that had happened was strange but small, not horrifying. As for Mom, well, I was thirteen, exactly the age when being free of your mom is just what you want, if only so that you can come to understand that being free of your mom is not what you want. I didn't know if the other girls at school knew about what had happened or where Mom was, but I half expected to be sitting in the girls' room and to overhear one of them saying, "Can you believe how lucky she is? She doesn't have to put up with her mom at all! If only that would happen to me!"

It wasn't until I went to camp in the summer—not to the one in Wisconsin, but to one on the other side of Lake Michigan, called Interlochen, which meant "between the lakes"—that I more or less woke up and began worrying about Mom. Mr. W. had suggested the camp. Apparently he told Aunt Louise that I needed more of a musical education if I wanted to catch up to other girls who happened to have the sort of range and "ambition" that I did. Time to stop dillydallying around and learn something in a systematic way. In other words, songs around the campfire weren't enough. Mom—we visited at the hospital once a month—completely agreed, as, indeed, she completely agreed with everything. She later told me that she was so ashamed of her action, and of the damage that she might have caused, that she was entirely willing to do whatever her doctors told her, whatever Grandfather or Grandmother told her, whatever Uncle Drew told her. And she never wanted to drive again. My fellow campers were much more friendly than the kids at school. They practiced all sorts of instruments, played in all sorts of groups. I sang in as many of those as I could. Every morning, for two hours, we had to take hikes or canoe trips, but no one preferred that, as they had at my camp in Wisconsin. All of them wanted to get back to the music. It seemed to me that at a place like Interlochen, if you could harmonize, you could have as many friends as you wanted. And, as far as I could tell, there was no envy. If someone played better than someone else, the worse player didn't bother hating or denigrating the better player—he or she simply learned something from that player. It also helped that the campers were from all over the country, and even the world—there were a few from England and two from Japan (they were excellent musicians—my guess was that they came in order to learn English while practicing, since, perhaps, their parents couldn't stop them from practicing).

I was there for eight weeks, and when I got home, Mom was back in the kitchen, back at work (someone had replaced her at Kiel, but then someone else had left Kiel, moved to New York to take a job at a new theater they were building, a very big project, right by Central Park), back to the woman I knew in elementary school—practical, mostly good-natured, a bit reserved, and ready to walk anywhere. Once a week, on Thursdays, I would come home from school and wait for her until almost seven, then we would go out to dinner, often to the Cheshire, which was across Clayton Road. She let the car sit in the driveway, but she didn't want to do the carpool. One of the other mothers took over for her, and in exchange, she made muffins two days a week instead of one. She had to go to her appointments, get assessed and watched, as a part of her rehabilitation. She went to the appointments for the rest of my time in high school, and maybe they did the trick, because she seemed, to me, at least, to have very few ups and downs, and to have resigned herself to the life of what she now called "an independent woman."

In ninth grade, my life, too, slipped into a pleasant routine, with fewer shocks, fewer anxieties, more things to enjoy (not only books, such as *David Copperfield,* but also certain algebraic formulas, as well as ancient history, with Mr. A.). I learned how to do my hair properly—not at school but at camp, where there was an older violinist who was already used to playing solos and even among the other students of the camp was known as a prodigy. Unlike the prodigies most people hear about, she was blond and pretty, as well as socially aware, so she knew how to wear rollers and style her "flip." Dizzy was eight. She settled down, too, and let us pet her.

Mom and I knew that there was chaos out in the world—she wept when JFK was assassinated, and, seeing her, I did, too. But for some reason, we had gone back to feeling sheltered by our brick house, by the trees in the park across the street, by the stability of our weekly dinners at Grandmother's house and the monthly feast at

Uncle Drew's. Even the Big Muddies got popular (though no recording contract). They had a gig somewhere almost every weekend (though never at Gaslight Square, which was the "coolest" spot for young singers in St. Louis, and not far from our house on Skinker—I saw Gregg Allman and Duane Allman at a bar there once, before they got to be famous). Peter, Paul and Mary; Joan Baez; Bob Dylan; Tom Rush were around. Brucie and the other Muddies were adept at learning the best folk songs, and one of the members now had a VW van, so they could take gigs as far away as Peoria or Rolla.

My record stack grew—Joni Mitchell; Gordon Lightfoot; and Mimi and Richard Fariña became popular, and sometimes came through St. Louis. They sang at the Kiel (not at Busch Stadium, as the Beatles did in the summer of '66). I would lie in bed every night listening to those songs, mouthing the words, letting them etch themselves into my brain. In the morning I would get up, pick up my tenor recorder, and play the first one that I thought of, beginning to end. On Saturday and Sunday, I would play three in a row, and then go to the piano and finger them. As far as I was concerned, it didn't matter which one, because I learned something from the traditional ones and from the new ones. I especially liked "The Last Thing on My Mind," "Blowin' in the Wind," "Urge for Going."

Brucie was not well-behaved, nor were the other Muddies. He got in trouble for smoking behind a wall at his high school twice, and he got in trouble for setting off cherry bombs in the tiny green spot where Oakwood and Park meet in Webster Groves—the boy who had the van lived there, which I thought was the best neighborhood in town. They set off four cherry bombs, and by the time the fourth one had gone off, the police, who had been notified by a neighbor, were arriving. Sparklers were okay in St. Louis, but cherry bombs were not, especially on a February Saturday morning when everyone was sleeping. The bandmate and lead guitarist had saved the cherry bombs from the previous Fourth of July. No damage, because of the wintry moisture, but plenty of annoyed neighbors in big houses, some of whom thought they were gunshots. He got in trouble for speeding down Lindbergh, was stopped at the intersection of Gravois, down in Sappington, charged with going eighty in a forty-five-mile-per-hour zone (he said he was going ninety). At least his friend wasn't driving—his friend was passed out in the back seat, and was taken in for underage drinking. Brucie did not do well in school and skipped classes fairly frequently. He flunked tenth-grade history and eleventh-grade math, so it was no surprise that when it came time to go to college, he only got into Missouri State, down in Springfield. Since that was where he had been born, and where his father still lived, the last thing he wanted to do was go to Springfield. So he joined the army. The lead guitarist sold his van and joined the navy. It was 1966.

AT THE BEGINNING of senior year, Uncle Drew said he wanted to take me on a college tour. The other kids went on college tours in August. Ours was at the end of September. Uncle Drew wanted to do it by car, so I think what he really wanted was to see the autumn leaves. He told the head of the upper school that we would be gone for a week, and we got into his Caddy (brand-new, needed an outing), didn't go anywhere near Northwestern, which I thought was my best bet, but he got on Highway 70 and went, basically, straight to the Waldorf, which was where he always stayed when he went to New York, and where, I noticed, the doormen and the people behind the desk were happy to see him—they smiled sincerely and gave us a suite in the penthouse, even though he'd reserved only two regular rooms on the fifth floor. We took naps, then got up and ate an early dinner at Peacock Alley—dover sole, Manhattan clam chowder, both of which I had never tried before. Uncle Drew said that between them, those two dishes would make me forget every catfish I had ever eaten. We then went downtown and saw *Man of La Mancha*. My favorite song was "Dulcinea," but I could mouth the words to "I, Don Quixote" and "The Impossible Dream." The next morning, we left the Waldorf at about eight, got to Boston before noon, drove to the Berklee School of Music. What I noticed about Berklee was how close the buildings were to one another, how the school did not look like a park surrounded by country clubs, as my school in Ladue did. There were pleasant parks, and we took a walk in one—Fenway—but I felt rather neutral about the school and the city. The next day, we ended up in Stockbridge. I thought living in Boston would be like being stuck in a closet.

We drove to the most prestigious school—the Eastman—and when we got to Rochester, the wind was screaming down from Canada over the lake. It was so cold and windy and cloudy that I didn't even want to walk around the campus. The next day, we went straight to Philadelphia, which seemed rather tropical compared to Rochester. Curtis Institute of Music? No. That night, I told Uncle Drew I was ready to go home. I think maybe he was, too, because he nodded, said he missed Aunt Louise and the kids, and so, first thing in the morning, about seven, we headed west. We stopped for breakfast in Middletown, talked about how beautiful the trees were, and then went the wrong direction at the intersection of the highways, headed north instead of south, across the river. Two hours later, I knew exactly where I wanted to go—Penn State. The closer we got, even after we realized that we were going northwest instead of west, the more beautiful the landscape. I knew nothing about Penn State—it was as if I looked around and wished for a college, and suddenly one appeared.

Senior year went along as I preferred it. I enjoyed glee club, I didn't mind Ellen L. singing "Mary's Lullaby" for the Christmas pageant (I had one solo and the gawky girl got to narrate the Bible verses), and it never occurred to me that many of the participants in the glee club, singing the Christmas carols, were Jewish students. I got into Penn State.

3

THE ONLY THING Brucie ever said about his time in Vietnam was that he was glad he didn't wait. When he first got there, in August of 1966, there weren't many American soldiers, and the ones who did most of the fighting were marines. For some reason that I didn't pay much attention to at the time, President Johnson decided to pour troops into Vietnam the previous summer. No one talked about it, and the occasional letters Brucie sent to Aunt Lily went on about the landscape and his friends, with a few remarks here and there about his commanding officers. I had just turned seventeen. My understanding of the war was that the Chinese Communists, with the Russians right behind them, were planning to take over the world in one way or another. I didn't know what Communism was, other than a launcher of atomic missiles that would, for some reason, come from the north, down past Canada, and straight to our house on Skinker. Perhaps we all thought that. There were a few kids in our class who were more enlightened—Nancy S. was one of them—but the last thing we wanted to talk about was atomic bombs. I preferred the Black Death, which we did talk about in Ancient History. The Black Death proved that there could be survivors of an epidemic. With intercontinental ballistic missiles, there wouldn't be any of those.

At any rate, Brucie was there for about eighteen months. The battle that I heard of, Khe Sanh, was one of many that he missed out on. I am sure Aunt Lily followed the articles in the *Globe* or the *Post-*

Dispatch more carefully than I did, and sometimes when we saw her at Sunday dinner, she looked a little haggard. She would take Grandfather aside, tell him something or other, and he would give her a squeeze around the shoulders. But Grandfather had served in the First World War, had been in the trenches at the Second Battle of the Marne, lost a good friend though he himself wasn't injured—what he survived was the influenza epidemic. He never said so, but we all had some sense that he thought the war in Vietnam was pointless and minor—not a real war. Thinking about it, he would often sing "Tenting Tonight on the Old Campground." He would sing the last chorus with special feeling: "Many are the hearts that are weary tonight, / Wishing for the war to cease; / Many are the hearts that are looking for the right / To see the dawn of peace. / Dying tonight, dying tonight, / Dying on the old campground." While he was singing, and afterward, we would think of Brucie, who was three years younger than Grandfather had been in World War I, but there was something soothing about the song, and looking at Grandfather—hale and hearty in his seventies—was reassuring.

Penn State reminded me of Burroughs, a meadow, rather than a park, where they had decided to put some buildings. And State College was surrounded by mountains and trees. To the depths of my heart I pitied the classmate who had gone to Harvard, the gawky girl at Vassar, all the boys at Amherst, the two at Colgate. Suckers, all of them! My roommates (there were three) were nice enough. Two had come from Philadelphia, and almost immediately started complaining about how far we were into the middle of nowhere. I gathered from listening to them that one had applied to Stanford, was accepted, but hadn't gotten any sort of financial aid, so her parents had sent her to Penn State. The other one had also applied to Stanford and had not gotten in. They tiptoed around their complaints, eyeing each other, but they did complain. When I said I was from St. Louis, one of them said, "Oh, wow! I thought of applying to Washington U.! I wish I had!" I said, politely, "It is a great school." The third girl, the one who slept beneath me in my bunk bed, was from Indiana. It took me two months to realize that she was talking about a town about a hundred miles west of State College, not the Indiana I had heard of. Her parents had a farm; she planned to inherit it.

I was well prepared for most of my classes—most of the books we read for freshman English I had already read, and I was happy to read them again, just to see if there was more there than I had realized in high school. I liked history—we hadn't talked much about the prerevolutionary period, and there was information about the Quakers and the Amish that I hadn't heard before. No math—not a requirement. I took Russian, because Russia wasn't the same as our archenemy, the Soviet Union, and I loved music by Mussorgsky and Tchaikovsky. I suppose that it escaped my notice that the "1812 Overture" was celebrating a war, and anyway, I played *Pictures at an Exhibition* over and over. I liked Beginning Anthropology because it showed me what was behind, or shall we say, underneath what I had learned about ancient and medieval history from Mr. A. The course I was not prepared for was Musical Theory.

I would have said that I was—thanks to piano lessons and playing without lessons, as well as reading music for concerts and solos, I knew what a staff was, what the treble and bass clefs were, what keys were (and which ones I could sing most easily). I knew plenty of people who played woodwinds, brass, strings, and percussion. I knew the differences between Mozart, Beethoven, and Stravinsky. Through Brucie, I even knew someone who played a mandolin and someone who attempted to play a hammered dulcimer. I would have said (though only to myself) that I had figured out how to use my jaw and my mouth to deepen my sound and make it richer, I would have said that once I had been an alto and my range had been about two octaves. Now I did not define myself, but I knew my range had expanded about four notes downward and three notes upward. I would have liked to have a bigger range—one of the girls at Interlochen had a range of four octaves. I didn't think I was going to get there, but I thought I had improved my vibrato so that it was better than that girl's. But music theory was not about music, it was about the history of music—how do you read Bach, how do you understand the music that Mozart composed as a child, how do Beethoven's symphonies evolve? The main thing I learned was that I wasn't a child prodigy, but that I was lucky to have grown up in a family that loved music. Would I have been better off if Grandfather was a classical pianist who taught me everything he knew and oversaw my practicing until I was ready at the age of five to play in front of others? I didn't think so.

I made some friends. One of them, Cathy Hawley, was in my Musical Theory class because she had grown up a bit like that—she had been playing the cello since she was six, had played it in her high school orchestra for four years, and in a string quartet, but she was now an English major, had left that cello behind, much against her parents' wishes. She said I was lucky to grow up with songs, because she couldn't remember a thing about any of the concertos, cantatas, symphonies, or quartets she had played. She declared that she was a word person, and what she liked me to do as we were walking around campus was to sing her a song with interesting lyrics—"Goodnight, Irene" (Why did the guy get married one night and dumped a few days later? Haven't you ever thought you might jump in the river and drown?) or "Banks of the Ohio" (I know why he killed her, but why did she go with him? Didn't she sense anything? And he says he was sorry, but did he get caught? Seems like an open-and-shut case!). Her questions always made me laugh. I thought she was the funniest person I'd ever met, and the best at walking that narrow line between an assertion and a joke. Her face was interesting, too—her mouth and her eyes looked serious, but the tiny muscles twitched just a bit, as if she was holding back her own laughter. She was from York, Pennsylvania, and all fall, she said to me, "You will never want to visit there. What a dump," then turned around and asked me to come for Thanksgiving, since St. Louis was too far away for such a short holiday. It turned out that York was beautiful, a miniature city with plenty going on. Once we got back, I said, "I will never believe another word that you say!" and we both burst out laughing.

One thing that the music school had was practice rooms and accompanists, usually juniors or seniors who were specializing in piano playing, but a few guitarists, who, I suspected, were pretending to be interested in classical guitar but were secretly in bands. I had memorized lots of folk songs, of course—that's what the Big Muddies sang—but I didn't know much about songs that Frank Sinatra or Doris Day or Dean Martin sang. Those guys were still out there—Doris Day was exactly Mom's age, and Mom had met her once. But the Beatles, and Peter, Paul and Mary, had, as far as my friends and I were concerned, erased them. The accompanists, who were about my age, straddled the line, and there was one, my favorite, a nerdy boy only fifteen, from Pittsburgh, who evidently had been a prodigy, and didn't mind it, though he seemed a little out of his element at Penn State. His name was Leon Diamond and his parents came every weekend and stayed in a house they had bought in Park Forest Village, toward the edge of town, in a small glade of trees. I went there with Leon once, and saw immediately that his parents had a brilliant strategy—he was too smart to keep in high school, too talented to keep in Pittsburgh, so they got themselves a vacation home, and used that as a way to keep an eye on Leon, which was a good thing, because Leon was about five foot four (I was four inches taller than he was), shy, and a perfect target for frat bullying. There were plenty of times when we finished our practice sessions late in the afternoon and I walked him to his dorm. He never said that he was bullied or threatened, but he did glance around. At any rate, Leon specialized in Mendelssohn and Stravinsky, but he knew, by memory, all kinds of songs from the thirties and the forties—"Blue Moon," "Anything Goes," "I Got Plenty O' Nuttin'," "Too Darn Hot." We both loved "Summertime" and Paul Robeson. I practiced with Leon three times a week, with some of the others every day but Sunday. On Sunday, I sneaked into the nearest Methodist church, which was in a modest building but had a good choir, and listened to the hymns. All in all, I was entirely satisfied with my musical education. I was being trained but more or less ignored, and that was fine with me.

I also slipped into having a boyfriend. It turned out that having a boyfriend at Penn State was much easier than it was at my high school. For one thing, the percentage of nerds was much lower at Penn State, and almost every boy I met knew how to drive, how to fix something, how to take a walk in the woods and notice the birds and the trees. I often overheard the freshmen boys talking about fraternities—which ones would they like, which ones would take them—and I could see why, since many of those buildings were some of the most beautiful buildings I had ever seen. I sometimes imagined having a huge amount of money and buying the Kappa Sigma house for myself. The spectacular one—Sigma Chi—was a Tudor building with a tower. I loved walking past it. But I had no interest in sororities, and neither did Cathy or the other girls we ate with, walked with, or talked with.

The boy worked behind the counter in the eating area, serving up food. He smiled at me every time I went down the line, and then, toward the end of September, he sat down next to me in our history lecture. I hadn't realized he was in the class because I always sat somewhere in the first few rows and he was always late and sat up in the back. When he sat next to me, he said, "So, tell me. Why is your hair always in your face?" Of course I was insulted, but then he gently moved my hair out of my face with his finger, and tucked it behind my ear. It crossed my mind that I had never been noticed before, at least by a boy. Then class started, and we stared at the teacher, took some notes. After class, he walked me to my dorm, smiled, didn't touch me. I thought he would be like some sort of genie—just show up from time to time—and that's what he did, the next time at a freshman dance. I was sitting near the door; he came over, offered his hand, and turned out to be a good dancer. Whoever was playing the songs alternated between something current, like "I Was Made to Love Her" and "I'm a Believer," and older songs that I liked, too. When a version of "Goodnight, Irene" by Little Richard (one I owned) came on, in three-four time, the boy swept me into a very graceful waltz, his right hand in the air, his hand around my waist, and his head tossed back so that his very long hair swung from side to side. We danced five times, then went out into the night air just as "Eve of Destruction" came on. I said, "Do you believe we're on the eve of destruction?"

He said, "I think a lot of people would like to believe that, but I don't. I can't."

I said, "Why not?"

He shrugged. Always, there was a small smile ready to pop out. I hoped he would show up again, somewhere outside of the eating area, but I didn't even squeeze his hand, I was so afraid to be "forward." And he did show up two days later, at the doorway when I was leaving history class. My first boyfriend. His name was Charlie and even though he could dance like Fred Astaire, he couldn't carry a tune to save his life.

Now that Charlie was around, I eavesdropped on my two roommates from Philadelphia talking about sex. Mom, of course, had made sure I knew the basics, but the reason I was to know the basics was in order to avoid them. When she had first gone to New York to sing and act onstage, she had understood how babies were made, but Grandmother and Grandfather had told her nothing about romance, and according to her, she had never even been kissed on the lips—in our family, you got kissed on the cheek or the forehead. My father, who had betrayed her, was also the one who had "deflowered" her, and she was twenty-four. I hadn't heard anything about sex when I was listening to my classmates in the girls' room at our school—having a boyfriend was about looks, status, parties, dances, and where someone lived. If anyone was having sex, I didn't know about it. My two roommates—I called them "Mary Stanford" and "Laurie Stanford"—differed in their experience but were similar in their attitudes: sex was nice enough, depending on the guy, be sure that you took your pill, sometimes you had to show the guy what to do and how to do it. Mary, as far as I could tell, had shown several guys how to do it, while Laurie had done it once, with a guy who knew how to do it quite well but didn't want to do it twice (and belonged to Sigma Chi—he was a senior). They regularly used words I never heard at home—"ass," "clit," "tit," "dick," "balls"—so listening to them, at first, was like listening to a foreign language. I would lie quietly in my bunk, with my lightweight blanket over my head, and try to understand what they said and how they felt about it. Sometime around Halloween, the roommate on the bunk below me sat up one morning after Mary and Laurie had gone off to breakfast and said, "I wish they would stop going on and on about their sex lives."

I said, "Why? I think it's sort of interesting."

Lisa (I thought of her as "Lisa Indiana") said, "Because what's the big deal? One of my jobs on the farm for the last couple of years, since I got stronger, has been to hold the ewe while my dad guides the ram and then, lo and behold! The lambs arrive, and they are damn cute, I will say. Dad and Mom talk about sex all the time, and not just bulls and cows, stallions and mares, rams and ewes. They also know who in the neighborhood might have the clap, who had a miscarriage, who had that miracle baby only six months after the wedding, who disappeared into a convent over near Philly and then reappeared a year later."

I said, "Who did that?"

"One of the girls in my sister's high school class. Everyone knew who put it to her, and he disappeared, too. He went into the navy."

I thought of Brucie and the lead guitarist.

I said, "Don't you want a boyfriend?"

"Not really. Not unless he can drive a tractor. That's why I came here. I also got into Swarthmore, and my mom was dying for me to go there, but my dad knows that my brother doesn't want the farm, and I do, so he said I could go here. Not to mention how much cheaper this is."

I thought of asking what might happen if she got the perfect boyfriend, but his dad owned a farm in, say, Lancaster, but I didn't.

Cathy liked Charlie, too, and was good at joking with him. We would walk across campus. They would spar and I would smile or laugh, their audience. To me, Cathy said that he was nice or, as she said, "Nai-ece," a combination of "nice" and "naive." That was not what she wanted in a boyfriend. What she wanted was two, or preferably three, professional degrees—a doctor during the day who worked as a lawyer by night, or a physicist who explored black holes by day and traded on Wall Street by night. I said, "No one trades on Wall Street at night." She said, "But that's how you cheat and make your fortune!" as if she was amazed that I didn't know that. Charlie finally admitted that he planned to be a teacher, preferably in some disadvantaged neighborhood in, say, Baltimore.

Charlie was affectionate, but, as they said then, didn't force himself upon me, which I took to mean kiss me without my permission or touch my breasts, as if by mistake, or pinch my "ass." He didn't even try to sneak me or himself a drink. He knew very well that the drinking age in Pennsylvania was twenty-one (he also knew that in New York, it was eighteen), but unlike a lot of the boys and some of the girls on campus, there was no sneaking around with Charlie. He was as circumspect as I was.

So, here I was, with the perfect boyfriend—funny, kind, fairly good-looking, excellent dancer, gainfully employed, as my Mom would say; and here were my Philadelphia roommates—getting it on, having trouble finding relationships, going from boy to boy, sometimes regretfully, sometimes angrily, sometimes happily; or my Indiana roommate, not caring at all, and then developing a secret crush on her assistant professor of entomology, who specialized in insect-plant interactions. I could tell that she was pining away for him. I never saw him, so I didn't know if he was good-looking or not, but I did know that he was married, because his wife (they shared an odd name) taught flute in the music department. With the addition of my visit to York, Pennsylvania, I would have said that the first semester was perfect—I even got a B in Musical Theory.

The hard part was getting back to St. Louis from State College. I ended up taking a bus to Pittsburgh, then a train to Chicago, then another train to Union Station in St. Louis, where Mom picked me up, even though I was so tired of sitting down that I was ready to walk home, except that it was sleeting and snowing. Vacations were not something that I had thought about when I chose Penn State.

Somehow, I thought I would flutter back and forth like a butterfly, or, as I had called them when I was in kindergarten, a "flutterby."

There was a run-down old airport not far from the university, and planes did land and take off from there, but no airlines came in and I didn't think Uncle Drew was going to buy an airplane to come and pick me up, though by this time, he could afford it, especially since no matter how much money he made, he and Aunt Louise continued to live as they always had. They even joined a country club for a couple of years—Greenbriar Hills, which was only ten minutes from their house—but Uncle Drew never took to golf, and Grandfather continued to prefer the golf course near our house on Skinker, so they let their membership lapse. Nor did the kids, especially Allison, when they got older, want to go to private school—they liked their neighborhood, and their friends, and their public schools, so Uncle Drew was itching to spend (they did take vacations in Colorado Springs and even Palm Beach, and one time, he left the kids with Grandmother and Grandfather and took Aunt Louise to Paris and Rome), but he didn't like the things that most people spent their money on, so he dished it out to the relatives—put a new roof on Grandfather and Grandmother's place, supported Brucie in Northern California when he got back from Vietnam, sent Uncle Hank money for some sort of business investment, paid for my education, gave money to Mom and Aunt Lily, as far as I knew. And he asked for nothing in return other than lots of laughs.

Which we got over Christmas, maybe the best Christmas ever because Brucie was back and when we gathered around the piano at Grandmother's to sing, we were all in tune.

And then I went back to State College, moment by moment, and I decided that twenty-two hours on the train, four times a year, would be the price I would pay.

I suppose that Charlie and I were too shy for each other; by spring break, our relationship had slipped away without any friction—so little, in fact, that we still greeted each other when I went down the food line, and sometimes waved if we passed each other on campus.

I did see him with other girls, but I could tell by his demeanor that he was still reserved, still thoughtful. Later on, in the 1980s, when the AIDS crisis blew up, I began to wonder if maybe he was gay, and I looked for some information about him, but I never found anything.

After spring break, which I spent in York with Cathy, I got another boyfriend, taller, stronger, a little more sexy, and obsessed with hiking. It was easy to be obsessed with hiking in State College, because there were forests and hills everywhere. My new boyfriend was named Allen, and he was from Scranton. His life plan was to hike whatever trails were the most challenging. When I asked how he was going to support himself, he said he would start out as a travel agent, then become a tour guide. Eventually, say, before he hit the ripe old age of thirty, he would climb Mount Everest. He paid no attention to politics (one of a kind, in those days) because he didn't want to have any opinions that would threaten his access to every country in the world. As for Vietnam, his birthday was August 30, so his lottery number turned out to be 333. He was saved. And Brucie would have been, too, if he had not gotten in trouble, because his birthday was January 22, and so his lottery number would have been 337.

I had continued eavesdropping on Mary Stanford and Laurie Stanford, and shortly after Christmas vacation, Laurie had begun talking about a junior she danced with at a mixer—he was an English major, of all things, had no professional ambitions, but he had a deep voice and a square jaw and was muscled all over. She couldn't stop thinking about him. Mary said, "Well, just do it and get it over with!" and Lisa Indiana said, "She doesn't know it, but it's his smell. How a guy smells is what turns you on or off. My cousin had this boyfriend, he was perfect for her, and she loved him, but every time he forgot to shower, she would smell his pits and decide to break it off."

I said, "What happened?"

"They got married anyway, and they have two kids, but they sleep in separate bedrooms. I think he's going to dump her in the end."

So let's say it was Allen's smell that motivated me that spring, two weeks after I met him, when we went to a mixer, danced twice (he wasn't bad but wasn't anything like Charlie), and then went back to his dorm room early because his two roommates (one had dropped out) were on some kind of field trip and wouldn't be back until midnight. We started kissing as soon as he closed the door, and then, button by button, we took off each other's clothes—he was wearing bell-bottomed jeans and a pink button-down shirt, I was wearing a plaid miniskirt with a wide belt and a tight neon-green blouse that, I thought, made me look like Twiggy (though of course it did not). Once we were down to our underwear, we fell onto his bunk and he undid my bra, then slipped off his briefs. Even before he slipped them off, I could see something poking out of the top, and then there it was, the "erection"—something I'd heard of but never seen. It was both intimidating and interesting, and at the very moment that I realized that he was going to put it inside me, he reached over, opened a drawer beside his bed, and pulled out a small rubber thing, which I suspected, from listening to Mary and Laurie, was a condom. He slipped it over the end of his erection and turned toward me. He must have still smelled good, because I lay back, spread my arms and my legs, and waited expectantly for something amazingly wonderful to happen. What happened was that he had a hard time entering, poked his way in, said, "Jeez, you're a virgin!" and then I said, "Didn't you know that?" and he said, "I didn't think anyone was a virgin these days!" But he smiled, as if he wasn't going to hold it against me, and then came after four thrusts and pulled out. The erection had turned into a rather cute thing that flopped to one side. The condom came out with the floppy thing, and Allen took it off and tossed it across the floor into the wastebasket beside his desk, said, "Score!" and gave me a hug. I lay there while he drifted off, but maybe an hour later, he woke up, said, "Jeez, they're going to be back soon!" It was about eleven.

Getting our clothes on was much more boring than taking them off. I envied him—jeans, a comfortable shirt—but I had, I thought, to look as good when we were finished as I had when we started.

I even took my hairbrush out of my purse and did the best I could with my tangly hair. We were outside the door of his dorm heading toward mine when he turned and greeted his roommates, "Hey, guys! How was it?"

"Shit, I'm done in," said one of them, and the other one yawned, and we laughed about that as we held hands on the way back to the dorm. The holding hands was the best part of the whole episode, and when I got back to my bunk, Lisa sensed what had happened, because she said, "You washed yourself inside and out afterward, didn't you?"

I said, "I couldn't. We were in a boys' dorm and I couldn't use their bathroom."

She said, "Do it now, or you will get an infection." She pushed me out the door and down the hall toward the girls' room, where I took a shower and did what she said as best I could. When I got back to our room, Mary and Laurie were there, but Lisa had not, apparently, told them my secret, because they treated me as they always did—friendly but distant.

From the eavesdropping, I gathered that the odds of my relationship with Allen continuing after my deflowering were low—a ten-to-one long shot, Uncle Drew might have said (and I did have my $86 roll of bills in my suitcase in the closet), but things went on uneventfully for the next month. We had sex a few times, once on a beautiful day in a remote spot on the campus. The frequency mostly depended on our roommates, and his were gone more often than mine were. We talked about getting a room at a local hotel, but neither of us could afford that.

There was unrest on campus—the Black students felt isolated, because there were so few of them and, I thought, saw no downside to staging a protest. There was an article in the *Daily Collegian* about how it felt to be Black on campus—the detail that struck me was the fact that counselors in Philly did not want their Black students to go to Penn State because of how they would be treated when they got there. How they were treated included being followed around the local Woolworth's if they tried to shop there, and one student being chased out of a town nearby. That some of the students had been called the N-word by members of the fraternities didn't surprise Allen or me. The list of demands the students proposed was published in May, and Allen and I thought they were totally reasonable. And then summer vacation loomed.

There were two things I worried about—how would I keep up my good mood without Leon and the other accompanists? And were letters between Scranton and St. Louis enough to maintain my love affair with Allen? I did promise to go on the pill, which Allen and I both thought would be safer. Allen was not going to hike that summer—he was going to work in a lumber mill. He had worked in a meat processing plant the year before and didn't want to do that again. I didn't know what I was going to do, but I supposed that Mom could put me to work at the Muny in some capacity.

It fascinates me to look back on those times, because I had no idea that I was about to get my big break.

I did go to work at the Muny—Mom got me onto a crew that kept the costumes and the props and some of the furniture sorted and dusted through the summer productions. My favorite room was where they kept the wigs—for men and women. Some of them were really old, others were made of plastic, but some were quite beautiful, especially the women's wigs for musicals like *Show Boat* or *Oklahoma!* And no one minded if I spied on the rehearsals and listened to the songs the actors were singing and how they sang them. I was paid $1.75 an hour. Mom kept saying she was going to charge me for breakfast if I didn't stop eating so much bacon, but she never did. I got a letter from Allen once a week, waited a day, then wrote back. His letters were steadily sweet and affectionate. Toward the end of June, someone else working at Kiel came into Mom's office and asked what I was doing for the next week. Mom told him, and he came back the next day and asked if I could learn ten songs in four days.

Mom said that I could. She was more sure about that than I was, but I assumed that it was a show or a musical, and I thought it was time to try that. It ended up that it was a band, the opening act for a prominent group (not the Rolling Stones, I'm sorry to say). One of the female backup singers had come down with a serious case of strep throat, and her doctor said that she could neither sing nor travel, because the antibiotics he had prescribed weren't working very well and he was afraid she was coming down with pneumonia. I showed up at eight the next morning, and we went straight to work.

Appropriately for a group from Kansas City, the music was a mix: one or two cowboy songs—"I Ride an Old Paint," "Streets of Laredo"; one or two spirituals—"Deep River," "Peace in the Valley"; three Dylan songs, "When the Ship Comes In," "One Too Many Mornings," and "Leopard-Skin Pill-Box Hat"; a Tom Paxton song, "The Last Thing on My Mind"; and "I Heard It Through the Grapevine." Our encore song, should we need one, was one I'd heard often, sung by Skeeter Davis, "The End of the World," which I often sang to myself when I was walking in Forest Park, especially in the foresty area not far from our house. Fortunately, I knew all of these songs by heart, from listening to the records and singing them on my own as well as with the Big Muddies.

I fit in with the band—there were two guys, one African American, one white, on guitar and bass, and two girls for backup, also one African American and one white, and a drummer, who was white. Their names were Rex, Jack, Arlene, Carrie, and Lou. They had me sit in a chair and watch them as they played through their set. My job was to substitute for the alto singer, who was sick. I listened to the first two songs, and, unable to stop myself, began to join in, first tapping my fingers in time to the music, then nodding my head, then humming, then adding some harmony here and there. Eventually, Rex and Carrie began to laugh, and Jack summoned me up to join them. I stood between Arlene and Carrie, and worked my way through the rest of the songs. When we got to "The End of the World," I couldn't help belting out the line, "Don't they know? It's the end of the world! / It ended when you said good-bye." My eyes were closed, but I did notice that everyone fell silent, and then Carrie put her arms around me and said, "You got it!" That was the first time I felt that my talent for singing was recognized, and, maybe, that was also the first time that I recognized it myself as something I possessed rather than something I was striving for.

We practiced until noon, took a rest, did it again the next day for an hour, so as not to damage our voices. I found myself a dress to wear in the closets at the Muny—black, unassuming—and then we did the show. The auditorium was full down below, maybe half-full in the balcony, it was lots of fun, and I thought that was that, but the next day, Rex and Jack showed up at our place and asked if I would go with them to Cincinnati, Cleveland, Chicago, and Milwaukee, then back to KC. Ten days on the road, in their Chevy van, hotels supplied. Their performances were booked, and the doctor didn't know when their sixth member would be back in action, but they were taking some time off anyway, and . . .

Of course I said yes. They were friendly and, I thought, ready to be famous, though they didn't have a recording contract yet. I wanted to sing with them, feel the harmonies and the rhythms they were so good at wash through me, and to go along for the ride, part of the group. Did I want a career of my own? I thought I would know once I had observed what it felt like for them, maybe especially for Carrie, who seemed to me to be the most likely one to move on to a solo career. I didn't ask Mom's permission—I told her my plan. She smiled, helped me pack. I wrote Allen an excited note, and he said he would hitchhike to Cleveland to see me, and us. What I needed was something to wear. Carrie went with me to Stix and we wandered around the aisles until she found a sparkly loose dress, short sleeves, miniskirt. She said I was thin enough to wear it, and she envied me—her dress was silver, went to the middle of her calves, and swayed back and forth as she sang. Arlene's was like mine, but red. The boys all wore black. It wasn't until the night before we left that I felt nervous, but I didn't know exactly what I was nervous about. I felt comfortable with the group and I actually felt confident about opening my mouth and letting it all out.

The van looked big, but with all of the drums and the guitars, I was amazed that we fit into it. Rex owned the van, and it was new—before the boys added the girls (and changed their name from the

Freaks to the Freak-Outs), they had gone everywhere in a VW bus. They got paid well enough to travel, well enough to make the rent, well enough to maintain their instruments and sometimes buy a new one, well enough to dress stylishly and get their hair done, well enough to stay in decent hotels, but not well enough to eat lunch anywhere but a Steak 'n Shake or a McDonald's. In some ways, the van had surprisingly good acoustics—we could practice as we headed down the highway, but the Freak-Outs were so experienced (they had been on the road for a year and a half, off and on) that they hardly needed to practice. It was as we were heading out of St. Louis in the van that I felt my nervousness slip away. Being a musician, for each of the Freak-Outs, was normal, and I felt that confidence seep into me.

The routine was to leave one town at about ten in the morning, stop for lunch around one o'clock, go to the hotel in the next town, eat at the hotel, practice for an hour the next day on the stage where we would be performing that night, then look around or visit friends (the Freak-Outs had friends everywhere), go back to the venue around six, do the opening act, watch the main act, sometimes party with that act, and sometimes not. The one who drove was the one who was least hungover, and that was usually Carrie. If I went to a party after a show, I would see her take a glass of whatever was offered, sip it once or twice, keep it in her hand in order to look sociable, and then leave it behind, almost full, at the end. I thought that was an excellent strategy. She told me that her father tended a bar at a club in Kansas City, and he had kicked so many drunks out of the club over the years that he had made sure that his kids knew the consequences. The only state where I could drink legally was Wisconsin, but I let the Freak-Outs believe that I was twenty-two, not nineteen. Carrie was closer to thirty; Arlene was the youngest at twenty-four.

They were kind to me, and friendly, but it was "work-friendly," where you know that you have to get along—to smile and say hi, and ask occasional questions, but not pry or, I observed, tease. The relationships between the musicians were fine from the outside, but

Lou, who was the drummer, did not want to be put down in any way, and evidently, he and Rex had argued with Jack in the past. Lou would actually say, "Keep it to yourself, shithead!" but he was such a good drummer that Jack didn't dare try to replace him. Carrie was in every way more agreeable. If Jack said something that she didn't like, she would roll her eyes and toss her head, like a teacher who knows her students need education and patience. Arlene was always quiet. I tried my best not to say anything unpleasant, but once in a while I would screw up and get an eye-roll. At one point, at the hotel in Chicago, I heard Carrie and Lou having an argument. Huey Newton was about to go on trial, and Lou said, "They always do it, one way or the other—kill 'em on the street or in court!"

Carrie said, "Doesn't help you to shove it in their face."

Lou said, "Help what? What do you think you'll ever get out of these people?"

Carrie said, "I got something already. I got a voice. I'd rather be Aretha than a Panther."

Lou said, "You ain't Aretha, bitch."

And then Carrie laughed.

It was evident that she enjoyed the singing, but it was also evident that Lou could lose himself in the percussion. He would lean back, lift his drumsticks, then lean forward and start pounding. It didn't matter how fast, he was always right in time, and every night, he had one or two solos, apparently off the cuff, since when he got that look on his face, Carrie and Rex would look at each other, pause, and let him take it away. Jack was the lead guitarist, and it seemed as though he and Lou were on the same page musically, because Jack had no trouble playing along when Lou was riffing. They did get a lot of applause, especially in Cincinnati and Kansas City.

As for me, I did my best to learn from both Arlene and Carrie. Arlene was the soprano, and she knew every tune and all the words. She could hit the high notes that harmonized with Rex and Jack from above, which gave their songs a heavenly quality. Carrie and I backed up the rhythm, sometimes just made harmonic noises, and other times sang bits of the songs, repeating lines Rex and Jack had already sung. The three of us girls got to lead two songs each night—the Skeeter Davis song and, oddly, "I Heard It Through the Grapevine"—Carrie led on that one and always got a standing ovation. She told me Gladys Knight & the Pips had sung the original version, but I'd never heard it.

Meeting up with Allen in Cleveland had its good sides and its bad sides. The first good side was that he made it, three hundred seventy-five miles in nine hours and two minutes. The first bad side was that somewhere he lost his wallet. He was sure that it wasn't stolen, only that it had slipped out of his pocket, whether in a car or by the side of the road he had no idea. The second good side was that the theater comped him a ticket when I told them that his wallet and his suitcase had been stolen (which was why he looked so disheveled). Since he was Allen, he didn't mind the long trip (plenty of time to walk along the highway and look around) and he was optimistic about his wallet turning up—and it did. Two days after he got home (eight hours and six minutes), the Pennsylvania Department of Transportation sent him a note, saying they had his wallet, which a woman found in a little gulch beside the highway and sent to them. It looked as though a lot of vehicles had run it over—it was flattened. But the money was still there—$52. When he got to the office the following Monday, they issued him a new license, since his was now almost unreadable. They also gave him the woman's name. He sent her a thank-you note, and she wrote back, saying she had pulled over because she ran out of gas, saw it there when she was waiting for the tow truck. Allen went with us to the party after the show, did not get drunk, stayed with me in my hotel room (Arlene stayed with Carrie), and the last thing I saw as we drove off to Chicago was Allen on the other side of the road with his thumb in the air. I heard Lou, who was sitting in front of me, mutter something about Allen being lucky he wasn't Black if that was how he planned to get around, but I didn't react.

Maybe the luckiest thing about the trip was that the van had air-conditioning. Even Uncle Drew's car didn't have air-conditioning—not because he couldn't afford it (Aunt Louise's did have air-conditioning), but because he was very fond of his 1963 Thunderbird. Since it was a convertible, he didn't think it needed air-conditioning, and anyway, what else were windows for? But no number of windows in the van would have kept us, or more important, the instruments, cool enough in that midwestern summer. It was always at least in the eighties, sometimes in the nineties, and humid humid humid. It was sunny for the whole ten days, even though we drove all over thunderstorm and tornado country, and when it was over, and Carrie put me on the bus to St. Louis with $250 in my pocketbook. She said it had been a big success, hugged me, and thanked me for coming along, and being so cooperative as well as "always on the beat." She didn't say anything about the woman I had replaced, but I gathered that she was feeling better. It was on the bus, as we were crossing the Missouri River not far from Overton, that the idea of having a singing career seemed to gel in my brain. The downside might be the traveling and the routine, but that sense of looking at the audience, feeling the song blossom in your brain, and then opening your mouth and having it come out, the pleasure of that, and also the pleasure of knowing, thanks mostly to Carrie, that I COULD do that, made the whole idea irresistible.

A month later, I was back at Penn State. The sororities had siphoned off Mary and Laurie Stanford. Lisa Indiana and I shared a room with a new girl, Janet-the-Baker. Janet was majoring in home ec, and her current project was to come up with the world's best Christmas cookie, and then become both rich and famous. She lured Lisa and me into being her "primary tasters"—she never ate more than a small bite. Freshman year, she had specialized in leftovers. Her favorite project had been cooking a Sunday dinner, and then eating only dishes made with leftovers until the following Saturday. I asked her what the last dish she ate was, and she said onion soup made from capon broth with croutons made from the leftover rolls. She had cheated, though, when she added some freshly grated Gruyère. She was thin as a rail.

The easiest part was getting back into the practicing routine at the music school. Leon was now sixteen, had grown two inches, still looked fourteen. He had given three concerts over the summer—one in Pittsburgh, one somewhere in New Jersey, and one in Boston. He said he was "circling New York, but wasn't ready to land." Since he was adept at every sort of music, he would play a Mozart sonata, followed by three movements of *The Seasons,* by Tchaikovsky, and then finish up with "Rhapsody in Blue," by George Gershwin. Since he liked Gershwin, we spent most of the fall practicing a ten-song concert, me singing, him playing. We didn't expect to go onstage. My favorite was "I Got Rhythm." Leon's was "I Got Plenty O' Nuttin'." It didn't matter if the song had been written for a male singer or a female one, I sang them all as best I could, and managed to lower my range by two notes and raise it by two.

As for Cathy, we had exchanged four letters over the summer, and she sounded like she was enjoying herself working as a camp counselor in Vermont, taking kids on overnight hiking trips. When we got back to school, I hadn't heard from her in three weeks. She did get to school a week late, and she said nothing at all about where she had been. She seemed a little distraught—her sense of humor wasn't as bright or aggressive as it had been. We still ate breakfast together and walked to class, but I did all the talking. It was Lisa who told me that Cathy had had to go to Colorado to get an abortion, though how she came to know that, I never learned. I wasn't opposed to abortion—no one I knew was, including my mother—but I didn't ask Cathy about it, for fear that Lisa was wrong, and she didn't say anything. Over the course of the fall, she got most of her old personality back, but she didn't go to mixers and she didn't date. Lisa didn't know anything about who the guy was who had impregnated her or when it happened, and no one else ever talked about it.

Everyone said that sophomore year was the easiest and most boring in college, but for us, it both was and wasn't. The African American students, who had formed an organization named after Frederick Douglass, were joined by the local Students for a Democratic Society chapter, and tents were set up on Old Main Lawn, where students lived who couldn't afford housing. There were also protests about the Vietnam War and Women's Rights. Allen and I participated, but Lisa and Leon stayed away, though Leon said he was sympathetic. Rather than being boring or easy, I thought the tents symbolized the world we were in as a maze that you had to make your way through attentively and thoughtfully.

It was rather the same with Allen and me. He still had those ambitions, but he didn't need to talk about them. I had gotten on the pill, and we were doing it when we could, depending on the weather and the roommates. Nothing was surprising, nothing was thrilling, nothing was terrifying, but everything required thought. For Thanksgiving, I went with Lisa to Indiana, and her mother was an excellent cook, rather in the same mold as my grandmother, except that she grew her own turkeys and Lisa slaughtered and plucked them (I actually helped a little with the one we ate). My favorite activities remained practicing and walking—whatever momentarily fazed me was erased by one or the other, or both, since I liked to sing while I was walking. I did hope that that New York City agent or that California member of a rock band might be lurking in the State College trees, so I belted it out as best I could, but no one popped up and I wasn't discovered. I even got used to the train trip back to St. Louis, then back to Pittsburgh and State College. The singers I paid attention to—Janis Joplin, Joan Baez, Judy Collins, Joan Sutherland, Aretha Franklin, and a new one no one talked about but I liked, Linda Ronstadt—didn't seem to bear any relation to me or my ambitions.

I wrote a few songs. The one about Allen was titled "Oh, There You Are." It was about looking into a ravine, seeing the loved one (it could be sung by me or a guy), thinking he/she was dead, seeing the resurrection—he/she was only taking a nap. The one about Leon was titled "Up in the Trees." It was about taking LSD (which Janet did once and told me about) and seeing an angel playing a piano that was balanced on the top of a large oak tree and watching the notes sprinkle down like rain, feeling them in my hair and on my shoulders. The third one was about an accident I heard had happened in St. Louis, a car going off the bridge over the River des Peres, which may have once been a river but was now a sewer. My challenge was to make sense of the story while sticking in a bunch of odd St. Louis street names—Skinker, of course, DeBaliviere, Bompart, Chouteau, Vandeventer. The chorus was about Big Bend. The song made me cry, but I never sang it to anyone but myself. I got an A– in Musicology (how classical music and African American music and jazz were related to one another), an A in Performance Theory Tutorial. And then it was 1969 and what Allen and I talked about most of the rest of the winter was whether we should spend the money from my set of gigs going to a ski area and learning to ski, and if so which one?

Leon continued to develop—he got to five foot ten and started growing a beard, which made him look older. He also changed his playing style—not how he interpreted the music, but how he looked sitting on the piano bench. It was as if he had watched Lou, the drummer—he swayed more, threw his arms around more, had different expressions on his face. He now understood that he was no longer required to be a well-behaved student, but to perform in a way that held the audience's attention and also expressed the feelings of the music he was playing. He didn't go to his parents' place on the weekends, but stayed around campus and flirted with some of the freshman girls. For a few weeks, he dated a girl on the freshman girls' field hockey team, bundled up and went to her games. There was nothing about him that suggested that he was fed up with playing or oppressed by being a prodigy—rather, it was as if he was in a huge diverse field of plants and trees and animals, and he wanted to find out everything he could about every one of them. He didn't accompany my practicing as a task, but rather as another mode of discovery.

Sometime in early November, I brought out "Oh, There You Are," which I had copied out as sheet music. I set it on the music rack. He stared at it for maybe four minutes, then lifted his hands, and played it through perfectly, as least as far as I could tell, but he looked a little dissatisfied, tried again, liked it better, and I did, too, because it was way more melodious than I had expected. I joined in. Four verses, four repeats of the chorus: "You were under the leaves, I stared in grief, / and then came a breeze, oh, my darling, my darling, / oh, there you were, now, here you are!" He played it through again, added a stronger beat in the bass clef, and in order to give this beat some play, I slowed down, paused, let the music take over. Either the music was better than I had expected or it was better because Leon made it better. We added it to the Gershwin set and played it once or twice a week. We played it twice again when we got back to school in January, and I was motivated to compose two more songs, "Trees in the Distance," about a girl who watches her boyfriend walk away until she can no longer see him, and "What Dance Was That?" in three-four time, about a girl at a school dance whose date teaches her to waltz around the room, and she is spellbound.

Just before Valentine's Day, which was a Friday, Leon told me that he wanted to take me to the family place in Park Forest Village. Since he was extremely reserved, he didn't say anything about a valentine, so I was a bit worried. I said, "I've got a date that night . . ." He gave me a startled look. I said, "It's Valentine's Day."

He said, "Oh, I forgot about that. We can go the next day."

I was relieved.

His mother was very kind and welcoming, as always. When we walked in the door, she said, "Oh, kids! Sit down right now and have some of this hot chocolate! It's French, and so delicious!" And of course there were rugelach, as well.

Once we were entirely comfortable and had put our things in our rooms, we wandered into the living room (where a Steinway grand took up most of the space). Mrs. Diamond was perched on the edge of her chair, and Mr. Diamond was sitting on the arm of the couch. The two men on the couch could have been twins, except that one was a little grayer than the other one. They stood up and introduced themselves—Max Gross and Lev Gross.

Small talk. I kept looking out the window at the snow. I had brought a warm coat and good boots, so I didn't want the sun to go down before I had a chance for a walk. There was a section of the Diamond property a little down the slope that was peppered with tall, thin river birches. The leaves were all on the ground, but the bark was white, rough, and fascinating. One of the brothers, I thought Max, said, "So, Miss . . ."

I said, "You don't have to call me Miss."

He smiled. He said, "Well, anyway, Lev, here, is Leon's promoter. Fact is, I'm a promoter, too. That's what two brothers do who love music but haven't got a speck of talent, hard as they try. Anyway, Lev promotes classical and I promote popular and someday you can ask me who's making more dough and maybe I'll tell you."

Now we all laughed, including Lev.

Max said, "Over the holidays, Leon played a song for us. Said you wrote it. Couldn't sing it to save his life, but I did love the melody and what I understood of the words, and I wonder if you might sing it for us."

Leon was already heading for the piano. He sat, opened the fallboard, spread his hands. I was a little taken aback, and wondered for a moment if I would actually remember the words to "Oh, There You Are." But of course, as soon as I was next to the piano, in position, it just rolled out. It lasted three minutes and forty-two seconds, seemed like half an hour, and I kept my eyes down until maybe a minute after I finished. Mrs. Diamond said, "Don't be shy, sweetie!"

I looked at her. There was a tear on her cheek—but maybe it was the sunlight. Then I looked at Mr. Diamond and the Gross brothers. Mr. Diamond looked impressed, Lev Gross was smiling, and Max Gross looked excited. The first thing he said was, "You have quite a voice. Good vibrato."

Finally, I felt comfortable. I said, "Believe me, I've worked on that." I stuck out my jaw, and everyone laughed. Thinking of the ravine in the song, I glanced out the window at the trees.

4

EVERYONE, including Mom, who had had one of her own back in New York just after the war, called it my "lucky break." Max Gross didn't push me, but he hovered nearby, occasionally wrote me a letter, brought me to New York to do a recording, for Elektra, of "Oh, There You Are" on the A side and the other song he liked, "What Dance Was That?," on the B side.

He said my genre was "folk rock." For the recordings, he hired a studio band, all of whom were about ten years older than I was and had hair down to their shoulders. They lived in Greenwich Village, smoked either cigs, as they called them, or spliffs, or both. Only one of them, the bass player, hit on me, but he didn't push it, and the next day the rhythm guitar player said, "Just so you know, he hits on every girl he meets, because that way, the odds are on his side." I thought, for the first time in years, of Uncle Drew's winning bet, and said, "Once in a while." When I got back to school, I looked for my wad of dusty two-dollar notes, and there it was, in the corner of my suitcase. I wiped it off, gave it a kiss, said, "Stay with me, dear ones," and put it away again.

Leon and I agreed not to say much about the recording. I told Allen, of course, as well as Lisa, who knew how to keep a secret, but not Janet-the-Baker, who wouldn't have cared, or Cathy, who would have kissed me, hugged me, congratulated me, but then sighed, as if I was the lucky one. I remained friends with Cathy, and walked and talked with her every day, but how to help her was still a mystery to me. She was getting more and more remote, and even when I was kind to her in a routine way—offering her a pancake that I didn't want or opening a door for her—she froze up, shook her head, waited for me to eat the pancake myself or go through the door. A couple of times, I taxed Lisa with a few questions—what was going on? Did Lisa understand this at all? All Lisa said was, "I don't think she wants to get over it, but I don't know why." Then, after taking a psych class (for which she wrote a paper entitled "The Psychology of Bovines"), she said, "She's an extreme introvert. She can't help herself." I knew what an introvert was, and I didn't think Cathy had ever been one, but it didn't help to contradict Lisa, so I kept silent.

IT WAS AMAZING that the record got any airplay at all, given all the other songs that were coming out at the time—"In the Year 2525," "Gimme Shelter," "Proud Mary," "The Night They Drove Old Dixie Down." Elektra pushed it, and Max Gross had a few connections here and there. I always wondered, later, whether they paid radio stations to play it, as they had in the fifties (and I even wrote a song about that).

"Oh, There You Are" came out in early May, a good time of year to be thinking about a ravine, and a few weeks later, I sang at the folk-rock festival near San Jose, out in California—my first visit to the West Coast. I had heard nothing about the concert they held the previous year, and maybe Max didn't know anything about it, either, because it had been chaotic and dangerous (though nothing like Altamont, still in the future). Elektra set me up with a local band, Santana Blues Band, and we sent them recordings and music for four songs. There were plenty of guys in the band, and they knew what they were doing (they had a gig of their own later in the day). They were friendly and professional, and the main problem (lack of audience) was due to the recent release of the single and the fact that it hadn't gotten much play on the West Coast (the Santana Blues Band was what most of the people who were willing to come to the fairgrounds at eleven a.m. were hoping to see). But I got lots of applause for my four songs, Max was happy, and I was happy, too—because, as always, it was like sitting in the corner in junior year (or eavesdropping in the girls' room) and watching the popular kids gossip, flirt, stumble, fall down, say mean things behind one another's backs, wear hideous dresses in orange or purple, put on their makeup, get drunk or stoned. The festival lasted only three days. My favorite parts were getting to walk up to Chuck Berry and say, "I'm from St. Louis, too. Skinker!" and having him reply, "Cards, baby!" and know that no one nearby knew what in the world we were talking about, and watching the New Lost City Ramblers. Elektra flew me back to Pittsburgh Sunday morning, and I was back in my dorm room by midnight. It was like taking off from one planet and landing on another.

The semester ended and Elektra sent me here and there, to a few clubs, mostly in St. Louis, Chicago, Minneapolis, Kansas City. By the end of June, the song was up to number 86 on the *Billboard* Hot 100, which was fine with me, because that equaled the number of dollars in my roll, and I thought it was lucky. There were a few local reviews of my performances—I was praised for my voice, though my "stage presence" was "a little reticent" and my looks were "forgettable" (no one said that about David Crosby). My favorite performance was at a concert in New York run by a brewing company (not Anheuser-Busch, though they could have used the same idea in St. Louis, which was easier to get to than Wollman Rink). I was the first act, Blood, Sweat & Tears was the second act. I sang six songs, and sang along with them on two other songs. The next day was when I was walking down Broadway and I paused, looking up at one of those exterior fire escapes, and a man in an expensive suit nearly bumped into me. I turned and apologized, and there he was, my father, wearing the very face I had looked at in the mirror an hour earlier. I followed him, watched him enter Zabar's, where I had never been. I got a tray, got into line right behind him. I wanted him to look at my face and see his own. I even bumped him in the elbow with my tray, and smiled. But he seemed to notice nothing, ordered his pastrami sandwich, scowled when I looked at him again. After that, I went downtown to East Tenth Street and Tompkins Square Park, looked around, tried to remember that time I'd run across the street to pet the cat and the car squealed to a halt behind me, turning Mom's hair white (or so she said, though it must have gone right back to being brown). Maybe I remembered the cat. An image sometimes flickered in my mind late at night, but nothing more than that. Otherwise, I didn't remember New York at all, and nothing on Tenth Street or in Tompkins Square Park looked familiar.

And that was that. A little vacation on the Jersey Shore with Mom—two weekends, five days in between—then a stop in Scranton to introduce Mom to Allen and his parents, then back to State College, junior year. It was 1969—every good thing that happened to me, Mom, and Allen was pretty much overwhelmed by what was happening all around us, blasted out by the TV: Woodstock; the moon landing; Chappaquiddick; Catherine Warnes, a singer from Australia who was my age, shot to death performing in South Vietnam; a TWA flight into LA hijacked to Havana. I was glad to get back to my room, to Lisa, to Janet, to Allen, to what I thought would be dull and normal.

When I went to the music studios to sign up for practice, Leon was standing right outside, smoking a Camel and looking more like nineteen than fourteen. The first thing he said to me after his smile was, "Now we're going to write a Christmas song."

I said, "There's nothing new to say about Christmas."

"That might be the first line."

The next day I got a note from Max, one sentence: "Time for a Christmas song." So I sat down in my room and took out a sheet of paper. The question was: Funny? Sad? Nostalgic? Traditional? Irreverent? One that we never sang at my grandparents' house for the Christmas Eve party was "Rockin' Around the Christmas Tree," but Brucie and I had put it on more than once and danced around Aunt Lily's living room. You never knew what was going to sell, whether the days of "White Christmas" had given way to the days of "I Saw Mommy Kissing Santa Claus."

And I wasn't in a Christmas mood. How could I be, when the

grass was still green and the leaves cloaked the trees, and a lot of the boys were still wearing shorts to class? Allen thought September was the best time to run, and he always ran in a sleeveless T-shirt and shorts that showed the hairiness of his legs. He would then come by the practice room and give me a kiss, the sweat pouring off him. There was something extremely not Christmassy about this. I looked out the window for inspiration, got none, went to the cafeteria for lunch, saw no candy canes, walked down the hall between the practice rooms, heard only Bach, Purcell's "Air in D Minor," Leon playing "Rhapsody in Blue," which always put him in a good mood. I went outside, and there it was, one of the professors, an old man walking slowly, followed by his dog, also evidently old. The man didn't look back; he knew the dog was there, and the dog didn't do what I had always seen dogs do—run to this bush or that tree, just to sniff something out. The only thing the dog was interested in was the white-haired man smoking his cigarette, making his slow way toward—I looked around—Ritenour.

I walked back to my dorm, sat down, wrote a song called "Our Last Christmas" from the point of view of the dog. I didn't know if it was a joke or not. I closed my eyes and let all the Christmas songs I had known over the years wander around in my brain, wrote down the words. The first few lines were, "The best thing I did as a pup / Was leap when my master said 'Up!' / My job was to catch whatever he threw / Old and tasty, fresh and new / And then—was he sane? / He tossed me that candy cane!"

That made me smile. I went on, "My mistress laughed, and her kitty cat yowled / Then stole my cane, pushed it under the tree / And now he's gone and it's only me / Staring through the frosty pane / Looking for a candy cane." Then I walked around the room, humming a few ideas for a tune. I thought this song was going to be a sad one, and I was reluctant to do that, but the song itself was leading me down a road, and I was curious about it, so I kept going. I decided that three-four time was the most soothing, so I practiced tunes in three-four time. When I was finished, dinner service was over and here came Lisa (I now had only one roommate, as Janet-the-Baker was working as a cook somewhere in New York City). She said, "Whatcha doin'?"

I said, "Not much." I wasn't hungry. I read some of my assignment for European Lit, *Madame Bovary*. Didn't understand a word, even though it was translated into English.

When it came time for bed, I tried not to get frustrated with my song—in fact, I tried not to think about it at all, but that was difficult. The other songs had more or less popped out, been written down, words and music, and the whole process had been a pleasure. I thought that was what it was supposed to be. I did not think writing songs was supposed to be like writing English papers or history papers, looking things up, scratching your head, trying to understand, feeling frustrated and bored. Our musicology teachers never talked about frustration. Evidently, even when he was deaf, Beethoven heard it all in perfect sequence and wrote it down. That was his sign of genius, and here I was, putting together a simple Christmas song, and it was taking me twice as long, three times as long, as Beethoven's Ninth Symphony took him (I had no idea if this was true).

When I got up first thing in the morning, it was just after daybreak, and the weather was damp, so the grass, which had been looking a little faded and worn, had greened up. I put on my jean jacket and slipped out—Lisa was usually up before I was, a habit that she'd gotten from milking cows, or so she said. The campus was almost empty. I walked over to the Arboretum, then up the hill, one of Allen's favorite places to run—around the park, up and down. I wasn't thinking of my song or Christmas. Mostly I was still in a sleepy haze, still not hungry, though I did find two Oreos wrapped in a napkin in the pocket of my jean jacket. I thought back to my little tour, and then to my littler tour with the Freak-Outs, and sang the songs we'd sung, all in a row—"I Ride an Old Paint," "Streets of Laredo," "Deep River," "When the Ship Comes In," "One Too Many Mornings," "Leopard-Skin Pill-Box Hat," "The Last Thing on My Mind," "I Heard It Through the Grapevine," "The End of the World." At the top of the hill, with absolutely no one anywhere around, I sang "The End of the World" again, belted out my favorite line, and nearly ran home. When I got there, Lisa was off to breakfast. I sat down and wrote, "Yes there was a rat in the fireplace / I saw it there in a tiny space / I barked and whined and jumped around / But my old man couldn't hear a sound. / The rat stroked his whiskers and looked me in the eye, / Then ran up the flue toward the big blue sky / But the snow came down and washed him out / On the living room carpet, where he rolled about / I jumped on him then, but little did I know, / That my talent for jumping was pretty low / So we rolled around together and the old man laughed / For the very first time since the old lady passed."

I was finished in time for my musicology class, and then lunch (by now I was hungry and they were serving a really good chili), and then I came back, wadded up the paper, and threw it away. That evening I wrote the Christmas song I got famous for, "Nothing to Say About Christmas." Leon helped me with the tune, Max loved it, and it was out the day after Thanksgiving. The DJs would say, "Here's a funny one," or "This one will get you in the mood," and it went up to 43 on the Hot 100 list, another lucky number.

I WONDERED IF I was going to have to live in Greenwich Village and become "part of the music scene," as Allen said, but Max said that those days were gone. Now it was all about going to festivals, wearing brilliantly colored outfits, and being seen as an oddball. There were, indeed, several kinds of oddballs. My favorites were Joan Baez, Judy Collins, Joni Mitchell, and Karen Dalton. But the more I learned about them, the more it seemed that they were not only older than I was, they were also more opinionated. I also listened a lot to Aretha Franklin, Nina Simone, and Tina Turner, but they seemed so much more experienced than I was that I viewed them as part of an older generation—not quite Mom's or Doris Day's but almost. The one I liked best was Joni Mitchell, who I later found out was about the same age as Aretha Franklin, but seemed younger and less self-confident than the others. I imagined her doing as I did, wandering around in the woods or lying in bed at night, singing to herself and enjoying that more than being onstage. Joan Baez was the one who seemed to me to have the most self-confidence. She had plenty of opinions, and wasn't shy about expressing them. This seemed to thrill her fans, but I imagined myself onstage, or at that rally the Black students and the SDS had staged during halftime at a football game in November that had caused a big ruckus, or maybe being interviewed by some magazine, opening my mouth and then having nothing come out of it, not even a song. When I mentioned this to Leon, he said there were ways to get over stage fright (what he did was look down at the keys of the piano and start playing), but I also knew that as a classical musician, Leon wouldn't be expected to express opinions. He and his parents had plenty of them, especially about Israel, but their place was not in the recital venue, or so Leon thought.

Sometime in the spring, as I was idling my way through Keats and Shelley, secretly reading *Frankenstein,* pronouncing French words as best I could, and analyzing how various instruments meshed (the best part was that the kids in the orchestra would come in in pairs and play together, both scales and tunes), Mom sent me a letter, or three letters in one envelope. Hers was short—all it said was, "You won't believe this." The other two were typewritten, from Max. One said, "Enclosed, a certified check accounting for the royalties from 'Oh, There You Are' and 'What Dance Was That?' The royalties for song A (lyrics and music) amounting to $65,857.52. The royalties for song B (lyrics and music), which had less airplay, amounting to $47,945.33." The other sheet of paper said, "Enclosed, a certified check accounting for the royalties from the song 'Nothing to Say About Christmas' (lyrics and music) amounting to $100,860.86." I stared at the number, thought of my roll of bills, and immediately began to think of a song that would use the number eighty-six in the lyrics.

If I had ever heard of that much money in my entire life, I could not remember when. Uncle Drew certainly had that much money and more, but he never talked about money, only about mortgage payments, rent, and presents. I had overheard one of the girls in high school talking about what her parents had paid for their house in

Ladue (five bedrooms, three acres)—$71,000, and the other girl in the bathroom was impressed. I suspected Mom's house on Skinker had cost maybe half that.

The next thing I did was panic—what did she do with the checks? I could imagine her leaving them on the kitchen counter, then opening the window, and there they went, out into the backyard. Of course she would run out to find them, but the wind would blow them over the fence, and she would write me a note, apologizing, but explaining to me that these things happen, and life is uncertain. It didn't help that calling home was difficult—there was a phone in our dorm that a parent could call us on, if that parent happened to be patient, and there were pay phones in town, but you had to have a roll of quarters, and even then, you couldn't talk very long. I couldn't go to Leon's house, because Leon was on his own now, and even though his parents still owned the house, they didn't come anymore (a few years later, after Leon was off to New York, they used the place as their vacation home, no doubt because of the beauty of the surrounding landscape). That night, I asked Lisa if she ever called home, and she said, "If I called home every time I wondered about something or worried about something, I would drive them crazy. Mom and Dad are good about keeping me up-to-date on what's going on. Do you remember that time last spring when I was gone for about four days?"

I nodded, but actually, I didn't. She said, "There was a crisis, a combination of lots of calving and lambing, and then realizing that there was something wrong with the well. It's only ninety miles to the farm, so Dad just jumped in the truck and came and picked me up."

"How did you know he was coming?"

"Mom sent me a telegram."

"Why didn't she call? They can call us here."

"She never said. At any rate, I helped with the calving and the lambing while Dad and his cousin fixed the well. The pipe that connected the well to the pump was corroded and broken, and a lot of air was coming out of the kitchen faucet. That was exhausting, and then I had to take a plant biology test the morning after I got back. Jeez."

Looking at her shake her head, I thought that I would not use the money to buy myself a farm.

And then, the next day, there was a letter from Uncle Drew, detailing his recommended investment strategy, which did not include withdrawing it from the bank in two-dollar bills, piling them in a trunk, and shoving the trunk into the back of my closet. Even as I was reading the letter, I was thinking of all the things Uncle Drew had given us over the years, and wondering if I should pay him back. Mom might know what at least a few of them cost. I knew I should do it, but I didn't know how to bring it up. Part of me wondered if he would be insulted by the very idea, and part of me wondered if he would be insulted if I didn't do it. Since he and Aunt Louise still lived on Argonne, and they had not surrounded the house with an ornate garden or built any huge additions, there was absolutely no sign of whether Uncle Drew was still prospering or not. The kids went to public schools. Mom had told Aunt Louise how great she thought my school was, but Aunt Louise said it was too much of a drive, and anyway, the kids wanted to go to school with the other kids in the neighborhood. It was a mile to the elementary school, and as soon as they were in fifth grade, they rode their bikes. Mom would never have allowed that, but both Uncle Drew and Aunt Louise thought that it was good for them to "learn about traffic until it was second nature to pay attention." I will say that Aunt Louise seemed like less of a worrier than Mom was. I think what they really wanted was for the kids to fit in, and I suspected that they thought that that was the very thing that I had never done at my school. And so, why pay all that money in tuition? Fitting in was the key to success, according to Uncle Drew, and indeed he did—there were plenty of business clubs around St. Louis, and Uncle Drew belonged to all of them.

As for Allen, our relationship was still official, but it didn't have much substance, so I didn't tell him a thing about the royalties, and it never occurred to him to ask about anything like that. He knew I got paid for the gigs and he didn't mind going out for a fancy meal and having me foot the bill, but no one told him how the music business worked. The spring term meandered on. I wrote two more songs. The first one started out being called "Oh, Blow Me," but before I gave it to Max, I changed the name to "Stop Making Me Mad." The second one was called "Pictures on the Wall."

The first song grew out of an incident I witnessed in the dining room where I usually went for lunch. The lines were fairly long. As I was pushing my tray past the beef stew, I heard a guy behind me say, "Hey!" in a sharp voice. I looked around. He wasn't talking to me, he was talking to the Black girl in front of him. He said, "Move it, n—— b——!" She stood stock-still, but she looked simultaneously frightened, angry, and resigned—obviously this was not new for her. Her look gave me the idea for the song. Some of us lifted our trays—I think I lifted mine more out of surprise than anything else, but a Black student in a parallel line lifted his (and it was full of plates and food), swung it around, and smashed the asshole in the head. He stumbled to his knees. The best part was that about ten other students, Black and white, surrounded the attacker and eased him out of the dining room before he could get any lunch. The girl the asshole had snapped at sneered at him as if he were a pile of dog shit and went on down the line. Did she get a few hugs? In my song she did.

The song was from the point of view of the girl. I did not say she was Black, but I knew that some listeners would understand that she was. The lyrics went, "I was standing there when he bumped me, looking at the peas / His face was scowling, but I was afraid of his knees," then, a bit later, "There were words on my lips—Screw you, Blow me—But Nathan had the zip. / He swung his tray around, knocked the asshole down, / I kicked him in the balls to rounds of applause." Eventually, there were three verses and a chorus. I listened to a lot of Aretha, Chuck Berry, and Little Richard to make sure I got the beat right—what you do is listen, forget about it, put it out of your mind, write the tune. The beat stays there, in the background. When I showed it to Leon, and he played it, he couldn't stop bouncing up and down on the piano bench. He was glad I had named the attacker Nathan, since that was his cousin's name. We went through it again, and laughed, not because it was a funny incident, exactly, but because there was something about the music and the beat and the language that was surprising.

"Pictures on the Wall" was the one I wanted to put in three-four time, and I thought it would be easy. My favorite key was the key of D minor—I had always enjoyed "A Sunday Kind of Love," sung by Etta James. By 1970, her version was only ten years old, but it seemed to me as old as the songs my grandparents sang. Another one was "I'd Rather Go Blind," which was in three-four time, so I went back and forth between the two, trying to put together the tune and the key. I spent a lot of time walking around in the hills, looking up at the sky and the trees, and singing to myself. The first verse turned out to be about not a picture on the wall, but one I had tucked into a book—a picture of Charlie, the vanished boyfriend. He was about to smile—his nostrils had flared and his head was cocked to one side. His hair was a little tangled and glinted in the sunlight. I hadn't seen him in six months, and I hadn't even thought about him until I happened to open my freshman musicology book. Then I looked at the picture on my desk, of Allen. He was staring into the camera, smiling, but it wasn't an amused smile—more a distracted, when-will-this-be-over smile. And I knew he hated to have his picture taken—another sign of how much more comfortable he felt in the wilderness than he did even on our campus, much less in the classroom or the dining area. It took me a while to come up with the chorus: "Pictures on the wall, / Are they good or are they bad? / If all I had was memories, would I still be this sad?" The last verse went, "I saw a picture of my dad once, / And he looked just like me / If he hears me sing this song, / What picture will he see?"

I didn't expect to put anything in about my father, and, in fact, I didn't have any feelings about him, though I'm sure some psychoanalyst would dig up something, using this song to do it. But a song is not yourself—it's a string of words with a beat and a rhyme that creates its own picture. Most often, it feels like a fire that is sparked—you might light the match, there might be a lightning strike, an electrical line might blow down, and then the fire burns for a few minutes or explodes all over the woods. One song that had come out in the last year reminded me of this. It was called "The Weight," by the Band. It had a great beat and didn't make any sense at all. My favorite line was, "Take a load off, Fanny / Take a load for free." Then there was the part about giving someone a dog, and saying it was okay if the dog only got fed once in a while. Hadn't they heard of Hill's Horse Meat? But it was a song that never stopped going through your head once you thought of a line, and even though I had never seen this nameless band, I knew they thought of it in the same way. Allen said they must have been tripping when they wrote it, and maybe so, but that just reinforced my theory—if it had a beat and a tune, it didn't have to make any sense at all in order to burn down the house.

The next day, I walked over to the practice area and found Leon. He was working on Piano Concerto No. 20, by Mozart, which was also in D minor. I listened to him play the last movement of the concerto, then sang my song. He listened closely to the tune, had me sing it again, and then came up with the chords and the beat and the background right off the top of his head. After we did that one twice, we did the other one, and then, when we were walking toward the eating area for some lunch, he said he would drive me to New York so we could play them for Max. It was a two-hundred-and-forty-mile drive, he had friends we could stay with (they turned out to be relatives), and he would take me to Katz's Deli for lunch after we saw Max, and yes, he agreed with me that the only true pastrami sandwich was at Katz's.

I left a note for Allen and another for Lisa, and we went to his car, which was a brand-new white Jaguar XKE. I said, "Did your parents sell that house to buy this car?"

Leon said, "No, but my mom was wondering if it came with its own coffin."

"Your mom has a sense of humor."

"Only dark," said Leon.

But of course Leon was a good driver. He played the car like he played the piano, and our trip was smooth, only ten miles above the speed limit. As we passed other cars on Interstate 80, I could see lots of drivers stare at the Jag in admiration. It took us three hours to get there and half an hour to find just the right parking spot not far from his relatives', a spot on West Eighty-Fourth Street where he could leave it the whole time we were there, where it wouldn't be towed away, where it wouldn't be jacked or defaced. We got out; buttoned up our coats, because it was cold and windy; and went first to the relatives'—Rafe and Leah Silver, who were Leon's cousins and maybe ten years older than we were. Leah's mother and Leon's mother were sisters, and I could see the resemblance between Leon and Leah. She was an assistant editor at Simon & Schuster and Rafe managed an art gallery on Fifty-Seventh Street. Leah was evidently pregnant, but we didn't ask about it and she didn't say anything. They were just about to get on the subway and go to a Chinese restaurant. I hadn't had Chinese food since the summer in St. Louis (my mom loved dim sum and broccoli beef). Leon was starving, and he ordered a feast: pot stickers, egg rolls, orange chicken, but also spicy dishes—Szechuan chicken, Szechuan eggplant—and pork fried rice. Then we walked (staggered) down the street, crossed Park Avenue, then Fifth Avenue, and walked into Baskin-Robbins, where I ordered a single scoop of mint chocolate chip and Leon ordered two scoops—peppermint fudge ribbon and pineapple sherbet. Leon was now taller than I was by about an inch, but he was still thin as a rail. Leah and Rafe bought a pint of pink grapefruit sherbet. We took the subway home, and as we were riding and Leon was talking to his cousins, I wondered why Leon wasn't my boyfriend. We connected much better than Allen and I connected, we knew each other well, and I did feel attracted to him now that he had grown up. I didn't have the sense I'd had with Charlie, that he was gay. We walked around the Jaguar when we got back, both of us looking at it very carefully, and then went inside and fell into bed—I slept in the second bedroom, the one that was going to be the baby's room, and Leon slept on a pull-out couch in the living room. Once again, I felt that there was something alluring about New York, in spite of the noise and the grime and the shouting in the streets (as well as squealing tires from time to time). And there was, but over breakfast, which Leah made because she preferred her own cooking to everyone else's, even for oatmeal, Leah and Rafe talked about how the corruption ran from bottom to top and every time a body was found in the East River, the two of them talked about getting out. Leah said, "We could move to Brooklyn. It's safer there." Rafe said, "How do we know? It's all so secret." Leah instinctively patted her belly and everyone sighed.

When we played the songs for Max, who didn't seem to mind that we had just shown up without an appointment, his reaction was more thoughtful than enthusiastic. He asked us to play them again, then sat there, nodding his head a little bit and staring out the window. Finally, he said, "All right. The A side will be the pictures song, and the B side the other one, but you've got to rephrase 'Screw you, Blow me.' These political songs, we don't know where they're headed."

I said, "Joan Baez is—"

Max said, "She is. I'm not saying it won't be a success. I'm just saying everything is up in the air. But"—and he glanced at Leon—"you got to get yourself a band. Grace Slick has got the Jefferson Airplane, and Janis Joplin was in much better shape when she had the Holding Company to watch over her." He glanced at Leon again. I said, "You know Leon has his own career as a classical pianist." Then Max said, with his usual good nature, "And you're good at it, Lenny. That's what we used to call him when he could only play *Eine kleine Nachtmusik*. His mommy was wringing her hands. She wanted him to move on to *Peter and the Wolf.*"

Leon said, "Yes, and she read me that story and it freaked me out. I thought that was going to lure the wolf right through the door. There were thousands of wolves all over Pittsburgh, you know."

We all laughed.

I said, "How do I find a band?"

Max said, "Keep your ears open. I'll ask around, too. I'll see what we can do for a studio band for this recording. In the meantime, you know . . ."

I said, "Six more songs, an album called *Rattle Me*."

Max said, "That might work."

We went to Katz's, a long drive, but the pastrami sandwich was indeed divine, and we got back to State College as dusk was settling over the campus.

The one who found me a band was Brucie. The Big Muddies had split up just after Brucie went into the army, but one of them, the bass player, had moved to Chicago. His real name was Nicolo Molinaro, but we called him Nick Miller. Some of his family lived on the Hill, and some lived in Clayton and Kirkwood. He did play several instruments, and, according to Brucie, when he got to Chicago, every local band was after him. He ended up with the Scats. The three other members were from Chicago: the lead guitar player was Reggie Koulinakis, the drummer was Jack Pell, and the rhythm guitar player was Gussie Busch—not THE Gussie Busch from St. Louis, but an entirely unrelated Gussie Busch who swore up and down that he had no idea what Budweiser was. Whenever Reggie and Jack practiced when they were teenagers, one of the neighbors next door to Reggie's house would run out into her yard and wave her arms, and yell "Scat! Scat!" It was Reggie's mom who named them the Scats. None of them were in college—two had finished, two had dropped out—and they were a pretty big band around the Midwest. They played concerts in Ann Arbor, Urbana, Columbia, Madison, and Bloomington, and backed up bigger bands in Milwaukee, Chicago, St. Louis, Indianapolis, Kansas City, and even Detroit. Reggie was very attuned to the differences in local music styles, and he could shift the rhythm or the way they sang so that it would be more like local music. Gussie was the lead singer, who could go back and forth between tenor and baritone as easy as you please. They had had a recording contract, but the guy who signed them had a heart attack, and the guy who took over from him was more interested in folk. They wanted me because of my relative success, but also because their previous singer, Eileen O'Brian, had been married to Jack and then left him. They didn't mind learning my songs if I didn't mind learning theirs. Gussie (I did like him) took me aside at one point and told me not to get involved with any of them because the departure of Eileen had nearly done them in. I agreed. I did not want to get involved with any of them.

Time passed. School ended, and so, I thought, did my relationship with Allen. The way I knew it was that we were sitting in the eating area. He was finishing his hamburger and I was picking at some spaghetti, and he said, "Wish me well."

I said, "Okay. Why?"

"I told you. Down the Appalachians from Bear Mountain. We'll see how far I can go."

I didn't say he hadn't told me, because I wasn't sure whether he had or not, but I did think that he might have told some other girl and remembered that as telling me. I said, "Is it a single trail?"

"Not yet."

"Three whole months?"

"I don't know how long it will take. The longer, the slower, the more I can see, but I don't know. Could get lonely."

"I wish someone was going with you."

He nodded. He didn't say he wished that person was me. We'd known forever that our likes and dislikes and interests diverged.

I said, "I wish the trail ran through Chicago." Then we both laughed—that was what had held us together, laughing at the same things.

He said, "You're going to live there all summer?"

"The Scats have lots of concert dates, so we won't be in Chicago most of the time. But we have to learn all the songs and use the concerts to get in sync. I guess Max is pushing the record company to put together an album at the end of August. It's going to be either 'Rattler and the Scats' or 'the Scats, with Jodie Rattler.'"

Allen said, "Okay. Well, I've got to get to my exam." He stood up, leaned down, and kissed me, and, oddly enough, that was the last time we spoke. All the girls I knew would have breakups that made them cry or made them rage. I was the only one whose boyfriends seemed to fade away. Once again, lucky, because that was how I liked it.

The Scats got along somewhat better than the Freak-Outs had—there was less arguing, but some tension. They were mostly kind to me, but all of them were irritable, and every one of them would snap at me, then apologize. The fact that they, and then we, harmonized as well as any band I had ever heard did not mean that we lived in harmony, but it did mean that I could forget about the arguments. A couple of years later, one of my favorite singers put out a song about having sex with Janis Joplin at the Chelsea Hotel, which was maybe two miles from Tompkins Square Park, in New York. I had never stayed there, but the more I practiced and toured with the Scats, the more I could relate to the line about "workers in song." I was not, I thought "running for the money and the flesh" (though the Scats were running for both, which I came to accept as standard band behavior). I actually wasn't quite sure what I was running for, other than the pleasure of opening my mouth, hearing the song come out, and having the Scats chime in like angels.

And the money wasn't bad. As far as I knew, whatever we got for gigs, we split equally. The manager of the band, Bill, I later learned, spent a lot of time gauging whether the band or Miss Rattler got the most applause, and depending on where we were, it went back and forth. There was a little bit of competition—I would stick out my lower jaw, get a little more vibrato in there, and I might get some shouts. Jack would take off on a riff, and people would jump out of their seats and dance. Nick would set down his bass guitar, pick up a banjo or even a violin, and replay the previous verse, knowing we could keep up. Reggie would do an ad hoc tune that seemed to me as complex as much of the classical music I'd heard Leon play. On some days, our competitions were fun and made us laugh, but if we were tired and depressed, they could be irritating. Gussie and I did pass the songs back and forth, with him singing the tune and me harmonizing or vice versa. We changed the pronouns, and a few of the lyrics, to make it work. Once, I think it was in Milwaukee, he cocked his head toward Jack, and then we sang one of the verses twice, first from his point of view and then from mine—it was a song about a breakup. The audience understood what we were getting at and gave that song lots of cheers. Bill told me later that he couldn't decide who "had more traction," that he told the record company that the more we competed, the better we sounded, and then he said, "But that's the way it is for lots of bands."

Gussie and I collaborated on two songs, "Out on the Porch," a murder ballad, like "Down in the Willow Garden," but the boy doesn't kill the girl—he raises his gun, the girl grabs it and kills the boy. Gussie said that a murder ballad had to have an irresistible melody, so that's what we worked on the most. The song is told from the point of view of the girl's sister, who finishes the song by vowing never to reveal what happened. We agreed that the second one had to be more upbeat. We called it "Studebaker Lark." It was about two teenagers driving a yellow Studebaker Lark convertible who go too far, get lost, realize they've never had as much fun before, and kiss, something neither of them has ever done before. We spent a lot of time discussing how old they were. The boy had to be at least sixteen. I thought the girl could be fifteen, but Gussie thought she should be sixteen, too. Had I gotten kissed by the time I was sixteen? I admitted that I hadn't, told him the story about how my sex education came from eavesdropping on my freshman roommates, and Gussie said he was a little late to the game, as well (though he gave me no details). Then he told me about a guy he knew who had been seduced at twelve by a girl down the street. At any rate, we decided that the sixteen-year-olds in the Studebaker were both shy and I said, "I guess they have no particular place to go," and we remembered the line about Chuck not being able to undo his seat belt. Gussie said, "Did you ever meet him?" and I told him about the one time, but I was in Chicago, so I didn't mention the Cards.

The Scats were quick learners—we performed both songs within three days of writing them, and they fit into our style. They also got onto the album, which we recorded at the end of August in Detroit, because we had to do it between gigs in Cleveland and Ann Arbor. Max flew in from New York and oversaw the recording: six tracks on each side, A side, "Out on the Porch," "Oh, There You Are," "The Foggy Dew" (one of Jack's favorites), "I Shall Be Released,"

"What Dance Was That?," and the Scats' best song, "Under the Rainbow." The B side began with "Studebaker Lark," then there were two songs by Gussie and Jack, "High Flyers" and "Over the Ridge," followed by "Stop Making Me Mad" and "Pictures on the Wall." The last track on the B side was Tom Rush's "No Regrets," a song I lobbied for, thinking of Allen hiking.

On all the tracks, we did what we did onstage—we competed, which gave the tracks energy, and Gussie and I passed the lyrics back and forth, which meant that I didn't fade into the surrounding guys. In the end, the record company titled the album *High Flyers, by the Scats with Jodie Rattler.* Max told me that the record company thought that the Scats and I had slightly different fan bases, and they wanted to appeal to both of them. On the cover, we were standing in a group, but the picture was set on the top of a cloud and the background was sky blue. Because almost everyone in the music business was talking about the Isle of Wight Festival in England, we imagined being invited in a year, traveling to England, and rubbing shoulders with Jimi Hendrix, Joni Mitchell, Leonard Cohen, and, for Gussie, Miles Davis. Huge number of fans, no violence. Ideal.

I went back to school a week late. I told Leon all about the tour and the album, but I didn't tell anyone else, even Lisa. Everyone assumed, I supposed, that I'd had the flu or something. As soon as I got back, I was happy to retreat into the woodwork again. I hadn't quite realized how exhausting the summer had been—traveling, singing, practicing, writing, recording—until I slept like a rock for seven nights in a row and woke up in English class (Eighteenth-Century Lit) and realized that I was reading Alexander Pope over and over without understanding a word. I came to when we moved on to *Robinson Crusoe.*

The album came out on the first of November and got a few decent reviews—not so much of our songs, but of our style, which was described as energetic, bright, funny, rhythmic, and upbeat. The reviewer for the *Chicago Sun-Times* complimented the album, but said, "If you want to really enjoy the Rattling Scats, a live performance is where you should go. The energy they toss back and forth like a flaming Frisbee invigorates the crowd in a way I've rarely seen." The *Trib* said, "Admirable local band. Much underrated." *Rolling Stone* acknowledged that we existed. My pleasure in the singing itself and the response was what kept me going—by the time the album came out, both Jimi Hendrix and Janis Joplin had died of overdoses, and the Beatles had broken up, which, it seemed to me, revealed the truth about being a band on the road. But much of our tour—singing with Gussie, listening to Jack riff, telling jokes, glancing at one another at the end of a song that both we and the audience knew had been well-done—was recollections I hoped never to forget (and Mom had often told me that you remember the good times better than you remember the bad ones). But even so, my overall feeling about the tour turned out to be gloomy. Possibly one reason was that I had adhered to the rule not to get involved with any of the band members, so much so that perhaps, except onstage, they saw me as wooden and remote, keeping to myself, hardly saying a word. The one I would have gotten involved with was Gussie—even when we weren't writing the songs, I felt a connection—but he did have a girlfriend, and anyway, rule following was one of my specialties.

Max was pleased with the sales, and he thought we might get invited to the Isle of Wight. He wanted me to take a leave of absence from college, or even drop out, because he said we needed to practice and tour to build up our name (the Rattling Scats), but I ignored him. We didn't get invited to the Isle of Wight, because that festival ended (Max said that the local inhabitants couldn't stand it anymore—the population of the island was under a hundred thousand, and six times that many, they said, had shown up for the festival). But we did get invited to a new festival in England, at Glastonbury. We practiced during spring break and I skipped graduation and went to Chicago to practice, also. It turned out that June was a wonderful time to find yourself in southwest England, even if your performance took place at nine in the morning, a day and a half after you arrived at Heathrow, and you were still jet-lagged. They invited us to stay on, though, and Jack and I did a little exploring. There was a beautifully strange wreck of an abbey, where, supposedly, King

Arthur himself was buried, as well as a lovely town, and hills and valleys everywhere. Jack didn't mind driving on the left side of the road (though I flinched at oncoming traffic about a million times). In the end it was worth it just to see the farmhouses and the hedges and the grazing cattle. Jack was also an adventurous eater, so he tried two or three new types of cheese every day, as well as Cornish saffron buns, Cornish pasty, and even Hog's pudding. It was sunny every day—Jack said this was incredibly lucky, and about that I kept my thoughts to myself. The fact was that the inconvenience of the performance was what turned out to be lucky, because once we had recovered from the jet lag and the effort of doing our best when we hardly felt capable of doing anything at all, we enjoyed the vacation and got along better than we ever had before.

Another thing I noticed was how differently everyone spoke. Our driver from London spoke differently from our escort; the people in the audiences sometimes had such different accents that they couldn't understand one another. Maybe this was why everyone seemed to have such revealing facial expressions. I loved walking down streets and watching the Brits react to one another. A man dressed in an elegant suit and hat walks down the street and two or three guys pass him, then mimic his walk, lifting their chins and pursing their lips, then lots of people laugh, or a man lets his cigarette hang out of the corner of his mouth, and after they pass him, another man hangs his pencil out of the corner of his mouth in exactly the same way. I was reminded of my mother's love of *My Fair Lady* and the way she would mimic the various accents we heard in the songs. We were there for five days. After I flew with the Scats to Chicago and then returned to St. Louis, I couldn't stop thinking of Glastonbury, of England. Mom gave me maybe three days to recover, and then, just before the first of July, she confronted me in the kitchen. She was putting away dishes from the night before while I was eating a piece of toast and drinking a cup of the Earl Grey tea I'd brought back from England with me. She said, "Well, what now?" in a tone of voice that was not unkind but was also insistent. I said, "I have to make a call, and then I'll tell you."

The call was to Uncle Drew. I asked him how my "investments" were doing (and these included another $46,981 that I got from the two songs on the album that I wrote and the two that I collaborated with Gussie on). He said, "Well, there has been a downturn, that's why there aren't any jobs." (I hadn't noticed that.) "But even so, the accumulated amount as of the last time I looked was four hundred and ten thousand dollars."

I thanked him.

At lunch, I told Mom I was making a reservation to go back to England. My plan was to travel around in England, Scotland, and maybe Ireland, researching folk music, and then, in the fall, I was going to apply to a musicology program and become a specialist in music history. Mom's face fell, and she couldn't help shaking her head. She said, "You are walking away from this? You have so many talents and connections! Why would you do that?"

I shrugged as if I didn't know, but I did know—whatever the pleasures I had enjoyed, now I wanted to be alone. The band, the touring, Max, all of that seemed to me to be simply an exaggeration of everything else I had known—school, camp, high school, college, the clatter of voices in your ear all the time, the sense that you had to be right or wrong all the time, the feeling of being watched and judged. But it was more than that. I understood in a way I never had before why Allen wanted to hike so much—to be in the middle of nowhere; it seemed to me that being alone in England and Scotland would be being in the middle of a much more interesting nowhere, and as for the pleasure of singing, I could do that on my own.

Mom said, "Well, you're twenty-two. You can vote for whoever you please, and I can't stop you."

5

I WENT TO a travel agent in Clayton and bought my ticket, then I wrote a letter to Max, saying that I wanted to take a break. The odd thing that I realized as I was writing was that Max hadn't said anything about bookings in the summer. I might have realized this if the end of school and the practicing hadn't been so driven and chaotic. And none of the guys, not even Jack in the car or Gussie over a meal, had said anything about our plans. Max sent a special-delivery-overnight reply—he hated to have to tell me this, but Eileen O'Brian was begging to come back. Her year away from Jack and the band had taught her a lesson, and she and Jack had reconciled, and now . . . She did offer to practice with me—we could be like the Mamas and the Papas. I already knew that Eileen had caused some strife in the band before I came along—that might not have worried me if I hadn't yet toured, but the thought of going back to all those towns in the Midwest that I was already tired of made me even more eager to go somewhere new. I wrote back and said I had other plans, and I hoped that they enjoyed being together again. I then wrote Gussie and thanked him for including me in the band for a while. Two weeks later, I was on the plane, first to New York, then to London. I had a backpack and a stack of traveler's checks, and my roll of two-dollar bills, shoved into a small cloth bag, resting in the bottom of my backpack. Mom set out my raincoat, but I left it behind—I wanted to buy one that would fit into the England that I was going to be living in. I booked myself a room at a hotel called the Langham, and I stayed there for a week. It was a peculiar hotel—lots of corridors and many pictures on the walls—but its allure was that from that neighborhood, you could walk anywhere, and that was what I wanted to do.

The first day, which was sunny and a Friday, I went out of the door of the hotel at about ten a.m., turned left, and walked around the block, which turned out to be around the hotel, which was as ornate, or maybe more so, from the outside as it was from the inside. Across from one corner of the hotel was a circular park enclosed by a hedge. They called it a garden, but I didn't see flowers. From there, I enlarged my circuit, keeping my eye on the people and the buildings and the names of the streets, which came to fascinate me. Yes, in St. Louis, I had grown up with Eager Road and Laclede Station Road and Creve Coeur, which meant "heartbreak," and, of course, "Skinker," which some kids in eighth grade had used to tease me by pronouncing as "Stinker." But here I was on "Chandos" and then "Little Titchfield" and then "Riding House" and after that, "Oxford Circus" (and not a carousel in sight). I would have liked to keep going in an ever-widening circle, but I got confused and lost. I understood that I should have brought a map along, but it was early in the day and I figured I would come to some store that would carry maps. I kept walking. On some of the houses I saw little blue plaques, and I went over to look at them, thinking that if anyone stopped me, I would open my mouth, say I was lost, and be instantly understood as an American ignoramus, at which point, I would be led down the street and pointed in the "proper" direction. The blue plaque across from a small park read, "Virginia Woolf House." I had heard of her, of course, but none of her books had been assigned in high school or college. I imagined her living right where I was walking around, and looking at these same scenes, so I decided to get one of her books. I went to a nearby corner, waited to cross, looked both ways, except that I looked the wrong ways, and as I lifted my foot to step off the curb, the man next to me threw out his arm and stopped me. A car passed. My heart was pounding. I took a deep beath and thanked the man. He walked across the street with me, and before we parted, I said, "Do you know where there's a bookstore?"

He said, "Indeed, miss. Foyles is your best bet."

He made it easy—pointed my way down the street I was already on, told me to turn left at Tottenham Court Road and keep going until I saw the bookstore. I did not look the wrong way again. At each intersection, I looked both directions about six times before crossing, and by the time I got to Foyles I had the habit of looking first right, then left, then right again. At the bookstore, which was huge, wandering around in a circle was much easier than it was on the street. I bought a map and a copy of *To the Lighthouse*. I knew from reading the opening page in the bookstore that I wasn't going to understand it the first time around, but I didn't understand anything else about London, either, so I didn't mind. I imagined my mother in New York just after the war, staring at Tompkins Square Park and scratching her head, wondering where she was.

I looked at the map, then walked down Charing Cross Road to Trafalgar Square. I did pass a bank, and as I did, I realized that I had to turn some of my traveler's checks into pounds. I entered the bank, handed the teller three checks. The exchange rate was $2.40 to the pound, and then there were all these other coins, most of them fatter than quarters and nickels—five-pence coins marked "NEW PENNY," twenty pence, fifty pence. But I was sorry the names had changed—no more ha'pennies, tuppence, crowns, the words I had read in *David Copperfield* and other English books, as well as that song by the Who, "Magic Bus," "Thruppence and sixpence every day / Just to drive to my baby." The song that started running through my mind, though, was "Christmas is coming, the geese are getting fat / Please put a penny in the old man's hat! / If you haven't got a penny, a ha'penny will do / If you haven't got a ha'penny, then God bless you!" In fact, the thing that I enjoyed about my walk was that everything was both familiar and completely unfamiliar. Because of the books we read in school, like *Oliver Twist,* and the Agatha Christie books I had read on my own, and because of history class, I had pictures in my mind that were linked to words like "Trafalgar" and "Charing Cross," but in fact I was completely out of my element. It was rather like singing a new song, struggling with the words and the tune but feeling my toe tap automatically to the beat. I walked around the square, looking at the buildings and the statues, then walked down Whitehall Street. There were so many statues and buildings to look at, and cars and buses and pedestrians to look out for, that it was overwhelming, and my ear, normally the sensory organ I was most attuned to, was overwhelmed also—the very thing I wanted to hear, the different ways people spoke and the different words they said, jumbled into a mess of noise, but I did eventually get to Big Ben, and then to Westminster Abbey, where I sat down in one of the pews and stared at the stained glass windows.

The abbey was not silent, but it was quieter than the street. As I calmed down, I imagined, thinking of Leon, the music that had been sung and played in this cathedral over the years. I vaguely remembered that it was first built at the time of the Norman conquest, which I also vaguely remembered was 1066, but when I thought of composers, the one that came into my mind was Ralph Vaughan Williams, one of Leon's favorites. And then I thought of Purcell. I calmed down even more, recalling whatever bits and pieces of the music I had heard Leon play. Leon had grown up playing Purcell's suites. He said they weren't very difficult, but, perhaps because he was so young when he started playing them, they were his "idling" music, as he called it, music he would tinkle through while he was sitting on the bench contemplating other issues, like when would be a good time to get some lunch. Sitting in the pew staring up at the arches and the dimly lit nave, I did my best to remember what he had played for me. Then I got up and started wandering around, and there Purcell was, right beside the organ. His epitaph read, "Here lyes Henry Purcell Esq., / Who left this Life and is gone to that Blessed Place / Where only his Harmony can be exceeded." I wandered here and there. There were lots of kings and queens, most or all of them lying on their backs with their eyes closed. Queen Elizabeth the First was buried right across from Mary, Queen of

Scots, which probably would have enraged both of them. I had had a little Mary, Queen of Scots, obsession when I was about ten and read a Landmark biography of her, so I stared at both of them. Mary had the palms of her hands together, sticking straight up in the air. Elizabeth was trying to hold up her scepter, but she had died, her hand had fallen open, and it had dropped to her shoulder.

I kept walking, and there was George Frideric Handel, who looked like he was dancing and pointing his finger at the band, counting the beat.

I thought of one of his suites, in D minor, that Leon loved to play, and of the time Mom had taken me to the St. Louis Symphony for a performance of *Water Music,* which was about the Thames, but stuck in my mind as a reference to the Mississippi. He was in the same area as Dickens.

There was something simultaneously exciting and exhausting about being in the midst of all these famous dead people, and I was suddenly famished. I left the cathedral and went looking for some food. I finally found a spot that didn't look like a fancy restaurant, and I could hear people talking in different ways going in and out of the place. It was a bit dark inside, but I went in, was shown to a seat, and was asked, after a few minutes, if I was waiting for someone. I shook my head. The menu was full of things I couldn't imagine, with no explanation—fish and chips, bangers and mash, cottage pie. I looked around, and when the waiter came back, I pointed to the plate in front of the man at the next table. It turned out to be something called a Cornish pasty, and then I remembered having a couple of bites of Gussie's when we were driving around Glastonbury. It was excellent, and gave me the energy to walk back to the Langham, which took a long time because first I lingered in St. James's Park, then I wandered over to Hyde Park and listened to someone on Speakers' Corner, then I wandered down Oxford Street, went into a store called Robinsons, and bought a raincoat, which was a good thing, because when I was walking to the Langham on another strangely named street, Wigmore, the rain finally began. I went into the hotel, asked for the key, went up to my room, threw off the raincoat, fell onto the bed, and slept.

I fell asleep completely disoriented and woke up oriented. It was early—sunup in London in July was around five a.m. I knew just where I was and what I had to do, which was empty my backpack and hang up my clothes, take a bath, wash my hair and comb it out, dry it, get some breakfast, and study my map. Even now, the day I remember most in London is that one where I didn't know a soul, or what I was doing, or where I was going, or what was next (hopefully not being hit by a car). That day sticks in my mind as one of the best days of my life, simultaneously utterly mundane and utterly lucky because of what I saw, what I ate, and what I enjoyed about being alone in a crowd.

For the next four days, I did what a tourist is supposed to do—went to the Tate, went to the Tower of London, went to the National Gallery, walked down Carnaby Street and the Strand, watched the changing of the guard at the palace, and wandered around Harrods. I went to Kensington Gardens and the rest of Hyde Park, where there were people riding horses, which I had never seen in Forest Park or Central Park. I went to a play, *The Dirtiest Show in Town,* which I had heard of in New York, and to a couple of movies. I kept my ears open and mouthed some of the words that I heard, but I hardly said anything to anyone, other than waiters or salespeople. I didn't buy much other than food and treacle toffee (candy in England was much better than a Milky Way) because there wasn't room in my backpack for more clothes or shoes. I did walk around shops that sold musical instruments, wondering if I might accompany myself once I learned the folk songs. A few instruments were tempting—not guitars, but lutes and mandolins. I asked to pluck a few, and looked through instruction manuals, but even as I did, I imagined myself carrying a lute around and becoming obsessed with it, as you might become obsessed with a baby—what was the temperature? Was it humid outside? Where might I put it if I had to, as they said in London, "go to the loo"? I decided not to accompany myself.

I got up Monday morning and checked out of the Langham. The clerk, whom I had gotten to know a little bit—Liam, his name was—asked where I might be going. I said Gloucestershire, and he said that Paddington Station was quite a walk—did I want a taxi? But no, I didn't. I was so used to walking by this time that the walk was what I was looking forward to, which was why I was setting out early, so I could find my way. I went by way of Portland Place and Weymouth, through the part of London called Marylebone, a residential area that I could see myself living in, except that the streets were narrow and there was traffic everywhere. I was looking first at the brick houses and buildings, with their ornate white porches and windowsills, some of them with rows of chimneys along the edges of the steep roofs, and then at the cars unable to pass one another, often because of the cars parked alongside the road (and where would they put parking garages? The city was full already). It was beautiful.

It took me a while to get oriented in the station—it was huge and busy and I kept looking up toward the ceiling—but eventually, I stood in front of the schedule and stared at the destinations. No one asked me if I needed any help or had any questions. What I was doing was waiting for someone to go by who might give me a clue, and then two women did, a mother and her daughter. The mother said, "Well, Ay haven't bin ta Bath in donkey's years."

The daughter said, "Was Ay a baby thin?"

"Nay. Before that, even."

They seemed happy, and so I decided to go to Bath. And even though I thought I'd had a good Anglophilic education, when I went there I was thrilled to discover all the things I never knew. The train trip was only eighty-five minutes. If I had left Union Station in St. Louis for Chicago, I would have ended up in some pancake-flat empty space in central Illinois. But to get from Paddington to Bath, I went past Wormwood Scrubs and through Ealing. Someone got off at Yiewsley. We went through Slough and Maidenhead, and then there was the countryside and the river Thames, trees and hedges and water, what looked like a golf course. I had my book in my lap, but I couldn't take my eyes off the view through the window. I must have muttered something about how beautiful it was, because the woman sitting in front of me turned her head and said, "Well, miss, you go on up narth! That's the beauty spot, it is! And don't be stoppin' in the Cotswolds! Go on up t' the Lake District!" I nodded. I thought that I certainly would. In Bath, the sun was well up in the sky, the weather was delightful, and I thought I would look around and find myself a hotel.

I walked up St. James's Parade, simply because it was a parade. The buildings were golden, solid, strange. They looked like they had been molded to fit into spaces created by early roads, and indeed, they had. My Baedeker travel guide said that Bath was as old as Roman times, which meant that the streets had been here for nineteen hundred years, in some form or another. I kept thinking, Well, that's the oddest building! First it was Lombard House, which looked perfectly triangular, but then, I passed two long buildings across from each other with rows of chimneys jutting out of their roofs. After that, I turned down a street called Westgate Buildings. There was a building with a beautiful dome, a square that I wandered into with buildings that actually looked Roman—lots of pillars—and then, at dusk, I was lucky once again, because I was glancing at one of those little "gardens," this one fenced, saw an awning across the street, and there was my hotel, and there happened to be one room left.

It was called the Francis Hotel, and had evidently been there since wallpaper was first invented. The lobby was small but ornate, opened into lots of other rooms for, it looked like, sitting by the fireplace or reading a book. Maybe the walls were thick—at any rate, everything was very quiet. I went up to my room. It was on the third floor (or the second floor, as they said in England), and the wallpaper was entirely interwoven privet blossoms that were so neatly done that I could almost smell them. I set down my backpack and went downstairs again, looking for the restaurant. When I found it, I saw that they were still serving dessert, and I chose the sticky toffee pudding. I understood that if I was going to maintain my figure in England I was going to have to walk walk walk.

My bed was a four-poster. I only smacked my toes on a post once, and I did get a good night's sleep. When I got up in the morning, I realized that I was about in the center of town—the perfect place to be, except that it was pouring rain; water was streaming down the window of my room as if it was being hosed. There was wind, too—the trees were lashing each other in the parklet across the street. In the lobby, people were drinking their morning tea and there was a pile of baked goods spread across a buffet table. I went to the front desk with a smile and said, "Good morning. I forgot to ask this last night, but how old is this building?"

"Ah, love," said the man behind the desk. "Georgian, 'tis. 'Bout two hundred years old now."

I said, "Thank you. Fascinating building." I walked along the table of delights and picked a crumpet, which I had had when we came to Gloucester. I smeared it with lime curd. Another temptation given in to. I also picked up what they called a piece of bacon, but after one bite, I left that on my plate. The rain continued, and as always, once I was up and about, impossibilities dwindled away and possibilities multiplied. I grabbed my slicker and my brolly and headed toward the door. As I was passing the front desk, the man said, "Ye might go to the baths t'day. Perfect weather for it."

I got outside, stood under the portico, and took out my Baedeker. The baths were indeed nearby. I put my Baedeker back in my pocket and turned up the street. But the first thought I had just then was not about the baths, whatever they were, it was about the fact that I hadn't thought about music since my first day in London, in the music shop. Not one thought, not one wish to write a song or sing one.

I turned right and walked to the corner, then turned left and walked down Gay Street. I walked past an old stone wall that I couldn't see over, then toward a green spot that was straight ahead. The buildings distracted me from the rain, which was steady now, but light. The narrowness of the street led me to believe that I was heading toward a copse of trees, so I was a little taken aback when I found myself looking at a huge sweeping row of buildings that curved around a grassy park with five tall trees in the center. Cars were driving around the park, or rather, the "circus." I had never seen anything like it. I didn't know what I thought of Bath—on the one hand, my favorite spots had always been in the countryside, even if it was humid and full of flies and ticks, like St. Louis. On the other hand, these beautiful rows of buildings looked like stretched-out castles, and a lot of them had lovely small gardens, or flower boxes. And there were parks and little squares everywhere, where there was plenty of grass. I wandered and wandered. I sort of forgot about the baths, and then I remembered, and found one, Thermae, it was called. The exterior looked rather like a hotel or a restaurant. There weren't many customers, perhaps because it was still early in the day. The woman who welcomed me was friendly, pointed to the dressing room. I changed into a swimsuit (which they supplied) and went to what looked like either a giant bathtub or a tiny swimming pool. There were three other people in the pool, two women and an elderly man. I slipped in, and after a moment, I was reminded of sitting in the bathtub for hours when I was a child—perhaps the temperature was similar, because I don't know what reminded me. I sat quietly, got a bit dozy, and then closed my eyes.

That was when the music came back into my mind, in the form of a ballad I had known for a long time—"I Never Will Marry." I had sung it many times, never meaning it, imagining some Irish girl or English girl looking into a lake and wondering what to do with herself (and at least she wasn't going to get shot, like the girl in "Banks of the Ohio"). I had always thought that it had a lovely tune, and sitting in that spa, I let the tune and the lyrics float through my mind. I must have also been moving my lips, because when I opened my eyes, one of the women was looking at me and smiling. I smiled back, but I didn't say anything. I was glad to have the music back, though, playing in my head, and after I left the spa and walked around (fish and chips for lunch), one song led to another. They seemed to come from the buildings and the parks into my head, and then to float out of my head into the air. It was an uncanny experience, and I appreciated not having to share it. For some reason, I felt that I was learning something about tunefulness and how to use my voice in a more elegant way. I felt safe and kept walking until it was almost dark, and then went back to my hotel.

When I woke up in the morning and looked out the window, the trees in the square across from my room, glinting in the moist sunlight (there had been a sprinkle overnight, but not a lot), convinced me that I wanted to get out into the countryside and see more of this area. I checked out and started walking. I walked for about an hour, then went into an art museum that had some interesting pieces. When it stopped raining, I went outside again, and into the "gardens," which were more of a park than a garden, but pleasant. I was walking past a couple, and I heard the man say, "Indeed, my view is that Winchester Cathedral is a good deal more elegant than Salisbury, but, darling, you are entitled to your opinion." He squeezed his wife's hand, and I nodded to them, not simply acknowledging the fact that we were passing one another, but, in my own mind, thanking them for two ideas—first Salisbury Cathedral, and then Winchester Cathedral. I went back to the hotel and reclaimed my baggage. The bus would be in an hour.

The road we took on the bus was two lanes, not four, and seemed to have been carved gently into the hills. There were trees everywhere (beautifully shaded by a light fog), stone fences, hidden driveways, sometimes a house or a stone building tucked into a valley beneath the road. Limpley Stoke was one of the little villages. After Limpley Stoke came wider, flatter fields, surrounded by fences and neatly trimmed hedges. Every turnoff drew me and made me want to walk or ride a bike through every town and up every road. Woods, fields. The trip lasted about an hour, but it was as immersive as a dream. Which was the best part? When the road ran along the side of a hill, and I could intermittently see green fields rolling into the distance? Or when the trees closed in and bright puffs of clouds floated over them? Or when I would see, briefly, a pale stone house nestled behind a hedge? Or the sun flickering through the leaves as we passed an area that the man behind me told his companion was Little Wishford. And then we passed some sort of fancy house, and we were back in civilization, and I woke up from my dream in a new world. It was about three in the afternoon, and I knew I should find a hotel, so I walked down High Street, but I was so enthralled by what I saw that I passed one twice, the King's Head Inn, before I even realized that it was a hotel. Part of the reason was that the hotel was on Bridge Street, and the bridge crossed the Avon River, and the river itself was shining, bubbly, flowing. I saw a staircase leading down to the river, and when I lifted my eyes, I saw the side of the King's Head Inn, and came to my senses. I went in and booked a room overlooking the river, left my bags, and walked out. I should have gone to the cathedral, but all I did was walk around town and listen to people talking. In the morning I went on to Winchester, but I thought I would be back.

The thing I found interesting but strange about traveling in England was that you never knew where you were. Back in the US, a lot of the roads were set out on some sort of a grid, and if you knew that the place you were headed was east, west, north, or south of where you were, you would probably get there if you kept walking. In England, the roadways seemed to follow the easiest paths from one spot to another. I had a sense that I was wandering, and I might get to my destination, but I might not, and if I didn't, I might end up somewhere that was weirder and more interesting than my destination. I knew why this was—hundreds of years ago, road builders had to make the best of what was around them, and of course the Brits weren't confused, but I enjoyed my confusion. Maybe for that reason, when I was on the bus the next morning to Winchester, I didn't even realize that we were going east. I thought we were going south, and I kept wondering how far we were from the ocean. The trip was shorter, and not as dreamy. Either I had gotten used to the countryside, or the countryside between Salisbury and Winchester wasn't as interesting as what I had seen the day before, but even so, the trip was enjoyable. I got to Winchester just after lunchtime, and went straight into the first pub I saw—the Green Man. I was a little dazed when I sat down, and when I looked at the menu, I had no idea what to eat. I had read the names of the dishes before, and even eaten a few, but I felt so disoriented that I had no idea what I wanted.

I took a deep breath, and then the server came up to me. He had a beautiful wide smile, and said, "May I help you?"

I said, "What would you eat?"

He said, "Where are you from?"

"St. Louis, Missouri."

He looked at me thoughtfully, and then said, "Toad-in-the-hole."

I laughed out loud, and said, "In St. Louis, we don't eat the poor toads. Or frogs, as we call them. We eat crawdads, though."

He smiled again, and said, "Well, it's really a sausage cooked inside a Yorkshire pudding. I am sure that it's so delicious that they named it that so the neighbors would refuse any invitation to a meal if that was what you were offering, so you could eat it all yourself."

I said, "I trust you."

He wrote down the order, and I didn't really look at him until he was walking away. Tall, slender, graceful, he was having a laugh with one of the other servers as he went to the kitchen. And he was obviously English, but he didn't really talk like the people I had heard walking the streets. I looked around. The pub was nicer inside than it was from the outside. They had made good use of the darkness (not a lot of windows). There were several chandeliers, and they lit up the shining wood of the tables and the chairs, which looked as if they were old, made of oak, but well taken care of. The bar (I didn't know what they called it in England) had five taps for various beers (ales—none of them Budweiser), and was made of a lighter, redder wood that shone brilliantly.

The toad was neatly housed in a puffy pastry, along with some buttered potatoes and onions and mushrooms. When the server set it on the table in front of me, the fragrance rose up and I took a deep breath. I looked at him, and said, "I owe you." He looked at his pad, and said, "Indeed. Six shillings, ten pence."

I reached into my pocket and pulled out a one-pound note and set it on the table. He picked it up, dipped his head, smiled, and then, when I had completely cleaned my plate, he brought me an apple crumble. I ate the whole thing. When I was finished, I felt more normal, and I was ready to wander around Winchester. I did find a hotel, not far from the pub, housed in a typical Winchester building, red brick, narrow windows, on a tight street. Then I walked around town.

In the summer in England you could walk around town until ten p.m.—even though the sun had gone down, there was still light glimmering in the sky, and there were plenty of streetlamps and lit-up windows to look into. At first I meant, of course, to go to the cathedral, but as I was walking, I was waylaid by a set of ruins inside a tall stone wall. There were a few plaques, but I didn't have a guidebook, so I only learned some things—built before William the Conqueror, then add-ons, the home of a bishop. I sang a song to myself as I walked around, mostly about women in the Middle Ages mourning their lost loves, and then went on to the cathedral, which was just down the street. It was a grand place, with beautiful arches and windows, but not as interesting, at least right then, as the ruins I had seen earlier. I looked around, decided to come back, and went outside. There were some people who were about my age scrounging for something in the green area to one side of the cathedral. One of them stood out, literally, because he was extremely tall and very cute, with long thick hair and one of those faces—prominent cheekbones, lovely jaw, blue eyes. But I was tired. I went back to my hotel and curled up with a book, but fell asleep. When I woke up, I was hungry again (I looked at my belly, but it was okay, I guess thanks to all the walking and the backpack). I asked the man at the desk if he had anything to recommend, and he said, "Have you tried Indian food? Curries and all that?"

I shook my head.

"Up the hill there's a lovely spot. As it's new to you, I suggest the chicken korma. A good introduction that you will never regret."

It was still light, of course, so no problem finding the place, but it was dark inside, just like everywhere else. I went to my table, picked up the menu, and the chicken korma was there, but it was interesting to look at the other names, too—tandoori chicken, chicken tikka masala, butter chicken (which made me think of Grandmother, who always said that butter was the best thing you could put into anything). Garlic naan. My eye went straight to that. By the time the waiter came over, my sight had adjusted to the darkness, and right behind him, I saw the face of that tall guy, leaning forward, and taking a bite of whatever he was eating. He was just as cute in the darkness as he had been in the light. The waiter left with my order, and I secretly watched the tall guy, but then the woman sitting with him, her back to me, laughed out loud, and her laugh sounded joltingly familiar. He said something else, and she laughed again and tossed her head, and her dark hair flew around, and the fact that it was something of a mess reminded me of the gawky girl in my high school class. I kept my eye on them.

A couple of times, they reached across the table and squeezed each other's hands. She said something that I couldn't hear, and he laughed. He smiled a lot, and I knew they were a couple, and I thought that even if the woman was not the gawky girl, I was already envious.

And then they got up, walked past me, and I saw that she *was* the gawky girl—glasses, mouth slightly open, smile, still gawky (she caught her foot on a chair leg and grabbed the tall guy's arm so that she wouldn't fall down). They left. The next day, I saw what they were doing in Winchester, England—the people in the green area by the cathedral were working on an archaeological excavation for medieval remnants (I asked questions when I went back to the cathedral, and the guy I talked to had plenty to say). I stood near one of the ramparts on the outside of the cathedral and watched the gawky girl and the tall guy. Her job was to carry a little notepad and a box around, and, apparently, when someone found something, he or she called her over and she recorded where it was, then carried it to some office. His job was to carefully scrape the soil, moving across rather than down, and then to pick things up and decide if they were actually things.

I walked away. And yes, she had a wedding ring on her finger. It glinted in the sunlight.

The gawky girl hadn't been a friend of mine in high school, but I hadn't minded her—in some ways, I even liked her, because she was herself. Either she didn't try to be the sort of girl we were supposed to be, or she didn't know how. If I hadn't been so focused on what I wanted to do in terms of music and going to college, I might have befriended her—some girls did. But I had never thought that she would precede me into marriage, into an evidently happy relationship with a drop-dead gorgeous man who made her look like a regular girl—when they left the restaurant, I saw that she came up to his chin and that he had to duck his head when he went through the door.

As I was walking back to my hotel by myself (and glancing around the narrow streets for someone who would leap out and stab me—usually, I wasn't that nervous), I thought that yes, I had wasted my life—not on music, but on bands, on performing, on doing what I wanted to do. Was she the lucky one? Maybe.

The next day, it rained, which made it worse. There were plenty of places to walk and some parks, and even though you had to go uphill, the hills weren't terribly steep. I was fairly used to walking wherever I wanted now. I stared out my window (there was only one), and went out into the downpour one time, but I was too depressed to do much. Fortunately, I did get hungry, and so at what they would call "teatime," I went back to the Green Man. It was Saturday, so there were a lot of people in there—I assume because the food was good, and yes, there were plenty of servings of toad-in-the-hole being taken around. But I wanted to try something else, so I was staring at the menu, going back and forth between the sausage roll, the Scotch egg, and the shepherd's pie. I heard his footsteps, and I knew who he was before I looked up—the server from my first night—and one thing I registered about him was that his footsteps were regular and even rhythmic. When I looked up, he was smiling, and I couldn't help smiling right back. He said, "I thought we'd lost you."

I said, "I had Indian food last night."

He licked his lips.

I said, "Chicken korma, naan bread. Lots of garlic."

He said, "Do you want to go out to dinner with me?"

I said, "What time?"

"About eleven, give or take half an hour."

He smiled.

I said, "Well, for now I'll take the Scotch egg and the sausage roll."

And then, he looked around, and suddenly sat down in the chair across from me, leaned toward me, and said, "I say. Tomorrow is Sunday. Let's do it then. I'm off for the day. Where are you staying?"

I told him, and he said, "I'll show up at the door around half two and we'll do a few things."

I said, "Yes, but, is half of two one?"

This time he laughed out loud and said, "No. It is two plus one half. Two thirty, you would say."

I nodded. He stood up, and a few minutes later, brought me my food. It was fine, but nothing like the toad. The place got busy, and so he didn't say much more to me, but he would smile as he went by, and then, when I paid, he touched the back of my hand just for a moment, and smiled again. As I was walking to my hotel (trying to avoid the umbrellas on the street), I felt like my world had flipped over, but I wasn't entirely sure if he would show up.

His name was Martin Leighmor, he had grown up not far away, he was very fond of Winchester (and Salisbury), not so much of London, and his favorite Beatle had been George, not because he was the cutest, but because he seemed to be the kindest. He was an only child, and had been working at the Green Man for about a month. He was interested in me and my background (he had even heard of St. Louis) but he didn't pry. He waited for me to dish out bits of information, and I did—bits. I didn't say anything about my records or my songs, only that I had sung in a band, that I liked traditional English songs, and also English composers, but I did reach into my backpack and feel the roll of two-dollar bills with my fingers.

6

NOTHING IN MY PAST had taught me what love was. And no songs or movies had, either, especially the ones I liked best (because they had the best tunes), such as "Mary Hamilton" or "The Foggy Foggy Dew." I certainly didn't want to find myself in the middle of a real-life "murder ballad" (but I did enjoy "Pretty Polly" floating through my head). I had been very fond of Charlie, but in some ways he was a repeat of Brucie—close, kind, friendly, but more like a relation than a boyfriend. Allen. Well, I admired Allen, but I always knew that he saw me as a distraction from his real purpose. At first, being with Martin was like sensing that you are "the chosen one," and being grateful and flattered. We would be walking down the street, and he would suddenly turn around and stare at me, then smile with pleasure. We would be looking at something, anything—a map or a tree or a green field—and he would put his arm around me and pull me against himself. There was a steady current of desire—he was very organized in the way that he took me to his place, brought me in, turned on the light, and then took me into the bedroom, folded back the coverlets, and undressed me gently but with plenty of desire. He felt my body all over, touching my face, smoothing my hair, feeling the shape of my shoulders and my hips, taking one of my hands in both of his. He was evidently experienced, but he treated my body like a wonder that he had never felt before, so there was a kind of frisson. And he didn't seem to have a temper, even at the Green Man. One time, I was eating there and some drunk who didn't like his food grabbed his plate and threw it at Martin as Martin was walking toward another table. Martin saw it coming, reached up, caught it, and set it back on the man's table, saying, "May I suggest something else, sir?" It was the manager of the restaurant, who was also one of the drinks servers, who came over and kicked the fellow out.

So, at first my love for Martin was a kind of appreciation of all of his good qualities, but as I got to know him better, I became enthralled by the narrative of who he was—two years older than I was, born in February of 1947, to a well-to-do family (his father was a baron who had survived four years in the Second World War, and his mother's father was a viscount). His uncles and cousins loved foxhunting and travel, but he preferred walking and reading. His father was strict, but had a kindly streak, and his mother had some sort of health issue and was very loving. Her greatest regret, she had told him, was not being able to give him any brothers and sisters, though he did have several cousins, so we shared that. He didn't know how to play an instrument, but he loved music of all kinds (and he had a stack of records about three feet tall in his flat). He said he was smart enough to get into Eton, not smart enough to stand out, and so he hadn't been pushed into some typical career path that would lead to standing for Parliament as a Tory. He had gotten into both Oxford and Cambridge, and had chosen Oxford only for the landscape. He'd lasted two years there, studying literature, and now (his father was rolling his eyes and his mother was very supportive) he was doing various jobs just to see which one he might like—he did not accept any money from his father or the estate because he wanted to understand what it felt like to be on his own. What he liked about being a server in a pub was that he interacted with a lot of people, and learned about human nature by doing that. At the moment, he was contemplating going back to college and becoming a psychologist—maybe research and maybe therapist, but he didn't know yet.

It was the psychologist side of him that, I thought, prodded him to more or less investigate me. He was curious about Mom's issues, of course, and got me to relate the details of her driving "episode" more than once. He was also interested in Uncle Drew's generosity and his choice not to display his wealth, climbing the residential ladder by moving to some prestigious neighborhood, or even to New York. Martin thought it was interesting that my private high school had had a significant number of Jewish students and that, as far as I could tell, they seemed comfortable there. Antisemitism in England was an issue the Brits were only beginning to confront. Since he knew where Missouri was, he also probed my thoughts about Black people and the history of slavery, and I learned more from him than I had at school about the English slave trade.

The downside of our affair was that I couldn't get the pill in the UK—it was illegal for anyone who was not married. I was still on the pill, but my supply was running low. Martin was aware of this. He didn't mind wearing a condom, and he didn't mind pulling out. And he would always make sure that the condom hadn't split after he used it. Our sex life fit in with everything else—it was relaxed and enjoyable, and I didn't have any sense that for him, having sex was making up for other things. He seemed to enjoy everything equally, as, perhaps, a psychologist should.

One time, maybe a month after we got together (and I had moved into his flat with him—his mother knew about it), we were walking along a stream in a park not far from the university, and we saw the gawky girl and her husband coming toward us. The path was narrow, so someone had to step aside. Martin was talking about the Cotswolds, but he didn't even pause—he put his arm around my waist and eased me to the left. The tall guy had intended to do the same thing, and he drew the gawky girl in the same direction, so there we were, nearly bumping into one another. Martin and the tall guy both laughed, and then Martin guided me around them. The tall guy, of course, didn't know who I was, but the gawky girl didn't recognize me, either, which I thought was interesting. When I told Martin about this—that we had gone to school together in a small class, sixty-five students all together—he said, "No surprise. Did you see her stumble when they were coming down the slope?

You didn't say anything, so she hadn't the chance to recognize your voice. You might not have recognized her, either, if she weren't such a beanstalk."

Martin had a few friends, but he wasn't much of a socializer. He told me that he mostly liked to observe people, and he did plenty of that at the Green Man. When he got back to his flat, he liked to think about what he had observed, and sometimes write it down. A member of his social class, in England, was expected to give parties and go to parties and make connections, but he didn't like that, and the only good thing about his mother's medical problems was that she wasn't up to the socializing that would normally be required of her.

Martin worked from about five until about eleven Tuesday through Friday, and then during the day on Saturdays. He had Sundays off except for festive holidays. I would go to the pub with him at five and have something for supper or dinner or tea—dinner in England didn't actually begin until six thirty. I would walk home in the early-evening sunshine, noticing, as the summer edged into fall, how quickly the daylight dimmed. Since I felt safe in Winchester (whether I should have or not, I had no idea), I enjoyed the changes. I always carried an umbrella, but I didn't always use it, even if it was raining. I was much more tolerant of rain, knowing that there wouldn't be any tornadoes (or actual hurricanes, Martin said, thanks to the Gulf Stream, which brought warmth and took the bad weather west).

When I got back to the flat, the first thing I did was clean up whatever mess we had made during the day, and then I sat down in a chair in the corner, with a wall on one side and a window on the other, and thought about music. Sometimes my thoughts were memories, and sometimes my thoughts were ideas. I wanted to write more songs, both the lyrics and the tunes. It was easy to hear songs on the radio in England, and Martin's collection was up-to-date—Little Feat; *Love Story,* by Johnny Mathis; *If I Could Only Remember My Name,* by David Crosby; *Songs of Love and Hate,* by Leonard Cohen; a live album by Aretha. The way I did it was to listen to music with Martin in the morning—I let him choose, and he often chose Leonard Cohen, sometimes Aretha. While we were listening, we would eat breakfast and read, then we would turn off the music and go for a walk. When I came back after dinner, I would sit down and do what I had always done—write down some thought that came to me, and then expand it. The first thought that turned into a song was "Why me?"

During our walk that day, because it was rainy, we had gone to one of the museums, and as we were looking around, Martin stopped to say hi, in his usual friendly way, to a blond woman who, I suspected, was a couple of years older than he was. I immediately noticed that she was happier to see him than he was to see her, and that she glanced at me, gave me a polite smile, and then went back to staring at Martin. He said, "Lidia! How are you, love?"

She evidently had a sense of humor, because she said, "You tell me, darling!"

He looked her up and down, and said, "Good health, evidently active, omelet for brekkie with a side of toffee."

She laughed.

He squinted, then said, "Ah—treacle toffee."

She said, "No, hazelnut," and all three of us laughed. Then she said, "And you?"

He put his arm around me and said, "Rice Krispies!" We all laughed again (for breakfast we had had porridge and bits of ham, plus a split scone). Martin said, "Where are you living now, love?"

"Still in London. In a flat in Greenwich, actually. I gave up on Carnaby Street." She looked serious for a moment, then smiled again.

Martin said, "Still designing tie-dyes?"

She said, "I've moved on to silk underwear. That's where the money is."

She kissed him on the cheek and headed for the door. Just by looking at her, I knew that she still loved him, that whatever had come between them seemed to her to have been a bad idea, and I guessed that maybe they hadn't seen each other in a couple of years.

Martin didn't tell me anything about her and I didn't ask. I looked at him a few times, but it didn't appear that he was holding anything back, only that he didn't think it mattered.

That evening, when I stared at the words "Why me?" the next words I thought of were, "She had such blue eyes / As blue as sadness / As blue as the skies. / Darling, I saw the tears. / Did you?" (Chords and percussion.) I thought up the chorus—"Did she know it? / Did I show it? / That I wished / Right then / To look like her?"

I tapped my fingers on my knees and wrote the second verse, "Darling, did you stare / As she fled away / Stumbling down the stairs / As she wiped away the tears. / Tell me, did you?"

Then the chorus, slightly changed, "Did you know it? Did she show it? / Even then, I still wished it, / To look like her."

I got up and walked around the room. It was almost dark, and the lights in the buildings nearby were turning on. I didn't turn mine on, because I was waiting for some sort of inspiration.

I sat down. "What do I see / When I look in the mirror? / Brown eyes, brown hair / Fading in the gloom / All of me sliding away." Then the third chorus: "Do you see it? / Do I show it? / What do you wish? / Should I look like her?"

I leaned back in the chair and closed my eyes. I could hear a few cars go by below (our street was too narrow for trucks) and then I could hear some people, men and women, laughing. I waited for silence, then wrote, "You open the door, / And switch on the light / My heart is sore, / But your kisses are slow / Your smiles are love . . . / Why me? Why me? / Only you would know."

Then I altered the final chorus again: "You see it, / You show it, / Love, for us all, / Is the ultimate riddle, / The great windfall."

I mouthed the words, so that I would remember them, and then read them over again and folded the paper. I knew that the rhythm was a bit off, but once you think up the tune, then you can fix it.

I turned on the light and felt a sense of relief as the room brightened. I picked up our copy of the *Guardian* and looked through the culture section. I still thought a movie, even a comedy, about a man with a transplanted dick would be too weird, so didn't want to see *Percy,* though Martin had shown some interest. I thought we could see *Carry On Loving,* since the village where it took place was named Much-Snogging-on-the-Green. The next night, though, Martin wanted to see *When Eight Bells Toll.* I thought that it was a little scary, but I loved the landscapes. Martin said it was "decent." I wasn't ready to sing him my song.

I WOULD HAVE SAID that central Pennsylvania had the most beautiful autumn colors, but there was something about the trees and the hedges set against the fields around Winchester that struck me when we went, in the early fall, to Martin's family's place (I had imagined a large farmhouse surrounded by wheat fields) for his father's sixtieth birthday. I was a little nervous, though Martin wasn't. He said that his mother ("Lady Leighmor" until she told me I could call her Ida) had told his father ("Lord Leighmor," and maybe I would never be able to call him Eric) that Martin had found himself a sweet young woman from a "prominent family" in the US (and yes, Uncle Drew now had plenty of money, and had been interviewed for the *Wall Street Journal* about his investment strategies). She said I was well educated and loved England—according to Martin, she piled it on. I had not met her, because she couldn't drive a car and hated buses, but I had spoken with her over the phone, and she had been friendly, and had even asked me about my songs—she liked music, and she had heard of "There You Are," but hadn't actually listened to it. Her favorite American singer was Etta James and her favorite English singer was Cilla Black. And she liked the Beach Boys better than the Beatles. All of this made me laugh, because she was British, and at least as old as Mom, whose favorite singer was, as far as I knew, Mahalia Jackson.

The night before we left, when we were cuddled up together after having sex, relaxed but still awake, I felt thankful that, for him, an orgasm was followed by a gentle laugh and a sweet hug. The sense of warmth and comfort felt natural and satisfying, and there was something about Martin that made him seem like actual perfection to me, whatever some shrink might say about human nature. I had been a little nervous about meeting his parents, but listening to his easy breathing caused that to drift away.

It was only thirteen miles to Nether Wallop, and I didn't know if there was a bus. I imagined hitchhiking, but when I asked Martin, he smiled and said, "You wait. You'll see." And indeed, I did. Just after noon, there was a knock on the door, and Martin helped me into my coat (yes, it was chillier in England when the leaves were turning than it was in St. Louis). Outside, pretty much taking up the whole narrow street, was a black Rolls-Royce, all square and flat and shiny, and a young man, maybe five years older than Martin, who showed us the way to the back door. Martin said, "Tyler! How are you, my man?" and the driver said, "Doing well, sir. Short ride."

And it was, if you were lucky negotiating the narrow streets we had to get down. Twice, Tyler turned onto a street and saw that there was another car, and he had to back up and try the next street, but yes, the thirteen miles to Nether Wallop were beautiful and smooth. I said to Martin, "If your father has a chauffeur, why doesn't your mother let him drive her?" Martin said that he didn't know why, but she never had, unless Lord Leighmor was with her. He held my hand as we both looked out the windows. Martin said, "I say, Tyler, how many guests have shown up?"

"Only two when I left, but I understand that forty-six have been invited."

I looked down at my dress and smoothed it along my legs. It was one I had brought in my backpack from home, and when we were invited to the party, I had taken it to be cleaned and pressed, but even so. It was a green A-line with a neat yoke and short sleeves, a little embroidery around the edge of the neckline and the sleeves, and the sweater I had brought along (because Martin told me his family's place was "on the nippy side") did not match it at all. Martin leaned over and whispered, "Be yourself. Everyone else will be tiresome as hell."

Well, maybe to him. I began to wonder what I was getting myself into, and my skin even prickled a little bit. I tried thinking of what

I was feeling as stage fright, and remembering all the times I had overcome that, but as soon as the Rolls drove through the gate, I knew that this was maybe a bigger deal.

The property was named Beech House. It was on the promontory of a small hill, facing south. There was an elegant glade of trees behind the house, and a long road that swept around the hill and then approached the house from the front. It was not surrounded by a wall or fencing. The landscape made it seem remote, even though it wasn't far from town. The main part of the house ran from a curved western end to an addition on the east side where the bedrooms (twelve of them) were. It was C-shaped, graceful, and imposing in a way that was unlike any estate I had seen in Huntleigh or Town and Country. The party took place in a large room (with three chandeliers and a fireplace at each end) that was in the back of the house, just behind the front hall and the entrance.

And yes, I was intimidated. I had sort of gotten used to the Rolls-Royce by pretending it was a taxi. And Lady Leighmor was sweet and friendly—she even gave me a kiss on the cheek when we went into the house. Maybe what worked me up was that everyone was "dressed to the nines," as Grandmother would say, and some were evidently wearing impressive "vintage" outfits that they still actually fit into. My favorite was a dress that looked like it was from the 1920s, sort of a gold color, evidently silk velvet, and beaded all across the front. When the lady wearing it saw me looking at her, she glided over and said, "Well, dahling, finally I can fit into this old thing again. My most beloved gown ever! You will discover, my girl, that there are a few benefits to wasting away in your elder years." She smiled, and she did look old enough to have danced around, doing the Charleston or the shimmy, some fifty years ago. She glided away, got herself another glass of champagne, and I kept trying to look friendly.

No one had bought his or her outfit in a shop on Carnaby Street, and certainly many of the outfits were straight from Paris, including the gown that Lady Leighmor was wearing, tight from the shoulders to the waist, with a gracefully patterned fabric—maybe silk—and then a huge skirt that floated down to her lower calves. I suspected it was a Chanel—that was the most popular designer. Oddly, Lord Leighmor was wearing his uniform (cleaned and pressed of course) from the Second World War. He looked something like Martin, though not as easygoing. He strolled around the party, dipping his head, lifting his glass, smiling but never laughing, thanking those who had come, sometimes having a bit of a conversation with one of the men who looked about his age. Sometimes Lady Leighmor would go to him, take him by the hand, and lead him to someone she wanted him to talk to, and he was always polite. And he was polite to me—his chats were like a bowl of porridge that he dished out, one spoonful at a time. Even so, I felt judged and found wanting (if only by me). The party lasted exactly two hours, and then everyone was gone. I knew that we were to eat dinner there, and spend the night (in separate rooms), then return to Winchester in the morning. I longed to leave. I tried to distract myself by looking out the windows, but it was so empty and windy outside that it actually made me a little more nervous.

I did not know that Lord Leighmor was going to startle me by grasping me by the elbow and guiding me into his study, sitting me down in a chair with a tall back, and interrogating me, but that's what he did. Lord Leighmor's study was on the "first floor" (something that had rather confused me when I got to England and had to learn the difference between the first floor and the ground floor) of the curved end, and through the three cathedral-like very tall windows, I could see the sun setting behind a hedge in the distance.

He smiled the way he had at the party, as if he knew he should, but he didn't have Martin's instinctive good humor. I looked at the seams on his uniform. I thought it was pretty amazing that what he had worn thirty years before still fit him perfectly. It was like a khaki suit, with incised metal buttons; neat shoulder pads, not too loose, not too tight; large flat pockets; and a belt that showed off his waist. He had his billed wool cap on. As he "chatted" with me, he walked back and forth in even steps, as if he was marching.

He said, "Well, Miss Rattler. It is a pleasure to meet you. I understand you grew up in St. Louis, Missouri. I knew an officer in the Italian campaign who grew up in St. Louis."

I said, "Did he ever tell you where? Every neighborhood is different, and it seems like that is always the first thing we say about ourselves."

He said, "Let's see. It was, indeed, an odd name. Da Pears? Something like that."

I coughed and said, "Yes, Des Peres. Lots of names in St. Louis are French. 'Some fathers,' I remember my grandmother telling me. I grew up closer to downtown. Near Forest Park."

Now came the clue—he smiled, and said, "I have heard that is a nice neighborhood."

I said, "I loved it."

He turned toward me. "And what, may I ask, brought you to England?"

I started a bit, and then I was honest. I said, "A fascination with music, especially traditional English songs. The Child Ballads list, that sort of thing."

"I understand you are a songstress."

I said, "If you emphasize the syllable 'stress,' that would be true."

Now he actually smiled. I saw that he did have a sense of humor and felt myself relax. He said, "It does seem like a difficult way of life."

"The touring can be a pain in the—" I stopped myself, and said, "Taxing. But writing and playing and singing the songs is a great pleasure."

He said, "I am fond of music, I must say, but I know very little about it. Sometimes I do take Lady Leighmor up to London, for a concert. The symphony orchestra there is quite good. Lady Leighmor does like Mr. Previn, though he looks like a child to me."

I said, "Isn't he about forty or something?"

"Perhaps."

He walked back and forth one more time, and I shifted in my seat. Then he said, "I must say, 'Rattler' is a bit of an oddity."

I didn't say a word about my father. I said, "When I was a child, I thought we were related to rattlesnakes."

"It is English, you know. I do believe that England has the oddest names on the planet. My favorite is Birdwhistle. I am quite fond of birds."

I said, "I enjoy birds, also."

We chatted back and forth as he walked around, and I began to appreciate looking out the windows as he pointed out a few deer and then the beeches that the estate had been named for and some hornbeam trees. I thought we were about finished when he walked over and turned on one of the chandeliers, but he suddenly turned toward me, and said, "Is there anything you are considerably averse to?"

I thought, Liver and onions?

But then he said, "This generation of yours, and not only in the US, is quite rowdy. I was in New York City on some business around the time of that Woodstock fracas." He shook his head.

I thought for a second, cleared my throat again, and said, "I didn't take part in that, if that's what you mean. Sir, I will be straightforward with you. Apart from music, and perhaps travel, I am a cautious person. I suppose some people would say 'risk averse.' I cannot say, to be honest, that I am proud of that." I thought of Brucie. I hadn't heard from him in a while, but he did have a job, and maybe a girlfriend.

Lord Leighmor looked at me and said, "I believe we are of a mind, Miss Rattler. I would say that the thing that saved me in the war"—he looked down at his uniform and ran his hands across the pockets—"was attentiveness to risk. I was good at seeing threats and pointing them out to my underlings. I survived, and most of them did, as well."

And so the "interrogation" had turned into an interview, and at the end of it, after about half an hour, I accompanied Lord Leighmor out of his study with a sense of pleasure. Although his demeanor was much different from Martin's and from Lady Leighmor's, he seemed basically decent.

I didn't want to say anything to Martin in front of the chauffeur when we went back to Winchester the next morning (after a breakfast that I thought would keep me full for the rest of the day), but when we were snuggling in our bed before he was to go to the Green Man, I told him about my conversation with his father. He said, "Love, I didn't wonder where you were, because Mother warned me ahead of time, and I also didn't suppose that he was going to frighten you in any way. If I had, please understand that I would have gone in there with you."

I gave him a kiss and said, "He is so unlike you."

"That's true, and I do sometimes wonder if Mother was so eager to have a child that she appealed to another source, but who knows?"

"Your mother is a sweetheart."

Martin gave me a little squeeze.

I said, "Your father said that he takes her to concerts in London. I wonder if she's ever sneaked off to a Beach Boys concert."

"She did! Twice! Five years ago, a friend of hers came by to take her up to London to do some shopping for the holidays, and she came back with very little." He laughed. "Then, in May, the following year, her friend showed up again. That time they went to a big event—Mick & Tich, Cream, Dusty, Cliff Richard, Cat Stevens—I don't remember all of them. Those two must have been the oldest people in the audience. I don't know what she told Father, but she was gone for two days!" Then he said, "But do tell me if he said anything that made you uncomfortable."

"Not really. He asked me what I was 'averse to.' "

"I hope you said sexual intercourse . . ."

"He would know I was lying!"

We both laughed and rolled around on the bed, and then he said, "He doesn't like political upheaval of even the mildest sort. He wants the Tories to keep everything in the UK exactly the way it always has been. He is a charitable old man—he doles out shillings and even pound notes whenever he walks down the street—but he's terribly afraid of some thin end of the wedge, as if Labour taking over Parliament will end with some navvy walking into Beech House and claiming it. He went with me to watch *A Hard Day's Night* when it first came out, and he sat there stiff as a tree limb the whole time. He did not want these northerners to get above themselves. Mother, on the other hand, always thinks the sedan is going to go off the road, or the eggs aren't sufficiently cooked, or the pooch walking down the street is rabid." He shook his head. "They sleep separately. His chamber is a shambles and hers looks like no one has ever been inside it, it's so neat. I know they appreciate each other's virtues, but they don't . . ."

And then he pulled me close, as if to say, This is my relief.

WE WENT BACK to Beech House on St. Stephen's Day, as they called it, and stayed until New Year's Eve, because Martin had gotten the week off. The Green Man had been very busy on both Christmas Eve (Martin said because of the eggnog) and Christmas Day (for the Christmas pudding). I had made a few of my grandmother's sugar cookies, but I hadn't been able to find any sprinkles, only some brown sugar crystals, but we both thought they were good. Martin slept most of the way to Beech House, and the chauffeur told me to be sure to eat as much of the haunch of beef as I possibly could, because "that will keep you goin' for the rest o' the winter." We did have a bit of a feast—served for teatime, all leftovers, but all delicious; the only thing I missed was mashed potatoes, as Lord Leighmor preferred sweet potatoes. Lady Leighmor played a few traditional carols, and, since I knew all the words, I sang and enjoyed it. The whole time I was singing, Lord Leighmor nodded in rhythm and Martin looked pleased but tired. He fell asleep around nine, or so he told me, because, of course, we still could not share a room.

My room was not far from the doorway to the larger part of the house, and even though the Leighmors seemed to have "retired" also, I felt comfortable strolling around, looking out the windows at the snow and the stars—it was a beautiful night, and I was reminded of when Uncle Drew used to point out Orion and the Big Dipper and the North Star. I had gotten a letter from him two days before

Christmas, telling me about this and that and saying that he was coming to England on business in late February. Where would I like to meet him? He wouldn't mind prowling around Yorkshire for a few days.

The house was indeed "nippy," but I was used to that now, so I didn't mind. I looked at the pictures of the Leighmors, and in one of them, of James Leighmor, sitting on a horse, sometime during the nineteenth century, I saw that he had Martin's smile as well as his hairline. He looked about the same age, too. But it did feel more like I was exploring, or even trespassing, than that I was in some sort of home. Maybe because it was winter, it seemed like the Leighmors didn't have anything to do. They didn't use the property as a farm—no cattle or sheep in the fields, and no crops, though there were two orchards, one for pears and one for apples.

The next day, when we went for a short stroll after breakfast, I said, "Where are the cows and the pigs and the horses?"

"Oh, it's never been a farm. Good heavens! The very thought!" Martin laughed. "Father is an investor. That's all he's interested in. Doesn't even go to cricket matches, though he played a bit before the war. Mother rode horses as a girl, but she turned out to be allergic. She doesn't like beaches or oceans, so there's no swimming in the sea. She reads and visits friends, but she grew up in Lincolnshire and went to boarding school in France." He glanced at me. "Common in her day. The thing that drew Father to her when she came out was everything she knew about French cuisine."

We turned toward the house. He squeezed my hand and said, "Her great legacy in Nether Wallop is that she persuaded the bakery to make croissants, pain au chocolat, and baguettes."

I said, "But what does your father do all day?"

"He reads the London *Times, The Economist,* and the *Financial Times* in his study, and takes phone calls and oversees his investments." I had noticed that the servants seemed satisfied—my guess was that their jobs were easy and maybe well-paid, and they did have pleasant quarters to sleep in. Lady Leighmor gave them books, if they wanted books, and subscribed to a few magazines. As we drove down the long driveway to the gate, I looked around. Quiet. Peaceful. Beautiful.

BOTH MARTIN AND I were thrilled to get back to Winchester—me because I hadn't thought of a single tune or lyric when I was at Beech House, and Martin because his life in the Green Man was much more dramatic and intriguing even when the customers were behaving themselves. His way of talking changed, too—in Beech House, he sounded a little stiff and upper-class, and in the restaurant, he talked like everyone else. And laughed like them, as well.

We still got along perfectly. I would have to say that Martin was the only man I have ever met in my life who didn't have a lick of a temper. I might have said that Uncle Drew qualified for that prize, but Uncle Drew could get annoyed, if only with himself—I even heard him shout, once when I was at his house, "Oh, fuck me!" I think it was because he couldn't find something he was looking for. Martin was more even-tempered than that, and seemed to see every frustration as an opportunity to be patient, including with himself. If I spilled something or stepped on his toe, or forgot something, he would say, "No worries." When he had taken me to a shop just before Christmas, to buy me "an outfit," he let me try on what looked good to me, and only steered me in the gentlest way toward what he liked—a below-the-knee, slender, pale cream cashmere dress with long sleeves, a high neckline, and a belt. I preferred the Marimekko, but certainly it would not have been warm enough. And both Lord and Lady Leighmor had complimented me on the dress. I had nothing to complain about, and it didn't occur to me to complain, or even wonder, until sometime in late January, when I was cooking something in our flat (Martin's evening off) and I glanced over at him. He was sitting in the chair beside our lamp, and he was staring at me. When he saw me look, he smiled and turned his head, but then, a moment later, I saw him staring at me again, rubbing his hand on his thigh, and then covering that hand with the other one. He was nervous about something.

That evening, in bed, he was affectionate and pleasant, but he still seemed a little reserved. There was some wave of energy that I felt, and all night long, I woke up and went back to sleep thinking that he was going to break up with me. What had I done? I couldn't think of anything. That afternoon, I went to the Green Man for lunch and watched Martin wander around among the customers and the staff, but I detected no signs that he was interested in another girl. I sort of hoped that the blonde—Lidia, it was—would show up and try to woo him, just to give me an answer to my anxieties. The Martin I watched was about 90 percent his usual funny and active self. At one point, he was carrying a tray, and some guy stuck his leg out. Without even thinking about it, Martin jumped over the guy's foot. The guy was startled, and exclaimed, "Blimey! Sorry, lad!" Martin turned his head and smiled.

I finished my toad-in-the-hole (still loved that) and went toward the front door. Martin came over, graceful as always, and kissed me on the cheek.

From that kiss, I knew he wasn't intending to leave me—it was light, full of feeling, sincere.

As I was walking back to our flat, I realized that he was planning to ask me to marry him. At first, my sense of relief was replaced by a sense of pleasure. I did NOT want him to know what I was thinking, so I decided to stop working on songs about my feelings, and to start with phrases that I heard when I was walking down the street, or ones that I saw on signs. The results were intermittent but interesting. My birthday was in a few weeks, and after that I would go to York to meet Uncle Drew, so I saw it as a nicely circumscribed experiment. The first one came to me when I had left the Green Man the next day and was turning from St. Swithun Street onto St. Thomas. It was dark, and I was carrying my umbrella, but I didn't have to use it, because the rain had tapered off. Behind me, a woman's voice called out, "Careful down the steps, love!"

I looked around and saw an old man wearing a porkpie hat do what he was told—he held the handrail and leaned on his heels. He made it safely down the steps, and turned right.

When I got to our flat, I sat quietly for about fifteen minutes, and then wrote down, "I can't keep him home / He still wants to roam / Where is he going? / He won't say / He can't say . . ." I knew it wasn't very good, and I didn't intend to work on it, but I enjoyed imagining the woman in her flat, trying not to fret, and the man wandering down St. Swithun Street. I imagined myself, the same age, staggering out of our house, ambling down Skinker, making sure to keep Forest Park to the right and the houses to the left, and then wondering where I was, and knowing only that I had to turn around and walk until I saw my own house. When would I be that out of my head? Twenty twenty-five? Twenty thirty? An interesting question. I was reminded of Jeane Dixon, who had prophesied the end of the world, I think in the 2020s. I remembered girls in high school talking about her, especially after Kennedy was assassinated. I smiled at the thought. She was rumored to have grown up in Missouri, but none of the girls knew exactly where—some said Joplin, some said Rolla. Nancy S., who had a great sense of humor, said, "Oh, yeah, Devils Elbow is what I heard."

All in all, I thought my experiment would be fun. A couple of days later, I told Martin about it, and he told me some of the funny things he had heard at the Green Man, but I wanted the phrases to be more random than that, so I wrote down what he told me for future ideas.

The only song that I came up with that I actually liked, and that actually inspired a tune, grew out of the phrases "He did spend all that time telling porkies, and now, seems ta me 'e's tikin' the biscuit!" I heard this on St. James's Lane when I was taking a walk. It was a lovely day, considering the time of year, and I was trying not to think of anything. A pair of men came out of a house on the corner and one of them said this as he turned and headed down Christchurch Road. I looked at them. They were a little older than me. The other one said, "We should uv told him ta sod off ages ago." I didn't hear the rest. I went to the nearby graveyard, a place that is perfect for coming up with a song, especially a graveyard that is a little run-down. Because I didn't understand what they had said, I made it up as I went along. The part I liked was at the end: "Ben gobbled up the biscuit, came to John for more / But Johnny didn't have one, and Li'l Ben was sore. / Johnny touched Ben's head, / and when he woke at two a.m., / Ben was in his bed."

The tune that came to me for this song—key of D—jumped lightly around. Four-four time (I had hoped for three-four, but that time signature doesn't lend itself to humor). By the time Martin came home from the Green Man, I was ready to sing it to him, and he did laugh.

The next morning, he said, "Well, love, what shall we do for your birthday?"

I said, "I'm looking at you, honey, and I am guessing that you have an idea."

"Ah! You caught me! I do have an idea. But let's see if we might be having the same idea."

In fact, I hadn't really been thinking about my birthday. My experience was that a February birthday was a pain in the ass. I was born on the twenty-second, and I knew that it was much worse to be born on the twenty-ninth, but even so, when I was growing up, almost the only fun things you could do on a birthday in February were go ice-skating or sledding, and your party had to be early so that everyone could get home before dark. In Winchester, the sun was pretty much down by half five, and it would be cold, so I really didn't have an idea. I said, "Go to bed at sunset and get up at dawn and eat only ice cream for dinner?"

Martin said, "I thought of that! But I have another idea. You think on it, love, and then we'll talk."

We got up and fiddled around the flat. Martin made a nice omelet for breakfast, and then we went to the shops for a few things and passed the day in our usual style—making jokes, talking about this and that, kissing, embracing. I accompanied him to the Green Man and ate the Cornish pasty, which always had a crisp and flaky crust that my grandmother would have approved of.

It was only when I was walking home that I contemplated my birthday—I would be twenty-three. Just thinking this got me thinking about other women singers—Janis, Joan, and Judy were always the first who came to mind, because we shared that J. Joan was thirty-one now, and Judy was almost ten years older than I was—thirty-three in May. Janis had died at twenty-seven. Others were younger, but even Lesley Gore was almost twenty-six. For a while, I had identified with Marianne Faithfull, who was less than two years older than I was—just turned twenty-five—but then her life had started to scare me. Since I had been in the UK, I had paid some attention to Olivia Newton-John, who was about five months older than I was, and looked like she was much younger. No one, that I knew of, was about to turn twenty-three. It seemed to me that if I actually wanted to make it in the music business, it wasn't going to happen for at least another two years, and, I thought, it wasn't going to happen in England, because there were plenty of beautiful English women singers—they didn't need a girl from St. Louis.

But what about my plan when I came to England? It was to learn about English traditional music, not to join a band, and all I had done about that was diddle around, listening to what I could find and looking up Child Ballads. My musical pleasure had been getting ideas, making up songs, and working on my voice, which I thought was getting richer.

Twenty-three! Mom had been almost thirty when she had me, and, as far as she was concerned, her twenties, on Broadway after the war, were the best years of her life. What would she have done if she'd gotten pregnant when she was twenty-two or twenty-three? Well, maybe she had, but in New York, away from her parents, she would have put that baby up for adoption, and the whole episode would have vanished into space.

Did I want to emulate Mom?

I walked away from that idea in a heartbeat.

And then I wondered if Mom had wanted to get married. I had always assumed that she had gotten herself pregnant with the Rattler guy because she hoped he would leave his wife out of some sort of passion—and it was true, looking at photos of Mom in her twenties, that she was very beautiful for her day: slender, perfectly made up, perfect haircut, a sort of elusive smile (neatly lipsticked) that a man of Rattler's age (judging by the time I saw him, he must have been in his late thirties when he met Mom) might not have been able to resist. I had never thought about his service in the Second World War, but maybe he had married his girlfriend before he left, come back with a few reservations about who he had married, and then become what my grandparents called "a man-about-town."

As I was walking (as it happened, on St. Swithun again), it occurred to me that I had missed an opportunity, in that deli, of connecting with Rattler—maybe not telling him who I was, but flirting with him a bit, chatting, finding out more about him, at least, perhaps, his temperament and his sense of humor.

When I got back to the flat, I turned on the light, and saw my backpack sitting on the floor. Maybe because I had been thinking about all those memories, I reached into the bottom-right corner, trying to find my wad of two-dollar bills, and it was missing! I panicked right then and there. My heart started beating fast, and I started breathing hard, and I thought that there was something about finally losing that eighty-six dollars that was about to wreck my life. I went into the loo and splashed some cold water on my face, then sat down and stared at the backpack. When I stood up again, my toe bumped the left corner, and I felt it, the roll. I pulled it out and opened it. Forty-three two-dollar bills, still clean and sturdy. I rolled them back up, and began collecting my clothes and rolling those up. The cream-colored dress Martin had bought for me didn't fit into the backpack. I left it on the hanger and closed the closet door. I didn't know if I was about to jump off a cliff or fly away.

When Martin got home, he saw the candle I had set on the kitchen table, flickering in the darkness. The door to the bedroom was open, and I was already under the covers. I'd heard the front door creak, and I could see him setting things down. He didn't know I was awake, and he was trying to be quiet. He blew out the candle and slipped into the room, took off his clothes, and slid into bed. After a moment, I moved toward him and hugged him. His body seemed a little chilled, and he cuddled against me. We didn't make love, but we slept that way all night, warmly nestled together. I drifted in and out of sleep, but I didn't turn over because I didn't want to miss a moment of this embrace. He got up sometime before sunrise, perhaps about half six, and when he came back, we did make love, calmly, gently, not passionately, but attentively, and we both climaxed (not common). I fell back to sleep.

When I woke up again, it was to the fragrance of ham slices cooking in the kitchen. I got up, borrowed his robe (he was dressed), and went to find him. I saw the leftover scones, some dried fruit, and I made him a soft-boiled egg, which he liked sprinkled with curry powder. Perhaps I had never felt such a smooth connection with another person in my life as I did while we were making breakfast.

We sat across from one another, and smiles kept coming to his face as he looked at me. When we were finished eating, he reached across the table and took my hand. Before he could say anything, I said, "Sweetheart, I have to tell you that I'm leaving today. I need to go back to the States."

He said, "Fuck! Is there something wrong? Is it your mum?"

I said, "There's nothing wrong that I know of, except that I need to go back and resume my career."

"I could go with you. I have a passport."

I shook my head. Fifteen minutes later, with tears on my cheeks, I kissed him good-bye and walked out the door. I spent my birthday alone in a B and B in Donington, in Lincolnshire. One thing I was glad of was that I had never given Martin my address in St. Louis, because I knew if he wrote me, I would come running back.

I met up with Uncle Drew in York a week later. I hadn't promised to bring Martin along, because Martin hadn't been able to get the time off, so Uncle Drew didn't see anything amiss when he met me at the train station and I was by myself. I got there before noon, so after getting a bite to eat at a pub, we checked into the hotel, which was right by the station. Uncle Drew said that he was nervous about renting a car, because he had had some close calls driving on the left side of the road over the years. He'd stayed in London for two days, and was no longer jet-lagged, so we went outside and walked on the path that ran beside the old wall, and then we went through the arch and wandered around. It wasn't until we stopped in a little place for tea (and crumpets, because Uncle Drew loved those) that Uncle Drew said to me, "Okay. Tell me why you look so down. I've never seen you like this."

I slathered my crumpet with lemon curd and took a bite, then wiped my napkin across my face, and said, "I walked away from the love of my life, and I am still trying to figure out why."

"Martin Leighmor? The young man you wrote me about?"

I nodded.

He said, "Jodie, I thought you were saner than that."

I said, "He was perfect. Sweet, thoughtful, handsome, smart."

"Couldn't carry a tune, though?"

"He could. We went to his family place at Christmas, and he was very good with the carols."

"Temper?"

"Not a lick."

"Okay. You've got me."

"I just turned twenty-three! How old were you when you married Aunt Louise?" But then I rethought my question. "I mean, how old was Aunt Louise when she married you?"

"Don't you remember? We're the same age to the day. We'd just turned twenty-five."

"What had she been doing before she met you?"

"Well, now she says she was looking for me, but she was passing the time doing secretarial work at a law office in Clayton. She'd dated a few men around town. It was 1956. She was watching *I Love Lucy* and *Ozzie and Harriet*. That was the life she wanted. Me, too.

Maybe that's the reason we've never moved to Ladue or the Central West End." He smiled, then said, "I think she was traumatized by *The Philadelphia Story* when she was eight."

I said, "What about *On the Beach*?"

"She did ask me if I thought I would like Australia, but I said I would prefer New Zealand."

As always, talking to Uncle Drew perked me up a little bit. I said, "I know what I am going to do with my career is a dilemma, and I haven't solved it, but . . ." It wasn't that I was searching for an idea, it was that the idea came to me. I said, "About two weeks ago, I had the sense that he was going as ask me to marry him and also that I wouldn't be able to refuse if he was holding my hand or if I was looking into his face. But the more I thought about it . . . Okay. I met Martin because he waited on my table at his pub. After I got to know him, he told me that he didn't have to do it, and his father didn't approve, but he wanted to understand what life felt like if you had nothing to fall back on, so he wouldn't let his father give him any kind of money."

"Sounds like he's heading for Parliament."

I said, "Not as a Tory, though."

Uncle Drew shrugged slightly.

"Anyway, he took me to see his folks for his dad's sixtieth birthday. His dad scared the pants off me at first. It was like he was made of marble, but his mom was sweet as could be. She's frail, though, because she has a lot of allergies, or maybe worse. Anyway, this whole huge house with umpteen bedrooms and lots of other rooms, and no one . . . I mean, it is in a beautiful spot, and they have help, but they don't farm it, and you can't even look out the window and see some light in the distance, except for the stars and the moon. One night when we were there, I went walking around the house in the dark, and it was so lonely that I started hoping for a ghost."

Uncle Drew smiled, then said, "Is he an only child? You know what that's like."

"I do, but I had all the cousins. I was always going to your place or Aunt Lily's place, or Grandfather's place, or you were always coming to us. I mean, I guess because of Brucie, I never felt like an only child."

Uncle Drew nodded.

The waiter came over and took our plates. Uncle Drew said, "What do you recommend for dessert?"

The waiter said, "I would go for the spotted dick, but we do have some parkin. That's right from Yorkshire, and is mostly ginger and honey."

Uncle Drew said, "Fine, thank you. One of each." The waiter nodded.

I continued. "I knew that even if Martin didn't want to move back to Beech House or take up the management of his father's investments, his parents would talk him into it, and then we would be lonely forever."

"You would have kids."

"Martin started boarding school when he was eight."

Uncle Drew said, "Lonely at the top."

I said, "Maybe especially at the top of a hill in an empty house."

The waiter brought the desserts. We passed them back and forth, and I did like them. They had more flavor than, say, Betty Crocker's white cake or Jell-O chocolate pudding. I could tell that Uncle Drew was thinking.

When we went outside and continued to walk around York, Uncle Drew finally said, "Sweetie, I have no idea whether you did the right thing or not, but you did do a decisive thing, and I think that was good, because even though you have to grieve, you don't have to go back and forth, changing your mind. You acted on your instincts, and who knows whether your instincts were correct. But I proposed to Louise the day after I met her, and I was acting on my instincts, too. I've never had a moment's regret, either."

I said, "What is your instinct that I should do next?"

Uncle Drew looked around, and said, "Take the train to Scotland. Drop-dead gorgeous, and amazingly different from England. Travel is a good way to grieve."

We kept walking, and then he said, "You have plenty of money."

I said, "How much?"

"Five hundred sixty-two thousand and three hundred and sixty dollars."

I nearly jumped out of my pants. I said, "What have you invested in?"

"Boeing. ITT. American Motors."

"Do I have to buy a Rambler?"

"You don't have to do anything, sweetie, except take a lot of deep breaths and look around."

I believed him. Two days later, I took the train to Edinburgh.

Thanks to my time in the UK, though, I did put out another album in 1974—*Fair Isle*—which included "Johnny Was a Strange Boy"; "Why Me?"; "Love Brings Him Home," about the old man, which I fixed up; and eight that I had come to love when I was traveling around, including "I Never Will Marry." It was supposed to come out in July, when there might have been some room for it, but the recording sessions didn't go well, and some of the members of the accompanying band had to be replaced. Eventually, it came out in October, along with plenty of others. I had a few gigs, sold a few albums and singles, got a little airplay. I didn't really know what to think or feel when the record company didn't renew my contract, but, I thought, at least it came out, and at least I liked it. At the time, I had wondered if I should include a song by Joan that I could truly relate to—"Love Song to a Stranger." But that one hadn't been out for very long, and I was intimidated by the bravery of her lyrics. "You stood in the nude by the mirror and picked out a rose . . ." And I thought at the time that someone might interview me about that song and I would reveal something or other that I wanted to keep to myself. Later, I wished that I had included it—beautiful melody, thoughtful lyrics. "Don't tell me of love everlasting and other sad dreams . . ." If I had included it, would the recording company have renewed my contract? Those are the things that you never know.

Part II

7

FOR MY THIRTIETH BIRTHDAY, because it was so cold in New York, I went to St. Thomas. I was completely used to celebrating my birthdays alone by then, and I was also so used to traveling alone that I didn't give it a second thought. The main reason that I wanted to celebrate my birthday by myself was that I was having simultaneous affairs with two guys, who may have suspected that I was doing that but didn't know for sure. From the time I left Martin until I was on St. Thomas, I had conducted exactly twenty-three affairs, which I defined as longer than four days. The longest one was six months, two weeks, and one day. I know because after the first post-Martin affair, I kept a record. I began doing that because of worries about STDs—if I got one, I wanted to have some inkling of who might have given it to me. It was a precaution that went along with other precautions—the man using condoms, me learning to wash myself inside and out. Nor, thanks to the pill, would there be a conception. The only infection I got was actually herpes, but it was from a kiss. I had met a very sweet boy, maybe three years younger than I was, in Boston, at a record shop. He was holding my second album in his hands—*Fair Isle*. He looked at me, then looked at the album again (the picture was of me sitting on a big rock, holding my guitar in my lap). He bought the album, and then asked if I would have dinner with him. He was nice. He didn't want to have an affair—what he wanted was to tell his friends that he'd met me and treated me to the best seafood in Boston. He gave me a kiss as he put me into a cab after dinner, and herpes on my lower lip.

I enjoyed looking at my list, because every time I did, I could remember each of the "fuckers" (calling them that made me laugh) pretty well, and each of them pushed my regrets about leaving Martin out of my mind, because I knew that I wouldn't have met or enjoyed any of them if we'd gotten married. I more or less didn't care how they looked, but I did care how they behaved, and it turned out that I had an instinctive ability to recognize decent and kindly guys (maybe that was something Martin gave me). That matched up very nicely with an instinctive ability to recognize angry or manipulative ones, too. The way I would test them was to make some slightly teasing little joke—if a fist clenched or even tightened, or if irritation passed across a face, I smiled, apologized, and eased myself away from that guy. Or I would chat about dogs and cats. If they had either one, I would listen to how they described them, or what anecdotes they told about them. I wanted my instincts about men to be as good as canine and feline instincts about humans. What I learned from my sexual adventures was that there are plenty of nice guys in the world, and if you treat them kindly and don't expect much from them, they reciprocate. I wish my mother had learned the same thing.

The two guys I was having those affairs with worked in New York, though one of them lived outside of Greenwich, Connecticut, and the other one lived in Harlem. The one who lived in Greenwich was a writer and the one who lived in Harlem was a studio drummer. I don't know that he had to live in Harlem, because he made a fair amount of money, but that's where he had grown up and that's where his family lived. The affairs overlapped—the one with Aaron (the drummer) began in October (I was walking in Riverside Park and he called out to me, because we had met once at a studio) and tapered off slightly after New Year's, and the one with Len began after a Christmas party and tapered off just as the forsythia was blooming in the park.

The first thing Aaron and I talked about was the Freak-Outs.

He had never met them, but he had heard of both Lou and Carrie. I told him a little bit about Lou's temper, and he said that was unusual for a drummer because usually the drummer was the steady one, who kept going, though he sometimes rolled his eyes when the others were having arguments. Aaron had started out with a band in San Francisco—the Falling Leaves—but he wanted to get back to New York, so the leader of his band had called his record company and gotten someone to help Aaron find a job. Aaron said that he was lucky, because not quite a year after he'd left the band, the other members were leaving a party, and they drove down Bradford Street, lost control of the van, and ran into a tree. The street was so steep that the van tipped over and actually slid down the street. No one was killed, but all of them had serious injuries and the Falling Leaves simply broke up. The leader of the band went back to school and became a physical therapist. I enjoyed talking to Aaron and I enjoyed putting my hand through his elbow and being glanced at on the streets of New York (and in the restaurants) because we were a biracial couple. He would say to me, "They're looking at us again!" and I would say, "Baby, they are looking at you, because you are the cutest." That would make him laugh. But everyone did say that he looked like Bob Marley's cousin, and they had met (I never had the chance to meet Bob Marley). When he came to my apartment on the Upper West Side, maybe every ten days or two weeks, we would play a little music together, eat something that I bought at Fairway, and then hop into bed.

I met Len at Zabar's one day when I was buying a pastrami sandwich. He had come to buy a half dozen bagels, and he saw me look him up and down. He lifted his eyebrows and raised his hands as if I had a pistol, and then we both laughed. Len was not as cute as Aaron, but he truly had an eye for how to dress, as well as plenty of money, and one of the things he liked to do was take me to Bonwit Teller and show me dresses and suits that he thought would flatter me. He didn't like what he called "hippie-style" outfits—all of his were custom-made and looked like they'd been designed in the late 1940s, but he was graceful and he wore them with what Mom would have called "panache." During Fashion Week, he took me to two shows, one in a loft in SoHo and one at Bergdorf's. He bought me a shirtwaist dress with long sleeves, about a zillion pockets, and a narrow belt, and he told me that I could only wear it when I was sad, because models always looked like they were about to commit suicide. Len had a wry sense of humor, and would also tell me that all his problems came from the fact that he was a nice Jewish boy, and was that bacon he could smell on my breath? What he liked to do was pick me up in his Caddy and drive me to his house in Greenwich ("You got your passport? They have border checks on the New York–Connecticut line"). His place was on the northeast edge of town, and looked something like Uncle Drew's place on Argonne, back in St. Louis. His house was perfectly furnished and completely clean. He said that he dusted it himself by wrapping towels around his hands and feet and jumping onto the furniture and backflipping off. Every time that I laughed at something Len said, he gave me a little startled look, as if I was offending him, but then he laughed, too.

His writing specialty was what he called "light mysteries"—yes, there would be a crime, sometimes a robbery and sometimes a killing, but the point was to make it funny. His detective was four feet eleven inches tall and was always perfectly dressed. His name was Hector Schmaltz. When I knew him, Len was thirty-two, and had published five of what he called *The Chicken Fat Series,* and they had a decent fan base. He had a contract for five more.

So, Len and Aaron were number twenty-three and number twenty-two. Number one was a man I'd met in Edinburgh. After my little visit with Uncle Drew, I did take the train, but I got out in Durham and then I got out in Newcastle upon Tyne and spent two nights in each town. Northern England was not a place Martin had ever talked to me about, and so I didn't associate Durham Cathedral or the closed-in, almost cozy, nature of the town with him. A river looped around the center of the city, the Wear, and various paths ran along the edge of the river. It was no longer icy, but I imagined what it might be like to skate on the river, looking up at the trees and the hills on either side. People nodded to me and I heard them speaking a form of English, except around the university, that I almost could not understand. That was fine with me. The way they talked was not like Martin talking to his parents or talking to his customers, and as I listened, I felt my longing for Martin slip to the side, still there, but not in the center of my thoughts. On the first night, as I was going back to my hotel from the pub where I ate, I saw a notice that a singing group was playing at a pub not far from the university, so I went and listened. They were singing the songs that I wanted to hear, ones that would remind me of my desire to learn more about traditional English and Scottish music. The three musicians were about my age; they sang some interesting tunes, but they were a little off-key, so I eased back out.

Newcastle upon Tyne was a completely different city from Durham in just about every way. I walked up Grey Street in awe of the beauty of the city and its evident sophistication. The variety of stonework and brickwork reminded me a little of St. Louis, but the sweep of the landscape was much different. And the light, in mid-March, had a kind of flicker to it. I imagined taking some of my money and buying a house or an apartment, and simply spending the rest of my life walking around. Two days of sunshine, two singing hinnys (fried scones), a lamb shank, and an order of pan haggerty, which was au gratin potatoes, but with cheddar and onions, then the train to Edinburgh, into the darkness and gloom. Which was fine with me.

I got there at night, and asked my cabbie to take me to the hotel he thought would be the most interesting. After about ten minutes, we arrived at a truly strange building with an elaborate portico, two parallel towers, and large windows. The cabbie said, "Na, this iz a pricey one, miss, but they's nuthin else like it." I paid him for the trip and walked in. Thirty pounds per night. My room was thick with paneling, coverlets, and drapes and upholstered chairs, and my window looked out on a green parklike area that was also studded with snow here and there.

In Edinburgh, there was also plenty to distract me from thinking about, or longing for, Martin, and it did. I went to museums and castles and cathedrals, up toward Arthur's Seat, and explored regular neighborhoods with trees and hedges and walls and cars beeping at me to get out of the way. In restaurants, I pretended I was French and didn't understand what the waiter was saying, pointed to items on the menu and nodded thanks. I tipped, which maybe was a clue that I wasn't French after all, but the waiters didn't mind.

On the third night, I was walking back to the hotel in the well-lit gloom of downtown Edinburgh, and a man about my age came up to me. I had seen him in the restaurant. I smiled but backed away, and he started chatting with me in French. As far as I could understand, he had visited not only Paris, of course, but also Marseilles, Bourgogne, and Nice, but, he said, "J'aime la Dordogne." I nodded and edged away, but then he smiled so kindly that I smiled back and we kept walking. He continued to speak French and I kept nodding for about ten minutes, then I said, "Monsieur, actually I am American."

He said, "I was beginning to see that."

So then we talked about where he had been in the US—Boston, New York, San Francisco. He was an avid traveler and planned, someday, to go to Chile. He didn't say a word about where he got the money to travel, and I didn't ask him, because what would I say about where I got the money to travel? He saw which hotel I was staying at, and he showed up the next morning. We continued to talk about this and that, and he took me to his apartment later that afternoon. Our affair lasted exactly as long as my hotel reservation. His Scottishness (he turned out to be from Dumfries) was appealing, and he spoke both French and English with a Scottish rhythm. I told him I was a traveling musician, but I didn't say anything about my career, and he said that he enjoyed music. That was all. And that was the best thing about him—he was kind but not curious, affectionate but not passionate, informative but not dictatorial, and perfectly happy for our five-day affair to end. His name was Alastair. As soon as I got on the train for John o' Groats, I pulled out my little book that I normally used for writing lyrics, and wrote a song: "Please Be a Ghost." The first line went, "I'm done with men, or so

I say / Women say that every day / But we want something / Something fine. And you are It, / Though you're not mine. / You came and went, so quick, so free / Please be a ghost and come back to me. / Please be a ghost—I am not scared / Please be a ghost and remind me, / Remind me, remind me, of what we shared."

My next affair began on the second of June, near Loch Lomond, but I don't remember it. I wrote that I slept with a slightly older man three times over the course of eight days, then went to Perth. I had another affair in August, in Liverpool, also brief—I do remember that man, Richard Lowman. I wasn't especially attracted to him, physically, but he was an amateur local historian, and he drove me around to all the interesting sites, both natural and cultural (including, of course, the neighborhoods where the Beatles had grown up). We shared the expenses for "petrol" and food, and there was something brotherly about him. He had wonderful hair—dark, thick, wavy, and smooth. I loved running my hand through it. I think he enjoyed introducing me to Liverpool and reciting all the things he knew about the place. I wrote a few of them down, and I also wrote down that it was more interesting than it looked. Maybe he was, too.

By the end of August, I was ready to go back to the US and start over. I wouldn't have said that I learned what I wanted to learn about English and Scottish folk music, but I went to whatever performances I happened to notice were on, both large and small, and I bought whatever records I could (they were hard to transport, so I sent them to Uncle Drew). On the way home, I didn't go into London or back to Winchester. I feared passing Martin on a street or seeing him from a distance. I felt guilty about leading him on and then dropping him, and I still sometimes felt a longing for his grace and the comfort of his embraces, but I didn't feel guilty for setting out on my own.

When I went back to the States, the first thing I did was buy a guitar, a Martin with a mahogany top. I looked through the instruction manuals and at the books of songs, but I decided to use my own ear to learn the strings and the chords. I bought a tuner and a capo; when I tuned it, I would adjust the strings so that they sounded good to me, then use the tuner to see if I was right. I always was. I spent an hour every morning and an hour every afternoon figuring out how to play along with my own singing, and, as always, I learned as much from my mistakes as I did from my successes. I was not planning to be a Joan Baez, who accompanied herself, but I knew I needed the guitar to help me through my own singing and songwriting.

The real question was where to live. I was drawn to St. Louis because I loved our house and our neighborhood, and I was also fond of the neighborhoods where some of my friends had lived when I was in high school—a spot I had thought was magical was Log Cabin Lane, in Ladue, and another one I was drawn to was Webster Park, which had lovely older houses and beautiful trees. But what singers who had wanted to get ahead had stayed in St. Louis? Josephine Baker had gone to France, John Hartford had gone to Nashville, Fontella Bass had gone to Chicago and then, I heard, to Paris. Chuck Berry may have had a house in St. Louis, but he was said to be on the road so much that he didn't even know where it was. LA was where the record labels were, but I didn't know how to negotiate that. Detroit? Los Angeles? I tried out each of them—visiting for a week, staying in a decent but not fancy hotel, renting a car and driving around, but also walking around, looking at the neighborhoods. I had one affair in each city, but not with any fellow musicians or producers. Mom did not normally offer advice, but she said, "At least try New York. You can afford it. You have to watch the in-crowd, even if you don't want to be one of them." She suggested somewhere around Washington Square Park, near Greenwich Village but not *in* Greenwich Village.

I chose the Upper West Side, mostly because I was fascinated by Riverside Park and Central Park—some days I walked in both, from my apartment on West Seventy-Eighth Street to the Riverside Park entry, then north to the monument at Ninetieth Street, down Ninetieth to Central Park, then around the reservoir to Eighty-Sixth Street and back down Central Park West, around the natural history museum, and back down Seventy-Eighth Street to my apartment. It took about an hour and a half, and was maybe four miles or a little more. Always, there was someone, usually a guy, doing the same route, but running. One day, one of those guys bumped into me when I paused to look at some trees, and we ended up sleeping together that night. He had an odd name, Horace, which I suspected was not his real name, which, judging by my friends, was either John or Bill, but maybe it was his middle name, imposed upon him by some uncle. Anyway, all he wanted to talk about was running next year's New York City Marathon. I never saw him again, so I didn't count it among my "affairs."

The friend I made was Jackie Grandon, who lived in my apartment building, on the third floor (I lived on the fourth floor). She was my age, she was from San Francisco and had gone to UC Berkeley. She'd specialized in anthropology, worked at the natural history museum, and couldn't carry a tune to save her life. She told me that all of her friends were "dissectionists" and I had no idea what she was talking about until she explained that they picked apart the remains of dead and sometimes long-buried plants, animals, and humans to investigate what the remains showed about the past, distant and not so distant. She herself had worked in northern Canada, northern Norway, and northern Iceland. Her biggest wish was to get to the southern tip of New Zealand and maybe to Antarctica. She wore glasses; she was persnickety, as my grandmother would have said—she was always correcting any misinformation that I might express (but with a smile); and I loved her. She told me that she could hear me playing my guitar and singing in my apartment, and she enjoyed it, especially since she didn't have a record player and never went to concerts. I took her to two—a performance at the Met of *La Bohème* and Summer Jam at Watkins Glen in July of '73. During *La Bohème* she fell asleep, and at Watkins Glen, she seemed to enjoy the Allman Brothers and the Band, but she also looked very nervous, because, she said, she expected to be trampled to death (and it was packed). She liked the drive, though—since moving to the city, she had never been out of town, even to the Catskills. When my album came out in October of '74, I didn't say anything about it, but she kept her eye on my place when I went away for the few gigs.

As for affairs, I did pay attention to Joni, Janis, Judy, and Joan. The rumors about Joni were that she had several relationships with other musicians, but the only ones I knew about had to do with David Crosby and Graham Nash. Which one would you pick? Well, they had both helped her along in many ways, but to all appearances, she had retained her independence. I didn't know much about Janis, except that she had an affair with Kris Kristofferson sometime before she overdosed, and who wouldn't, if you had the chance? Or that was what I might have thought before Martin. And then there was Stephen Stills, the handsomest of his band, who had not only had a relationship with Judy, but had also written one of my favorite songs about her (and she left him for an actor who, to me, looked a little sinister). Judy was ten years older than I was, and the way that she claimed all sorts of songs from all sorts of points of view was an inspiration. I imagined her always doing what she wanted to do and having "no regrets" (a song I sang to myself every time I remembered Martin).

When "Chelsea Hotel #2" came out, we all knew that Cohen was singing about Janis. I imagined what I would think if he was singing about me—"I don't think of you that often"—and I knew that at first I would be insulted, but then I would understand that he maybe was choosing not to think of her that often because thinking of her and her death was too sad. I wrote an alternative version just for myself, about Martin—

I remember you well in that sweet little pub
You were laughing—so charming, such grace
And then shaking our sheets on the unmade bed
While you teased me about my long face.
That was Winchester, deep in the mist
We were searching for love and for beauty.
And that was the goal that we had as we kissed,
Probably still is for those men I have left.
Ah, but I ran away, didn't I, dear?

I just turned my back on the dream.
I got away, I dared not hear you say,
I need you, please don't leave me
I need you, please don't leave me,
Stretching your arms, avoiding this harm.
I remember you well in our little flat
You were darling, your heart was unique,
I told you I didn't know what to think,
That for you, I might make an exception.
But I packed up my bag and I went out the door
The worst thing that I've ever done.
Did you fix yourself up? Did you say, never mind?
I am damaged, but I still have the music
And you got away, didn't you, babe?
Have you now turned your back on our love?
You got away! Don't think of us saying,
I need you, I don't need you
I need you, I don't need you—
Both of us telling the truth.
I don't mean to forget that I loved you the best,
Or to replace you with somebody else,
I remember you well in the Green Man pub.
But I don't dare to think of you that often.

AFTER I WROTE that song, I played it at one gig at a small bar actually in Chelsea. By that time, Cohen's song was popular. I had also used my version to help myself get a little mastery of the guitar. At that gig, I sang ten songs—three that were on *Fair Isle,* six that I was working on, and that one, which I introduced as a tribute to Leonard Cohen, but also, I said, to another friend of mine. It got a fair amount of applause, but when you scan the audience after you sing a song, you can tell whether they really like it or not, and it was clear to me that of the twenty-five or so people in the audience, only four appreciated it, so after that, I only sang it to myself when I was thinking of Martin. I will say that it helped me set my decision in stone.

The song did something else, too—it got me to go, occasionally, to the Chelsea Hotel, once in a while on foot. I enjoyed the walk, and just after Thanksgiving, I got involved with the desk clerk, who, as it turned out, was in the process of a divorce and was both lonely and without any desire for a long-term relationship. His name was John, he was from Pittsburgh, and he wanted to become an actor. I could tell that working behind the desk at the Chelsea was part of his training, because the real John was shy but the desk clerk John was friendly and, sometimes, when he had to be, stern. There was always the chance that someone would come in off the street to try to steal something, or to lie down on a sofa and fall asleep. John watched the door like a hawk, and he knew who the guests were and who the intruders were. If he wasn't checking someone in, he would scoot around the desk, grab the guy, turn him around, and send him out the door. Also, because he wanted to be an actor, he was physically fit, about five foot ten, and strong enough to guide and push even the bigger ones out onto the street. If he was checking someone in, he would glance at the intruder, and then, as soon as the lobby was empty, he would go over, poke the guy with the toe of his shoe, wake him up, and then help him out the door.

When I first saw him, I liked his demeanor, and it was me who waited around (he happened to be on the day shift) and then went up to him and smiled. I said, "Interesting hotel! I'll bet there are some fun spots around here."

He knew I was coming on to him, and he blushed and looked away, but he did nod, and then, out on Twenty-Third Street, he straightened up and put my hand through his arm, adeptly avoiding addicts and beggars along the way to Twins Irish Pub, which turned out to be his favorite spot. The pub was just what I had been wanting—a nice glass of hard cider and an order of shepherd's pie, which I hadn't had since I'd left England. John did not get the fish and chips—he got the Cuban, which I'd never heard of but looked good. I won't say that he hardly said a word—what he did was increase the number of words that he was willing to say in a cautious but orderly way. For example, when I asked him where he lived, he said, "Bryant." Then, a moment later, he said, "Bryant Park." Then, a moment after that, he said, "Near Bryant Park," and then, "Sixth Avenue and Thirty-Eighth Street." I sensed that if I talked too much, that would shut him up, so I was reserved, too—"Seventy-Eighth Street." Then "Riverside Drive." By the time he walked me to Penn Station to catch the subway, he seemed relaxed and friendly. As I went to the gate, he said, "Tomorrow I get off at eight p.m." I smiled and nodded, and the next day, I showed up at 7:55. I knew he liked order.

Our affair lasted exactly a month. He told me a little about his wife (she was five years older than he was and wanted children, which he did not. They had come together to New York, but now she was back in Pittsburgh and ready to get married to someone else) and about his job (not as stressful as it looked) and about his ambitions (Broadway, not movies), the Lee Strasberg theater institute (not as picky as the Actors Studio), his favorite bands (Pink Floyd, the Jackson 5), and his favorite operas (*Nabucco* and *Yevgeny Onegin*). He gently inquired into my tastes. He had never heard of me, though he had a vague memory of "Oh, There You Are." My favorite part of our affair was that on nights when we met up and slept together (seven in all), he would act out the behaviors of different sorts of men (including his own bashfulness). He never asked me which one I preferred, and if he had, I don't know which one I would have chosen. Looking back now, the one that sticks in my mind is the "soigné monsieur français."

When I opened the door, he smiled in an elegant and ironic way, tipped his head, waited until I stepped back, and then strode gracefully into my room. When I laughed, he turned his head, and said, "Pardon, mademoiselle?" For the whole night, he put on a French accent (he told me later that he didn't know much French, only greetings, but his accent was believable). The best thing was that when it came time for sex (after he told me a few of his desk clerk adventures in his French accent), he was both determined and polite. Usually, he undressed himself and let me do the same, but this time, he undid my buttons and zippers, helped me out of my jeans, and let down my hair. At that point, my hair was down to the middle of my back (and thank God, I thought, I had washed it the day before and actually brushed it that afternoon, because you didn't want your French lover to think you had no sens du style), and then he ran his fingers through my hair, which he hadn't ever done before. We had sex twice, once before we fell asleep and once in the middle of the night, when he said, "Ma chérie, are you, ah, what is the word, awake?" (which made me smile). In the morning, he was still French, though he did get up early and go to Zabar's for bagels (he told me in his French accent that they had no chocolate croissants). I made the café and our breakfast was affectionate and good-humored. I think that the episode I didn't like was when he put on a southern accent and swaggered around the room, and kept calling me "sugar." He did a good job of it, though. We split because he got a part in a play in Westport, Connecticut, which I did not see. He was insightful—he knew the run of "our play" was up when he left. I stopped visiting the Chelsea Hotel, and I didn't see him on the streets, but I did hope to see him on Broadway. Once in a while he shows up on IBDB, but not on IMDb.

Uncle Drew occasionally came to visit me in New York. He would take his usual room at the Plaza and meet me in Central Park, at Bethesda Terrace. He never asked me about my love life, but I could not help telling him about the various members of what he called "the Jodie Club." He didn't push me to marry, and he didn't push me to stop sleeping around. I think he knew that the times they were a-changin', and I think he also knew that I wouldn't take his advice anyway. As for me, I thought it was politically correct to sleep around, because I was a feminist, and I thought that the essence of feminism was to claim the same rights and privileges that men had, and always had had. One of them was, of course, to control your own finances, one of them was to control your own reproductive choices, and one of them was to have a free and exploratory sex life. I thought

I had three models of what not to do: Mom—get attached to the man who took advantage of you and then spend your life feeling forgotten and ashamed; Aunt Louise—get married and have kids, but marry a kind and decent man who agrees with you, lets you do what you want, and listens to what you have to say; Lady Leighmor—get married and discover that you are isolated, lonely, and obedient for the rest of your life. I didn't want to follow any of these models, even Aunt Louise.

I did ask Uncle Drew about Aunt Louise and the kids but he understood what I really wanted to know—he would give me a precise account of my "financials," which, no doubt because of him, kept going up. I would say now that I was naturally thrifty. It was not only that I didn't care about fashion, I also didn't care about guitars—one was enough (when George Harrison's superband, the Traveling Wilburys, came out with "Cool Dry Place" maybe ten years or so later, I laughed all the way through it, because I knew so many musicians over the years who couldn't resist trying and buying new guitars, and even pianos). Whenever Uncle Drew told me what was in my "portfolio," it was clear that I was spending less than I was earning. Sometimes, after we talked, I walked around Central Park and the Upper East Side, which was more elegant than where I was living, and closer to Bonwit's, Altman's, and Lord & Taylor, but I didn't want to live there or go to those stores and try anything on. I also knew that because I wasn't "runnin' for the money," I didn't have to "run for the flesh." Lucky again. Every time I saw Uncle Drew, I went back to my place and kissed the roll. Uncle Drew never asked whether I had spent it or lost it, and I never told him anything about it.

WHEN I'D GONE to St. Thomas on my thirtieth birthday, I knew that I had to think up some way to push my career—just a little—not to make more money but to use my performances to get to places I hadn't been before, to explore. St. Thomas was a good introduction, because, for one thing, it was one of the most beautiful places I had ever seen, and the contrast with gloomy, midwinter New York was thrilling. However, I spent the first couple of days trying not to get killed, because I hadn't realized that they drove on the left, and even though they did that in England and Scotland, I hadn't done the driving there. Once I was familiar with the driving, I still didn't feel I could safely look out the window, so I pulled over whenever I could, got out of the car, and took in the view. Sometimes the roads were too narrow for pulling over, so I didn't see everything, but I had nothing else to do, and so I drove to as many places as I could. Of course, Magens Bay is legendary, and I went there three times, and I did go into the water, which was warm. I preferred the mountains, though. I think I stayed for more than an hour at Drake's Seat, turning around and staring, turning and staring. Drake's Seat is just about in the middle of the island, and from there, it seems as though you can see everything.

One of the effects of being in paradise all by yourself when you are just reaching thirty is to wonder if you should go ahead and throw yourself off a cliff and get it over with, and this was something I felt for about three days. For one thing, since I was single and without children, I didn't have any obligations to fulfill. My friend Jackie was single and without children, too, but the more I got to know her, the more I understood that when she got up every morning, curiosity about whatever it was that she was dissecting or investigating pulled her out of bed and onto the subway. Would she have called it "a mission"? She did call it her "career," but I think that really it was her destiny. Same with John—I knew from our relationship that whatever his level of success as an actor, he wasn't going to judge himself according to that. His goal was to satisfy himself and his own standards. During our affair, I had connected to that and felt that was part of our affinity, but in St. Thomas, I understood that acting in plays was different from being a musician because onstage in the plays John liked, you are never alone—your job, even if you were a loner, was to play out the part of being a member of a group, and even for someone as shy as John, the interactions were stimulating and made him feel connected. For those first three days in

St. Thomas, what I felt I had done with my life was put myself in a box and close the lid, shutting out all of the things that most people live for, and that the money that Uncle Drew oversaw was the gold leaf covering the box—sparkly but not meaningful.

Gradually, as I drove around St. Thomas, sometimes to new places and sometimes to places I had been before, I realized that each place was different, including the ones I had been to the previous day. It might be the light—one day, I pulled over on Frenchman Bay Road, got out of my car, and looked down the hill and out over the cove. It was late in the day, the sun was shining across the cove and lighting up the houses and the trees. The water in the cove was pale blue, flickering. The next morning, I drove past there at about nine, and did the same thing. This time, the trees cast shadows downhill, the grass was greener, and the water in the cove was deep blue. Or the difference might depend upon who was out and about—one night, I went to a restaurant on the east end of the island that specialized in oysters and house-made ice cream, and I had a pleasant meal of ceviche and prawns. I watched the staff joke around, smile at the customers, and bring out a series of elegant dishes. For dessert, I had a chocolate pot de crème as delicious as anything in Paris (not that I had tasted the pots de crème in Paris). The next night, I hurried back, and things went smoothly until one of the cooks lost his temper and threw a spatula at one of the other cooks, and, to top things off, all the pots de crème were gone. Or I would be walking along the beach or down a street, and I would hear some people chatting, and because I had a good ear, I could make out what they were saying. If I didn't understand the words, I was still fascinated by the sounds—how their voices rose and fell, how the pronunciations differed, not only from what was normal for me, but also how the man's words differed from the woman's, or the child's words differed from his mother's. The more I listened, the more all of the conversations sounded like a form of music. And there were bits of stories, too, that I knew I could turn into songs if I went back to my hotel room and picked up my pen.

Once I started paying attention to these small daily adventures,

I wanted only one thing, which was to see more of them, and to understand how they all fit together. I did find out that the cook who threw the spatula was the nephew of the man who owned the restaurant, and that he had discovered that he was not being paid as well as the other two cooks. He was also known to have a hot temper. With just this little bit of information, I went back to my hotel and wrote a ballad, not about the cook, but about a Wild West outlaw who started out as a rancher's son, and verse by verse exiles himself from his family and their property, until, as the ballad ends, he and his horse are alone on a mountain. He is looking down on the family ranch and expressing his regrets.

By the end of my trip to St. Thomas, I had discovered a reason to live—curiosity.

I understand now that everyone who is around thirty goes through the same thing—even women with a couple of children sometimes look at the children and wonder if this life they have chosen is worth continuing, but at the time I thought I was the only one who didn't have any idea what she was doing being alive.

On my way back, I saw someone on the plane who, when it was time to disembark, searched all of his pockets for, I assumed, his wallet. But he had his wallet in his hand, and kept looking at it and turning it over. I didn't find out what the problem was or if he solved it, but I thought his behavior was interesting. He was maybe forty, so some sort of dementia didn't seem to be his problem. And he was alone—no wife or girlfriend as far as I could see. The stewardess was patient, and I saw her talking to him. Since the taxi trip from JFK to the Upper West Side took a while, I kept thinking about the panicky expression on the man's face, even as he looked at his wallet (I didn't see him open it), then, after I went to bed, it occurred to me that "Who am I?" was a question that anyone might ask, and that the regular answers—your name, your age, a photo of yourself—might not suffice to answer the question. Yes, I was back in French existentialist territory, and yes, when I got up in the morning, I walked around my apartment looking in my mirrors and at my reflection in the windows. What I liked the most, and what seemed the most meaningful, was my reflection in the windows—light, not really visible—so that night I wrote a song ("Who Am I?" of course) about a ghost who wanders around New York City, not trying to scare people, just trying to find some information about how she became a ghost, who she was before she became a ghost, and whether she is slowly fading away. In verse one, she scares a child on the street, and in verse two, another child on another street sees her and approaches her, and that scares her, because she doesn't want to hurt the child, and she doesn't know her powers. She is a solitary ghost, and so she can't ask her question to anyone she sees. After I wrote the song, I turned the question over in my mind for a day or two, and then, when Jackie and I went for dinner at the restaurant in the New-York Historical Society, I asked Jackie if she ever played around with those thoughts. She painstakingly dissected her ravioli and shook her head. She said, "Maybe anthropologists never ask that question, because we have no sense of 'I' as opposed to 'us.' At any rate, just listening to the question makes all sorts of findings about human beings jump into my head, and I know it would be infinitely boring for you to hear them all." She went back to her ravioli, and I didn't contradict her, but I thought maybe she would tell me some of them a little at a time.

All of these thoughts were running through my head the next day, along with dim memories of the churches in St. Louis (it seemed like there was one on every corner), when I came up out of the subway right in front of the First Baptist Church, on the corner of Broadway and West Seventy-Ninth, which was a striking building, and I thought, for maybe the first time ever, that the point of religion was to answer those two questions—who am I and what is my reason for living?

There was a chilly wind. I pulled my scarf over my nose and stared at the church. I didn't go in. I didn't want to go in. But as I walked home, I sang a few songs to myself that were religious—"Amazing Grace," "Bringing in the Sheaves," "I'll Fly Away"—and I suspected that many of the singers who were recording those songs were as indifferent to religion as I was, and yet the music and the words were tempting, so they sang them. I understood as I sang them that the words don't make you believe, but they do make you imagine a wretch being somehow saved, a group of people happy at the richness of the harvest, taking a plane to St. Thomas. Music makes you happy, even when the story in the lyrics would be hard to handle without the tune. Now I laugh when I think of how brief my "existential crisis" was, but however brief, I accepted my results and never thought again of throwing myself over a cliff.

8

EASTER THAT YEAR was on April 15, a good time to be in St. Louis, where the weather was warmer than in New York and the trees were blossoming—dogwood, redbud, the last of the forsythia, the beginnings of the apple, pear, and cherry trees. I decided to take the train instead of a plane, and I went via a route I hadn't taken before, up to Albany, then to Chicago, then to Union Station. It was a pleasant trip through lots of different landscapes and I got to Union Station late in the afternoon, just in time to take Mom to dinner at the Cheshire, which was one of her favorite spots. She dressed more carefully than I did, but she didn't turn her nose up at what I was wearing. The restaurant at the Cheshire, the Fox and Hounds, was always dark, but that was true of a lot of restaurants in St. Louis. I was a little hesitant to go there, because of the English-pub theme, but that was where Mom wanted to go, so I kept my mouth shut and ordered the fish and chips. Mom ordered the bangers and mash. What made me smile was that our waiter was a handsome Black guy with an impressive Afro but when he served us, he did a wonderful and amused imitation of a posh English accent. He and I exchanged a wink after he said, "Don't order the Yorkshire pudding, it's a frightful bore."

I was in a good mood as we walked home—it was still light, but the sun was going down and the trees in Forest Park were shimmering in the light breeze. I kept looking at the trees, then toward our house, and Mom saw me. She took a deep breath and said, "I have to sell the place."

I stopped and whipped around and said, "Why?"

"You know perfectly well. I need the money."

"And you know perfectly well that I can give you the money. Do you have a mortgage?"

"No. It's not that. It's the upkeep. It's that I think my job is a little too much for me now. I don't really—I don't really like the shows that the Muny is putting on these days."

I tried to summon up both patience and sympathy. I said, in a low voice, "Where would you go?" I dreaded that she would say New York City, but she didn't. She said, "I saw a house in Kirkwood that I liked. Half the size and half the price of mine."

"How far from Uncle Drew?"

"A few blocks. It's only one floor."

I knew this was a good idea, but how was I going to give up the house on Skinker? And how was I going to keep up the house on Skinker? As lovely as the trees were, I didn't want to move back to St. Louis, and I knew what Mom was feeling about being one person in a large, empty house.

She said, "It keeps me up at night. I always think I can hear someone sneaking through the front door, even though I know I locked it, and what would prevent that person from breaking the lock, or a window? What do I have that anyone would want? I don't know, but then, that person doesn't know either. I live in a beautiful neighborhood. I must have something . . ." She sighed, then said, "It's amazing to me that I've lived alone for so many years, and always, before now, not even thinking about pushing the back of a chair up under the doorknob to my bedroom, or wondering if I would rather be attacked or jump out a second-story window." Then she looked at me again and said, "You're in New York! Don't you have those kinds of fears?"

I shook my head, and just at that moment, it seemed amazing to me that I didn't, or that I wandered around the city whenever I felt like it, day or night. I said, "Well, it's a small apartment. And the floors creak. I have this friend, Jackie. She's in the apartment right above mine. She can hear me sing and play my guitar, and I can hear her walking around, so I suppose that we could hear something bad happening, too."

"But that's what I'm getting at. This house"—she pointed to our house—"is so heavy and thick that I never think anyone could hear me or save me." She sniffed. "And I know that maybe I always thought of its sturdiness as its safety, but now I can't stop imagining an invasion."

I didn't say anything, because I didn't know what to say, but I did stare up at the house as we approached it, so odd and so beautiful and in such an interesting spot. The next day, we went to Grandmother and Grandfather's place for Easter dinner (always ham). They were both in their eighties now, and I suspected that Uncle Drew was looking after them in some way. I hadn't seen them in almost two years, and I looked carefully for bad signs. Mom would be sixty in a couple of years; she was almost the same age as Charlie Parker and Dave Brubeck—did that make her old? I noticed a couple of things—the ham was way too large for just Mom, Aunt Lily, Grandmother, Grandfather, and me (Uncle Hank and his family sometimes came for Christmas, but never for Easter); it was so large that Grandfather had to carry it to the table. Grandmother didn't say much—she would smile and then look around as if she was, I thought, trying to find what it was she was going to say. Grandfather was a little thin, but mentally, he was his regular self, meaning smart, funny, and willing to tease. He ate his usual amount of food, while Grandmother just picked at this and that. After dinner, Uncle Drew and Aunt Louise showed up with a dacquoise, a French cake that was basically a stack of sponge cake and cream. Aunt Louise had been taking a course in French cooking. As soon as she saw the cake, Grandmother perked up, struggled to her feet, and brought in some vanilla ice cream that she had hand-cranked. After dessert, she seemed to get herself together, which meant leaving the dishes in the sink for future washing, and going straight to the piano for some songs. Grandfather sat while singing—the rest of us stood—but his baritone voice was still vibrant, and he still remembered all of the words, just as Grandmother still remembered all of the notes on the piano. I thought this was interesting, but I realized that it was one of the benefits of "force of habit"—if your habits were musical, you could keep singing and playing even if you were losing your mind.

We left before sunset—Mom said that this was one of the things she had always disliked about Easter, that you had to eat dinner at four, for some reason. We drove Aunt Lily home, and I sat in the back, listening to them talk about Grandmother and Grandfather.

Mom said, "They have these homes . . ."

Aunt Lily said, "Never in a million years."

Mom said, "But that house has so many stairs!"

"You saw Daddy walking around. It's like he never aged. When I was over there the other day, I saw him run up the stairs to get something, and then run down without even holding the handrail."

"But Mom—"

"He watches out for her. You saw him carry the platter with the ham on it. He does all sorts of things like that. Around Christmas, I thanked him for doing that, and he said, 'Why wouldn't I? She watched out for me when we were young, and for God's sake! She took care of you kids when I didn't have a clue about babies or kids!' "

Mom said, "Even so, I still worry a little about them."

Aunt Lily shrugged. "What don't you worry about? Name one thing." She glanced at me. Mom saw her do it, and smiled, then she said, "I am trying to stop worrying about one thing."

Aunt Lily said, "I must have showed you how, because I stopped worrying about Brucie years ago. All I do now is bite my lips."

I knew they knew I was listening, so I said, "How is Brucie? I haven't heard from him in ages."

Aunt Lily said, "Did you know he moved to Texas? He went to visit Hank and Carol in Houston, and then fell in love with Austin. He's got some job there in construction. Apparently, a lot of people are moving to Austin. He likes it. Some girlfriend, too. She's about your age. I'm hoping they'll get married."

Mom said, "You haven't even met her."

"I should have said, 'I'm hoping *he'll* get married.' I do want him to settle down. Whatever girl it is, it's his pick, not mine."

Mom nodded, then she glanced in the rearview mirror, at me, and said, "Did Mother ever tell you how she and Daddy got together?"

I shook my head.

"Well, he'd been in St. Louis for a Cards game. He was visiting a cousin in Belleville, who was working at some factory. Mother was visiting a friend of hers that she met at the teachers' college in Normal. When she got on the bus, or trolley, or whatever it was, to go back to her friend's house, she happened to sit next to Daddy, and he thought she was darling, so he joked around and talked her up, and they kept going and she kept looking out the window, and eventually, she realized that she had gotten on the wrong trolley. She said that she was completely lost, and he asked her where she was trying to get to. She told him, and, since somehow he knew the trolley routes, he got off with her at the next stop, and walked with her to her friend's house. He always said they had to change trolleys twenty-three times." Mom laughed, then said, "I guess that was their inspiration for moving to St. Louis. Daddy preferred the Cards to the Indians. I remember when I was ten, he took the train to St. Louis to see the seventh game of the World Series, which was against the Philadelphia team. He was gone for three days."

I thought, sometimes you're lucky in ways you never knew, because none of us, driving in this car and laughing, would be alive if Grandmother hadn't made that mistake.

Aunt Lily said, "Well, they set a good example. They've been married for sixty-two years!"

And then Mom said, "But we never followed that example. Do you ever wonder why that is?"

Aunt Lily said, "I don't wonder—I know! What man that you've met is as kindly and responsible as Daddy? Only—"

And then they both said, "Drew!"

They nodded and I thought of Martin, who was, I thought, as

kindly and responsible as my grandfather, but the thought of living in his house and his world for sixty-two years made me shiver. I sighed.

Aunt Lily glanced at me and said, "Maybe you'll find someone."

I sighed and said, "I did."

Aunt Lily said, "You did?"

And I said, "Brucie!"

We laughed at that, but we all knew that women didn't marry their cousins anymore. At least they weren't shocked when I said his name, and that meant that I didn't have to say a word about Martin. I knew Mom would have been over the moon if she had known anything about Martin, and I also understood that Uncle Drew hadn't told her anything. We dropped Aunt Lily off, and after she got out, as I was moving to the front seat, she kissed me on the cheek in thanks for my compliment to her darling boy.

She must have written to Brucie, because about a week after I got back to New York, I got a letter from him. He didn't say anything about his girlfriend or what he was doing to make a living, but he said that he liked Austin, that it had a great music scene, and that he was part-timing as a rhythm guitarist in a band called the Random Picks. He liked the band. The two guys who had started it, the main singer and the percussionist, had searched around town for other musicians and then played with them to see what sorts of songs they knew. The whole group numbered about ten, and the leaders of the band got themselves gigs, and then sent out notes, seeing who could join them. Sometimes the band numbered three, sometimes six or eight. He wrote, "You ever hear of Marcia Ball? She lives in town, and we did backup for her a couple of months ago, at a festival gig. All of us played. She should be your model, even though she accompanies herself on piano, not guitar. Anyway, find one of her records." He also wrote that the Random Picks prided themselves on doing what you had to do in a place like Austin—play country, cowboy, rock, soul, pop, and even a little jazz (they had a trombone player). Brucie said that he performed about once a month, but he regularly went to the venues when the others were playing, and even though it was hard in Austin to have a sizable audience, because of all the music groups that there were, the Random Picks did pretty well. He liked Austin. A guy from St. Louis didn't care about the humidity, and he was looking at a house up by Lake Travis, but he didn't know whether to make an offer. If I wanted to come there, he would be happy to put me up. I knew Janis had gotten her start in Austin, and now there was another interesting guy, named Willie Nelson, who had spent time there. Brucie's last line was, "Kiddo, LA is about movies, New York is about money, Austin is about music. You would like it here. Love, B."

The first thing I wondered when I finished the letter was what the temperature was. In New York, it was chilly—about fifty, very cloudy and windy. I had already played my guitar for about two hours and worked on a couple of songs, and I was planning to take my usual walk around the park. Jackie and I were going to meet for dinner at a Chinese restaurant we liked. In other words, for New York, a perfect spring day. I knew that with the money I had I could get out of town whenever I wanted—back to St. Thomas, or to Austin, or to Hawaii or the Riviera, for that matter—but maybe I had to choose a home, and maybe Brucie was right about the place where he lived and played music. New York was a place where you could enjoy anonymity, but I had to decide if that was what I wanted to enjoy. I picked up my guitar and fiddled with the tuning, then continued to work on a technique that I really liked—not exactly accompanying what I was singing, but playing in harmony with it, as if the guitar was a partner whose notes contrasted with the tune I was producing. It interested me because it was complex, and I had to keep two different tunes in my mind at the same time. Fortunately, I knew the words and hardly had to think about them. When I glanced at the clock once I thought I had it figured out, another hour had passed in its usual musical way, slowly and quickly at the same time. I set the guitar on its rack, put on my coat, and went outside.

I decided to go uptown and walk around the section of the park that they called the North Woods. It was a long walk, but I liked that spot because it reminded me of the part of Forest Park across from our house that was a little wild, a little hilly, and full of trees. Of course, even then, Central Park had better upkeep than Forest Park, so the roads and trails were clean. There was a rather large pond up there, and also a spot called the Ravine that I liked to walk in, because it seemed so wild. I could hear the sounds of the city, but even so, I felt like I had been airlifted to a bit of wilderness. Because it was the end of April, everything was flourishing—leaves on the branches, and plenty of wildflowers huddling near the roots of the trees. The people who walked around there must have been careful to keep to the trails, because the plants—white and yellow, mostly, but a few tiny red ones—were flourishing. I looked at some, then closed my eyes and said to myself, "Buy a plant guide." I think I walked around the park for about forty-five minutes, then emerged at the corner of 110th and Central Park West. It was interesting to walk downtown on the sidewalk that went along the west side of the park, because on your left, it was green and full of trees, and on your right, there was one interesting building after another, some old, with exterior fire escape stairs, and some of them were sturdy and simple while others were ornate. My favorite one was a huge, European-style building on the corner of Central Park West and 106th. It wasn't square at all, rather very ornate, with huge towers with pointed roofs and arched windows along the upper story. There wasn't anyone in it, and it definitely looked abandoned, but at the time, I didn't know why. It looked like the perfect place for ghosts, and every time I passed it, I amused myself by imagining a few fluttering white wings of sheets or feathers showing themselves in the windows. I saw that some of my fellow pedestrians did not even look at the building—they just stared at their feet and hurried on. As I was glancing up, a guy came around me, saw what I was doing, and said, in a friendly way, "See that balcony? Last fall, I was walking right here and I heard someone call out, 'Can you help me?' There was a guy up on the balcony! I do not know how he got up there, but I did pause and say, 'You trying to get down?' and he said, 'Nope. I just need a buck or so.' I couldn't figure out how to get it to him, but then he pointed to a pail on the other side of this fence, and I dropped a couple of bucks into it. I still don't understand how he got up there, but maybe the doors are falling apart or something. It was funny."

New Yorkers never mind telling you something that they think you ought to know, but this guy was more laid-back than a lot of them. He walked along beside me for a few minutes, and then smiled and sped up. I kept walking, looked at the buildings and the park, and then went into Zabar's to pick up my weekly pastrami sandwich. As I was paying for it, a voice said, "You are Jodie Rattler, aren't you?" I turned around, and there was that same guy. I nodded.

He said, "I realized it was you! I have your records."

I said, "Well, I'm glad someone does."

"You live around here?"

"More or less." Yes, I felt a little suspicious. I still remembered Leon's cousins chatting over breakfast about corruption and bodies found in the East River, and I knew that there was always the chance that someone was going to pick your pocket in some way or another (I also sort of admired the ones who were deft enough to bump into you, smile, and walk off with your wallet, though this hadn't actually happened to me).

He must have noticed the look on my face, so he backed away and went out the door.

The fellow who was checking me out at the cash register said, "You know who that is?"

I shook my head.

"Sylvester Stallone!"

I said, "Oh, shit! You're kidding!"

The guy rolled his eyes. I took my bagels and went home, and I thought that it was truly strange that someone like Stallone would recognize me, and yet I didn't recognize him. Jackie and I had a good laugh about that when we were eating dinner that night. But the odd thing was that after that incident (and my walk in the Ravine), I didn't think any more about moving to Austin. There were surely famous people in Austin, but that wasn't the point—the point was to live in a place where you never knew what was going to happen next, or how you were going to experience that. I looked up that weird building with the balcony, and I discovered that it had been a cancer hospital and then an asylum of some sort, and now the city was trying to figure out what to do with it. I wrote Brucie and told him I missed him, and that I would come for a visit, but that New York was the place for me.

I didn't forget what Brucie had told me about his band, though, so I put the word out to both bands and record companies that I was available as a backup singer, that I was adept at various styles, that I could play rhythm guitar, and that I had a good range. I knew that most of the bands, at least the ones who were my age, knew these things about me, and so did the record producers, but I saw it more as an invitation, and maybe they saw it more as an act of desperation (no one in New York, even Jackie, knew about my funds). When agents would call me up and ask me if I could play at this gig or that gig because someone was out sick or in rehab or had finally had it with his or her band, I named a price, which I had to do, but I made it reasonable and similar to what any guy would ask for, because I didn't want to mistakenly set a kind of "girls are cheap" example. I also didn't want to assert, or pretend, that I was a star. All I wanted was to work and to meet other musicians and to try various types of music.

Music, of course, was changing. The bands I grew up with were pretty much gone, though the Rolling Stones were hanging on. Janis was dead, Judy was fading away, Joan seemed to be working more for causes than for music, and Joni was trying new things. But folk had given way to pop, and I knew I had to pay attention not only to Tina Turner, but also to Dolly Parton (and when it came out the following year, I did see *9 to 5* three times and learn the lyrics of the song, even though I didn't want to perform it). I did not want to become a pop singer—I was still drawn mostly to folk, to the sorts of songs that Bob Dylan was writing about his own senses and his own experiences. What the singers of the time really succeeded at was ramping up the beat, and I loved that. I got two gigs in the summer, one at a music festival and one down in SoHo. The bands were working regularly, but they weren't well-known, and most of the band members were four or five years younger than I was. After I practiced with them a couple of times, I saw that the issue wasn't whether I could play or sing, it was what I was going to wear. If I wore my usual simple dress or jeans onstage, I was definitely going to look like I was the band's seventh-grade teacher, some old stick-in-the-mud. And then there was the question of hairdos. No more just letting it hang down your back, to your waist, or, if you were lucky, to your hips (but be careful not to sit on it). Also, no pixie cuts, thank goodness. But Jane Fonda and the other stars were wearing huge wavy hairstyles that undoubtedly required stylists, and maybe sleeping upright all night so that you wouldn't smash the curls. I solved this problem by having my hair cut so that it was just below my chin, then washing it, bending over, and throwing it around, squeezing it into semi-curls, and never combing it—messy looked cooler than long and straight. I was cooperative and knowledgeable when I did my gigs. Every so often, I offered a modest suggestion about rhythm or harmony, and the other band members would come around, so I got compliments and more gigs. By October, I was working once a week, Friday night or Saturday night, sometimes repeating my gigs with a band. I got pretty adept at different music styles, but thank heaven I wasn't often asked to sing, because in 1979, low-level bands were beginning to do what the eighties are remembered for—shouting, screaming, jumping around, and pretending to be crazy.

Since playing along was becoming second nature to me, what I really enjoyed was looking at the other band members, being struck by how handsome some of them were and how weird others were. The music business was like Hollywood or Broadway in the sense that the singer had to have stage presence, but stage presence for a musician isn't merely looks or talent, it's also the ability to act strange, as if you represent the coolest cohort of the human race. I did not have this ability, so I stood a little toward the back and represented, in some sense, the organizing principles that the band was simultaneously making use of and leaving behind. I was asked by a couple of band members, and by a manager, too, whether I suffered from stage fright, and I had to say no. Over the years, I had seen lots of musicians with their hands over their faces, or huddled in a corner, or more or less stiff with anxiety, and then the curtain went up and they jumped onto the stage and sang with an amazing energy. Maybe I would have had stage fright when I started out on the little tour with the Freak-Outs, but at the time, I had kept my eye on Carrie and pretty much followed her example in all things, and she seemed to see the stage as a kind of open door—that was where the light was, that was where the other people were, and so you walked through it with pleasure and anticipation. Maybe Arlene had had some stage fright—she used to take a few deep breaths before the curtain went up (or we walked onto the stage). But for me it wasn't only a good example or good habits, it was also that the pleasure in making or listening to the music overwhelmed every other feeling. I think it was like that with Leon when we first met, and he was such a youthful prodigy. His parents were much more nervous than he was, because he was so used to entering into the music that, it seemed to me, he didn't even notice the audience, large or small. Maybe I should have had stage fright doing these substitute gigs, because even though we rehearsed together, I was still newer to the music than the regular band members were. But I trusted my ear and my sense of rhythm, and, to be honest, I wasn't a perfectionist (some musicians are). If I made a mistake, I would roll my eyes and toss my head and fix it when we sang the next verse. I think in the music business, that is how you get forgiven for making a mistake onstage, and, frankly, everyone does, because something distracts you (some guy losing his temper in the audience, some girl falling out of her seat, someone stumbling down the row to his spot and stepping on lots of toes), and even though it does, you have to keep playing, and you hope that the number of times you've played and sung that song will just carry you through the distraction.

But maybe it was an inherited characteristic, too, because I had never heard of Uncle Drew being nervous about investments, or, for that matter, playing poker. Aunt Louise had told me that he was one of those guys who had an instinct about cards. One time she and

Uncle Drew had been playing bridge with some friends, and he was dealing. He glanced at the cards in his hand and then looked at the floor, bent down, and picked up a card. When one of the other players asked about it, he said that he could tell by the weight of the deck that a card was missing. I supposed that he had an instinct about investments, too, because it seemed like he was always ahead of the market, choosing what to invest in before other investors sensed that that company—let's say Boeing—was going to boom. Another thing I suspected of Uncle Drew was that he didn't cheat, because my experience of cheaters was that they were more jumpy than people who didn't cheat. And that applies to music, too. People don't "cheat" at music—you've got to play the notes or sing the melody, but if you are tipsy or high, then you are cheating, and while you are playing you have this simultaneous sense that you don't know what you are doing and you do know what you are doing.

I flirted a little with some of the cuter guys, because that's how you show that you are not their seventh-grade teacher, but, rather, a knowledgeable older woman. I didn't take up with anyone, though. I did keep my eye on Ross Valory, who was in Journey. There was something about him that I found both interesting and appealing, and then discovered that he was almost exactly my age, and had some interesting ideas about playing the bass guitar that weren't that different from what I was trying to learn about playing harmony with myself on my own guitar. In the eighties, I would say, the lyrics to Lenny's song "Chelsea Hotel" were even more apropos to "the workers in song." Most of the bands that I met looked desperate. They had to put out a lot of albums, do a lot of tours, write a lot of songs, and always seem as far-out as they possibly could.

Unfortunately, I was not asked to step in on Lenny's tour that year for *Recent Songs,* which was too bad, because I loved that album so much that I could have performed every one of them standing on my head. I especially loved the one about the horse. I went to two concerts, though, and said hi to Garth. I saw Lenny from a distance but I didn't approach him, though I should have, to thank him for the inspiration. I even took Jackie to the second concert, and I could see her sort of wake up as the music progressed. When we were driving home, she said, "My! That was eclectic!" which gave me a good laugh. So the answer to the question of "What should I do?" was "Something or other," and I had the money to do that.

It was Jackie who told me about the Americans who were taken hostage in Iran. Was I lucky to be blissfully ignorant of what was going on in the Middle East? I thought so at the time, because although Jackie was confident that the issues would be sorted out and the hostages released, I felt the Cold War, in a sense, pour down upon me all over again. I had voted for President Carter, and I appreciated some of the things he had done, especially giving amnesty to the draft evaders from the Vietnam War. He seemed like a decent guy, and I trusted him enough not to pay a lick of attention to him. As I remember, Uncle Drew had voted for Gerald Ford, and I teased him by saying that he'd only voted for him because of his looks. Jackie understood more about Carter—he'd grown up on a farm, even growing his own peanuts when he was young. She said that no doubt he had an excellent immune system, having been exposed to so much dirt. She also thought he had navigated the Georgia tradition of segregation and slavery very neatly, because he was that nice person I thought he was, and maybe that was why he seemed so surprised by the hostage-taking—he couldn't imagine someone doing such a mean thing.

For a few days, I hardly practiced my music—I sat in front of the television and read the *Times,* waiting to be told when the bombs were going to arrive (though I didn't understand who would be sending them). Then I got a call, asking whether I could do a gig in a few days—the girl in the band who was the usual backup singer was down with the flu, could barely speak, and it was a lucrative gig that the band didn't want to give up. I said that I would, and when I hung up the phone, I thought, Well, better to be bombed while you're singing your heart out than when you're lying in bed worrying. One thing I liked about the band was that they were sort of disco-ish, and while I was singing (and I had to wear red and have my hair done), I did not play my guitar, so I was free to dance around on the stage.

A lot of the members of the audience got up and danced a bit, too, or at least swung their arms and kept time bobbing their heads. For an hour and fifteen minutes, I forgot completely about imminent death.

And after the Cuban Missile Crisis, didn't we get used to looking around for that mushroom cloud, all the while going to pick up some groceries or being carpooled home from school? I remembered listening to a couple of the girls in the back seat of the car, whispering about where the mushroom cloud would be—off to the west, because they would be striking the atomic facilities in Colorado or wherever they were, or off to the east, because they would be destroying Washington, DC, or Wall Street (one of the girls said that the main thing Commies hated was "the stock market"). We had all agreed that they might bomb Chicago, but not St. Louis, because there was nothing worth destroying in St. Louis. And the gawky girl talking about her stepfather saying it wouldn't be worth it to live. All of these memories ran through my head as the time passed and I walked around Central Park when it wasn't terribly snowy.

Jackie got more political, and kept me informed about the primaries. As 1980 went on, she got annoyed—she would never vote Republican, but what she didn't understand was why the Dems kept arguing while the Reps got together behind their candidate, "brainless idiot" (her words) that he was. I did see Uncle Drew and Aunt Louise over the summer, when they rented a house up in the Catskills, in the countryside not far from Woodstock, for two weeks, but all we did was drive around. We never talked politics, we only talked about their kids and Mom. Being Uncle Drew, he was curious, and so we took a trip to what turned out to be my favorite spot, Roxbury, where, Uncle Drew said, the real John Burroughs, a naturalist that our high school was named after, had grown up. We drove past the house, which was tall and interesting, but somehow Uncle Drew had discovered that when he was a boy, John Burroughs had gotten his love of nature from going up Old Clump Mountain, which wasn't far from the house. As I looked around, I thought, Well, around here, any mountain will do—they were all beautiful and even in the summer, whatever humidity there was seemed to be blown away by the breeze. We looked around some other spots, too—Woodstock, Fleischmanns, Big Indian—and I wondered if maybe I should spend some of my money on a small house, say, a log cabin, that I could use to get out of the city.

Aunt Louise was worried about Mom, but Uncle Drew wasn't. She had decided to stay in the house on Skinker. That night, when we were having dinner at a restaurant in a town called Saugerties, Uncle Drew said he thought it was because she didn't think she would get enough money for it, and Aunt Louise thought it was because getting rid of, or moving, all of the stuff that had accumulated over the years, in the attic, the closets, under the stairway, was too intimidating. Aunt Louise was good at keeping things neat and sending things that she no longer used to the Salvation Army. I didn't say so, but I thought Mom's problem was that she didn't want to be reminded—of anything. Once, on the phone, she asked me if I had heard the phrase "Live in the present." I hadn't. She said she had been shopping at Schnucks and two girls walked by, obviously hippies, and she had heard one of them say that phrase and then sigh. She thought it was silly at the time—an impossibility, really—but the more she thought about it, the more she decided it was just the thing for her. And yes, all of her plans, over the years, had gone awry. Then Uncle Drew said, "I think I made a mistake." Aunt Louise and I looked at him. He said, "When she was talking about moving down the street from us, I said, 'You know, I'm happy to support you.' She said, 'How sweet!' but her face kind of closed over and I knew I'd embarrassed her. Here's the thing about your mom, Jodie: there was never a moment, as long as I've known her, when she wasn't hell-bent on supporting herself and making her way in the world. Thirty years ago? The 1950s? That whole idea of the sweet middle-class family, where the wife does all the ironing and the cooking and the husband brings home the bacon, repelled her."

I said, "But Grandmother and Grandfather were like that."

Uncle Drew said, "Well, that's why."

I said, "But they love each other. They are wonderful with each other."

Uncle Drew and Aunt Louise exchanged a glance, then Uncle Drew said, "I'm not saying there weren't arguments when we were growing up—there were—but we all knew that Daddy's income went up and down and that made Mama worry. That's why I got my first job when I was twelve. I wanted to stop her from worrying, and I did, sort of, at least in front of me. I made five dollars a week, and every Friday, I handed four bucks to her."

I said, "What was your job?"

"Washing cars at a gas station. On the way there, I would walk past Burning Bush Church. That always gave me a laugh. I thought it was lots of fun seeing the cars, and of course, it was the guys with the newest cars who wanted to keep them sparkling clean. Your mom got a job in a factory, because women had to do that during the war—all the men were at the front. And she liked it. She made some money, and that's how she got to New York. She paid for some dance lessons, worked in a few shows, and then the guy who was teaching the dance classes sent a letter to a friend of his in New York, and your mom had enough money to take the train. She was so sure she was going to make it to the top." He looked out the window. "She worked in shows at a few of the hotels up around here, too. There was quite a scene, because a lot of the Jews in New York came up here for the summer, and the hotels had theaters and put on shows. You know that town we drove through yesterday, Ellenville? There was a big resort there. I think that might have been the one where she went."

I said, "That's where that church was with the really tall spire. That was a beautiful spot."

Aunt Louise said, "What spot isn't, around here?" Then she gave me a look, and I knew she was thinking that she did wish somebody, maybe me, would buy a summer place.

Uncle Drew said, "At any rate, I never knew anyone that had higher hopes than your mom did, and was, in a lot of ways, more disappointed." We shared a look, and he knew what I was thinking. He said, "I never met your dad. I overheard Daddy and Mama talking about her when she was pregnant—maybe halfway along. I remember Mama saying, 'Is he going to marry her?' I thought she was talking about Lily, and I remember saying, 'I thought they were already married!' Daddy laughed, and understood what I was getting at, and he said, 'They are! Don't worry about it,' and waved me away. After you were born, your mom sent pictures and Mama went for a visit, and they always said how cute you were, and how great it would be if, and then when, you two moved to St. Louis; they didn't say a word about your father. To be honest, I thought he had died somehow." He laughed. "I thought that being shot or offed by gangsters was the norm in New York City." We all laughed.

I said, "Did I tell you that I saw him at Zabar's?"

Uncle Drew shook his head.

"I think it was about ten years ago now. I saw him on the street. I was waiting for the light on the corner of Eightieth and Broadway, and this guy passed me who seemed really familiar. I wondered how I knew him, and raised my hand to say hi, and looked at him again, and I thought, Geez, he looks just like me! I followed him into Zabar's, and he walked like me, too. It was uncanny. I felt like Sherlock Holmes or something. Anyway, I got behind him at the counter. I even got close enough to bump into him. He glanced at me, looked totally pissed off, and left. I ordered the same sandwich he did—pastrami on rye, with a touch of mustard. Could be his wife was there, because a woman went out the door with him."

Uncle Drew said, "I bet we know some of the same people. I should ask around."

If Uncle Drew ever found him, he didn't tell me. Later on, when I saw the yearbooks online (Trinity and St. Agatha's) and then walked uptown and looked at those schools, I thought I was lucky to have gone to my school-in-a-garden and then to Penn State. Even then I believed that it was better to have been born on the outside and then to make your way inside, if only because what you see is not something you know or understand and so you listen and look around, trying to figure it out, and maybe notice things, and people, that the ones who are used to the inside are not in the habit of noticing.

I loved our trip, and I was pretty sure I would buy some house up there, but when we got back, I wrote Mom a note asking if I could come "home" and see Grandfather and Grandmother. Of course she said yes. So I took the plane to St. Louis in mid-September. Mom picked me up at the airport and we went straight to my grandparents' house for a late dinner, a chicken stew with homemade rolls and the first apple pie of the season, made, Grandmother said, with Arkansas Blacks, her favorite pie apple. The food was good and tasted exactly the way it always had. I watched Grandmother a little bit, trying to figure out if she was declining, and there were a few times when she didn't seem to understand what we were saying, but anything that had to do with dinner or doing the dishes seemed to be so ingrained that she could do it without a single hitch. Grandfather was careful to let her, I assume because he didn't want to insult her.

On the way back to Skinker, it turned out that the person Mom was worried about wasn't Grandmother, or herself, it was me. The first thing she said was, "I don't think it's a good idea to keep to yourself too much."

I said, "I have some friends. I mean, it's not like I go to lots of parties, but . . ."

"Sweetie, that's not what I'm talking about."

I glanced out the window. We were on Hanley, passing the small woodsy area where Deer Creek and Black Creek come together. The leaves were just beginning to turn and even though we were in the middle of town, I was impressed, as always, by how thick the trees were. I finally said, "Then what were you talking about?"

"Sweetie, I know you have regular gigs and you are making some money, but you're in your thirties now. In our business, the only way you can push your career into middle age, especially if you are a woman, is to be more aggressive."

I smiled and said, "You mean by beating up a few people?"

She stared at me, realized I was making a joke, and tried to laugh, then said, "No, I do not mean that, though I know that sometimes it's tempting."

We drove past Bruno and then Elinor, and finally she said, "I mean two things. One is a recording contract and the other one is an image."

I glanced at the side mirror, but it was too dark to see my face. She noticed what I was doing, though, and said, "You still look great."

I said, "As far as I can tell, the girls who want to get ahead these days have to act as crazy as possible, and look it, too. I don't know what my image would be."

"That's what a recording contract is for—the company shapes your image."

And yes, I looked down at the belly that was beginning to take shape. It was true that the time of Twiggy had passed. The models in *Vogue,* say, were a little more fleshy, a little more fit, and didn't look like they were about to commit suicide, but my fondness for Twiggyness continued, and I didn't like that belly.

Mom said, "That's part of it. But not a big part."

We crossed highway 64 and did what you always did in St. Louis, went from a sparse area filled with buildings and parking lots to a luxurious area filled with woodlands and brick walls. Mom didn't say anything more, turned right on Clayton, and then left on Skinker. When we went in the house, I said, "Okay, I will go through all the junk in this place and figure out who I am. Can I throw out the rest of it?"

Mom said, "Please do!"

I started the next day. I'm not sure whether Mom was a hoarder, as they are called now. Maybe she was lazy and maybe she was a "hider." My apartment in New York was clean and spare. My clothes didn't fill my closet, and I had eight pairs of shoes—two for each season. One guitar, a stack of records that I actually enjoyed, and no books or magazines under the bed. In the kitchen, I had a frying pan, a medium-size cooking pot, and a larger one for boiling pasta. I had a hand mixer and three wooden spoons; I had one cookbook, *Joy of Cooking,* but I only consulted it from time to time. Everyone in St. Louis knew that Irma Rombauer was a St. Louis girl who had had a sad life but had done what she was supposed to do—get ahead by doing just what she wanted. The flour and the sugar and the butter stayed in their bags and boxes. My kitchen looked unoccupied, which was fine with me. Mom also had a copy of *Joy of Cooking,* as well as sixteen other cookbooks in a stack under the sink, and evidently the sink pipe dripped, because the top one was kind of wet.

My plan was to get rid of all of Mom's stuff, but I had to act as if I was curious, which meant that when I went down into the basement for the first time in years, I had to stay there, even though it was dank. Fortunately, since it was St. Louis and mid-September, it wasn't that cold, and I could see some sky and grass through the tiny windows below the ceiling. There were two old-style trunks and lots of boxes lined up along the wall, some of which I'd carried down there over the years, but the thing that looking around reminded me of was when we fled to this spot during the 1959 tornado. February, middle of the night, dark, a candle that kept flickering, and total silence, because of the thickness of the walls. Dizzy in the corner, her ears up, looking here and there, our sentinel. I remembered calling her and trying to get her to sit in my lap, but she knew she had another job. I also remembered shivering, and Mom putting her arms around me. I looked over at the furnace, which still worked, though Mom turned it on only in the middle of October, and then turned it off again in March—I remembered the trucks that used to deliver the fuel oil, though now it ran on natural gas. I was sure that if Mom had said "natural gas" to me in 1959, I would have assumed that the house was about to blow up.

I opened a couple of the boxes and lifted the lid of one of the trunks, but I didn't want to go through anything. I was focused on my goal, with Uncle Drew, of getting Mom out of the house. Now I regret that I didn't read through whatever was in those containers and come to some understanding of Mom and her past. Instead, I sat on one of the trunks and composed a song, "Too Much." It went, "I should be in the woods, walking down a path, / Loving the trees, having a laugh. / Instead I'm stuck here, drowning in this box / Of ancient words and forgotten socks. / I'd like to live my life, but I'm stuck living yours. / Please tell me one last time, why can't we close the doors? / They creak in the wind and let old storms return / To blow out the tiny fires that we would like to burn. / We smile and chat and act like friends, / But here and now, I feel that my capture will never end. / The windows are small, the walls are cold, every word that flies around is old old old. / Come with me, walk down the street, fly with me and see what we might meet."

I didn't write down the words, but I memorized them. I knew it was a mean song, and, really, it didn't reflect my feelings as a thirty-one-year-old—it was as if the basement had taken me back to being fourteen. That was the only interesting thing about the song. I never set it to a tune or performed it, but I kept it in my memory because of how weird it was. When I went upstairs around one or so, Mom had left, so I went back downstairs and carried the boxes and pulled the trunks out the basement door and threw everything in a trash bin.

It was easier to go through the clothing. They really were the sort of dresses that I might have bought at a used-clothing store in the midsixties. They were elegant, some made of silk or cashmere, and maybe the most interesting thing about them was how narrow they were—just the sort of thing Bette Davis would have worn in a movie, and yes, there was also a box of girdles, which were what Mom would have had to wear when she was sliding into those dresses. Silk stockings, lots of those, some with runs, and lots of high heels. Looking at those made me think of Ginger Rogers, dancing along with Fred Astaire, him getting the credit, but her doing the same steps in heels and getting overlooked, except as his "partner." Thinking of that made me wonder if there were any pictures of Mom dancing on Broadway. I went and looked out the front door and the back. No sign of Mom, so I then went through her desk and some of her drawers to see if she had some sort of picture—maybe a newspaper photo or a program, or something like that—but I didn't find anything. I thought I would ask Uncle Drew if my grandparents had saved anything, or if he had.

I kept one of the dresses. It was medium-blue silk, tight waisted, buttons down the front, a loose and comfortable skirt, maybe just below knee-length. It even had a couple of pockets at the waist. It looked businesslike and flattering. I held it up, looked at my belly, and hoped that I would be able to get into it someday. I took it to my room and put it in my suitcase. I put the other clothes and shoes from the late forties into a box. I put it into my room. My plan was to not mention it unless she did, and then give the dresses (and girdles) back to her if she wanted them. But what would remind her more of my stupid father than those fashionable dresses? I didn't want her to be reminded of him, even when she looked me in the face.

She still wasn't home, so I went into the kitchen and started working on the refrigerator. I doubt that anything in the fridge actually went back to the forties, because I remembered when Mom bought a new one around the time I graduated from Penn State. But there was enough mold so that some of the contents could have gone back to when she first got it. There were maybe six things that looked recently purchased—a pound of butter, a bottle of milk, a jar of strawberry jam, a head of broccoli, a bunch of carrots, and a fillet that was wrapped in paper. I got rid of everything else—spaghetti and sauce covered in white, some apples that were crinkly and blackened, some oranges and lemons that were rotten and soft, a half quart of milk that was old enough to be hard, and lots of moldy cheeses. Some of the stuff in the freezer was so frozen solid that I couldn't tell what it was, but that went out, too. And then Mom did what I wanted her to do, which was to walk in the back door, notice what I was doing, and say, "Ah! You sweetie! I was hoping you would clean the fridge out! I don't have room for any groceries anymore."

She gave me a little kiss, went over to the sink, and drank a glass of water. I didn't ask where she had been and she didn't ask what I had thrown out. When I was done, she helped me carry the mess to the garbage can, and when I suggested we go to Viviano's to get something for dinner, she said okay, but maybe instead we should just go to the Hill and have real Italian food instead of our own attempt. This sounded good to me, because the Hill was my favorite place for Italian food, and that included New York. And it didn't matter which restaurant you chose—all of them were great. Unfortunately, Mom wasn't up to walking (it was about two and a half miles), so the hardest part was finding a parking spot, but we did, and then I had the veal in a cream sauce with gnocchi and Mom had the lasagna.

We didn't talk about what she was going to do next, but two weeks after I got back to New York, she wrote that she had put the house on the market, because Uncle Drew told her that autumn was a good time to sell, but you couldn't wait too long, since the buyer would want to move in by Christmas. Sure enough, a buyer showed up just before Halloween, walked through, made a good offer, and that was that.

What I realized was interesting (though, oddly, it took me a while) was that I was happy about the sale and not as upset as I had thought I was going to be when she first suggested it. And I did look at my investment accounts and I did realize that I could have bought it, but I was glad I hadn't. When I thought of it now, it seemed like a giant, heavy object that would hold me down no matter what else I wanted to do. I saw that cleaning everything out had gotten me used to the idea of getting rid of the house, too.

Just after Thanksgiving, Uncle Drew wrote and said that Mom was moved into her new house on Argonne, a small, one-story brick house with a front yard, in good shape, not much maintenance required. A day later, I got a letter from Mom saying that she was very happy in her new place, and the clothes she still had actually fit into the small closet in her bedroom.

9

RIGHT AROUND EASTER in 1984, I ran into Martin in maybe the oddest place, the city least like England, least like Winchester, that I could think of at the time—Los Angeles. I was there making a music video, maybe for MTV, but maybe for another channel that became VH1, for older viewers. At any rate, I had been intending to go to the LA County Museum of Art, but I was loitering, walking down a sidewalk that passed some interesting houses and a row of tall palm trees as well as other trees that we didn't see in New York. The cars zipped by, I got a little hungry, and I saw Molly Malone's Irish Pub across the street. I looked both ways about a zillion times and then zipped across the street. When I got inside, it was dark, and I felt kind of panicked, but lucky to have survived. I was imagining not falling under some car, but flopping onto the hood and then, because the driver couldn't stop and didn't care whether he could see or not, being driven to Laurel Canyon and dumped over the side. I went to the bar and sat down to catch my breath and think about whether that could be a song. The bartender said, "I guess you ran across Fairfax." I nodded, and he set a small bowl of nuts in front of me. Then I felt the presence of someone behind me, and I whipped around.

Martin said, "I thought that was you."

Well, what was I to do? I threw my arms around him.

He was stiff, and then he melted, and then he said, in a sort of Irish accent, "Nay, I dawn't work here, if thet's what yer thinkin'."

I laughed and then he did, and he sat down beside me. He looked good, for thirty-seven. He still had plenty of hair, no gray, and his face was lively and friendly—a little more chiseled around the cheekbones, but his eyes were even more expressive. He wasn't wearing a jean jacket (I was), or a leather jacket, or high-waisted baggy pants (I was wearing high-waisted jeans because they did a good job of confining my belly and I didn't have love handles yet). He had on a blue and white shirt, nice collar, sleeves rolled up, real trousers, a pair of Chelsea boots, and an argyle sweater vest. I said, "You look great! Are you playing an English aristocrat in a movie?"

He said, "No. I'm just doing these folks a favor by walking around and showing them what they should be wearing."

I kissed him, then said, "You are definitely setting a good example."

The pub didn't have any toad-in-the-hole, nor did they have Irish coddle. We ended up eating regular old burgers and then walking to the museum, carefully, each of us watching the other one to make sure that we crossed the street safely.

I can't say that I paid any attention to the works in the museum, because I was so aware of Martin being next to me. We wanted to stay quiet (there were a lot of people walking around), so we didn't say much, and I think that was good, because it helped us get used to each other's presence. When we ambled out into the street again around four, he answered all of my questions without my asking. He said, "Charlotte and the kids are back home. Poor Charlotte—she's stuck with caring for both Mother and the twins for a week without me, but we do have a nanny who comes for about four hours during the day, and a nurse comes, too, to help Mother first thing in the morning, and then later in the day, so Charlotte gets some time to rest. Livvy and Lauren just turned one, so they aren't walking yet, but they are sweet and active, and they seem to enjoy one another, I must say." He turned right on Curson, and there we were at the tar pits, and I followed Martin into a new museum that was full of findings and information about the mammoths and saber-toothed cats. Right up Martin's alley, I thought. We didn't stay long because it was about to close, but we did look at the area around the museum as the sun began to go down. I said a few things, too—"New York City is such an intriguing place to live. And in the summer, I love spending a month or two in the Catskills. There are so many little towns and each one is beautiful, so I can't decide where to buy a house, or a cottage. Something small. My two singles are doing pretty well, and I'm getting ready to put together another album, half traditional songs and half ones that I wrote, like the last one. I don't want to do covers, though my producer would like me to."

He said, "You're in great shape, love," which I took to mean that Charlotte was not, and then I said, "I'm impressed with how graceful you are, still." And that was that. He followed me back to my hotel, where I got my things and my guitar, checked out, and then went to his, the Prospect, which was interesting, not in perfect condition, but very very LA.

We went straight to his room, dropped my things by the door, and fell down on the bed, where we began kissing and hugging. Twelve years since I walked away from him, and he was as familiar to me as my own feet. We didn't undress or make love—I knew that was for later—but we didn't have to, to feel like we had joined up once again, and also to feel like that was temporary. A wife, twin daughters, his mother—Martin was nothing if not responsible, and even as I thought that, I knew I was still lucky—lucky to have met him, lucky to have left him, lucky to have run into him again and to now understand that whatever resentment he felt toward me had faded away.

He was in LA to have some detailed conversations with a financial manager about how to invest what he had to make the best of the property, where he was now living with Charlotte and the girls. He was also thinking of "going on 'Change"—becoming a stock trader on the London Stock Exchange—but he thought that he needed some coaching, so he had come to visit with the manager. When he told me this, he looked a little blue, but then he said, "Half of me says we're stuck with Maggie and half of me says we're lucky to have her, and I've no idea which half is right and which is wrong."

There was no part of me that thought well of the guy I called, to myself, "Little Ronnie," but I didn't say anything, because I depended on Uncle Drew, and Uncle Drew was a Reagan fan. Because of the slight hint of blueness in his face, I wondered if it was Charlotte who was pushing him to earn more money and had sent him to LA, but we didn't talk about that, or talk about Charlotte at all. He did say a few things about the girls, though—they were identicals, they were active and looked like Charlotte mixed with his father's eyes, which I didn't remember, though I remembered the chat I had with him in his "study" and how pleasant he was, even though he was all dolled up in his World War II uniform. That was his sixtieth birthday, so, twelve years later, he would be seventy-two, but Martin hadn't mentioned him, so I assumed he had died, and that would make Martin Lord Leighmor. I didn't say anything about that, either. I did venture to say, "Girl twins! I always wanted to be a twin! Are you going to try for a boy?"

He shook his head and said, "Love, those days are gone. I actually wonder if a pair of girls as sweet as they seem to be would be willing to inherit the place. That's part of the reason I need the money. Upkeep."

I said, "That's why I didn't mind when my mom sold the house I grew up in, and I also remember when my uncle, you know, the investor, looked around St. Louis at a lot of elegant houses and then decided to stay exactly where he was."

When we were in bed that night, and he got up to go to the bathroom, I saw that there was a piece of paper on the bedside table with the information about his reservation. He was leaving in a week. That, I thought, would be the length of this affair, and all I wanted to do was to make the best of every minute. Beside the piece of paper was a little bottle of lavender hand lotion. I picked that up and rubbed it over my hands and face. When Martin came back from the "loo," he got into bed with me, and said, "Ah! Lavender! My favorite."

We cuddled, and I fell asleep as if I was a baby who had been swaddled. We woke up simultaneously at about four a.m., still dark, and I heard him reach for something that turned out to be a condom (and why did he have those with him?). My first lovemaking since the end of those twenty-three affairs, and I felt as though I had been revirginated. But Martin was careful and slow, as he had always been. I could see his face, because of the light from the street, and there was a new beauty to it, as if some sculptor had come in and remolded the angles of his chin and cheekbones. Peter O'Toole looked dull by comparison. Our intercourse was slow and pleasant until the very last second, when Martin seemed overwhelmed by ecstasy. I did not orgasm, except at the sight of his passion. Luckily, the condom did not break.

He fell back to sleep but I did not. I just looked at his face as the sunlight began to enter the room. After breakfast, we took separate taxis to the jobs we had to complete, and then we met for a late lunch at Musso & Frank. Martin had rented a car, but he was a little nervous about driving it, so it had been parked by the hotel for three days. I said I would drive, so that afternoon, we started our exploration of LA by visiting the Getty and then driving down Sunset to a beach. I was glad to be driving, because that way Martin could be staring out the window at what you might say was the real LA. Occasionally he would say, "Ah! Hold up, love! We have to look at this!"

I knew how to drive on the right side of the road, but otherwise, it may be that I felt as out of place as Martin did—the giant hedges, the soaring palm trees, the constant traffic that was not like New York City traffic, when you were stuck at intersections for what seemed like hours. My favorite thing was that we engaged in small talk as routinely as we had before—remarks, observations, jokes. I wondered if married people did this. The only marriages I had seen very much were my grandparents' and Uncle Drew and Aunt Louise's. In my grandparents' marriage, my grandfather did most of the talking and my grandmother did most of the winking, eye-rolling, and amused smiling. Aunt Louise had a lot to say, and Uncle Drew listened to her, but they always talked about what you might call "implementation"—the children, the house, the finances. Aunt

Louise didn't tell Uncle Drew how to invest, but she did tell him what they needed and that she truly hoped that they would be able to afford it (they always were). As we chatted, Martin seemed to feel a sort of relief and relaxation. He didn't tell me what he was learning about finance and becoming a stockbroker—maybe our afternoons together were relief from that very thing. Every day I was tempted to tell him to get in touch with Uncle Drew, who knew all about it, but I didn't want Uncle Drew to have an opinion about our affair, or our breakup.

We explored every afternoon—Pasadena, Manhattan Beach, the Griffith Observatory, even the Mount Wilson Observatory, which was maybe my favorite place, because it was so high up, and there were spots that we crept to where we could stare in amazement at the rough, sharp peaks that overlooked the city. The difference between us was that he wanted to look through the telescope, or at least see displays of what the astronomers had discovered, but I preferred sitting somewhere near the observatory and just looking around. I suspected there was inspiration all over the place, and I wanted to find some. Since we went late in the day, the birds were out and maybe the mountain lions, too—I thought I saw one slinking through the brush not far from where I was sitting on Mount Wilson.

I was glad that we didn't run into anyone we were acquainted with—or anyone who recognized me as a singer. I had sort of given way to the idea of presenting myself onstage and in the video as a little crazy, or maybe just daring, but I didn't wear any of those clothes (or fake eyelashes) when we were wandering around. In fact, I wore my glasses, which I had started wearing the previous year. I had been tempted to buy Cazals, which I could afford, because they were huge and I thought that maybe I wouldn't lose them (or sit on them) if I could see them from across the room. Eventually I didn't buy those—I bought something simpler—which turned out to be lucky, because in New York people were having their Cazals stolen off their faces, and a few people had been shot for them—apparently in New York, people would shoot you for anything. Sometimes people glanced at us when Martin said something, because he still enjoyed talking in various UK accents (he put on a good one when he told me about going to the observatory in Scotland). One night, when we were in a bar, we saw two musicians, both men ("Benny and Denny," they called themselves). The third song they played was "Ballad of the Absent Mare," by Lenny, of course, and I couldn't help singing along—"And she steps on the moon / When she paws at the sky." I knew all of the words, and Benny and Denny were easy to harmonize with. Benny smiled at me and nodded, so I kept going. They clearly didn't recognize me—they looked like they were in their early twenties. But I saw one man turn and look at me for a fairly long time and then look away. Judging by his expression, he recognized my voice but then decided that this plain Jane couldn't possibly be me.

I think Martin was a lot more comfortable having an affair with me in LA than he would have been in London. He was good at keeping in touch with Charlotte, asking about the twins, doing it every other day from the hotel at about noon, when it would be about eight p.m. at their place. He would tell her what he had learned that morning about going on 'Change, ask her how things were, listen to whatever she had to say, try to comfort her, and then ask to speak to Livvy and Lauren. It took about half an hour, and I'm sure it cost a pretty penny, but I found that reassuring, too. He didn't mind that I was there, and whatever I learned about their marriage, I learned from listening to the tones of his voice. I later wrote a song (of course): "I'm looking in the window / She's walking across the room / The woman that you married / Carrying a broom. / She drops it, turns around / Distress fills up her face / Does she know that you are with me? / That I am her disgrace? / I know what love is / I hope she does, too. / I hope that she gets it, every day, from you. / But here you are with me, / So graceful, by the door, / Staring in my direction / As if you never saw me before. / For men, love is strangeness, / Something fresh and free / For women, / Love is what you know, as simple as a tree / In your backyard, that you look at every day / I would be her friend, if I had the will / I would pass your love to her in a tiny little pill. / Her face would brighten, turn into a smile / And you would look at her / As you did, as you did / When you walked her down the aisle."

Nothing Martin said indicated that he was cheating on Charlotte (apart from this time). It was more like he was following her rules and doing it for Livvy and Lauren, which was what responsible men did, of course, and this got me to wonder if my father had faced a similar dilemma and made what he considered the most responsible choice. After that, I no longer thought of him as a nasty cad, but as a regular postwar American husband, choosing what he had to choose, no matter what he really desired. My sympathies shifted toward him, or rather, they expanded. I still understood how Mom had felt, but I also saw that it was an impossible situation that both of them had had to navigate.

After I wound up filming my video, I spent the mornings walking around the neighborhood of the Prospect, and it was more interesting than I had expected. Usually, when I was walking along, looking at some plain modern buildings and thinking how boring LA was compared to New York, I would turn up a street—say, Whitley, which was near the hotel—and walk into a hilly, woodsy world made of bushes, trees, and Spanish houses with clay tiles and sometimes circular towers, gardens, palms, and flowers everywhere, even in the summer. The hills were steep, hard to walk up, easy to walk down, and for two hours I let them draw me on, if only slowly. Then I went back to the Prospect and played my guitar for another two hours until I felt I was starving to death, and then Martin would show up and we would find someplace to eat. Martin wanted to try different cuisines every day, and not what he was used to—Brit, French, Indian. We started with Chinese, then went around the world in a way—Russian (chicken Kiev), German (schnitzel), Spanish (paella), Brazilian (moqueca de camarão), then back to LA, and steak, when we found Lawry's. Lawry's had a kind of Brit air to it, not only the interior, but also the Yorkshire pudding, and Martin and the waiter had fun going back and forth in different accents, Martin's English and Scottish, the waiter's American—his best was a kind of Boston Brahmin. When I asked how soon the steaks and the Yorkshire pudding would be ready, he lifted his chin and said, "Immeddeahtlih," and then added a few remarks about how exquisite the "Yawksha" pudding would be. He also did a flat St. Louis accent that ("thaaaaT") made me laugh. Every meal was good, and so it was great that I did those two hours of walking every day, because I worked some of it off. And we worked some of it off each night, too. Because of the twenty-three affairs, I understood more about the idiosyncrasies of sexuality—that it was related to love, but it was not love itself. When we were growing up, all the girls I knew, because we were told this over and over, thought that getting fucked was at the absolute heart of real love, which was why you had to wait and give the boys a few love tests before you allowed them to kiss you, then fondle you, then touch your privates, then enter you. Not all of the boys passed those tests, of course, and some got angry that you had been "leading them on" and then rejected them. They were the most obvious ones who didn't pass the test, and even though you had to be careful, you still had to administer the test. The girls who liked sex just because they liked sex were looked down upon—fast, sinful—but then women's lib came along, and the fast girls got more respect because they were claiming the privilege that men had always had.

At least half of my twenty-three affairs were with men who were used to sleeping around, and were charming about it. They made it clear from the beginning that they weren't interested in a relationship, but they were interested in having some fun, and they were happy to make it fun for you. Usually they were the good-looking ones and the ones with a good sense of humor. There was one guy, I think in late 1975. I met him on a beach in Boca Raton when I was taking a break from the cold weather in New York. He looked maybe thirty, was good at beach volleyball, was the sort of guy who would smack one of his fellow players on the ass and then laugh. Everybody laughed—evidently, they all liked him. I had been watching the game for maybe twenty minutes, then I went to my beach chair and sat down with my book. Five minutes later, he came over and sat next to me. I hadn't had an affair since about September, so I looked at him and smiled and he knew exactly what I was thinking. He held out his hand, I took it, and he walked me over to the beach bar and ordered me a piña colada. Our affair proceeded in the normal way—chatting, walking, ruffling each other's hair, a kiss on the cheek, and then a real kiss, then his arm around my shoulders and my arm around his waist. Lunch one day, dinner the next (deviled lobster at a restaurant that specialized in Caribbean food). One thing that surprised me was his readiness to correct my technique—how to kiss, how to stroke his dick (up and down the sides), how to give him head more effectively—but I appreciated his efforts (as did, I think, the men I had subsequent affairs with). But the thing that really surprised me was that he would not, under any circumstances, tell me his name. He wasn't wearing a wedding ring, and he didn't look familiar, but after it was over, I started thinking of him as some politician or movie star who had to keep his affairs a secret (in the nineties, I stared at several pictures of Bill Clinton, trying to convince myself that he was the one, but I didn't succeed).

Because of what I would call "my education," I had become more knowledgeable about what I liked sexually (my nipples were especially sensitive, and that plus stroking the guy's dick was what pushed me toward an orgasm), but Martin seemed to be the same as he always had been. I could tell that what turned him on was simply being with me, once again, and maybe discovering that twelve years hadn't destroyed my looks. During our week together, the sex wasn't what thrilled me, it was being with him, and maybe (I remembered Lisa Indiana telling me that in college, and that guy in the seventies said the same thing) his odor (which he said women were sensitive to, and which was why he showered every day and used a men's cologne that gave him a sort of fruity smell with a hint of cookie). I didn't see any bottles of cologne in Martin's luggage, so whatever his fragrance was, it was natural and delightful, at least to me. Maybe that was when I understood that there was a divide between sex and love, and even though the sex Martin and I had was routine, just having it with Martin was exquisite. But there was more—for the entire week, Martin was the kindly and amusing man I remembered and loved. But I also saw that I had been right about leaving him—just as I had suspected, he was trapped in the place and situation I had known he would be, and he was simultaneously making the best of things and doing what he had to do. He felt a lot of responsibility toward his mother and toward the estate and he was fulfilling all of those responsibilities. I could not say that I was doing what I had fantasized when I left him—becoming a star—but I was doing a bit of this and that, and enjoying myself without worries, thanks to Uncle Drew.

Before we went to bed on our last night together, he asked me to get out my guitar and play a few songs. I chose three of my own and three that I was fond of, old songs from when we were young. One was Joni's, "The Circle Game," and one was Judy's version of "Four Strong Winds." Then I was tempted to sing "Piece of My Heart," but instead, I sang the Tom Rush song that I had thought of so often to reassure myself that I had done the right thing—"No Regrets." "No regrets, no tears good-bye, / Don't want you back." I don't know whether Martin was familiar with that song, but when I was finished, he had tears on his cheeks, and so did I. We went straight to bed, didn't say a thing, didn't even make love, just cuddled and kissed, and drifted in and out of sleep. In the morning, I drove him to the airport, and sang, to myself, "Leaving on a Jet Plane," slightly changing the lyrics to "I know you won't be back again, / Oh, babe, it's time to go."

ON THE WAY back to New York, I stopped in St. Louis and stayed with Uncle Drew, because Mom said that her place didn't have air-conditioning. I kept my affair to myself—yes, I was four days late getting to them, but I said it was because of editing issues with the music video. While we were there, I did several St. Louis things—Uncle Drew took me to a Cards night game, where all we had for dinner was hot dogs and popcorn; we went to the zoo with a couple of their grandkids, and then to a good barbecue joint; took the kids to Grant's Farm, then went swimming. Even though I didn't say anything about Martin, I realized that being with him for that week had what you might call a spillover effect—I was in a good mood and easy to please, I felt loved and loving without the responsibilities that loving Martin would have entailed if we had gotten married, and I felt a renewal of my lifelong faithfulness toward Martin. I felt like I couldn't have him, but I did have him, and that was enough.

Another effect the affair with Martin had on me was that I went to my bank and took out a bunch of five-dollar bills. When I got home, I folded them across and then lengthwise, so they were easy to put in my pocket and also easy to remove. When I passed a beggar or a busker on the street, it took me only a couple of seconds to pull one out and put it in his or her can or basket. I was usually three or four steps down the street before they managed to unfold the note and see that it was a fiver. In those days, you could take five bucks into Zabar's and get a good-sized sandwich. At first, I was afraid that some other guy would notice, follow me down the street, beat me up, and steal all the money, but that never happened. Instead, the local buskers, and some of the beggars, saw me coming and gave me a smile. One of the buskers, who played regularly at the corner of West Seventy-Second and Riverside, where the park spreads out, sometimes played "Oh, There You Are," so if I was walking in that direction, I would take along a ten for him.

One result of handing out the money on a regular basis was that I got more aware of what the buskers and the beggars looked like, and I began trying to sense what had gotten them on the streets. All of the buskers were men, though some of the beggars were women with children. Oddly, I had more sympathy for the men. Maybe that was because the women looked more distressed. Eventually, I got past that. I realized that if I thought those women shouldn't have had those children, I was also erasing myself. After that, I gave each of them—the mother and however many kids were with her (usually it was one or two)—a fiver. Thinking these thoughts made me also think about being glad that I had been born. That was an intimidating thought. It was not exactly remembering wonderful experiences large and small, it was also understanding the nature of pleasure—a walk in Central Park on a beautiful day in the fall was a sustained pleasure, but walking around in London on your first day there and being prevented from stepping in front of a passing car by a kindly fellow pedestrian was also a pleasure, even though it had tints of fear and shame. Spending time with Martin was a pleasure, and welcoming our unorthodox relationship was a pleasure. Seeing cute little kids on the street was a pleasure, and not having any of them screaming in my own apartment was a pleasure. I understood Jackie's pleasures (investigating) and I understood Uncle Drew's pleasures (exploring) and I understood Brucie's pleasures (making jokes and playing tricks). I understood my own pleasure, first and foremost, music: making it, listening to it, understanding it, belting it out. I realized (and maybe this is true for all musicians) that audience applause was not much of a pleasure, because when you finish your set, you are thinking about the mistakes you made and what you might have done better.

I also understood making music as, perhaps, the justification of the human race, a bunch of mammals that didn't deserve the power they claimed and often misused it, sometimes to the point of earthly destruction. Songs, riffs, cantatas, operas, symphonies, murder ballads, lullabies, drum solos, duets, barbershop quartets, hymns, make us enjoy that we are living and, as we learn them, give us a sense that we will continue living, in the way that the beat goes on. One of the things that I remembered as I was thinking these thoughts was what I thought of Tchaikovsky when I was growing up. Mom liked Tchaikovsky, and would often play *The Seasons* and *Pathétique* on our record player in the late fifties. I loved them, but I knew that the Russians were bad people and might kill us all. I didn't know anything about Tchaikovsky's own life or problems. I remember asking her when I was eight or nine if listening to *Pathétique* was "treason." I don't remember where I heard that word, but maybe on TV. She put her arm around me and said that it wasn't, because the feeling it was giving me was not making me hate my country, it was making me love everyone in the world.

As I worked my way through all of these thoughts, I understood more and more about how lucky I was, and I decided to spread my luck around in a slightly more organized fashion. I looked at my budget, my tax documents, my investment returns, my rent, and what I was handing out, and decided to make regular contributions to various charities. At first, I had a hard time figuring out which ones, but then I walked around Manhattan and looked at the buskers and the beggars more—not after I gave them the fivers, but as I approached them—and I tried to figure out what organizations might help them. It worked a little—Save the Children, International Rescue Committee, Helen Keller, the Hunger Project. Later, I did more research. What I did not want was to be hounded with requests, so I did it in sort of the way that I gave out the fivers—I set up an account at my bank under a slightly different name with a post office address and mailed all the checks from that address. When the mail came rolling in, I just tossed it.

Part III

10

About a week after I got back to New York, the production company in LA invited me to go to another production company they were associated with over in Brooklyn to have a look at the music video. I loved going to Brooklyn. I had some friends who lived near Prospect Park, where I liked to walk. There was something about Brooklyn that was more relaxed than Manhattan, and it was a pleasure just wandering around, so I used the appointment as an excuse to get on the C train just before nine and then visit my friends, have lunch at a restaurant I hadn't tried before. Mostly what I did while I was walking around was appreciate the fact that I wasn't in LA. There was something homey and welcoming about Brooklyn, even though I did see one guy, who looked maybe my age, punch another guy and knock him down. I turned the corner and went the other way, but I could still hear them yelling. When I got to the production company, and told them who I was and what I was there for, the guy said, "Oh, yeah. Okay. Let's see what's going on"—none of that LA welcome into the studio. He went away and came back, said, "There's just you, right? Tony's gonna set it up. When it's done, you know how to get out, don't you?" I nodded. Whoever I was, the guy was unimpressed, and I knew he would be exactly as unimpressed by, say, the Rolling Stones.

After I sat down in front of the screen, which was not a movie screen, but about the size of a large painting, I heard the guy say, "Hey, Tony! Hit it!" and the video started rolling. I had done the performance standing up and I was wearing high-waisted black pants and a silk jacket with shoulder pads. The first shot was long—I looked like I was standing on a cliff in the distance (I had actually been standing on a small platform in the LA studio), and two or three times I stepped forward as if I might go over the cliff. I don't know where they'd shot the images of the cliff, but it didn't look very LA. It was green and quite beautiful, actually, and I wished I had gone there. The accompanying band was at the bottom of the cliff, and periodically, the drummer would look up, as if he was looking at me. The amusing part, for me, was that as my song got sadder and more desperate sounding, the drummer looked up at me more often. In the meantime, the lead guitarist was doing one of those guitarist dances where he leans way back, looks as if he is going crazy, and the music squeals all over the place. The rhythm guitarist bounced to the beat. Every so often, the camera passed over the hands of the pianist. I thought they sounded good, and my experience of them (they called themselves the Garter Belts, which made me laugh as it was intended to) was that they were competent and sane, and when the producer was picky about every little note, they did what they were told with amused smiles.

As the camera moved closer, I felt satisfied with the sound of my voice and also the tones of the guitar as I fingerpicked the harmonic melody—yes, I thought, it was in tune! What struck me was that I didn't look like myself. Yes, I had seen the beginnings of a few wrinkles, especially to either side of my lips, but it was that my lips looked weird as I opened my mouth, and it wasn't because I thrust my jaw out in order to deepen the vibrato. I stared at my face, letting the music go in my ears without paying much attention to it—and music does become automatic the more you play it. After the second verse, the camera backed off again, and I was in a different place—in a city, with a wall and windows behind me. I closed my eyes and lifted my voice toward the crescendo, and the last few notes throbbed in the dark. Apart from how I looked, I was actually impressed by how dramatic the camera work was, and how it followed the song but also differed from it.

Two minutes after it shut off, the guy opened the door and said, "Okay, babe, that's it. Hope ya liked it," and ushered me out onto the street again. I turned around to remind myself where I was and how to get back to the C train, and then I saw my face in the window and realized that the reason I had been surprised by what I looked like in the film was that I was used to seeing my face backward, in a mirror, and that was what looked normal to me. I don't think I'd seen a photograph of myself since before I'd turned thirty.

The song was inspired by my love of the Catskills, but it couldn't just be about some pretty landscape—all songs in the eighties, and maybe forever, had to have some drama. I didn't want to write a murder ballad, so I was stuck with writing a "left behind" ballad. There was a farm just north of Roxbury that I thought was in the most beautiful spot in the world, up a slight slope, not a cliff, from a branch of the Delaware River, with majestic wooded hills in every direction. I often looked at it as I drove by, and that was where I set the song. It was titled "You Knew."

You knew I married you and not the farm
I thought I would lure you back someday
To the busy street where we learned to play
That little game we loved, Let's go, Let's stay.

But when I saw the lovely trees
The clouds fluttering in the breeze
When I walked in through the door
Saw the knots in the piney floor
And smelled the billowing wind
I wanted to stay, and never to go.

We planted the beans, we planted the thyme
We deepened the well and enjoyed the grime.
It was you who got restless and eager to go

Back to noise and life on the go.
I grabbed your hand, took you up the hill
I looked into the distance, but you got a chill.

Then you were gone and you never returned.
Life on the farm is deathly quiet,
The house is as empty as if it had burned,
With my ashes inside it, drifting in the air,
I can't leave, I won't leave this beautiful place
But nothing fills up your empty space.

Do you see me down the street, looking your way?
Do you hold out your hand or run away?
And then you turn, and it's me who has gone
Back to the farm, to the sun at dawn,
Glowing with love, perfect in the sky
Giving me beauty till the day I die.

I think if that farm had been for sale, I would have purchased it on the spot, but it never was. Instead, I bought a small log cabin near Roxbury, six acres, woodstove, one bedroom for me and one for Jackie or Brucie, nestled in the hills, with a flourishing garden that I thought would keep me occupied (and it did). I also bought the car that I needed to get there, a Toyota Tercel, which I shared with Jackie. She was really good at noticing when a parking space opened up, and running out and moving the car if we had to. I loved going to the cabin, especially because, though I hadn't thought about this detail when I bought it, it had great acoustics and was a terrific place for practicing.

The video did reasonably well, and so did the album it accompanied. I played a few gigs here and there. Since St. Louis always liked me, I went there, and then to Minneapolis and then to KC and then to Chicago, and I was the opening act for two gigs, one in Philly and one in Chelsea. Lisa Indiana actually showed up for the Philly one and she was, of all things, pregnant. She waited for me after the concert, and we went to a bar for a drink (we both ordered piña coladas, and Lisa told the bartender to go easy on the booze). She saw me staring at her belly, and said, "Six months along. Guess what number this one is."

I said, "Fourteen?"

She laughed and said, "Not quite. Four. I made a little mistake."

I said, "What was that?"

"I married a good Catholic boy."

I didn't know what to say, and she saw what I was thinking, and said, "It turned out that I like them! I couldn't believe that feeling I got when Mary was born! I just looked her in her face and fell in love. Mark says I was really jealous if he picked her up when she was crying, and I say that I was just wanting to nurse, but he was right. I'm better now about not being so possessive."

I said, "So you converted?"

"I had to in order to get married. It's okay. Michael enjoys being an altar boy and getting off the farm, and Mary loves her school. We'll see about Markie. He's a handful!" But she said this with such pleasure that I knew she appreciated his active nature.

I said, "Does your husband enjoy living on the farm?"

"He does. His grandparents had a farm near Smicksburg, and then his dad moved to Pittsburgh and worked in a steel factory. Mark thought he had to get out of town." Before I asked, she said, "I met him in Punxsutawney, at a groundhog festival." She laughed. "He asked me if I lived in Pittsburgh, and as soon as I said I lived on the farm, he said, 'Can I date you?' And I'll tell you, he didn't know a thing about planting or harvesting, but he knew a lot about fixing this or that." She glanced at me. "As well as making do. That's the best part. My folks adore him, and they help with the kids. We built them a little cottage in the orchard, and they love living there. I run the farm, Mom raises the kids, Dad is in charge of the animals and the compost, and Mark is in charge of keeping everything in good shape."

I said, "Sounds like paradise," and Lisa Indiana said, "I knew it would be."

That's how I felt about my life for those two years after the album came out and I bought the cabin, but that all changed in 1987. Uncle Drew and Aunt Louise were now in their late fifties, and for years they had been talking about a long trip all over Europe, as a follow-up to the short one they had taken to Rome and Paris when I was in college. They finally made the reservations and bought the tickets at Christmas in 1986. Aunt Louise and Uncle Drew planned the trip for April, May, and June, which was not tourist season, but was the best time to enjoy the landscape, according to Allison, who was now almost thirty and loved to travel—her favorite spot was actually Morocco. Sometime in March, Uncle Drew sent me a map of their plan—flight to Frankfurt, then a clockwise circle: Munich; Vienna; Budapest; south to Athens; across the Adriatic by ferry to Bari, Italy; then a winding trip through Italy to places they hadn't been before, like Terni and Perugia. Allison and her two kids were going to meet them in Florence, and then, after Florence, Barcelona, Madrid, Porto, then Bordeaux; Tours; Brussels; a week in London, where Darryl would meet them; then back to Frankfurt by way of Amsterdam and Hanover. When I went to St. Louis for St. Patrick's Day to see them off, Aunt Louise had a stack of language guides and she was busy talking to herself in German, Italian, and French when I went to visit. We did have a St. Patrick's Day dinner, but there was no corned beef, instead some lamb shanks and potatoes au gratin. I had never seen Aunt Louise in such a good mood. Usually, she was kind and thoughtful but reserved. This time, she was sort of jumping around the house, grinning and laughing.

Uncle Drew and I walked up the street to Mom's new house, to accompany her to the dinner, and she seemed a little disorganized. As we walked back down the street, she stumbled, but she was between us, and we caught her. She had an excuse—a tree root had pushed up the paving. At dinner, she didn't eat much, and kept staring at her glass of wine. Nor did she say much. More than once, Aunt Louise looked at her as if she was irritated, but then she glanced at Uncle Drew and relaxed. Grandmother and Grandfather weren't there, so when we were walking back from taking Mom home, I expected

Uncle Drew to tell me that something bad was going on with them. Instead, he said, "Jodie, sweetheart, I've got a big favor to ask."

Given that my account was now worth four and a half million dollars, I didn't think that any favor would be too big. I said, "I accept."

"I haven't told you what it is."

"Hand all the money over to Allison and Darryl?"

He laughed, then said, "Not yet. Maybe later. No, I need you to come back to St. Louis and watch over your mom while we are away."

"What about Grandmother and Grandfather?"

"They are in better shape than she is, but I do drop by every couple of days just to say hi."

His request was one of those things that seem like a big deal for about five minutes and then sort themselves out. For one thing, I didn't have any gigs until August (a couple of festivals), the cabin in the Catskills was closed up until June and could wait, and I could always bring my guitar. I said, "Your place?"

He nodded.

I said, "I love your place."

The odd thing was that I didn't ask why he wanted me to watch over Mom. I assumed it was her mood swings and that memory we shared but never talked about, of her veering into the left lane on Brentwood Boulevard and rolling down the hill. And yes, Aunt Louise and Uncle Drew needed a break from those concerns. I went back to New York and told Jackie I would be gone for three months. No dogs or cats to watch over. All I had to do was lock the door. I got back to St. Louis on the thirtieth and Uncle Drew and Aunt Louise flew out on the morning of the thirty-first. Grandmother and Grandfather knew I was coming, so they had Mom, me, and Aunt Lily over for dinner that night. Uncle Drew had left me the keys to Aunt Louise's Acura but not to his own Audi. I drove Mom to Webster, not far. It was Aunt Lily who interested me, and not just because she had a few things to say about Brucie, but also because she still looked about my age and was up and about all through dinner—

bringing the food, serving it, taking away the plates, helping Grandmother to the bathroom (which was upstairs), cutting the pie. She and Grandfather traded jokes back and forth, and Grandmother laughed at some of them. It slowly dawned on me that even though my grandparents hadn't served any booze, or any wine, Mom was drunk. She didn't fall out of her chair, and she didn't slur her words, and maybe that was the scary part—she was so used to being drunk that she was an expert at containing it, and probably that was what she had done when I had come to clean out her house—that time, she had seemed both odd and herself. But in order to do so now, it appeared, she had to not laugh, not make any remarks, barely eat a bite, not stand up. When Aunt Lily was handing out the pecan pie, Mom put both her hands on the table and closed her eyes, and Grandfather and I shared a look, but she didn't pass out. She opened her eyes, sat up, ate just a bite of the pie. I saw that Grandfather knew what was going on, but Grandmother didn't.

The key with Mom, of course, was for me to pretend again that nothing was wrong, and just try my best to fix whatever I could, but since I didn't drink myself and didn't really know anyone who preferred alcohol to pot, the only way I could start was to go to her place the next day and offer to help her clean up. The back door was unlocked, which surprised me, but Kirkwood wasn't Manhattan, and if you were a criminal and looked at Mom's house, you would see that the back hall was piled with trash and the kitchen sink was full of dishes—why bother? And the refrigerator was almost empty—a carton with three eggs, a pint of milk that smelled sour, some bacon, a bag of English muffins, and some butter. The dining area needed sweeping and in the living room, the TV was still on and there were magazines and a few books everywhere. When I turned off the TV, there was total silence. I thought about going to Mom's room, but I didn't want to scare her, so I stacked the books, organized the magazines, lined up the pillows on the couch, and straightened the curtains and the blinds, which were askew. After I was done, I picked up one of the magazines, a copy of *Time,* and thumbed through it. It looked unread.

When I heard Mom's footsteps in the hall, I looked at my watch. It was nearly noon. I waited, picked up one of the *Vogue*s. She came into the room. I listened closely, but I didn't hear her stumble. She saw me and said, "What are you looking for?" She didn't sound drunk.

I turned around and said, "Nothing. I thought maybe you might want to do something today, and the back door was unlocked . . ."

She was haggard. She pushed her hair out of her face and glanced around. She didn't seem pleased that I had straightened things up, but I saw her reorganize her response bit by bit, until finally she smiled and said, "Thanks, sweetie. I know I have too many subscriptions. You have anything to eat yet?"

I told a lie, and said, "I got a sausage biscuit at McDonald's on the way here."

She nodded, then made her way into the kitchen. I followed her and watched. She opened the fridge and stared at what was inside, then fried herself an egg and toasted one English muffin, which she put a little bit of butter on. No bacon, no cereal, not even any jam. No wonder she looked so thin. We didn't say much. I remarked, "Looks like a nice day. I guess I'll go for a walk." She didn't offer to come along, but she perked up—I could tell she was glad to see me go. A few minutes later, she said, "The park is pretty nice. Worth a look. You wait any longer and it's going to be crowded."

I stood up and said, "It is a nice park." Mom stayed in the kitchen, and I went toward the living room as if I was going straight out the front door, but I slowed down, and then paused and waited. I heard her open a cabinet. I looked at my watch. It was about one. Early to be starting the booze.

I stayed away for three hours—walking and then playing and singing. When I got back to Mom's place around four, I knocked on the front door and she opened it, gave me a little kiss on the cheek, stepped aside. She still looked haggard, but she was smiling. The TV was on, some afternoon news show. There was an empty glass beside her chair. I said, "I'm not going to stay. I just wondered if you wanted to come to Uncle Drew's for dinner. There are tons of leftovers, and they all look good."

She said, "Oh, I don't know. If I show up, I show up."

I nodded. At what point do you say to your mother that she looks like a war orphan?

I kissed her on the cheek and then walked back to Uncle Drew's and got into the Acura. It was about five—perfect time of day to drive around a place I hadn't driven around in maybe twenty years, at least not on my own. I went north on Kirkwood Road, also known as Highway 61, which, in our neighborhood, was just a four-lane street that ran smoothly between pleasant houses, fenced yards, and plenty of trees. Of course Dylan's song rambled through my head—I knew the lyrics by heart, and it was fun to sing to myself, even though I'd always thought it made no sense. I crossed Manchester, which I had heard was once Route 66—the version of "(Get Your Kicks on) Route 66" that I remembered was by Chuck Berry, and I did turn my head once or twice to see if he was walking down the street. And then, the way it always is in St. Louis, businesses and modest houses turned into mansions with gates—Huntleigh led to Frontenac. I turned right on Clayton, which would have taken me to the house on Skinker if I had let it, but instead, I drove down Price to my old high school, turned up the driveway, and parked. School was out for the day, the front area still looked like a lawn. I got out and started walking around. In a few weeks, it would be twenty years since I'd graduated, more than half my life. Looking at the front steps, the door, the windows, and then at the trees on the hill to the left, I remembered all the details of the inside—to the right, English with Miss Fieselman in seventh grade, with Miss Damon in eighth grade, then down the hall to the sculpture class at the far end, and then down the hall of the right wing to the painting class. The steps to the lawn behind this building.

Even as I stood there, I could hear some noises, and there were a few cars parked in the lots, so some team was practicing—maybe the track team. How overwhelming it all had been! Not only the size of the building, but avoiding glares from the teachers, trying to get A's on papers and tests, reading books that I barely understood, watching the other girls talking to one another. But also yelling and screaming at Bombers football games, secretively looking at the cute boys, and watching to see who they looked at (never me). As I lifted my gaze, I could see myself on the second floor that time, in algebra class, staring out this very window, and then hearing Mr. Yeager bark my name and me jerking so that my pencil flew out the window. There were bushes in front of the building. Had the pencil been found, or rotted in the dirt? As I looked toward each window, the classrooms filled up in my mind—David O. in front of me, Fred G. in the front row, Nancy S. to my left, Debby P. and Carol P. whispering behind me, the gawky girl sniffling in the second row, Tom D. making a joke in a low voice, Albert S. moving around in his chair. The images were not all from eighth grade—it was as if they had been resurrected at exactly that moment I noticed one of them and they were all sitting in the same room, ages twelve, thirteen, fifteen, seventeen.

I looked upward, and there was the music room, and we were sitting in rows, with Mr. W. playing the piano and staring at us, nodding as we sang, and I felt all over again those first pleasures of harmonizing, opening my mouth and hearing all the notes rise together, and then listening to the soloists, one at a time, pour out their own feelings, and me being given the chance to do the same. Yes, there was a feeling of relief when Mr. W. nodded, and you knew that you were in tune, but the real pleasure was in hearing the notes that you made attach themselves to the notes that the other students were making. And I did remember that when music class was right after lunch, I felt good for the rest of the afternoon. I would let the tunes we had made wander around in my head and they always took me away. How many times had Mom said that I should be eternally grateful to have gone to this school? So many that I had decided, sometime while I was at Penn State, not to be grateful at all, because, I thought, my whole life at this school had been made up of watching the other kids and knowing that I was an outsider from beginning to end. But now, thinking of the music room and remembering those pleasures, I was grateful. I opened my mouth and sang a song, I think by Haydn, that we might have performed in tenth grade, or we might have simply sung in class. I couldn't remember any of the details, but I remembered the words and music perfectly. And it perked me up.

Which was a good thing, because when I got back to Uncle Drew's, after wandering through Brentwood, Maplewood, and Webster, it was almost six thirty, and Mom was sitting on the front porch. Her eyes were closed and she was leaning against the back of the deck chair, and as I was parking the car in the driveway, I felt a tingle of fear.

But she was neither dead nor passed out. She was a little addled, though. I unlocked the door and helped her into the kitchen. Aunt Louise had left some beef stew with dumplings and some homemade chili in the refrigerator and plenty of things that I hadn't really checked out in the freezer. Mom chose the beef stew, which I heated up on the stove. I would have chosen the chili, but I thought I would eat that for lunch. I was hungry, so I ate lots of stew and three dumplings. Mom had three bites of stew and she poked at the dumpling but didn't eat it, saying that it was "too loose." There were cupcakes, too, with chocolate icing, but Mom wouldn't even touch one of those. She said she was "watching [her] figure." I did not say that her figure was disappearing, or that I worried she would pass out from starvation.

As soon as dinner was over, before I even cleared the table, she stood up and said, "Do you mind walking me home? Walking in the dark makes me nervous."

"I don't mind, but why don't you stay? We could watch something together."

Now I saw her dilemma—if she went home, she could happily drink herself to sleep, but if she seemed too eager to get away from me, I would suspect something. However, I had a dilemma, too, which was what to do and how to do it.

I asked her if there was some show she liked to watch, and she said, "Tell me what day it is again?"

"Wednesday."

"I like *Highway to Heaven*."

That was one I hadn't watched, but I said, "Oh, that's a fun one." As it was only a little after seven, and it didn't come on until eight, I had to figure out a way to get her to stay. I turned on the TV. Mom sat down on the couch with her glass of water beside her and I took the dishes into the kitchen and actually washed them, since I wanted to set a good example. When I went into the living room, she said, "This one is pointless."

I said, "What is it?"

"Something about a guy named Aaron." She got up and changed the channel, but couldn't find anything she wanted to see, and went back to the first one, which I hadn't seen and didn't understand, although I did notice that the characters were dressed like Amish people in Iowa. By the time *St. Elsewhere* came on, Mom looked like she was asleep. I had often enjoyed *St. Elsewhere,* but I didn't watch it very often, because in New York, it came on at ten. I enjoyed the whole episode, but I kept glancing over at Mom. Maybe fifteen minutes before the end, she jerked out of her sleep and said, "Dammit, take me home!"

I said, "Okay," very mildly, helped her up, and walked her down the street. I kissed her good night at the door, and then lingered, and yes, she turned on the light, went straight to the cabinet, and pulled out what looked like vodka or gin—something clear.

The next day, I called Jackie, my only source of believable information, and said, "Do you miss me?"

She said, "Are you gone?"

We both laughed, and then I said, "Do you have any relatives who are drinkers?"

She said, "Not anymore. It was my uncle, but he discovered Bill W. because of some friend of his, and he seems to have worked for him."

I said, "Do you sound skeptical?"

Jackie said, "Always. It's not a scientific approach, and as far as I know, no studies have been done, but even my aunt and my cousin Rita swear that Uncle Chuck has quit, and that it's been about ten years."

"How did they get him into it?"

"That was the worst part. He had a drunk driving accident and woke up in the hospital with a concussion and a broken shoulder. I guess he ran a red light and didn't see a guy making a left turn. He ran into that guy, but fortunately, that guy was driving a pickup and wasn't hurt. Anyway, he did get into a lot of trouble, and as soon as he got out of the hospital, Aunt Gracie and Rita took him straight to an AA meeting and stayed by the door to make sure he didn't try to leave. He could see them there. I think that was what stopped him. I mean, it's supposed to be voluntary, and you have to say a lot of things that indicate that you want to stop, but maybe by that time, Uncle Chuck did want to quit."

I thanked her, and we talked about the neighborhood, the weather, what she was doing, what I was doing. I missed her. But the gist of her story was that her uncle got into trouble and regretted that. Judging by how Mom acted, I didn't expect her to get into trouble and give me an excuse to do something for her.

I asked around Kirkwood to see if anyone knew where there was an AA meeting. I had to ask strangers, because I didn't know anyone, and I had no way of asking Uncle Drew or Aunt Louise. It sort of made me laugh, because most of the people I asked looked me up and down, as if I was asking for myself. Someone did point me to a church that wasn't far away, and said, "Try that place. I've heard they do that." But he wasn't pointing at the Episcopal church, which my mom went to once in a while, he was pointing at something called Community of Christ. In that title, there were two words that would offend Mom—"community" and "Christ."

I walked over there, though. It was on Highway 61, across from one of my favorite houses—a brown and white Tudor, with steep roofs that I had looked at often when we passed it. Some man, maybe the pastor, was inside when I opened the door, and he was a kindly guy. He said that yes, they did host AA meetings, and he gave me the name of the parishioner, or whatever they were called, who had brought the meetings to the church. He said that the meetings were every day at five p.m. He, too, assumed that I was the alcoholic, because he smiled and said, "You can show up anytime."

And so, since I was used to performing, I showed up the next day, a Friday, at five. I walked in, sat down, and watched the members come through the door. I had told Mom that I was going shopping. Eventually, I counted thirty-two people, mostly men, but ten women, also, who came in and sat down. At exactly five, one of the men stood up and said, "Welcome to Alcoholics Anonymous, a worldwide fellowship of men and women who help each other to stay sober. This is a closed meeting. You are welcome to stay if you have a desire to quit drinking." He glanced at me and smiled. I smiled back. I decided to do what I always did, which was to listen and imitate. There was a long pause, and then one of the men, who looked about my age, said, "I am an alcoholic." He sighed and said, "I'm sorry that I missed two meetings, because I found myself more tempted yesterday than I did four days ago. I was walking past the Fireplace, and you know it's so out in the middle of nowhere. I haven't been there in six or eight years, but just seeing it made me want to bang down the door and go in. Plus it was raining. But I made myself turn around and walk back to Big Bend, even though that little tunnel you go through sort of creeps me out. I mean, we all know it's tiny. But anyway, I kept saying, 'Okay, Jimmy, it's only one step at a time.' But it was really hard to get the memories of that joint out of my head." The others nodded sympathetically, and one guy said, "You did it. Now you've just got to put it behind you."

The rest of the hour was filled with similar stories and reminders of "the Twelve Steps," which I didn't know anything about. The man to the right of me kept looking at me, until finally the woman to my left said, "Bobby, she doesn't have to say anything until she wants to." I nodded and smiled. Then that woman said, "Hi, I'm Marie. I don't have much to say, but I did want to confess that I've been hiding two bottles of Cointreau in my basement for the three years since I started coming here, and yesterday, after our meeting, I got them and poured them down the sink."

A few people said, "Good for you!"

There were some people who didn't say anything, but they nodded and paid attention to the Twelve Steps. I also understood from what a lot of people said, especially "Let go and let God," that this was some kind of religious organization, and that would put Mom off for sure. But it was friendly and welcoming, and I knew that Mom was a loner. I wondered if the sense of having some friends, or at least some acquaintances, would offset the religious aspect—what she liked about the Episcopal church had only to do with the architecture and its connection to English history.

When the meeting was over, everyone was nice to me as I left, and then, as I walked down the street toward West Argonne, the guy who had been sitting next to me ran up and said, "You're Jodie Rattler, aren't you?"

I nodded and smiled, expecting him to say that he had one of my records or had seen the video, but he said, "You're Bruce's cousin. I remember meeting you such a long time ago. Fun guy, your cousin. Where's he now?"

"He's living in Austin, Texas. He likes it."

"Well, the next time you hear from him, say hi from Bobby Schmidt."

I said that I would. I also thought I would talk to Brucie about this AA thing.

Mom showed up for dinner just after I got home. I had thawed out some slices of Aunt Louise's always wonderful meat loaf. I hadn't had time to boil any potatoes, so I made my two slices into a sandwich. Mom picked at her slice and turned down the bread. I didn't know which part worried me more, the drinking (she was very quiet—always a sign) or the starving. I thought there should be an organization called Caretakers Anonymous, where we would sit around and complain about our parents, or our kids, or our boyfriends, for that matter. She got up and left before sunset, and I didn't stop her, but I did watch her walk down the street. She was steady on her feet, as her career as a dancer had taught her to be. I wished Uncle Drew would give me a call so that I could ask him what he thought, but he wasn't going to, I was sure. Three months! A long time. I spent the rest of the evening playing my guitar. Not practicing, just enjoying, a relief rather than a task.

The next day, I dropped by my grandparents' house to say hi. Grandfather was sitting on the small front porch, looking at the lawn, which did need trimming. He stood as I came up the lower steps. He met me there and gave me a hug. He looked amazing for someone who was eighty-nine—when he trotted down the upper steps, he didn't even look down once. Just as we walked in the front door, he gave a little burp and said, "Too much apple pie."

I said, "Apple pie already?"

He said, "If she makes it for dinner, I eat a big piece for breakfast the next morning. The quicker I eat it, the sooner she makes another one."

I nodded at that, since Grandmother's apple pie was legendary, at least in our family.

Grandmother was in her chair, sitting quietly, with yesterday's copy of the *Post-Dispatch* on her knee. She looked at me for a moment, then smiled. I went over and hugged her. It was clear that she wasn't doing well—she looked confused. She didn't say anything to me. She picked up the paper and looked at it again. Grandfather went over and whispered in her ear, and she nodded, then said, "Hi, Jodie. I—I didn't recognize you. Did you change your hair?"

I said, "I forgot to comb it. Mostly I just pin it up to get it out of my face."

Then she said, "Are you married yet?"

I shook my head, gave her another hug, and said, "Grandma, that's not going to happen."

She said, "You don't want to be all alone when you get to be my age."

I glanced at Grandfather and said, "But Grandfather's already taken."

She didn't get the joke, but Grandfather laughed, then took me into the kitchen for a piece of apple pie. I expected the kitchen to be a mess, but Grandfather was an orderly sort of person, so all the cabinets were closed, the dishes were in the dish rack, and the table was wiped down. There was even a little vase with two tulips in the middle of the table. I smelled the tulips, and he said, "Come outside and have a look at the lilacs. They're great this year." We went out the back door and around to the side of the house where the lilac bushes had pretty much taken over. The blossoms were radiantly purple and I could smell them from ten feet away. When I stepped into a small space with flowers on both sides and also over my head, the scent was intoxicating. Grandfather said, "Too bad they only bloom once a year."

The side yard and the backyard weren't as well taken care of as the house—there were weeds everywhere and the grass was maybe six inches high. He saw me looking, so I said, "You want me to help you mow the lawn?"

"Well, the mower's broken."

"You want me to take it to be fixed?"

"You could. Fact is, I don't feel comfortable behind the wheel anymore."

"Did you . . ."

"Nah, not exactly. But, see that tree over there, next to the garage? I had the car parked kind of beside the house, and I was going to back down the driveway, and I put it in gear instead of in reverse, and scraped the tree. Took some paint off. Bit of a dent. But I knew it was a sign. I still go for groceries once a week, but I always go maybe around two in the afternoon when there isn't much traffic, and I know I'm going too slow. The cops don't like you to go too slow. Can't parallel park worth shit anymore, so I don't do that. If there isn't a row of parking spots in the parking lot at the store, then I just wait. Makes me nervous as hell."

"Can you call a cab or something like that?"

"Around here?"

Another question to ask Uncle Drew, along with, "Do you have any idea what's going on with Grandfather?" I said, "You need groceries? I could take you."

"Nah. We went yesterday."

"Grandmother goes with you?"

"Can't leave her home."

I nodded.

We went back inside, and Grandmother was in the kitchen. She looked at me and said, "Ah, sweetie. I didn't know you were back in town." It was as if she had spent so much time in the kitchen over the years that that's where her memories were stashed, and when she went in there, she had access to them. She offered me a piece of the apple pie. I glanced at Grandfather and said I wasn't hungry, so she got up and went to the refrigerator. It was about noon. She said to Grandfather, "How about a grilled ham and cheese. We got any cheese?"

He helped her slice the cheddar, and she made the sandwiches with complete expertise, frying them in a little bit of butter until they were brown and crispy. I was sorry I had turned one down. By the time I left, they were chatting about the yard. I said I would pick up the lawn mower the next day and see if I could get it fixed, but what I really intended to do was buy them another one.

I went back to Kirkwood and stopped to see Mom, but I didn't tell her about AA. I walked into her kitchen, saw the bottle—it was vodka—on the table, and went to the bathroom. When I got back to the kitchen, the bottle was gone. We had a chat about Grandmother, and then I left to go see Aunt Lily.

She must have noticed me approaching her front door, because she opened it before I knocked. She was dressed up, and said, "Hi, dear. I have to leave in twenty minutes, but how are you?"

I said, "I have no idea. I mean, I'm worried about Grandmother and Mom, and I miss New York and I haven't had much time to play any music, but Aunt Louise left some great food in the freezer, and the weather is beautiful."

Aunt Lily gave me an affectionate squeeze, and then said, "I know what you mean about Grandmother. What worries me is that they seem to be stuck in their house, and I know Grandmother sort of perks up if she gets outside. The funny thing is that she always liked to go to the zoo more than Brucie did. I think she still does."

I asked her if Grandfather had told her about his accident. She shook her head, then I told her, and she said, "Well, that's a good reason, for sure. I mean, Jesus, he's going on ninety." She stared at me, and then she did what she always did, which was to walk around me and go to her car, a ten-year-old VW Rabbit. I watched her drive away, and I admit that I was sort of seething because I was thinking that she never took care of anyone or anything, including the Rabbit, which looked like it hadn't ever been washed. Then I glanced at her house, which was about as big as an outhouse, the smallest on the street. She hadn't locked the door when she came out, so I opened it and walked in. It was almost the same as it had been in the fifties, when we visited—I think she'd replaced the sofa, but not the dining table or the bookcase. The stove in the kitchen was gas, looked ancient, and the faucet was dripping, even after I tried to turn it off. Her bed was made, but the bed in Brucie's old room was just a mattress lying on the floor. The TV was in what you would have called the third bedroom, but all the rooms were tiny. When had Aunt Lily ever had the time or the money to worry about other people? She was friendly, worked hard at her job, didn't get paid very much, and did the best she could. If she had been in New York, she would have been one of the people I'd have handed money to—after giving my waiter a large tip, say, I would have given Aunt Lily, the maître d', a tip also. I also seemed to remember asking Uncle Drew if he'd ever given her any help. He'd said, "She wouldn't take it."

My irritation slipped away, and I went for a walk down Kirkham, then up Gore to Old Orchard. Old Orchard was the first shopping district that I ever knew, and I still loved it. By the time that I was six and Brucie was seven, we were allowed to walk to the drugstore and buy some Dots or a Hershey bar. As we were walking, Brucie would tell me all sorts of things about the train tracks, the little creek, the auto repair place, and why, if we went to the soda fountain in the drugstore, I couldn't ask the server to not put the cherry on top. Gore dead-ended at Lockwood, and you could go right or left. Brucie and I sometimes turned left and then walked to Glen Road and all the way to our grandparents' house, through the neighborhood that I loved where some of the Big Muddies lived. The walk was at least a mile, but Brucie was so active that it had seemed routine to him, and I did my best to keep up. Two or three times, we knocked on Grandmother's front door and she came out and looked around, then said, "What are you two doing here?"

I would exclaim, "We walked from Old Orchard!"

She must have known that Aunt Lily had no idea where we were, but she didn't get mad at us, she just opened the door and took us to the kitchen, where she gave us a cupcake or a cookie and called Aunt Lily. I did hear them chat about it one time—Aunt Lily said, "The neighborhood is totally safe!" and Grandmother said, "What about cars?" Aunt Lily said, "Brucie would never cross the street without looking both ways." Grandmother said, "I just don't know," and Aunt Lily laughed and said, "Yup—you just don't know what I got up to when I was Brucie's age!" And they both laughed. Good memories. I wandered around for about an hour, then went back to Aunt Lily's and got the car. When I dropped in on Mom a little after lunch, she said she needed to do some shopping, so I took her to the grocery store, but she said that wasn't what she meant—she wanted to go to Famous-Barr, in Clayton. As I was driving her there, she told me how she had always preferred Stix, but Famous had gotten more stylish. I had no idea what she would buy, and I thought that she would look very strange in big shoulder pads, which maybe would come up to her ears. When we got to the parking lot, I put my hand on her knee and prevented her from getting out. I said, "I think we need to talk about Grandmother and Grandfather."

"We do, yes."

I didn't tell her about the accident, because I knew it would scare her more than it did Aunt Lily, or even me, but I said, "Grandfather is worried about driving, and he should be, I gather from Aunt Lily, but Aunt Lily also says that Grandmother hates being stuck in the house."

Mom nodded.

I said, "I'm guessing she's lonely. I think we should go over there once a day and help with things. I'm going to go back tomorrow and take the lawn mower to see if it can be repaired. You know how picky Grandfather is about the yard."

She said, "I'll come with you."

We went into the store, and I watched her wander around, fingering the dresses and sorting through the underwear. I pretended to be looking for things, too. She spent a lot of time in the shoe department. I knew that if we wandered and wandered, that would put off Mom resuming the day's tipple, so some of the time I hid so that she couldn't find me. I managed to keep her there until almost five, then I let her find me, and said, "Jeez! I'm starving. Where do you think we should go for an early supper?"

She said, "Schneithorst's isn't that far. I love their Wiener schnitzel, and they have some kind of potatoes . . ."

We were there in ten minutes. And I was hungry. We ate (Mom ordered a beer, but only one, and actually finished her schnitzel, and I had both the schnitzel and the shrimp cocktail), and then I said, "Let's get some takeout and go to Grandmother and Grandfather's and give it to them." We got Grandfather the paprikash and Grandmother the meat loaf and the apple strudel. When we showed up at their house, Grandfather was sitting at the kitchen table, watching Grandmother peel a potato, and when we told them what we got, Grandmother smiled and tossed the potato into the wastebasket. We told them we had already eaten, but we sat with them at the table while they ate, and then I said, "I would love to sing some songs."

Grandmother was as good at the piano as she had been in the kitchen, and although it was a little out of tune, I didn't say anything. We sang "Oh, Shenandoah" and "Comin' Round the Mountain," "John Henry." Grandfather did a wonderful job of singing "Beautiful Dreamer," and I did the best I could to harmonize. I wished I had my guitar, and said I would bring it next time. Grandmother seemed to be a little exhausted after the four songs, so Grandfather took her over to her chair, and we chatted until she fell asleep. Grandfather nodded, and Mom and I left. When we got to her place, it was eight forty-five. She had gone maybe seven hours without anything but a beer and she hadn't seemed irritated. I thought maybe that was the key. And when I got back to Uncle Drew's, I picked up my guitar and played for two hours. I felt my first sense of pleasure since coming to St. Louis and a big part of it was remembering those walks Brucie and I had taken down Glen Road, me with absolutely no sense of danger or worry, and Brucie telling me this and that as we walked past the trees and houses, stepped across the shadows of the trees, and enjoyed the sunshine.

The next day, I took the lawn mower to a hardware store, and left it there. Grandfather was pleased with the replacement, and immediately went outside to mow the lawn.

I now accepted my task, which was to take care of my grandparents and my mom, and to keep Brucie informed about whatever I noticed about Aunt Lily. It had taken a week to understand it, get used to it, and realize that I didn't have much else to do.

I got into a routine. I would get up early, play music, and write whatever lyrics I could come up with, then Mom would show up, sometimes with a headache and sometimes a little sleepy, but apparently capable of walking down the street. I would let her choose whatever it was in Aunt Louise's cupboard or fridge that she might like to eat, and she would eat a few bites. At that point, almost lunchtime, we would head over to Grandfather and Grandmother and do whatever they wanted to do. Grandmother got used to it, and recognized me every time. We started out bringing her something, but then it turned out that she preferred being taken somewhere for lunch, and she did enjoy Schneithorst's, but what she really liked was a kind of weekly tour of her favorite restaurants, including Steak 'n Shake, a place called Mugg's, and even McDonald's, if we left early enough to get a sausage biscuit. I do not know whether she enjoyed the food. Mom and I laughed at the way she always said, "This one could use more salt," or "I would have left the fries in the grease a little longer." On special days she would say, "Oh, let's just go straight to Velvet Freeze. I need something sweet." She always ordered the pecan krunch, and Mom was most tempted by the strawberry cheesecake. Grandfather let us go without him, and I think, though he never admitted it, that he was glad to have some time off from taking care of Grandmother. Sometimes Mom would try to get her to go to Famous or some other department store, but Grandmother seemed afraid of them, so we didn't push it. What we pushed, at least in May and June, was a little walk somewhere, but the park had to be small enough for Grandmother not to feel that she was lost or in danger. There were two she felt comfortable in, both of which ran along Deer Creek. Mom and I would take turns helping her along. Every Sunday night, Mom and I had dinner with Aunt Lily at Grandmother and Grandfather's. While Grandmother was cooking, the four of us would talk a little bit about how she seemed. We all agreed that the exercise and the variety were perking her up, and in some ways, it looked like she was enjoying going places that she had been to many times but didn't recognize. It was as if she was exploring and enjoyed it. And, according to Grandfather, she was sleeping much better, and he wasn't as afraid as he had been that she would get up in the night and fall down the stairs.

What I didn't say was that our efforts seemed to be working for Mom, too. She got used to putting off the booze until late in the afternoon and she began to eat more and talk more, even to tell a few amusing stories. We didn't sing every day, but we always sang on Sundays, and Grandfather said that Grandmother was spending more time at the piano—she had even told him to call a tuner, which he did.

My time for exploring was between about four and about seven—the light was perfect, and I drove all over the place. It was during one of those drives—after I crossed McKnight and was passing Tilles Park, going down Litzsinger—that I remembered that I had left my roll of two-dollar bills in New York, stuffed under a floorboard. I hadn't thought of them in a while, but I had thought of them right after I made my one-way reservation to St. Louis with the doomed feeling that my luck had run out, and I was like a dog being dragged on a leash back to my cage (Mom's house). But now, after a month of shopping, eating, singing, and wandering around with Mom and my grandparents, I felt lucky again. I felt that my luck had spread out and touched my relatives, and that had renewed my love for them and my understanding of them. Grandfather was frustrated and a bit ill-tempered because he was angry at himself, not at other people—if I paid attention to him and noticed how he was acting, he wouldn't bark at me if I interrupted him. If we let Grandmother do what she was used to and wanted to do, she knew how to do almost everything so well that she could get through it and feel pleased with herself. Most important, Mom was well aware of her drinking problem, which was why she was so circumspect about it. If I didn't nag her, or even seem to notice, she would do her best to regulate herself, and also to eat more and get more sleep. Maybe the key to understanding our family was that everyone was determined to do whatever they wanted to do, but they could actually modify their wishes if they had to. Just thinking this made me relax and, yes, feel lucky.

In mid-June, Brucie came for a visit, and he brought his new girlfriend. They had driven up from Austin, stopping overnight in Tulsa. Obviously, they had to stay with me, since Aunt Lily didn't have room, and I was happy to receive them. I put them in the master bedroom. I thought I was welcoming, but maybe I was too welcoming, and maybe I hugged Brucie too enthusiastically, because I saw at once that the girlfriend, Lynne, her name was ("Spelled with an E," she said sharply as Brucie introduced us), was jealous. Every time I said, "Brucie . . . ," she turned to him and said, "B . . . ," making sure that I knew that I was completely outdated. Brucie seemed oblivious to our rivalry.

I guessed she was in her thirties. Brucie was thirty-nine. She wasn't very revealing and she didn't like questions. I didn't understand why a sweetheart like Brucie would be with her, but then I woke up in the middle of the night and heard a rhythmic banging coming from their room. I lay quietly and listened, then I heard what sounded like a simultaneous orgasm and a laugh. After that, quiet. That gave me a pleasant memory of lover number seventeen, a guy from Minneapolis who called himself Pistol Pete. A good-looking, well-endowed assistant professor of history at Trinity College, in Connecticut, he was in New York City doing some research at the Morgan Library into Mesopotamian cylinder seals during spring break. There were a lot of pubs I liked in that neighborhood, and he was one of those guys who looked you right in the eye, smiled, and said, "Hey!," which meant "Let's do it!" The spring break lasted a week, and so did affair number seventeen.

In the morning, Lynne was already making breakfast—she had found the waffle iron, the eggs, a couple of sausages, and two apples. She sort of flinched when I entered the kitchen, and I realized that she hadn't intended to include me in breakfast. I wasn't that hungry—I was intending to make myself a piece of toast—but because she was such a bitch, I sat down at the table and said, "That looks good." In the end, she made me a waffle and Brucie gave me half of his apple and a lot of smiles, so she said, "Well, we have to get going," and left the dishes for me. They were gone all day, and when they came back, Brucie said that they had seen Aunt Lily, but Mom and I didn't see them at Grandmother and Grandfather's as we went about our regular routine (and Grandmother did say, two or three times, "Have you seen Brucie? Where is Brucie?"). After two nights in Uncle Drew's house, they moved to the Cheshire Inn. Brucie came along with Mom and me to Grandmother and Grandfather's twice, but Lynne wouldn't let him do it every day, and by the end of their trip, when we were having our regular Sunday night dinner, he looked fed up. They left the next morning without saying good-bye to me, but they did stop by Aunt Lily's and say good-bye to her. That was the last I heard of Lynne, and Brucie never talked about her again.

WHEN UNCLE DREW and Aunt Louise got home from their trip at the end of July, he took me out for a walk, and before he told me about the adventure, he asked after Grandmother, Grandfather, and Mom. I told him what we had done, and what my theory was, and after a bit of skepticism, he smiled, gave me a hug, and said, as if he was joking, "So, you want to stick around?"

I said that I did, and he thought I was the one who was joking. But I wasn't.

It turned out that Uncle Drew had real estate investments, too, and one of them was a row of apartments not far from my grandparents' house—a pleasant fifteen- or twenty-minute walk. By the first of September, I had done my August gigs, sublet my apartment in New York to a friend of Jackie's who wanted a furnished place, gotten a new bed and some used furniture for the apartment, and moved in. The next day, I flew to New York, picked up the Tercel, spent two weeks in my cabin in the Catskills, and then closed it up for the winter. Jackie wasn't sorry to see the Tercel go—she said keeping it on the Upper West Side was a pain in the ass, and showed me a little dent that she had found one morning. The drive back to St. Louis was pleasant. My new apartment had a garage in the basement, which seemed like a luxury.

Aunt Louise and Uncle Drew agreed to follow my schedule with Mom and my grandparents, and so they integrated themselves into the program, and what I felt afterward was that we wove ourselves together as a family once again.

II

OVER THE NEXT six years, I knew what was going to happen, and I also came to understand that being present for sad events teaches you to accept them and learn from them, even if you don't know how they are going to pan out. I thought of this recently when I unearthed a paperback that I bought about a year after I moved back to St. Louis. Unbelievably (at the time I saw it at Left Bank Books) it was written by the gawky girl from high school, the same girl I had seen in a park in Winchester, tripping over her feet. On the back cover of the book were bits of praise, so even though I hadn't heard of it, it must have done well. Five stories and a novella. I read the novella first, and as I was reading it, I thought, Gee! She decided to become a dentist, because the main female character was a dentist (so was the husband). As I read the novella, I congratulated myself on not becoming a dentist, not getting married, and not having children, because the dentist's three young ones, six months, I think, to four years old, were the main source of the chaos and maybe the reason why the wife was having an affair that the husband refused to recognize. I liked it at the time, even though it was depressing, but then, the other stories were depressing, too. I thought maybe the gawky girl was having even more problems than I was.

Aunt Louise took over Mom's morning ritual of showing up for something to eat and I finished my practicing around ten, then walked to my grandparents' house. I would help with whatever they needed, and then, if the weather was pleasant, sit with Grandmother on the porch while Grandfather worked in the yard. Around twelve thirty or so, Uncle Drew would show up with Mom, and Grandfather and I would help Grandmother down the steps and into the car. Allison had moved to Kansas City, and Darryl was living in Chicago, where he also worked in finance. There were now five grandchildren—Allison had three, Darryl two. When they came to town, we used that as an excuse to take Grandmother to the zoo or the botanic garden. Grandmother had always liked children and we had always liked her. The botanic garden was old and odd, and therefore a lot of fun for us all.

Bit by bit, I began to reconnect with kids I'd known in school. I wouldn't say this was intentional; mostly I would recognize someone at a store or in a park, or someone would recognize me, and we would say a few things and maybe have lunch. Everyone I met was married, had kids. But, although I enjoyed the occasional meetings, I didn't want to be distracted from our efforts to take care of Mom and my grandparents.

One of the things that Uncle Drew liked to do was take us to local parks. There were a lot of them. His favorite was Babler, which was really a forest, a little past Chesterfield, and not far from the Missouri River. Since he had decided to buy a minivan, he would pick up all of us, saving the front seat for Grandmother, and take us up to Babler. Then Uncle Drew and I would get out and walk some of the trails, while Aunt Louise drove Grandmother and Grandfather around in the woods. We did have a rule—after every trip, we had to look for ticks, especially in our hair, on the backs of our necks, up our sleeves. And of course there were a lot of flies and mosquitoes, but Uncle Drew said that was the price for living in such a fertile and wooded area—would we rather be in Phoenix? Uncle Drew had traveled all over the world, and, from what he said, he had never found anywhere that he would prefer to live. Then he would name the cities he enjoyed—Istanbul, Fez, Oslo, Melbourne, Hong Kong, Buenos Aires, Quebec City—"great places to visit, but I only want to live here." I understood what he meant, but just hearing the names made me at least want to have a look. And I knew that I had the money. But for now, I had a job.

The first song I wrote was called "I'm on My Way." It was about my morning walk from my apartment to my grandparents' house on a rainy day in late September. I knew the lyrics were not something that anyone would care about (no murder ballad or successful love song), so I knew that I had to make the tune mesmerizing. One of my inspirations was an older song with a great beat and an interesting climax, "Come a Little Bit Closer," by Jay and the Americans. It was a good example of a complicated story/song, where a man goes into a café south of the Texas border and is drawn to a Mexican woman, but when her boyfriend enters, the guitar player in the band says to the man, "Vamoose, José's on his way!" The man runs, and then hears the woman say to José, "Come a little bit closer . . ." The narrator of the song thinks that the woman is evidently a two-timer, but I thought it was pretty clear that she has no option—she has to make up to her lover in order to save herself. I decided to use the tune I made up to expand my range, which wasn't easy, but if there was going to be a potent finale, I had to be able to get higher without screeching. It was enough of a project to keep me going, and that was all I wanted.

GRANDMOTHER WAS the first to pass on, which we all knew was what she wanted. In May of 1990, she had her ninetieth birthday. She kept it to herself, maybe hoping that we wouldn't remember (or maybe she herself didn't remember). The challenge was that someone had to bake a cake that she would actually like, and Aunt Louise, Aunt Lily, and I went back and forth about what to make. Grandmother had written down some of her favorite recipes, but none of them were cake. We also didn't quite agree what her favorite was—Grandfather said chocolate, Aunt Louise said strawberry sponge cake, and Mom said some sort of Bundt cake (and Grandmother had the pans for all of them). I decided to make the ice cream (vanilla, we all knew that) with her old crank freezer, and eventually Mom and Aunt Louise decided on chocolate, because there was plenty of cocoa in the cabinet.

We were there for dinner, but no one brought a present or said anything about the birthday until Aunt Lily got up, went into the kitchen, and brought out the cake. She set it on the table, and Grandmother stared at it, then took a breath and smiled. Mom set a candle in the middle of the cake, and Uncle Drew lit it with a lighter, and then Grandmother said, "I'm way older than that." She smiled and we all laughed. Aunt Louise watched to see if Grandmother ate her slice, and she did. We all breathed a sigh of relief. After dinner, we helped Grandmother into the living room and sat her down at the piano. She put her hands on the keys, but she didn't start playing—it seemed as though her hands were too stiff (or maybe painful) to play, but that was where she liked to sit, and I was the one, with my guitar, who played the tunes. We sang for maybe half an hour. Grandfather's voice was getting a little raw, but he still knew how to stay in tune and all of the lyrics. What pleased me was listening to Mom, who had decided to sing more often, and had gotten less shy about showing off the talents that had helped her get on the stage in New York. She was a sturdy alto with a decent range, and I liked harmonizing with her.

After we finished singing, Aunt Lily and I helped Grandmother up the stairs. She was small and light, so it wasn't hard to do, but it reminded us that their house wasn't built for old people. Downstairs, there was the kitchen, the living room, and the dining room, none of which could easily be turned into a bedroom. And, in case of a tornado (a thought we always entertained in St. Louis), it was almost impossible for them to get to the basement.

Aunt Lily and I helped Grandmother put on her nightgown and then get into bed. We each kissed her good night, just as she had kissed us good night when we were children. She closed her eyes.

We then glanced at each other. We knew that we had to talk with Grandfather about getting out of this house, and we also knew that Uncle Drew had suggested it over and over and had always been resisted. When we got back downstairs, it was clear that Uncle Drew was suggesting it now, and Aunt Louise was backing him up, because she said, "Our house has a room you could live in. That office to the right of the dining room."

Grandfather said, "Where's the bathroom?"

Aunt Louise said, "Well . . ."

And Uncle Drew said, "We can add one. We need one downstairs. You know that house Allison lived in for a while after college? I guess it had started out with an outhouse, and then they put a bathroom in the closet off the living room."

Grandfather didn't say anything.

After Aunt Louise and I had done the dishes and put away the leftovers, Grandfather looked like he was ready for bed, and we all watched him climb the stairs. That was getting harder for him, too. When they took me back to my place in the minivan, we all agreed that Grandfather was beginning to listen, and it was time to look for some sort of old folks' home, or to figure out how to add a bathroom to the office at the house on Argonne.

Since I went to my grandparents' house every day, I knew that Grandmother stayed in her room some mornings, and one of us brought a muffin or a scrambled egg to her. We also helped her to the bathroom when she asked for it, but after the birthday, it seemed that she stopped going downstairs altogether, and our job when we went there was to make sure that she had something to eat, that her sheets and blanket weren't soiled, and that her nightgowns were clean and loose. All she wanted to eat after the birthday was cake or muffins—soft and sweet. Mom put a radio in her room and tuned it to a station that played all kinds of music.

We all knew what was happening, including Grandfather. He looked distraught and resigned, and he would sit in her room, in her ancient rocking chair, chatting with her even if she didn't say anything. It took about two weeks. Aunt Lily was there when it happened, and Grandfather was in the chair. They said that Grandmother moved in her bed, put her hands on her chest, and looked at Grandfather, who knew that she was having a heart attack. He went over to her and knelt down, kissed her, and put his hand over hers. She slipped away. Aunt Lily closed her eyes. Outside the window, the lilacs were waving in the breeze, and Grandfather went to the window and opened it, so that the scent would flood the room.

Something that I hadn't thought of before was her burial. I had imagined singing at her funeral in the church we had sometimes gone to when I was young, but I now woke up to the fact that you had to bury your loved one somewhere. Grandfather's family had lived in and around Akron for a hundred and fifty years. He told us that they took up half the local cemetery, but then he looked out the window and said, "Don't want to be stuck there." Uncle Drew revealed that he and Aunt Louise had reserved plots in a public cemetery about a mile from their house. I liked the name, Oak Hill, so later that afternoon, I went over and walked around. It was ideal—a kind of rolling park with numerous gravestones and monuments, but also beautiful grass and plenty of trees. Uncle Drew found the people who ran the cemetery and talked them into trading the plot he had reserved for a larger one. That was all he told us. We also had to look for a funeral home. I would have thought that my grandfather, in his nineties, had made a plan, but Aunt Louise said that he had not, even though Uncle Drew urged him. What he said to Uncle Drew was, "Do what you want," and then had joked about being taken up to Weldon Spring, tossed into the Missouri, and allowed to finally take that trip down the Mississippi that he'd always wanted to do.

I was hoping that the funeral home would be close to my grandparents' house, so that at least some of their friends could show up, but the nearest available one was a couple of blocks from the botanical garden. Not many friends could get there, and the service was short, though there were plenty of tears. The lucky thing about it was that afterward, all of us—Grandfather, Uncle Drew, Aunt Louise and the kids, Aunt Lily, Brucie, Uncle Hank and his family, Mom, and I—took a walk through the botanical garden on a beautiful day, the first of June, and talked about Grandmother. Then, in honor of her, we went to Velvet Freeze first and Schneithorst's second, for dinner. I kept my eye on Grandfather. He seemed quiet but accepting. When we took him back to his place, I stayed with him until he went upstairs to bed, then listened for a while to make sure that he was moving around okay. It was just dusk when I walked back to my place, and it was the perfect time of day to wish your beloved grandmother well as you saw the shadows stretch across the lawns and through the trees and then fade into darkness.

THAT BECAME my routine—stay with him watching TV or singing some music or playing a game of checkers or gin rummy until he was ready to go to bed, watch him as he climbed the stairs, then show up in the morning about nine, watch him as he came down the stairs, and make him something for breakfast. More music, a few minutes of cleanup, and hand the responsibility over to Aunt Lily, who stayed until about three thirty and then went to her job. Over the course of the summer, I got interested in cemeteries, and of course there were a lot of them. I got more interested in walking around them than I was in walking around parks. I noticed, though, that Grandfather started to change after the funeral—Aunt Lily noticed it, too. He didn't seem to lose his senses or to stumble more. It was as if he didn't know what to do with himself now that he didn't have Grandmother to care for. A couple of times when I arrived, I looked all over for him, and then found him sitting in his car, staring at the garage. The key was in the ignition, but the car wasn't turned on, and the window wasn't rolled down. Since St. Louis is hot, I thought this was dangerous, but since the car was parked under a tree, at least there was a little shade. And it was a hot summer, or so I thought, being used to New York. I would find Grandfather sitting by an open window, swatting flies with his hand and sweating. I said, "Maybe an air conditioner in the window would work." He glanced at me and said, "Hate those things. You know, sweetie, you got to get used to the seasons as they pass. Can't be hiding out from the weather all the time. This idea that you've got to make every minute just right so that you can do the same thing day after day is a bad one. When I first came to St. Louis, I worked for Ralston Purina, in the mill downtown. Those guys were good about understanding how each year goes by. Of course we had to work hard around harvesttime, and things were a little easier in January, when we'd processed most of the grain. In the summer, they eased up on us, let us walk around and get some air. We got used to it. When I worked for Goodyear, in Akron, during the war, of course we had to keep at it all year round, all day long, and we understood that, but doing the same goddamned thing over and over nearly made me lose my mind."

Aunt Lily once found him lying on his back on the lawn, not far from the lawn mower, which was running. She thought he was dead—maybe had a stroke or something and fell down—but he was just lying there, looking up at the clouds. And when she went over to him, he didn't even take her hand—just got up on his own, gave her a smile, and went back to mowing the lawn. I knew what she was thinking. If he didn't come down the stairs pretty soon after I got to his place, I would be afraid to go up and find him (and the first thing I did when I walked into the house was look at the bottom of the stairs, to see if he'd fallen).

OVER THE SUMMER, he started opening up about his memories. I didn't ask questions, because I wanted to see where his own thoughts would lead him. Of course, a lot of memories were about Grandmother. Of meeting her on that trolley, he said, "You know, I looked at her and then I looked about for her ma. She was such a shrimp I thought she was about twelve, but then when she smiled and said, 'I can move over,' she had such a beautiful, deep voice that I realized she was grown-up. But the fact was, she was still such a shrimp that I felt somebody had to keep a watch over her. Good lord, we were on those trolleys for at least an hour, but it was perfect for a first date." A day or so later, he said, "Did she tell you she was at that teacher's school up in Normal? It was hard to get there, too, but she had a friend who lived in Chicago, in Oak Lawn. It was easier for me to get there, so she would take the train up from Normal, stay with her friend for the weekend, and I would meet up with her. Can you believe this? We had about three dates! I mean, I did write letters, and we knew each other that way for about five months, but I knew from day one that I wanted to marry her."

I said, "Lucky for us that you did."

He said, "Lucky for me, too."

He didn't say why until a few days later, when he said, "There was this girl after me back in Akron, and she was just about to wear me down. My ma thought she would be good for me, and the girl knew that. The thing about her was she was always telling me what to do. Couldn't stop. Your grandmother wasn't like that. I mean, she got me to do stuff, but it was by suggesting, or even just smiling and tossing her head toward something. There was one time when she was cooking and I was reading the morning paper, and I heard a little thump from the next room—didn't even think about it, but I saw your grandmother look that way, and then she tossed her head, and I jumped up. Your ma was pulling little Hank around by the feet. I think she thought it was a game. What was she, five? And Hank was two. Well, I put a stop to that. But there were plenty of other times, too, like when I saw your grandmother look out the window when we were passing that movie place on Brentwood, and she looked just long enough for me to know that she wanted to see that picture. It was *Singin' in the Rain*. That was a good one. We sang some of those songs for years."

One day, he said, "I'm not saying things were easy."

In fact, he hadn't been saying a thing. I put down my notebook (I had been writing a song). He went on, "There were plenty of times in the thirties when I thought Goodyear was going to shut down, because we always worried about a rubber shortage. I tried to keep it to myself, but Grandmother knew everything that I was thinking. She made the money last and she made the food last. I never saw so many types of beans in my life. I knew all about black-eyed peas and chickpeas, but I'd never seen a lentil. She used to make a stew with those and some bacon that I would have chosen over a pork chop any day. She'd walk into the pantry and look around and come up with something, no matter what. She even made a few crab apple pies from crab apples she picked in our neighborhood in Akron. I never thought those would be any good, but they were." I thought he was going to continue, but he sighed and looked out the window.

I was hesitant to take him for walks, mostly because there were lots of steps from his house down to the street, but a few times when I was walking toward his house in the morning, there he was, making his way up the sidewalk. Most of the time, I went right to him, gave him a hug, and said, "Hi," but one time, I walked along maybe ten steps behind him, just to see where he was going. He paused and looked at a few houses, especially one, almost to Bompart, that had a For Sale sign in the front yard. The sidewalk went uphill, but when he wasn't stopping to gaze, he was walking steadily. Because we went slowly, I actually appreciated the landscape. Some of the houses were set on small hills, others were right by the road. At Bompart, I caught up to him, and he didn't seem surprised. He said, "You know, most of these places were built in the twenties. I think that was the best time for building, myself. The builders knew what they were doing, and they put the bathrooms inside—didn't have to run out to the backyard in the middle of dinner or in the middle of the night, for that matter. Though when I was growing up, we had piss pots, as we called them. Mom and Dad's was in a cabinet beside the bed, and ours was in a corner beside the door of our room. But then you had to take them out and empty them. Didn't enjoy that."

We kept walking. The houses got nicer. We passed an interesting brick one, about the same size as Grandfather's house, but with a steep roof, and he said, "You know how once you buy your house, you like it well enough, but then you start walking around the neighborhood, and you get to envying some of the others? This was the one I always wished we'd gotten." He laughed. "Tight yard, and this big old tree blocking the view. You'd think I would have envied that one on the corner. Big square chunk of bricks. Looks roomy. But, no. There was something haunting about this one." We kept walking to Summit, and when he glanced up at the street sign, he laughed and said, "Always thought it was funny that if you were on Clark, you walked downhill to Summit." I wondered if we were going to keep going to my place, which he hadn't been to, but he turned around and headed back. He kept looking at the houses, but he didn't say much more. He didn't slow down or seem taxed, but he did take a nap when we got back.

I told Aunt Lily about our walk, and she said, "Oh, heavens! You should head down Bompart toward Old Orchard! One interesting building after another!"

I didn't remember seeing anyone on our walk—perhaps I was too focused on Grandfather—but two days later, when I was at the grocery store, a woman who was pushing her cart down the vegetable aisle looked at me, squinted, then smiled and said, "That old man you were with the other day is a wonder!"

I shifted the boxes I was carrying from one hand to another (I hadn't thought I needed a cart, but I did) and said, "He's my grandfather. We think so, too."

"He went to our church for years! I sang in the choir, too. Such a melodious voice." She smiled again and went on—evidently not in good shape, because she was limping and using her cart as a prop.

The best time to get Mom to help was in the afternoon. I would show up at her place before or after her first drink and tell her that Grandfather had asked for her, and she would get in the car agreeably enough. The first few times, I let her sit with him while I washed the dishes or did some dusting, but one day, when he wasn't feeling well and didn't want to come downstairs, I said, "You know, we ought to look around up in the attic, to see what's worth saving." We told Grandfather what our plan was, and he said, "Well, I'd like to see some of that junk!" but the attic stairs were steep, so what we did was, Mom opened the boxes and I took whatever she found down to him. He got himself out of bed and went over to his chair. The best thing, I thought, was an old stack of dusty photographs, black-and-white, of course, of what looked like his family in Akron. I handed him the largest one, of his parents, maybe an uncle, and all of the children standing in a row outside of their house, with some sort of fruit tree blooming in the background. He gazed at the picture, and then laughed, and said, "You know, these folks are us—my pa, and ma, and all the kids, and Uncle Harry—but it doesn't look a thing like us, because no one is laughing or jumping around. My brother Frank couldn't keep still for a minute! In those days, the photographer wouldn't let you smile, because then the picture would blur, so you had to stand still as a post. And it cost a mint, too. I remember when Pa brought this picture home, and passed it around, and then said, 'I forget. Was this taken at a funeral home?' "

There were old shoes and jackets and dresses Grandmother must have worn in the 1910s—one, green, felt like pure silk. She had also saved what looked like her wedding dress—it was white, about ankle length, with a high neckline, long sleeves, and beautiful embroidery that was also white. Grandmother had folded it neatly and put it into its own box. But it was dusty, so Mom held it up and I wiped it down. We stared at each other, and I knew we were both wondering if seeing it would be painful for Grandfather. We went down to his room, me carrying the dress, and then we put on a happy face—I said, "Look what we found!" and held it out to him.

He ran his hand across the silk, and as he did so, something, maybe his fingernail, made a small rip. Mom began to take it away, but he pressed his hand on the dress and said, "When it's my time, you wrap me in this, okay?"

Mom and I nodded, then I folded it up again and set it in his lap. She and I glanced at each other, and then went back up to the attic.

I was hoping to find more photographs, and we did find a few, from the thirties, when Mom was in her teens. In one of them, she was smiling and standing next to Uncle Hank, with her arm around his shoulders. He came up to her chin, and they had identical smiles. In another one, from a few years later, she came up to his chin, but they still had identical smiles. She stared at the two photos, and said, "Hankie! I was the one who called him that—he hated it. But we had fun. I admit that I was a terrible tease, but it always made him laugh, so I kept at it. When he was little, I used to tickle him all the time. And then he shot up, and one time I was sitting on the carpet, reading some magazine, and he came over and pushed me down and tickled me until I was squealing and laughing at the same time. I learned my lesson, for sure, but he was such a funny boy!"

I said, "I always wondered why he moved to Texas."

"Well, that's where Carol is from. She grew up in Beaumont, which isn't far from Louisiana. She told me that her family went to Mardi Gras every year. So, anyway, when she got together with Hank, she said she wasn't going to leave. Mama and Papa hadn't decided to move to St. Louis yet. Oh, I mean they talked about moving all the time, but one day it would be Chicago, another day it would be Cleveland, or even Louisville. They may have considered Beaumont. I think Hank decided that Beaumont was fine for him."

I said, "Now they live in Houston, though."

Mom said, "Between you and me, there are so many places to work in Houston that you can jump from job to job, and that's what Hank likes. He says the place is booming."

"How did they meet?"

Mom smiled. She said, "There was this fancy art school in Columbus, and Carol went there during the war. I think it was drawing she wanted to specialize in, and her parents didn't mind. Anyway, boom, they closed down the school during the day at the end of the war, but she could still take classes at night. So one night, Hank was walking past the school, and this girl comes out, and she turns in his direction, and he smiles at her and then he stumbles and falls down, and it was Carol who helped him to his feet, not the other way around. He scraped his elbow, and it was bleeding, so she took him back to her place and cleaned up the scrape and put a bandage on it. That's Carol all over. I do think she's the sweetest person I ever met, but when we see her, I always say, 'Carol, honey, I can't understand a word you are saying!' And then she speaks Italian, because she took a class in that."

"Did she keep drawing?"

"She's made some pictures of the kids, but she's a bit of a perfectionist, so none of them ever suits her."

We showed Grandfather a few more things, and he recognized

them all, including a porkpie hat. When we brought that down to him, he put it on his head, moved it around a little to make it look stylish, then took it off and showed us a little button and a string that went all the way around the hat, above the brim. He told us how he had gone out some night and the wind got really strong. He had to hold the string in order to keep the hat from blowing away. When he decided to take a nap, I told Mom I was going to Old Orchard to buy a few things, and that I would pick her up and take her home after Aunt Lily showed up.

When I got into the car, I reached into my glove compartment and pulled out a CD. I stuck it in the slot without looking at it, and the first song that blared from the speaker was "I Want to Know What Love Is," by Foreigner, a song that I had loved when it first came out, and I had thought about the fact that, at the time, I did know what love was, and had walked away from it. The song went on forever, and I had always loved the way that the singers sounded more and more desperate (and loud). I enjoyed it, and when I got out of my car in front of the bank, where I parked, I thought that Grandfather, Grandmother, and even Mom were giving me a new lesson about what love is, a lesson that maybe I couldn't learn when I was twenty-five, or twenty-three. This did not make me regret my decision about Martin, but it did make me think of it slightly differently, and wonder if I had leapt to the wrong conclusion when I was eavesdropping on his talk with Charlotte when we were together in New York. Maybe he did know what love was, and Charlotte, and the twins, had taught him.

Sometime in July, Uncle Drew decided to take Grandfather to a Cards game. They were playing against the Pirates, and it was a night game. The day didn't start out too hot, and Grandfather was clearly looking forward to it. He said that he hadn't been to a game in maybe twenty years, but the last one he had been to had been terrific—Bob Gibson pitching against the Giants, and winning seven to two. He said, "Well, they came over from San Francisco, and the game was in July, just before the Fourth, and I'm guessing they couldn't take the heat." We ate early (Mom cooked some hamburgers), and then Uncle Drew picked him up. Mom said she would stay at Grandfather's place until Uncle Drew brought Grandfather home, and then Uncle Drew would drop her off. I knew there wasn't any booze at Grandfather's house anymore, so as I walked back to my apartment, I thought Mom was secretly cooperating with my plan to wean her off the booze. The sun was going down, and my walk was breezy and comforting, but about an hour after I got back to my apartment, the phone rang, and it was Uncle Drew, sounding rattled. He said I needed to get over there as quickly as I could, but he couldn't pick me up. I thought of taking my car, but I decided it would be quicker to run. It took me about eight minutes. It wasn't uphill all the way, but it felt like it.

When I got there, things had calmed down. Grandfather was sitting in his favorite chair, and Mom was sitting across from him, where Grandmother had always sat. Uncle Drew was in the dining room, pacing around, and though he was looking at Grandfather, he was trying to keep that to himself. I went over and kissed Grandfather on the cheek and said, "How was the game?"

He said, "Good enough, I suppose."

Uncle Drew raised his hand and summoned me into the dining room and then took me into the kitchen. I said, "Did . . . What . . . ?"

He said, "We were sitting in our seats at the bottom of the second inning, and he stood up and started walking away. I said, 'Hey, Pop!' but he didn't hear me. I figured he was going to the restroom or something, so I followed him, but there was a guy who didn't realize I was coming, and stuck out his leg, which stopped me, and then I saw the old man turn to go down the steps—he stumbled and fell. There is a handrail, but he wasn't holding it, and he bumped his head on it. By the time I got there, a couple of guys had helped him up, but he seemed a little woozy. Just then, there was a big to-do when Ozzie Smith hit a homer and the old man started looking around like he didn't know where he was, so I took him back to the car and brought him home. And I had to help him up the steps. That's when I called you. I was sort of panicking."

We went to the doorway to the living room, and looked at Mom and Grandfather. Grandfather was laughing, and then he said, "No, that's not exactly how it happened. Truth is, Brucie was out in the backyard, and I saw out of the corner of my eye that he was running down the driveway, so I went after him. He did not step into the street, but the car that was coming down the street screeched to a stop, because the woman who was driving it thought he was going to. I picked Brucie up and took him over to her side of the car and she rolled down her window. My goodness, she was in a state. Sweat pouring off her brow. Brucie must have been three. I apologized and I made Brucie apologize, too. He said, 'Am I sorry?' I said he was, and he said, 'What am I sorry for?' and I said that he had scared this lady and then he looked at her and said, 'Boo!' Oh, we both laughed! Lily always said that he did run into the street, but he knew better."

Mom said, "I always imagined the car hitting him and then just rolling over him. Scared me. Maybe that's why I didn't tell you about what happened to Jodie in New York."

Grandfather said, "Sweetie, you are the one who scares yourself. You been like that since forever. I remember in the house in Akron, there was a window that you wouldn't go near. You swore up and down that there was a ghost outside that window. Thing was, the way that room was set, some times during the year, if you stood in front of that window, you would cast a shadow on it, and yes, you were afraid of your own shadow. I mean, you got over it, but you did that on your own. When Mama and I tried to explain it to you and show you what we meant, you didn't believe us."

Uncle Drew and I ambled into the room while Grandfather was telling this story and sat down. We both kept an eye on him, but he seemed to be himself, so I decided not to worry, for now. He told a couple more stories, then yawned, and I put him to bed while Mom and Uncle Drew were straightening things up, and then I heard the door close. I made sure he was asleep. Around nine thirty, I walked back to my place. It was warm, but the moon was out and I enjoyed it. A couple of families were finishing up their backyard barbecues and waved as I passed.

When I got home, I started playing my guitar and working on

some chording that I didn't really understand very well, so by the time I went to bed, it was past midnight, and I didn't get up at my usual time. When I did get up, I saw that it was late, threw on some clothes, and ran all the way again. When I got to the house, it was after eight thirty. I felt guilty, because I thought that Grandfather would be wanting something to eat, but when I walked in the door, it was way too quiet. I ran upstairs, and he was still stretched out on his bed, on his back, with his mouth open, the covers partly thrown off. I stood in the doorway with my heart pounding. I could see that he was breathing, but that didn't really comfort me. I waited for a minute or two, then went over and touched his shoulder. He opened his eyes, and I smiled and said, "Would you like some oatmeal with raisins?" He just stared at me, even though he always liked that, and for a long long minute, I thought he didn't understand what I was saying. He had a bruise, and maybe a bump on the left side of his forehead, and I thought, Concussion, but then he shook his head and sat up, and said, "Double portion, if you don't mind. I'm starving."

At the time, I would have said he seemed okay. He came downstairs and had his breakfast at the table, then he walked around the living room and the dining room, picking up this and that and putting them in different places. There was an old cabinet in the corner of the dining room where they had kept the plates and glasses they used for Thanksgiving and Christmas, and he opened that and looked at the dishware, then he said, "You should take this." He handed me a plate. An elaborate green-and-yellow-floral pattern ran around the edge and the rim looked as if it was etched with gold. The plate itself was cream colored, not white, and I remembered so many meals of turkey and stuffing or ham and mashed potatoes that we had scraped off of these plates. I turned it over. Lenox. I wondered how they had managed to afford that. I said, "Grandfather, I'd love to, but I don't have anywhere to store it, and I wouldn't want it to break." He nodded and wandered away.

Aunt Lily showed up about ten minutes later. I told her about the fall and she nodded. As she was standing there, he said, "Where've you been?"

"Just work and home. Did some laundry, if you can believe that."

He shook his head, but then smiled.

She said, "Even I have to clean up sometime."

He laughed and said, "Now you've reminded me!"

"Of what?"

"Well, we had this potty chair that we used for all the kids, and Martha and Hank used it before you did. I don't know what they say now, but back then, you had to start as soon as the kid could sit up. So your ma would set you on the chair and wait until you had done your business. It went fine, but then you started crawling and you were fast. And then you started walking before you were even a year old! It took you about two months to decide that you wanted the potty chair in the living room so that you could talk to us while you were doing your business. I can't count how many times your ma or I carried it to the back hall, because the bathroom was upstairs, and you pushed it back to the living room!"

Aunt Lily grinned and said, "Well, at least I got my way sometimes!"

But as the summer went on, it didn't seem as though Grandfather was out of his head, it seemed as though he was more and more depressed. Uncle Drew and Aunt Louise agreed with me; Mom said, "Who isn't?"; and Aunt Lily said, "Don't ask me. I have no idea."

We stopped watching the news because of the killings—first Dahmer, then the shootings in Utah, then in Killeen, Texas. I had to explain to Grandfather three or four times that Killeen was seventy-five miles north of Austin, so Brucie wasn't in danger, and nowhere near Houston, so Uncle Hank and his family weren't either. Each time I explained, he said, "Everyone has guns in Texas." I asked him if he had had guns, and he nodded, but then wouldn't say anything more about them. Just before Thanksgiving, when I was sitting across from him at breakfast, he said, "Your grandmother ever tell you about Leo?"

I said, "Who's Leo?" I was wondering if there was a lost child, born before Mom, dead at six months or something like that.

Grandfather said, "Leo Conrad. That was her boyfriend when I met her. Fact is, she did tell me when we saw each other the second time that she was already engaged, and even though she liked me, well . . ."

I didn't say anything, and Grandfather looked out the window and sighed. "Never said a thing about him after that. One time, maybe around the time your mom was born, I got a little frantic with jealousy. Don't know why, so I went through all of her things, and I did find a photo of a young man, her age, I would guess, spitting image of Jimmy Cagney. I wanted to tear it into shreds, but I put it back. I never asked about him and I never, I don't know, asked whether she really and truly loved me." He swallowed hard, as if he was choking up, and turned away.

I said, "She did. She told me she did. She said the best thing she hoped for me was that I would find someone like you."

He said, "What do you think of dreams?"

I said, "I don't know."

He said, "The only dream that I have had that I remember is of your grandmother on some street with Jimmy Cagney, glancing at me and then walking away." He closed his eyes and shook his head. I thought of Martin and Charlotte, but I didn't say that your own feeling of love is what matters, because you can't know what someone else's feeling of love is. I leaned toward him and took his hand. We squeezed. When Aunt Lily showed up, I didn't tell her what he had said, but I did tell her that he seemed depressed, still. She said, "I'll go get him a Big Mac. That perks him up, even if he doesn't finish the whole thing."

After she left, I went over to him and said, "Come on, let's have a little walk. It's not as gloomy as it was this morning. I think we both could use some sun." We went carefully down the back steps and walked around the yard, past the fence, along the driveway, around the back porch, and then toward the lilac bushes, and then we stood where the yard began to slope down to the street and I said, "I just love this house." He kissed me on the cheek, and I put my arm around him as we went back inside. I sat him at the kitchen table, and I heard Aunt Lily pull in. I said, "Aunt Lily has a surprise for you." When she came in, I kissed him again and left.

The next day it was raining. I had a good raincoat, and I didn't mind walking in the rain. I put on some sturdy shoes and headed out at the right time. I always wanted to get there between seven thirty and eight because that was around the time he woke up. I tried not to pay much attention to the trees and houses along the walk, but the rain always made the leaves and the trunks and the houses more vivid than sunshine did. The fall foliage was almost gone, but what was left glistened. The house was once again silent. I went to the back hall and took off my raincoat and my shoes. On my way through the kitchen, I grabbed a muffin that I'd bought two days previously, and a napkin.

As I walked up the stairs, I listened for sounds, in Grandfather's bedroom, or in the bathroom, but I didn't hear anything. I thought maybe the rain, or some wind, had kept him awake. The roof of the front porch was right outside his window, and I had often heard the rain pounding on the roof and then sort of bouncing off his window. The door was half-closed. I pushed it open.

In the morning gloom, Grandfather was lying in the bed, on his stomach, his face deep into his pillow, which he liked to be thick, because he said sleeping on a thin pillow hurt his neck. I spoke, and then I touched his arm. It was cool and stiff. Uncle Drew later told me that it takes a body about three hours to start to stiffen up, so we all agreed that he had died sometime after midnight. My first response wasn't shock, or even sadness. Maybe because of the day before, or maybe because of the rain, I felt myself nodding, and then I pulled his sheet and blanket up to his shoulders and kissed the back of his head. His hair still smelled like the shampoo we had used to wash it. Then I looked at my watch. It was 8:23. I went over and sat in the chair that he had sat in when Grandmother died, and I waited until nine.

I knew Uncle Drew was at work, so I called his office and told the secretary, then I called Aunt Lily and Mom, who were both still sleeping. Aunt Lily jumped out of bed, but I had to explain what I had seen three times to Mom before she understood. When she did understand, she said, “Oh, no.” Then she said, “There’s someone at the door,” and put the phone down without hanging up. I could dimly hear talking in the background. I waited for another two minutes, then I hung up. Aunt Lily was there in five minutes, and Aunt Louise showed up with Mom in about fifteen minutes. Uncle Drew had moved his offices to Clayton, so he didn’t take long, either. We stood by the door to Grandfather’s room, staring at him, then we hugged and went in. That was when the crying began.

But it didn’t last. We all knew that we were crying for ourselves, not Grandfather, who we knew was glad to go. He had said more than once that looking around at not only Grandmother, but also at the other old people he saw in stores or parks, or even old folks’ homes, didn’t make him want to live for very long. And then he had lived until he was ninety-four, sane, smart, but lucky? Only in some ways. At least, I thought, walking back to my apartment later in the day, when the sun had come out and the clouds floated like cotton candy, he had known that we loved him.

The funeral was gloomy and small—no preacher, some music, lots of eulogies. Uncle Hank and Aunt Carol came up from Texas, as did Brucie. Allison and Darryl were there, and one of Mom’s cousins from Akron, who came with his wife. It was close to Thanksgiving, so this was our substitute—a sort of banquet at the Chase Park Plaza, near the Muny and our old house on Skinker. No one talked about whether Grandfather had somehow killed himself. I suppose we all thought that it was none of our business.

12

I CONSIDERED MOVING back to New York. My apartment in St. Louis was cheap, so I didn't have to sublet it. And I missed the Catskills and my little log cabin. In the spring, I drove there and stayed for two weeks. I was hoping there would be leaves, grass, and flowers, because St. Louis was blooming, but there was mostly fog, a bit of snow, plenty of daffodils, and at least no ice on the roads. I had told Jackie I was going there, and she had talked about meeting me and staying for a few days, but since we no longer shared the car, she didn't call me and ask me to come get her.

The first day, I took the circular route to Russell's in Bovina, northwest through the mountains and the state forests, then home by way of New Kingston. It took me about an hour, but I loved winding around through the mountains. I bought what I could—some eggs and bacon and milk. Then, the next day, I took the easier trip to Margaretville, put my groceries in the car, and walked down Main Street. I was a little surprised by how the people, mostly tourists, I thought, who were walking the streets and looking around in Margaretville, sort of perked me up. I went into shops, even though there was nothing I wanted to buy, and watched people chatting and laughing. Every so often I smiled at something someone said, and sometimes they smiled back at me, but more often, I got a glance, and then the person would turn away. It was midafternoon when I drove back to the cabin, and as soon as I walked in, I went to my guitar and started playing and singing. The cabin still had good acoustics. When the sun began to set, I lit all the lights and went into the kitchen. But even though I had bought a filet mignon and a bag of frozen onion rings, I wasn't hungry. I went to the door, opened it, and stared out at the mountains that rose to the west. The sky was clear, with plenty of stars, and I looked at them, and at the dark limbs of the trees swaying as the wind strengthened. I left the door open and walked around to the back of the cabin, which was maybe twenty feet from a hillside that went up gradually for a while, then turned into a mountain. Everything was fragrant, though at this time of day, I couldn't identify any odors in particular, nor could I see the wildflowers. It was heaven on earth, but, I thought, if this was heaven, then it was a lonely heaven. I got into the car and drove into town. There was one bar, and I remembered it being crowded in the past, but for some reason, there were only three or four customers—maybe it was too early in the day.

The bartender looked familiar, but he asked me if I was new in town, and I said that I was. I had no idea what to drink, because I didn't like beer and I had to drive home. There were locally sourced wines on the menu, which I had never had, so I ordered a glass and drank it slowly. It was sort of hard to get my head around the idea of New York growing its own wines, but who wasn't, these days?

I behaved exactly as I should have—one glass of wine, some sort of tomato soup, and some crackers with an artichoke spinach dip. I paid, left a good tip, and drove home. And guess what, I had forgotten to close the door. But the cabin was so isolated that it never even occurred to me that anyone would walk in. And no one did, but there was a bird, not a crow or a cardinal, but some type I didn't recognize, perched on the back of one of the chairs in the kitchen. It turned its head and cheeped as I entered, but didn't move. It seemed to be staring at something.

I watched it for a minute or two, and even thought I would let it stay, but I didn't want to leave the door open because I knew it would get too cold to sleep. I stepped toward it and raised my arms, and it flew upward and landed on one of the beams that crisscrossed the room below the roof. I didn't know what to do, and there was something about this, added to my lonely meal and my sunset walk around the house, that changed my life.

I was practical. I put my guitar in its case and turned out the lights. I went into the bedroom and closed the door, and I put on warm pajamas and got into bed. I listened as best I could for any sounds, but I didn't hear much. I hummed myself to sleep, and when I got up in the morning, I went straight to the front door and opened it wide. The bird, which was then perched on the back of a kitchen chair near the eastern window, flew straight out the door. I got out a mop and a rag and cleaned up the droppings, six in all, including one on the kitchen table and one in the bathroom, which gave me a laugh. Then I threw the rags in the bin, took a shower, and made myself some breakfast. The valley was filled with bird noises, rustlings in the bushes, the sounds of deer creeping here and there. I knew that there were bears and coyotes and even cougars around—and I lived far enough into the valley to see them, but I never had. However, I realized, I lived too deeply in the valley to see many people, and even those I did see were never close enough to recognize. The cabin I had bought was my dream house, but then I remembered how the previous owners had had it for maybe three years, and the Realtor had smiled and said, "Well, they were not unhappy to leave. I think they found a spot down by Fleischmanns, not far from town."

I had said, "How could anyone leave this spot? I've never seen a place so beautiful!" And she had smiled, and said, "So, you're ready to sign the purchase agreement?" I had signed it with a flourish. But now . . .

But now I realized that even though I loved the cabin and the spot and, in some ways, the isolation, I was heading down a path that was getting narrower and narrower, or, let's say, lonelier and lonelier. I had family members, but not friends, or so it seemed.

For the next ten days, I practiced, not my guitar, which I was addicted to—I cut that practice down to two hours a day, though when I was in the woods, I did sing. I practiced being friendly, walking in more crowded areas, and actually visiting towns. I also tried to get Jackie to come, but she said that she was so busy that she couldn't take the time off. I could tell by the tone of her voice that she didn't want to take the time off. The key was to pay attention to whether I wanted to go into town or to stay in the cabin. If I wanted to stay in the cabin, I got up, put on a jacket (or a raincoat), and went into our town, or to Margaretville or Fleischmanns, and walked down the street. The first couple of days, I watched how people reacted to and greeted one another. I also paid attention to the people who were walking together—how they talked and what their body language was. Then I would walk past a store window and observe myself. I saw that there was something about my posture that might seem intimidating, or maybe unwelcoming. My neck was straight and my chin was down—I am not that tall, five foot eight—but my natural way of walking made me seem taller. I suspected that I walked this way because I had lived in the city for so long, and if you walked alone at night you had to indicate with your posture that you could easily be carrying some weapon for self-defense. But it was also true that over the years, I had ignored random flirtations and just walked on. I went into a few shops and asked for things—not because I wanted them but because I wondered what my habitual way of inquiring was. It was this: stand up straight, no smile, a little impatience if they didn't have the item, and maybe a scowl (I didn't look in mirrors, but I could feel that cross my face). Surely that was the reason that some of the shopkeepers I had talked to over the years had gotten irritated. In a grocery store in Fleischmanns, I eavesdropped on a woman who came in looking for penne pasta. She said, "Sorry, I am looking for the penne. I can't find it anywhere. Could you help me, please?"

The stocker said, "Don't have that. There's fettuccini, fusilli, and farfalle."

She said, "Okay, thanks. Do you recommend any in particular?"

He said, "Me, I like the farfalle."

She smiled, and he said, "Good with a Bolognese sauce."

She said, "That sounds great! Thank you!"

In the space of a minute or so, the stocker had gone from being gruff to relaxing, and then he watched her pick up a box of fusilli as well as a bag of farfalle. I followed her to the counter and then out of the store (I hadn't bought anything). She walked down Main Street, past the shops and the church on the left, and the gaily painted late-nineteenth-century houses on the right. She waved to and greeted the people she met, stopped a few times to chat with people who were tending their gardens or standing on their porches. Eventually she turned up Little Red Kill Road, and just after she did so, a woman about her age came out of a nice redbrick house, greeted her, and walked a ways up the road with her. I stayed behind them. The hill steepened, and that woman turned around. I kept walking, consciously adopting my usual manner. The woman glanced at me and looked away, then sped up. I waited until she went into her house, and then turned around, resisting the temptation to continue up Little Red Kill. When I walked back down Main Street toward my car, I made myself relax, look around, smile at whoever I saw, and I even traded a glance and a laugh with a woman who was holding both of her toddler's hands as he tried to pull away from her. She rolled her eyes and picked him up.

After the first two days, I went into shops and did my best to chat up the shopkeepers. I asked about the products, but also the history of the shop—how long had it been here, who had started it, how was business in the winter. The fact was that as I acted curious, I got curious, and I actually bought some items, especially handmade ones (and there were plenty of those in the Catskills). The shopkeepers loved to talk about who had made a certain clay pot or knitted a certain scarf or pair of mittens, and it turned out that I enjoyed hearing about them.

On the days when I wanted to explore the towns, I wandered around the valley, or found a trail and stayed in the wilderness areas. I did this because I loved nature, but also, I could think about why I was so reserved, and why, in fact, I resembled Mom in this way. I thought maybe that was why she was so adept at hiding her drinking—she was adept at hiding everything. I wondered if maybe AA would have been good for her, would have helped her make some friends.

After those ten days, I closed up the cabin and gave myself a test. I drove into the city, parked not far from my apartment, and waited for Jackie to get home from work. It was getting late, and here she came, walking from the subway station, umbrella in one hand and briefcase in the other. I jumped out of the car and ran over to her. I said, "There you are! How are you?" I was much more effusive than usual, and maybe she thought I was faking it, because she laughed and said, "Are you really Jodie? Are you drunk?"

I said, "Not yet! Where do you want to have dinner?"

She said, "Who's buying?"

"I am!"

She said, "I have a better idea."

We went to her apartment and ate leftover risotto and leftover lentil soup. I realized that I had forgotten something and said, "Oh, shit! I didn't make a hotel reservation!"

She put me up (which meant sleeping on her couch wrapped up in a blanket), but that also meant that we enjoyed chatting over breakfast (early, because she had to get to work by eight) and I felt like we were friends again—one step in the right direction.

I left at seven thirty and took the route past State College. I'd planned to walk around the campus, but the closer I got to St. Louis, the more eager I was to get there, partly because I began to be a little worried about Mom. Even so, of course I followed the speed limits. I stopped for gas outside of Pittsburgh and Terre Haute, ate a couple of hot dogs, and got to my apartment, wide awake, at exactly ten thirty, put the car in the garage, and fell into bed. In the dark, the landscapes I had seen sliding past the windows all day ran through my mind. I think I fell asleep somewhere between Dayton and Indianapolis, with the sun going down in my eyes, and the shadows stretching along the roadside.

When I opened my eyes, I was looking out my bedroom window toward the row of one-story houses set on the hill across from our building. The grass was damply green but the sun was beginning to shine through the trees off to the east, and the street glittered. The first thing I did was walk over to Deer Creek Park, and after walking around there, I was hungry enough to walk to Big Bend and have a muffin and some bacon for breakfast. When I got back to my apartment around ten, I was ready. I got into my car and drove to Mom's, feeling guilty every inch of the way that I had left her alone for twelve days, and hadn't even called her to tell her I was back.

I parked about two doors down from her place, and saw when I started walking there that her front door was open, another bad sign. I looked around the steps and on the porch, imagining that she had gotten so smashed that she fell down, but there she was, coming out of the door, neatly dressed in a black skirt and, of all things, one of the sweaters that Grandmother had knitted over the years for anyone who would wear it. She didn't see me—she turned, closed the door, tested the lock, and then she heard me and looked.

The unimaginable happened—I ran to her and we hugged. I said, "How are you? Are you okay?"

She said, "How do I look?"

"Like you're happy that someone knitted you a sweater!"

"Well, I did always like this one. Cables are perfect for this time of year. Don't tell Lily that I sneaked it out of Mama's closet. It was way too big for Mama, but she liked to wear it in the winter like a blanket."

We walked to the street and turned toward Uncle Drew's place. I said, "Are you going to Uncle Drew's for breakfast?"

"No. I had breakfast. Louise is taking me somewhere."

She glanced away, then glanced back, and said, "AA meeting."

I stopped and said, "When did you start doing that?"

"The day after you left. For now, I go every day. There's this one group that meets in the morning, because it helps the members stay sober all day. I like that part." We got to Uncle Drew's place, and Aunt Louise was already by the car. She waved to us, opened the door for Mom, then gave me a kiss and said, "How was your trip? You can go on inside. The door is unlocked, and there's a coffee cake on the counter. I'd love to hear all about it."

They drove off, and I recoiled, but then I did what I had done in the Catskills—I made myself relax my posture, smile a couple of times, and then go in the house and wait for Aunt Louise. I was glad I did, because I was reminded that this house had always been welcoming—neatly decorated but not intimidating, clean but not sparkling clean. I remembered that one time, in the sixties, Aunt Louise had hired a maid, because that was what people did then. Her name was Lizzy, and she looked about Aunt Louise's age, so she would have been in her thirties. She was African American, her family lived in Florissant, and at Aunt Louise's place, she had her own room, which was off the kitchen. On the weekends, she stayed with her family. Aunt Louise gave her a TV, which we could hear when we came into the kitchen late at night. I think she worked for Aunt Louise for about a year, but then she was gone, and Aunt Louise went back to doing her own work. I walked into Lizzy's old room and looked around. One of the kids was using it now.

When Aunt Louise got back, I said, "You know who I just was thinking of? Lizzy."

Aunt Louise said, "Oh, I think of her, too. She put up with a lot."

"Really? Too many kids?"

"No! She had to put up with me! We paid her well, but I was always following her around and suggesting she do some job in a different way. It wasn't just the cooking. I took that over after about a week. Back then I was so particular about how clean everything had to be, and how many times she had to mop the floor or even wash the windows. About ten years ago, I ran into her at some Kroger's, and I apologized to her. She laughed. She said that the woman I had set her up with, who lived in Creve Coeur, let her do everything her own way, and she worked there for twenty years, until her back started to go. I was so relieved that she didn't remember me as a royal bitch!"

"Did she ever have kids or anything?"

"No. Her sister had five, so she had to work to help her sister raise them. I think the youngest was just born when she came here. I will say that she didn't really approve of the way her sister was raising her kids. She spanked them a lot, as I remember. Lizzy talked to me about that a couple of times. Even then, I thought she was more patient than I was, especially with me!"

That was a good start to our conversation, which circled around Uncle Drew and the kids, referred to Grandfather and Grandmother, and then homed in on me, in the Catskills, and finally, on Mom. Aunt Louise said, "What did she tell you?"

"Only that she was going to AA now. I thought about getting her to go when I first came back to St. Louis. I even went to a meeting and pretended I was the alcoholic to see what it was like, but I didn't think it would work for her."

Aunt Louise said, "I never thought she would listen to anyone in our family, so I think you were right. It wasn't me or Drew who suggested it. What she told me was that the day you left, she got up and started in with the stingers first thing in the morning. Then she was walking down Argonne—she didn't remember where she was going—and she fell off the curb. Thank God there was only one car at that corner. That guy jumped out and picked her up. Then he realized she was smashed. He drove slowly down the street and when she recognized her place, he took her inside and closed the door. Then he came by the next day and took her to that AA meeting."

I said, "I can't believe she let him do that. She always thinks some stranger is going to pull out a knife and do her in."

Aunt Louise laughed. "Well, you should see him. Incredibly handsome guy, I'm guessing about your age. He lives over near Mary Queen of Peace. Three kids. The wife invited your mom for dinner this Saturday. You should go along."

The way we managed to include me was that I drove Mom to the house, a sweet house with a big yard and a long driveway on West Lockwood. I got out, said hi (in a smiling, friendly way), and went around to help Mom out of the front seat. Then I introduced myself, and of course they invited me to stay for supper. His name was Dave Rogers, the wife's name was Ava Kingston, and he looked like Jim Morrison might have looked if he had managed to reach forty, but with a smile. Ava looked like Alanis Morissette as a blonde. As we walked into the house, I made myself relax, actually said hi to the kids, who were maybe twelve, nine, and six (all boys). There was a piano in the living room, open, with some music, so that was how I started the conversation—Who was taking the lessons? It turned out to be the oldest boy, Davie, and when I asked him what he was playing, he got that look, the look of someone who has been sucked into music and will never get out. Ava glanced at him and said, "Let's eat dinner first, Davie, while it's still hot. You can play for us after, okay?"

He nodded, but reluctantly.

Dave, Ava, and the two younger boys, Fred and Jonathan, were very good at talking, laughing, complimenting, asking questions. Davie kept looking at the piano, and I could see his fingers wiggle as if he was practicing various chords. I was sitting across from him, and I said, "I'm a musician."

Ava said, "That's what I wanted to be, but I could never make myself practice. Maybe if I . . ." She laughed, then said, "I was obsessed with the harp. Do you remember Dorothy Ashby?"

I nodded.

"She was my model."

I said, "So you liked jazz?"

Ava nodded. Davie scowled, and Ava laughed and said, "Davie is all Bach and Beethoven, with just a little Purcell thrown in."

I wondered if Davie was a Leon in the making—Leon had gone on to have something of a career, performing regular concerts and putting out a few records.

Then Fred piped up and said, "I'm going to play for the Cards. Shortstop." I thought, You're way too cute for that, but I didn't say anything.

Mom didn't say much, but she laughed at the right times, and nodded and smiled. She was friendly toward Ava, but more often she looked at Dave, and when she did, her face was suffused with pleasure. He didn't look like anyone in our family, nor did he look like my father. I thought that maybe he looked like the son Mom had hoped for, and then she'd had me. It was Ava who drew Mom out. The way she did it was to alternate a tidbit about herself with a question for Mom—Ava had grown up in one of those brick houses on Juniata Street. Did Mom or I know where that was? South of Tower Grove Park. She had always loved the botanic garden. Where did Mom grow up? Mom said, "Akron," then, "Ohio," as if Ava didn't know that. Ava said, "Oh! We have relatives in Columbus! My brother and his kids live there." Mom said, "My brother and I loved to go to Columbus once we could drive. I would sneak away . . ." Then she tapered off. Ava said, "My brother's kids preferred the house there to the one where their mother lived, in Cincinnati, but she was nice. I liked her." Mom said, "It's hard to be stuck with only one parent." She glanced at me. Ava said, "Between you and me, I wasn't surprised she dumped him. You know that song 'Lazy Bones'?"

I began to sing, in a low voice, " 'Lazy bones, sleeping in the sun. How you 'spect to get your day's work done?' "

Everyone laughed, and Dave gave Ava a kiss on the cheek.

By the time we'd eaten dessert (strawberry ice cream), Mom seemed as relaxed and friendly as I had ever seen her.

Davie played a gavotte by Bach. He was dedicated, and he got the rhythm right, but he wasn't a Leon. I watched him carefully, and he went at it like I did—with dedication and concentration, traits that I thought might make up for his lack of natural talent.

ON THE WAY HOME, I said, "Dave doesn't seem like an alcoholic."

Mom said, "Well, he's been going to meetings for a couple of years. His mom is Irish."

I said, "I don't think you should say those sorts of things . . ."

She said, "No, it's him who told me that. He said that some people inherit what you might call a resistance to alcohol. You drink as a kid, and it doesn't affect you, so you keep at it, and you become addicted before you understand it, because you don't fall down or even feel woozy, but then one day, you're reaching for the bottle and you feel like you can't stop yourself. He said that when he met Ava, two beers or a single shot of bourbon would knock her out, so she never went too far."

I made a left turn, and she continued, "A couple of years ago, when the boys were in bed, she said something that offended him, and he turned and lifted his hand, and realized that he was going to hit her, and that's what stopped him. Our AA was the first one he found, and he still goes."

Mom made another friend in AA, too, a woman who taught math at Washington U. Nancy was about forty, unmarried, from Chicago. She was a full professor, specializing in algebra and trigonometry, and lived in an interesting house on Lindell—the bricks it was built with were different colors, and the entryway had a tall, arched window that could have been stained glass if Nancy had decided to start up a religious sect for calculators. She had a good sense of humor, and said that she had taken up drinking because math was boring, but she didn't dare tell that to her students. I enjoyed talking to her. She had been in AA for three or four years, and she told me that what she liked about it was the way that the members turned their daily experiences into stories rather than equations. But she also talked about how, when she was in high school and college (New Trier, Smith), she had seen mathematicians as detectives for scientists. It was as though the physicist or astronomer was Dr. Watson and the mathematician was Sherlock Holmes. The scientist was interested in what and the mathematician was interested in how, in the logical system that would solve the problem. She had also been aware that very few women became mathematicians, and that there was a long-standing prejudice against women as not being logical enough or smart enough, and that had pushed her on, too—in grad school, she had been the only woman in three of her classes, and she had shown off her skill at being able to do math in her head. She remembered a game that she and some of her classmates had played, where they had to multiply and divide complicated numbers without even a pencil, and she had almost always won. So, impressing the guys, and also her professors, had driven her on, too. But then she had gotten bored and started running—got up to six miles a day, because running was easy for her. She said to me, "I always thought I was lucky because I had talent, or gifts, or whatever. But if it's too easy, then it's not interesting enough to hold you. I'd always liked liqueurs, you know, Chambord, pastis, because of the use they made of herbs and fruits, so, believe it or not, I started mixing cocktails as a game. I was even ready to buy a house out in Chesterfield and start my own herb garden and go into the business, but then I found that I had a problem that I couldn't solve on my own." Then she said, "That was a piece of luck."

One time, Mom and I were at Nancy's place for dinner, and Mom went to the bathroom, which was upstairs, and Nancy said, "I love hearing the stories your mom tells about her life. They are so much more interesting than mine."

I nodded and smiled as if I knew what she was talking about, but I realized that in fact I didn't. Mom had never told me any stories. Sitting around the dinner table at Grandmother and Grandfather's, Mom had been the silent one. Sometimes, someone told a story about Mom. (Uncle Drew told one from when he was seven and Mom was seventeen—he was running around, and he stumbled and almost fell down, but she caught him. He fell against her stomach, and it was as flat and hard as a rock. He didn't say anything, but he went into her bedroom after dinner, when she was helping Grandmother with the dishes, and discovered what a girdle was. Mom hadn't laughed at that one, but she did say, "Lastex! Your very own rubber!" Then she shivered.)

Mom came back from the bathroom. When she sat down, she said to me, "Jodie, sweetheart, what did you think of that incident on *Saturday Night Live*?"

I said, "I have no idea what you're talking about."

Nancy said, "Oh, the Sinéad O'Connor thing?"

Mom nodded, then she explained to me that Sinéad had sung a basically a cappella protest song, then torn up a picture of the Pope in front of the camera.

I said, "I'm sorry I missed that. Was it funny?"

Mom said, "Not at all. She was dead serious. She looked so beautiful, even without hair. Do you think she has alopecia?"

I said, "I think she shaves it. I love some of her songs. Of course 'Nothing Compares 2 U.'" Then I said, "Frankly, I hope she isn't as sad as she looks in the video. I hope that the guy who directed the video told her to put it on."

Mom said, "She isn't faking it." We all sighed.

It was interesting to me as a singer to see the reactions, especially the pushback to the incident on *SNL*. I guess I had never thought about anyone in the music business defending the Pope—Madonna did. But of course, sales of O'Connor's music shot up—and I bought an album, too, but not because of her protest, simply because I wanted to see what younger women artists, especially edgy ones, were doing. I can't say that I was practicing in order to resurrect my career. I didn't have to resurrect it, thanks to Uncle Drew, but thinking about little Davie playing the piano made me want to try new things and see how I could understand them. Because it was October, the perfect time of year to wander around Webster, I wrote some songs about that time of year—what I remembered compared to what I saw now. One day, I even walked all the way to Mom's on Argonne, which was a good five miles, but then I couldn't walk back because I was so tired. Mom gave me a scoop of chocolate ice cream and called Aunt Louise, who took me home.

NANCY AND AVA taught me to make friends. On the Saturday morning after the World Trade Center bombing I realized I had to get out of my apartment, because I had been going back and forth all night about what might happen and where. I called Jackie, who was not as freaked out as I was, and I even calculated how many blocks it was from the World Trade Center to the apartment (ninety-three). It was not the event that 9/11 would be, but somehow, it was more shocking, maybe because that was when the impossible became possible once again. I suppose that in the thirty-one years since the Cuban

Missile Crisis, I had gotten used to being alive, and thinking of death as a thoughtful moment, as it had been with my grandmother and grandfather.

I drove around a bit, then I dropped by Ava's house. The two younger boys were jumping into a pile of leaves that was in the front yard. Ava was watching them from inside the house, and she saw me come up the walk and opened the door. I could hear Davie struggling through something on the piano. Ava said, "How lovely to see you!" I did my best not to look like I was panicking, so maybe I looked like some determined missionary trying to recruit her. I squeezed her hand, stepped inside. She looked out the window again. I said, "Are you nervous about the Trade Center bombing?"

She said, "Of course, but for now, I'm just watching Fred to make sure he doesn't push Jonathan around. At least they're both in the same place. The hardest thing is when one is in the backyard, one is in the front yard, and one is on the roof." She smiled.

I said, "On the roof?"

"Well, at the piano, but do you remember going on the roof of your house or your garage when you were a kid?"

I shook my head, and just then, she stepped out the door and called out, "Fred! Watch it!" Fred stepped back, and Jonathan ran in a circle around the pile of leaves. She said, "We did that. There was a gap between the top rail on the fence and the roof of the garage. We had to grab the edge of the gutter and pull ourselves up. I don't know how we did it. Or why!" The way she talked about these things made me believe that life goes on.

Just then, Davie barked out, "Goddamn it!"

Ava and I exchanged a glance. She rolled her eyes, and without asking, I went into the living room. Davie was sitting on the bench, his hands raised, staring at the music. When he saw me, he said, "I'm not supposed to say that."

I said, "Musicians say that all the time."

Davie said, "How do you know?"

"That's what I am."

"Oh. Yeah. You said that. What instrument do you play?"

"Guitar."

"Classical?"

"No. Different styles. Pop, folk, jazz." He looked unimpressed, so I said, "I've put out a few records."

That did the trick. I bent down and looked at the music. It was a Bach cantata. I said, "Did your piano teacher assign that? It looks hard."

Davie shook his head. He said, "All the stuff she assigns is boring."

"You want to show me one?"

He reached over to the music stack and handed me a Gershwin piece, "Walking the Dog." I turned it over, and, in a way, I could see how it might look boring, but I remembered hearing Leon, or someone in one of the practicing rooms in college, playing it. I had paused, impressed by the peppy good nature of the piece and the performance. As I remembered, it was repetitive, yes, but it was also short enough not to get boring if you played it in a lively, and even amusing, manner. I said, "Oh, I always liked this one! It's one of those pieces that puts you in a good mood."

Davie said, "Can you play it?"

I said, "I don't play the piano, but I can sing the melody." I started, "La la la la la LAAh!" reading the sheet music. Then I said, "Sometimes, when it gets played, people stand up and dance around." I handed it to him and said, "Try it. Make it bright!"

He set it up and started playing, and he did follow instructions. After the first three measures, I started dancing around the room, and he was familiar enough with the music that he could watch me a bit. When he finished and I sat down again, he said, "My mom and dad put on records and dance like that."

I said, "Dancing is so much fun!" I did not say "good for you." You never tell moody boys that something is good for you.

Ava didn't come into the room. I said, "Okay, let me see what you can do with the cantata." He put it on the rack and played the first two pages slowly, and then, when he reached up to turn the page, he knocked the music off the rack. I picked it up, turned the page, set it on the rack, and he went on. He was able to get to the end, but then he sighed and looked sort of blue. I said, "Davie, it's a beautiful piece, and you do a good job with it, but if you want to really make it work, you can't play it over and over—at least, that's my experience—because then you stop hearing what you are actually playing, so you don't know if you're improving. What you are hearing is all the times you've played it kind of melting into one another. I think you need to take a break."

He reached for another piece. I said, "No, I mean go outside and take a walk or something."

He said, "Well, I go to school all week. Saturday and Sunday are my only real practicing days."

I said, "Even so. Around the block a couple of times. When you're walking around the block, you'll hear what you just played."

He sighed. Then I said, "Here's a funny thing. Lots of times, the thing you want to do is disappointing, and the thing you don't want to do is fun. That's maybe the best thing I learned from going onstage."

Davie said, "Okay."

There was a silence, and then Ava knocked on the door between the kitchen and the living room. She said, "Lunchtime! Baloney." Davie stuck out his tongue, but he did laugh. Ava said, "Oh, sorry! I meant grilled ham and cheese!"

He jumped up. At least he liked to eat.

Ava said, "Jodie! You want to stay?"

I knew she meant: Do you want to tell me what happened?

I didn't know many mothers outside of my family, though of course I had seen them everywhere, and I thought they always looked frazzled or tired or annoyed. I decided that if I was going to let her ask me questions about Davie, I was going to ask her some questions about being a mother. The boys ate their sandwiches (and I ate mine, too). Davie went back into the living room, but then he came out again and said, "I'm going for a walk."

Fred said, "I want to come along."

Ava said, "Okay, but just go around the block. Algonquin, Jackson. Don't go near the tracks." She looked at me and said, "They go to Clark, and they have to cross the tracks to get to school. But I don't want to worry about them every day of the week." Then she said, "Jonathan, you should finish your Lego building. Dad said he would buy you another set if you finish this one." Davie and Fred headed out the door (Davie was the one who was careful to close it), and Jonathan skipped up the stairs to his room. Ava said, "Fifteen minutes of peace!"

She put the plates in the sink, and turned toward me with her automatic smile. I said, "He's got the right set of talents, but I can tell that there is someone he compares himself to."

Ava said, "I'm guessing Sheila Bancroft. She lives on Sherwood. But she plays the violin. Everyone says she's a genius."

I said, "I had a friend like that in college. She started playing the cello when she was six, and everyone, she told me, had made a big deal of it, so much so that when she got to college, she became an English major. I was crazy about her, and we really related, but she got so remote that we all started to worry about her. I wish there was some way to keep track of your old friends." I didn't say anything about the abortion. "Anyway, my guess is that she had played in so many orchestras by the time she got to college that she felt like she was used, and maybe used up. My experience is that it's better to have to work on it and solve it like a puzzle. Then you get to stay in the background and figure it out for yourself."

"Did you tell him that?"

"More or less. I told him to take breaks and, I don't know, work on putting some feelings into the music instead of trying to do it exactly right every time."

Ava said, "That sounds good to me."

I said, "Remember when everyone you knew had seventeen brothers and sisters and half the time, the mom didn't have any idea where they were?"

"Like on the roof," said Ava. "Yeah. When Dave and I tied the knot, we agreed on two, because Dave had read that book, *The Population Bomb*. Remember that one?"

I shook my head.

"Basically, it said that we would all be starving to death by now. But not so far. Anyway, we agreed on two, but then there was an episode of too much booze and where is the rubber and oh, that doesn't matter, didn't you just have your period? And then, out of the blue, here comes Jonathan. Well, he is a darling, and why wouldn't he be, given who his father is?"

And now I was moved to make a confession. I said, "I was afraid to have children. Just panicked." And I realized that I had been—it wasn't just Martin's future, isolated in the countryside, it was the thought of being surrounded by beings that I had no understanding of, and, since I was an only child, had never known. Would there have been a nanny? I hadn't thought of that, but I also wouldn't have wanted some strange older woman telling the kids what to do.

Ava said, "Well, you do have a career."

Now I felt stuck, because I didn't know what to say or what to ask. She helped me. She said, "These days, you shouldn't have to choose between a career and children, but it turns out that you do."

"Did you have a plan?"

"Dave and I met in law school, and I got my degree. I was going to specialize in environmental law and live in Washington, DC, and make those congressmen do their jobs. I did get hired by a firm there, and Dave got hired here. But, you know, a long-distance relationship isn't very eco-friendly, and I missed him. I also didn't think that the firm I was working for was having much impact." She sighed.

I said, "Did he think about joining you there?"

"He says he did. I can't say for sure. But if you have a family, it's hard to choose where to live around there. And then you drive around Webster or Kirkwood and you can't resist."

I said, "I know what you mean."

The boys came back in the house, and Davie said, "We went around twice. Once each way." Ava and I glanced at each other. I think we both noticed that he seemed more relaxed.

Fred said, "We saw a fox!"

Davie said, "It was a fox terrier!"

The next time I talked to Ava, she said that they argued about this for three days, which included many more walks around the block, looking for that dog.

When I left Ava's, I realized that I hadn't thought about the bombing at all, not even when she mentioned that book. That was a comfort.

This conversation made me think of Nancy, but the first person I told about it was Mom. My plan was to help her understand Dave and Ava a little bit, but she linked it directly to me—not the current me, but the me she was stuck with when she was twenty-seven. She said, "What was that show I was in? Oh, *Meet Me in St. Louis*! That made me laugh. Some hotel in the Catskills. Well, I was so wrapped up in rehearsals that I couldn't think of another thing. 'Skip to My Lou' was really fun, kicking up our legs and then dancing around. It wasn't till the show was over and we were back in New York that I realized that I was pregnant! What a putz, as they would have said at that hotel. But you can't regret that sort of thing, because then you wouldn't have the ones you love!"

I realized that she was talking about not having gotten an abortion, but I didn't say anything. Instead, I said, "There must have been some sort of show that you missed . . ."

"Well, there was, but it was Off Broadway. *Oklahoma!,* which I had never liked. Anyway, I had some money, and your dad . . . well, he fulfilled his responsibilities. That was a sweet apartment we lived in. On the second floor, with four windows that looked out on the park. They had screens, so I opened them and let you listen to the birds calling, which you liked to do. The stairs weren't terrible. There was a library nearby, and a bagel shop. Your dad told me that if you lived on bagels your entire life, you would make it to a hundred and twenty. Oh, he was funny." She smiled and then sighed. She glanced at me. I must have looked concerned, because she said, "Honey, I got over him. He was sweet and all, but in those days, especially in New York, almost every man who could lived a double life, and if you were from Akron, then you weren't going to be the person on the homemaking side of that life, because they had to marry for status. Us girls, we were the relief from the lives they had chosen, and we knew it. I thought I was lucky that he took any interest in us at all."

I knew she meant "you and me."

"He did tell me a little about the wife—that she was hard to handle—and in those days I was on his side, but now I see that maybe she had some mental issue. She was all about order and cleanliness."

I said, "Neat freak."

Mom nodded. "Well, as I remember, she was descended from the Stuyvesants, but I don't know which one. I'm sure she was obsessed with her image."

I said, "Was she pretty?"

"He said she was plain. Plain Jane, he called her, but I don't think her name was Jane. It might have been Janet. For a long time, he made me feel like I was his true love, one that he had finally found in his forties. When he broke it to me that he had to go back to her, he actually cried. I think it had something to do with the estate. I mean, he had a good job, but even if you had a good job in those days, you couldn't necessarily afford to live the high life in New York, and if you wanted to be a well-known success, you had to live the high life. And of course, everything we did would have been scandalous, and you never knew what Walter Winchell knew."

I vaguely remembered Walter Winchell.

She laughed.

I thought maybe she had learned to talk about herself by going to AA, and I also remembered that in the meetings, you offered your information—no one pulled it out of you—so I didn't ask any questions. And sure enough, as time went by, she offered more information about not only me, but herself. She talked about things that she wouldn't talk about in meetings, which were mostly for confessions, so my guess was that her confessions and other people's confessions reminded her of things, and she felt more comfortable letting them out. Since she still didn't want to drive, we had plenty of time to chat. One time, we were passing through Old Orchard, and she said, "I remember when Mother and Father wrote me that they were moving to St. Louis. None of us were surprised. Hank had already left for Texas, and anyway that's where they first fell in love, on the trolley. I had taken you to Akron a couple of times to meet them—you weren't yet two. And then I decided to see what St. Louis was like, in case I needed to get out of New York. Oh, that train ride was exhausting, but at least I had the money to go in the sleeper car. I took the lower bunk and put you between me and the wall. I was up all night, but you slept a little bit. Then I took a taxi to their new house, except that I had written down the address wrong—got the numbers backward and went to nine forty-one. But there wasn't a nine forty-one. Their street ended at Yeatman. So I just stood there, staring at the houses, until I remembered the real number, and I started walking, which I was used to. Such a pleasant street! I kept looking at all the different houses and saying, 'I hope it's like that one!' I could just imagine having a porch, and sitting there in the late afternoon, enjoying the weather."

I said, "I can't imagine doing that carrying a baby and a suitcase."

"You were walking. The suitcase wasn't big. And you were willing to hold my hand. I guess you had learned your lesson that time you ran across the street and that car screeched at you. I'll tell you one thing about that walk. I think if the taxi had dropped me off at their house, I would have been disappointed, but after the walk, I was so glad to get there that I loved it. Nice introduction to their neighborhood."

I didn't ask how she ended up at the house on Skinker, but a few days later, when we were having dinner at the Cheshire, she said, "Let's drive past the old place."

I said, "I miss it."

"I do, too, in some ways."

I drove north, then turned around at Wash U. and drove back. Mom stared at the house, which looked exactly the same, but she didn't say anything until we were almost to her place. She said, "The thing is, your dad came for a visit. I think he told Janet that he had some business deal that required a personal meeting, and he told her it was in Chicago, because maybe she would have been suspicious if she thought it was here. Anyway, he came for three days, and met me at the Chase Park Plaza. I brought you along, and he was nice to you."

"How old was I?"

"Just turned two and a half. He'd rented a car—a Caddie, of course—and we drove around. Since it was summer, I was working for the Muni by then, but it was Sunday when he came, so I had the day off and also Monday. When we were driving around Forest Park, he turned onto Skinker and we went past that house, and there was a For Sale sign on the lawn. He looked at me and said, 'This is the least I can do for you.' Then, I guess, he did all the lawyer stuff and wrote a check, because a house, even a nice house, in St. Louis would look like a bargain to someone from New York." I didn't ask what he thought of me, or how he treated me, though I hoped that would pop out someday. I turned down Clayton, and as we were passing Carl's Deli, she said, "Remember everyone coming in and out, staying the night, or even for a few weeks? I liked that about the house, and Mother and Father liked that, too. We all thought that we had the best of both worlds—the Forest Park fancy world and the Webster Groves easygoing world. You don't remember this, but after Hank moved to Texas, he and Carol brought the boys for Christmas, and they stayed with me. One day, I was walking down the stairs and I heard them arguing about moving back to St. Louis. I didn't say anything, but that afternoon, they did walk around the neighborhood, and then they came back and got me and you and I walked with them over to that house on Grandview that faced the corner, not the street."

I said, "You mean that stone one, with the porch in front and the tower on the Clayton Avenue side and the other tower on the Grandview side?"

Mom nodded. She said, "I thought it would be weird enough for Carol, and might lure her here, but I guess she didn't like the traffic noise of Highway 40 going under the bridge."

Other memories she told me about were ones that I suspected she had intended to keep to herself for her whole life, but suddenly, after we had been shopping at Stix, she told me about Danny Delane.

We were at my apartment, and she said, "Oh, heavens! Have you ever seen some stranger and become totally convinced that he was someone you'd once known?"

I said no.

She said, "Okay, so I was in the shoe department looking for some boots that might be more comfortable than these, and this guy walks by. There was something about his way of walking that, how should I say this? Turned me on!" She laughed. "So I watched him walk around the men's shoe area, and I realized that he was some kid—I'm guessing maybe your age. Thick, dark hair, great haircut, sort of a beaky nose. The next thing I thought was, What the hell is Gabriel Byrne doing in St. Louis?"

I said, "You mean the Irish actor who was in *Into the West*?"

She nodded, then said, "I didn't see that, but I loved *Miller's Crossing*. Don't get me started! If I could have picked any movie to be in, even as an extra, it would have been that one. Anyway."

She looked out the window, then looked at me again, and said, "Your father wasn't the only guy I was fond of in New York. There was an actor about my age from Vermont. I was already involved with your father, but I wasn't, you know, pregnant. We had gone to an audition, and we were leaving the theater. He smiled at me and held the door open, and then I stumbled, because the step was steeper than I expected. He grabbed my elbow and asked me if I wanted to get a cup of coffee. I did. Oh, God! He was funny! We got a cup of coffee, and then we walked around Bryant Park. We immediately connected, but it was more like friendship than love. We had so many things in common—I mean, just looking at the same things, laughing at the same jokes. How many rabbis could possibly walk into a bar? He loved those jokes about walking into a bar. He asked for my phone number, but I shook my head. I mean, I was going to the Catskills for *Meet Me in St. Louis*. But we kept running into one another. I thought about breaking it off with your dad, but then I realized . . . Well, you know."

I said, "Didn't you once tell me that someone named Danny Delane was the love of your life?"

"Did I? That was him, but I don't quite know what I meant about 'the love of my life.' I was always glad to see him, and he always made me laugh. It was pretty clear that he wasn't going to make it on Broadway, even as far as I did, because his dancing was a little stiff, and he was too tall. Back in those days, they liked the men to be about five foot eight and us to be about five foot five so that we could wear heels but not be taller than the men were. And he was a good singer, but he didn't have much range. He was so obsessed with James Cagney. He said that his dancing style was very Irish."

"Was he Irish?"

"Could have been, because there are plenty of Delaneys from Ireland, but we didn't talk about that, and I never met his folks."

Then I had another thought. I said, "So you got along really well but he never made a pass at you?"

Mom said, "Not once."

I said, "Maybe he was gay. Maybe that's why he came to New York and tried to get into the theater, because he thought he would find some connection that he didn't dare find in a small town in Vermont."

Mom said, "Well, he was always dressed to the nines, so maybe he was. Plenty were. I suspect Broadway was where they felt comfortable being themselves while not being themselves, because that's what we had to do."

She went on in an amused and friendly way, as if she didn't remember feeling passion when she was in her twenties, as if she had nothing to hide, from me or from herself. A few days later, I told her a little about Martin, about the estate, about the parents. She took my hand and said, "Drew told me about that, but he told me to keep it to myself. What was that, fifteen years ago? I was worried at the time, you know, about your regrets, because regrets always pop up too late for you to do anything to fix them."

I said, "I ran into him a few years ago. I got to realize that I didn't regret my regrets."

She said, "Lucky you."

I said, "That's me. Lucky." I didn't tell her about the roll of two-dollar bills. However, after I took her home and came back, I did get the roll out of the suitcase in my closet and count them, smooth them, and sort of marvel that they were still in good shape. While I was fiddling with them, I realized that I had come to appreciate Mom, and even to love her. It was sort of like opening an old book that had been lying around the house your whole life, and you had tried it a couple of times and put it away, and then it had gotten aged and sort of smelly, and then, just because you were thinking that you might give it to Goodwill, you opened it again, and it turned out to be interesting and readable, and there you were, pulled into a narrative, or a life, that you had always avoided.

We both got more affectionate—exchanging kisses and hugs. I hadn't ever thought that was possible.

MOM'S HOUSE ON West Argonne was small, but once we sorted everything out and actually put away all the clothes and shoes and magazines and dishware, Mom decided that she wanted to invite her friends over for dinner. She also decided that she wanted to try cooking new things, so the first cookbook she bought was *A Taste of India,* one that Jackie had back in New York. The recipe that Jackie liked was chicken cooked with coriander leaves and dill, but the one Mom chose was shrimp cooked in coconut milk. She invited Nancy at one of their meetings, and then she invited Ava because, Mom said, she needed a break from the children, and then she invited Aunt Louise. Mom made the list and I went to Schnucks, and I was sort of amazed that I could find all the ingredients except the tamarind, but Madhur Jaffrey herself said that lemon juice was a decent substitute. Well, we read the recipe over and over, and did the best we could, and it turned out fine—perhaps anything full of coconut milk would turn out fine. What I enjoyed about the meal was sitting around the table with these different women and listening to them chat. Nancy and Ava talked about the kids (I said a few things about Davie's musical progress since I had been going over to Ava's house and chatting with him once a week); Nancy and Aunt Louise, who hadn't met before, discovered that they both liked gardening, and talked about raised gardens vs. flower beds; Mom and Aunt Louise talked about how busy Uncle Drew was these days—he was helping some shoe company finalize a deal with a company in China, and had actually gone there. Ava, Nancy, and Mom talked about the music they liked to listen to (U2, Mary J. Blige, Mariah Carey), but also how odd band names had gotten to be (Nine Inch Nails, Public Enemy, Widowmaker). Then we all talked about what I could name my band if I started one, and we decided the most appealing name would be Deathbed Codgers. Everyone cleaned their plates, as Grandmother would have said, and so there were no leftovers—a pleasure. And no dessert. Aunt Louise said we were too old for dessert, and we all laughed.

As I listened, I was a little surprised by the jokes everyone made, but then I realized that making those jokes—at our own expense, and even at one another's expense—was an expression of freedom and relief. All day long, all of us had to behave properly, and here we were, having some fun in this small and secluded space. We decided to do it again, in two weeks. This went on through the spring and into the early summer, and it got to be sort of a club. I learned how to say more about what I was thinking, and also to make a few jokes. I started to see Aunt Louise as herself, a former girl who had ended up taking on Uncle Drew's ambitions and helping him fulfill them. I learned to see what he owed her because in a lot of ways, she was the most observant person I had ever met. If a fly landed on the window, she glanced at it. If a pot in the kitchen was boiling too hard, she heard it, got up, and went to turn down the burner; if someone was walking down the street, she took a look. One day, I asked her what her favorite newspaper was, and she said, "I always read the *Wall Street Journal*," and I saw that maybe it was Aunt Louise who kept her eye on the market and was the reason that my portfolio was now closing in on six million.

Sometime in June, Nancy brought another woman to the party who was new to AA. She lived somewhere near Fairground Park and she knew Nancy because she also worked at Wash U. Her name was Alberta, and she seemed quite reserved at first, and eventually she told us that it had taken her two dozen AA meetings before she managed to open her mouth and say anything about herself. Once she did, though, I could see that she had a good sense of humor—every joke made her laugh—and she also had some good stories. One thing that I thought was interesting was that when she was ten, her favorite uncle had died in a car accident, and had been buried in Bellefontaine Cemetery. Her family didn't live far from there, so every Sunday after church, they walked around the cemetery and said a few prayers for her uncle. The name of the cemetery had gotten her interested in learning French. And then, after telling us this, she smiled and continued her story in what sounded like very conversational French. Aunt Louise had been practicing her French ever since her trip, and so the two of them turned their heads, nodded, smiled, and finished the story with five minutes of French existentialist performing, then "À bientôt!" and "Mais oui!" Since we had turned the biweekly into a potluck, Alberta was the one who often brought the most interesting or sophisticated dish. My favorite of hers was the paella.

I also reconnected with a few of my friends from school. The oddest one was Linda Sullivan, who had been my friend in kindergarten and first grade. She had lived on Buena Vista, across the street from the house that was behind ours. She had a sandbox—her first attraction for me—and had usually walked to school with me when we were in first grade. But the most fun was that there was an alley that ran behind her house, and we were allowed to run up and down on it (and Dizzy enjoyed that, too). We ran maybe two houses down and back, but it seemed very long and exciting at the time, and I did remember one time when we went all the way to where the alley turned and ended on Alamo. We looked at each other and got scared, and then ran all the way back to her yard, jumped into the sandbox, and never said a word about it to her mom when she came outside to see if we wanted some peanut butter sandwiches. Just before second grade, the Sullivans moved to U. City, and so we hadn't seen one another in almost forty years, but when I saw her walking around Famous-Barr, I recognized her because of the shape of her eyes and her chin. I dared to say, "Linda?"

She was startled, but then she recognized me, too, and said, "Jodie! What are you doing here? The famous musicians move out of St. Louis!"

I said, "But if you want to stay famous, you have to shop at Famous-Barr twice a year, no matter where you live. It's the law."

We laughed, and I went into the shoe department, but when I headed out the door toward the parking lot, she was outside, searching her handbag. I said, "Everything okay?" and she said, "Maybe, but I might have dropped my wallet when I was at the cashier." We went back inside and looked around, and then she discovered it in her pocket. We kept talking, and then we walked down Forsyth to Shaw Park. We exchanged phone numbers and I walked back to get my car at Famous. The next one I connected with was a woman who had been two years ahead of me in high school, the singer I had watched and envied at the time. It turned out that she was now a member of the symphony chorus and did a lot of other gigs, too. Through her, I connected with a few others I had known in high school, and maybe because I was now less reserved, we occasionally met for lunch, or sometimes I got invited to a party. What interested me about all of this, which lasted for about two years, was that I was comfortable and relaxed. Contributing to conversations became automatic, and so did asking questions or showing concern.

I went back to the cabin in the Catskills in July, just to get away from the heat and humidity. The drive didn't bother me—I would leave around six a.m., stop in Columbus for something to eat, and get to the cabin around ten. At some point, I would see Jackie—I would pick her up in the city, drive back to Roxbury, put her up for a week, and catch up on all the news, and then take her back to the city. Now that Mom had AA and her friends, I wasn't afraid of her being left alone, and even though I invited her to come to the cabin with me, she still didn't want to go back to the Catskills and be dumped into all the things that she didn't mind contemplating from a distance. This time, the cabin didn't feel so isolated and lonely, and I knew that was because I had learned to show an interest in people and to feel a connection. I wondered if I would ever have learned that in New York or, say, Chicago. Maybe, I thought, there was something about St. Louis, so small and large at the same time, that offered friends if you could learn how to take them.

In a lot of ways, I had never felt so good, so relaxed, so happy. I even wrote a song about it—"Nobody Told Me."

"Nobody told me it would feel so fine / Leaving all of that behind / The worry, the hustle, the fear, the bustle. / Nobody told me that day to day / Doing nothing would be okay / Just having a chat and a piece of pie / Is always as good as flying high. /Everyone said, Just get out of town / But here I live to look around / At the mansions and the beggars, at the Caddies and the trees / At the birds rising and diving in the breeze. / Nobody told me the pleasures of fading, / That success requires evading. / Nobody told me, so I'm telling you—ignore what you want, look into the blue."

13

ON HER DEATHBED (though she didn't call it that), Mom told me how she had allowed her cancer to progress. There had been a point, maybe six months before we were having this conversation, when she had sensed that something was wrong, because she wasn't hungry, even for, say, Ava's grilled cheese with bacon or a piece of apple crumble. She had started to lose weight, and she was thrilled, because she had spent years looking down at her belly and wishing it would go away. Yes, she had felt aches and pains, but she was seventy-one. Everyone who is seventy-one feels aches and pains, and she had thought those would be worse for women who had spent years dancing. According to her, Ginger Rogers was one of a kind, thirteen years older than Mom and still going strong. Mom had paid lots of attention to Ginger Rogers, partly because she was from Missouri, and partly because it had always seemed that she could do whatever she wanted. At some point, when Mom was working at the Muny, they had talked about trying to get her to come and act in some musical, but they hadn't succeeded, so Mom never met her. She also talked about admiring Josephine Baker's ability to come back to dancing after the war, when she was in her forties, but said that she had tapered off after that (I had no idea if this was true). We had talked about Josephine Baker a few times during our dinners, but the other women were more impressed by her bravery and her politics. And then, when Mom realized that maybe something really was wrong, she had put off looking for a doctor. I suspected that this was because she didn't want to drive, and also didn't want to tell me.

It was Ava who took her to a doctor. I had gone with Mom to their house. I was in the living room with Davie, who was working on two pieces—Mozart's Piano Sonata No. 1 and "Criss-Cross," by Thelonious Monk. He liked going back and forth, and told me that he was willing to take a walk around the block, but it was actually more "productive" (his word) to switch "genres" (also his word). I sat quietly and listened to him play, and only said things like, "Listen to the rhythm a bit" or "Let's have a little more pop." I liked listening to him and watching him. While Davie and I were doing this, Ava and Mom were chatting. Ava told me later that Mom looked a little weak, so in order to gauge whether this was something to worry about, she said, "Oh! Come look out the window at the garden! I found the most interesting roses—they're lavender colored, and they smell so good." She helped Mom to the window, and then, because of the light, she said, "May, you look strange. I don't know, a little . . ." She put her finger on Mom's cheek and said, "Jaundiced."

Mom said, "I know. I'm sure it's cirrhosis."

Ava said, "What does your doctor say?"

Mom admitted that she didn't have a doctor. Without even telling me (Ava knew that Davie hated to be disturbed), she took Mom to her own doctor. Mom told him about her drinking problem, so he tested her for cirrhosis, but because he had a lot of patients in the waiting room, he didn't test her for anything else, and gave her another appointment for ten days later. She did not tell me about the appointment, so I didn't take her, and it was only a few days after that, when I was putting a clean handkerchief in her purse, that I saw the note about the appointment. I called the office and scheduled another one, in a week.

So, it turned out to be stage four pancreatic cancer. Ava's doctor set her up with an oncologist at Barnes Hospital, and I went with her so that we could both understand and discuss the recommended treatments—chemo, radiation, two types of bypass surgery.

The doctor made a stent sound doable, but then he described it in more detail, and Mom got up and walked out of the room. I said, "I'm guessing that she has a case of oppositional defiant disorder," and asked about pain. He said he could relieve the pain for the time being, and maybe we could talk her into one of the other procedures. I said, "How long?" He said, "A year, maybe two, is most likely."

When I got to the car, she was sitting there, with the windows open. I said, "You have Medicare, and I can pay if that isn't enough." She glanced at me, very calm, and said, "I deserve it—I smoked for years and drank for years." She actually shrugged. As I drove her to her house, she was so even-tempered about the whole thing—not nearly as anxious as she had been when I was moving her out of the Skinker house, or even when she was living there and thinking robbers or kidnappers were sneaking in—that I was perplexed. But she could read my mind. When she got out of the car, she said, "I would rather go now than have you watch the same thing happen to me that happened to Grandmother. She was about my age when I started to notice that she looked confused. One time, she went to the door when the mailman was putting the mail in the box, and said, 'What are you doing here?' He showed her the mail, and she said, 'What is that?' Grandfather was in the yard, fixing something, and he was the one who told me about it. He ran up the steps and apologized to the mailman, then took Grandmother inside."

I said, "But he was razor-sharp to the end. Maybe you take after him."

She said, "What good is that?"

I was about to say something about how we would miss her, and she said, "Do you really want to take care of me for years? Do you really not want to move back to New York and get on with your life?"

When I paused before answering, she said, "Be honest."

I was. I said, "I don't know."

I drove her to her place and then drove to Uncle Drew's. He wasn't home yet, but Aunt Louise came to the door and said, "Ava told me her doctor recommended an oncologist. Did she see him?"

I nodded and she picked up the phone. Uncle Drew was home in minutes.

Uncle Drew was ten years younger than Mom, and had never had a drinking problem, and for most of his life I would have said that he looked twenty years younger than Mom did, I suppose because of the way he always looked excited about starting something new, whatever it was. But as he came through the door, I thought he looked stressed. As far as I knew, he didn't yet know the diagnosis, and neither did Aunt Louise, or any of the women in our little club. He said, "What is it?"

I said, "Fourth-stage pancreatic cancer."

"Is she in a lot of pain?"

"She won't say."

He said, "Typical."

He took his coat and hat to the hall closet and hung them up, then closed the door. He said, "Let her do what she wants."

Aunt Louise nodded.

Uncle Drew said, "We both have filed DNRs."

I said, "What are those?"

"Do not resuscitate. Do not try to start my heart up when my heart has had enough, basically."

"Or," said Aunt Louise, "do not cover my mouth with yours and blow into my lungs. Imagine the old days, when your family sat in the room with you, and everyone, including you, knew you were breathing your last, and they kissed you and held your hand, and then some doctor came storming into the room and started pounding on your chest until you sort of woke up again but were never the same."

Uncle Drew said, "About half of your relatives would thank the doctor, and half of them would shake their heads, and then they would get into a big, but low-voiced, argument about who was going to change your diaper and spoon caca into your mouth for the rest of your life, or pay for the poor soul who you hired to do that. No thanks."

I said, "Would you two talk to her about it? I think she would be more honest with you."

Uncle Drew said, "I need the walk. You go tell her I'm coming."

When I got to Mom's place, the front door was half-open, and Mom, still wearing her jacket, was sitting on the couch. *Guiding Light* was on the screen, but the sound was off, though Mom was looking at it. She glanced at me, but didn't say anything. I said, "Uncle Drew is coming."

"Is he going to talk me into something?"

I said, "I doubt it."

He knocked on the door, and I went into the kitchen, then out in the yard. The thing I feared about Mom having to make up a plan was that we might have to stick with it, even if Mom changed her mind, because both Uncle Drew and Aunt Louise were great believers in planning ahead. I doubted that Grandmother and Grandfather had made a plan—it always seemed as though they were taking it day by day, which meant that each day they adjusted to what they were feeling like and what was happening. Whatever was going on with them, neither of them ever seemed afraid. Frustrated, yes, sad, yes, but accepting, and therefore affectionate to us and to each other. But Mom's case was different—there could be a lot of pain, and there could be other effects of her disease that we now didn't know about, and were not manageable. I imagined various doctors shrugging their shoulders if Mom decided she needed care and saying, "Not my business."

Once I went back into the house, they told me that they had agreed that Mom could do whatever she wanted, and we would all help her along. Uncle Drew then said he would stay with her for a while, which I knew was a signal that I should be on my way. The good thing about Mom's house was that it was one story and in a safe neighborhood. We could all go in and out, as we had with Grandmother. I drove to Aunt Lily's restaurant, since it was almost five in the afternoon, and she seated me at a table not far from the kitchen. There was a family at one of the tables near the window—

a woman and a man about my age, and three children, all under five. Two of them looked like they might be twins. Aunt Lily was good at chatting with me while she was doing her job, and I ate some tasty bruschetta while we said a few things about Mom's condition. When I had paid, she came back and escorted me to the door. She said, "Just in case, there's an old folks' home around Webster that used to be a convent."

I said, "I bet there are a few of those."

We agreed to go have a look the next day, and we did. It was a beautiful historic building, and the employees sitting in the front area were welcoming. We explained what was going on with Mom, and they nodded, and said that the rooms available for seriously ill residents were limited, but they would show us around. The outside of the building was green, leafy, and arresting, but the inside was what a convent was supposed to be—not rooms but "cells" with a bed and a window, but no chair and not much space for storing anything. Given that some of the residents that we saw as we walked down the hallway (the doors were left open during the day) looked to be in their nineties and had walkers and even wheelchairs, the worst thing about it was that the rooms didn't have bathrooms of their own (and given the age of the building and the size of the rooms, how could they), so even the weakest resident had to find her way (it was all for women) down the hallway, which was narrow and poorly lit. We thanked the employees for their kindness and left. I decided that this was a good example of Mom making the best choice, even if it might be painful.

AS WITH GRANDMOTHER and Grandfather, Mom's deathbed was in her own house, in her own bedroom, also right next to the bathroom and across from the kitchen. She had two windows that looked out into her backyard, facing south. There was a pin oak and an elm, and also a redbud and a young Bradford pear, which she had planted when she moved in. I often found her turned toward the windows, looking at the yard, which was small but closed in and quiet. I had always appreciated Uncle Drew's house, which was larger, but after I moved into the second bedroom, which also looked toward the backyard, I appreciated Mom's house more than I had.

One thing I did without asking was to move her CD player into her room. Then I went through her stack of CDs. The collection of 45s that I remembered from when I was growing up (and could still sing) was *My Fair Lady, West Side Story, The Sound of Music,* and a few others, and Mom had those in her stack of CDs, but there were plenty more—*Fiddler on the Roof, A Little Night Music,* and *Sunday in the Park with George.* She had CDs of James Taylor and Carly Simon, and the four J's, as well as one Beatles album, one Rolling Stones album, and all of the Eagles albums, including a live one. The classical albums were mostly Chopin and Purcell, but the one that looked like it had been played the most was Vaughan Williams's "The Lark Ascending." That was the one I put on first, when Mom was sitting up, looking out the window at a pair of cardinals, and nibbling on her blueberry muffin. She listened as the violin solo rose, and then, when the orchestra kicked in, she looked at me, smiled, and looked out the window again. That became our way to start the day. I bought her a few of my favorites—*Pictures at an Exhibition,* by Mussorgsky, and Tchaikovsky's "1812 Overture," but we only played those in the afternoon. I did notice that after we played those, perhaps because of the way the energy ramped up at the end, she would eat more. Once in a while, I played one of my own CDs. I even sneaked in a CD that Ava and I recorded of Davie playing his favorite piano piece, a suite by Ravel called *Le Tombeau de Couperin.* Davie loved how lighthearted it was, and I hadn't told him that it was in memory of Ravel's friends who had died in the First World War. I expected Mom to cringe a little bit when Davie happened to make a mistake, but she didn't, nor did she ask who the musician was. She simply enjoyed it. Ava and I were both surprised that Davie could play such complex (and quick) music, but I doubt that anyone, including Mozart, had ever worked as hard as Davie did. Ava and I talked about taking Mom to their house, for supper and "a concert," but we couldn't figure out how to do it, because she was declining quickly.

Ava dropped in about twice a week, and so did Nancy and Alberta. Aunt Louise came every day, bringing leftovers from whatever she had made the night before, and they were always terrific. She was easing Uncle Drew away from having meat every night, and so sometimes the leftovers were broccoli quiche or artichoke bisque. Mom ate a little of everything and I finished the rest, even though I, too, often gazed down at my belly and wondered whether I could get rid of it without coming down with a fatal illness. Nancy and I sometimes talked about this. We both remembered Twiggy and Veruschka, not to mention the Beatles on *The Ed Sullivan Show,* skinny legs, top to bottom. Nancy, of course, remembered numbers, and she had read in a *Washington Post* article that when she was a model, Twiggy was five foot six and a half, and had weighed something like ninety pounds. Which, Nancy said, was about like a famine victim. I thought it was interesting that we didn't remember the actresses from the same period as well as we remembered the models. Nancy said, "The models were the ones we were supposed to look like, and the actresses were the ones we knew we would never look like." Then she said, "I wanted to be Vanessa Redgrave. She always looked so determined, and when I was taking those math classes where I was the only female student, I would think about her and try to give off the same vibe, as we said." Then she said, "Did you see *Little Odessa*? She looks a million years old in that one, but it's really interesting. Did you ever go to Brighton Beach when you lived in New York?"

I shook my head. She said, "That's a little conclave of Russian Jews."

I asked Aunt Louise if she might stay with Mom for an hour while I went for a walk, and even though the walks didn't do a damn thing for my belly, they were interesting. The thing I didn't do was practice my guitar or sing unless Mom asked me to. Every two weeks, the dinners we had had at Mom's place resumed. Ava and I would help Mom get dressed and then help her to the most comfortable chair in the living room, then Aunt Louise, Alberta, Nancy, and Aunt Lily would arrive with something to eat. They only lasted maybe thirty or forty minutes. Mom didn't say much (when I mentioned this to her, she said, "What do I have to say?") but she enjoyed listening to what everyone else had to say.

We could all see that Mom was going fast, and Alberta offered to call a doctor and to bring him over, but Aunt Louise said, "That's what would kill her."

I wasn't so sure of that, but the next morning, I put my hand on Mom's forehead and said, "You want to see a doctor?"

She said, "No. Did you hear me?"

I nodded.

Aunt Louise must have told the relatives, because Uncle Hank and Carol showed up a few days later. They pretended that they were there for the opening game of the baseball season, and sat with Mom for maybe half an hour. Brucie showed up the next day. He said that he was moving Aunt Lily out of her house (he wasn't—she was stuck there). He chatted with Mom, and then we sang a few songs together. The next day, he came and said, "It's so beautiful. Please let me take you for a drive."

Mom looked doubtful, but we helped her to his car, which was a Dodge Caravan, and the best thing about it was that we could put Mom's seat back so that she was comfortable, and she could still see out of the windows. Brucie drove in a widening circle—first around the block, then along the railroad tracks and around the park, then past the spot where the weird Frank Lloyd Wright house had been built, then north and west through the fancy neighborhoods—I had always thought that it was strange how some of the fanciest houses I had ever seen were maybe three miles from Mom's modest house and about half a mile from Grandmother and Grandfather's place. That was St. Louis. As we drove, Mom said various street and village names in a low voice—Bopp, Lindbergh, Huntleigh, Des Peres, Creve Coeur, Litzsinger, Rock Hill. It was the perfect time of day, and the drive both perked Mom up and wore her out. We got back to her house, and Brucie and I helped her in. Aunt Louise and Aunt Lily sat with her and put her to bed, while Brucie and I went outside and had a chat.

I knew I was forty-five, but it was hard to believe that Brucie was forty-six. He was working in construction now. He wasn't doing the actual building, but he was overseeing the plans, making sure that they aligned with the spaces where they were being built, and making sure that they were up to code. These were important issues around Austin, because of the variety of landscapes and the weather problems. Also, there were a lot of people moving in from other states, and they complained if the houses they built turned out to be not as plush as the ones they'd left back in, say, Minneapolis. He was about to get married to a woman who had shared custody of her two children. The ex-husband was a friend of his. He looked at me and said, "He cheated on her, she didn't cheat on him." And then he looked at me again, and said, "But she was glad he did." The wife-to-be was Vicki, the kids were twelve and fourteen. She worked in a law office, and the fourteen-year-old wanted to play professional football while the twelve-year-old wanted to have a farm and grow hemp for housebuilding. I said, "Where did he get that idea?"

Brucie said, "She. Her name is Fern. She got it from me. I was reading about it somewhere, and she asked me, and I told her about how you grow the hemp, then you turn it into something called hempcrete. A lot of people are working with it, and Fern is hot to trot."

I said, "Isn't hemp marijuana?"

"Related, but no. That's the problem. The builders that use standard materials will push strict drug laws to get rid of the competition, because it's much cheaper to build with hempcrete than concrete, and fuck the environment." He scowled.

I said, "Are you still playing any music?"

He shook his head. "That band broke up. We all looked at one another one day and said, 'Jeez, we're old,' and Billy, one of the members, said, 'And when we sing, we sound like trucks running over gravel roads.' I had to agree with that. That's the bane of a singing career, looking at the audience and watching them wince when you can't hit the high note, and the low note sounds like a grunt."

I nodded, and said, "Tell me about it."

He said, "You're not singing either?"

"Only to Mom."

He said, "That's a shame."

I said, "Maybe, maybe not. I'm still writing songs. That's the thing I can't help doing."

He said, "No surprise."

I told him about Davie, about how hard he was trying. He said, "Good habits die hard."

"I had a friend in college who is a pianist. He still is doing concerts. I mean, as far as I know, he hasn't performed at the Met or Carnegie Hall, but I think he has regular work. He's put out a few records." Then we watched a couple of cars go by, and I said, "Maybe Davie will be content to play at the Muni or at the orchestra in town. A friend of mine from high school sings in the chorus."

Brucie said, "Some people never want to leave this town."

"Do you think that's weird?"

"Actually, I don't. I mean, if you have air-conditioning, or enough money to go somewhere in the summer, you might as well stay. There's always something going on. Including the Cards, but also not including the Cards."

I said, "I remember when I was in college, two of my roommates were from Philly, and I asked them if they were baseball fans, and one of them said that she liked to go to games with her brother, but whatever the players did, they got booed if it wasn't a homer. I didn't notice that when we went to games with Grandfather."

He said, "The Cards never get booed."

I knew he was joking, but I thought that was an interesting aspect of life in St. Louis.

Uncle Drew came over every few days, and when he was with Mom, he told jokes and was also comforting. Mom loved to hold his hand and remind him of when he was two and she was twelve, and she would hold his hand whenever they were outdoors. She said that she had known Grandfather and Grandmother were worried about the Depression, but somehow, just holding Drew's hand and keeping him safe reassured her. Uncle Drew said, "It reassured me, too. You know, nobody remembers much about being two, but I do remember that comforting feeling that someone was taking care of me."

Mom said, in a soft voice, "That's what I feel right now when I am holding your hand."

BUT UNCLE DREW continued to look, not exactly nervous (that would come later), but uneasy. One day, Aunt Louise showed up to help with Mom, and after we had changed her, washed her, and put her back to bed with some Eagles music, we were in the bathroom, cleaning up, and I said, "So, I wish you would tell me what is going on with Uncle Drew. Does he have some regrets about letting Mom go out in her own way?"

Aunt Louise shook her head. She said, "It's all this Clinton stuff. Vince Foster. Whitewater. Clinton was the first Dem he's ever voted for, but Drew thought that since Bob Dole is eight years older than he is himself, it was time for the old guys to step aside. But now, oh, you know. Your uncle always feels like everything is his responsibility. I keep telling him that his one little vote wasn't what put Clinton in the White House."

I said, "What about you?"

Aunt Louise said, "I've never been the optimist that he is, but the last thing I want is an I-told-you-so moment. And all of this conflict in the Balkans. I mean, you know he loves Italy—we both do—and when we went on our trip, we traveled to Trieste and Split and Sarajevo and spent a couple of days driving here and there. He doesn't want to see it wrecked. I don't either."

We finished up the cleaning, and I went to check on Mom, who had fallen asleep. Her shade was up, and the sunlight was spread across her quilt and her face. She was snoring a little. For the first time in my life, I thought she looked beautiful.

When I got back to the living room, I said, "You guys lived through the Second World War."

She said, "Well, I have to admit that those wars seemed far away, and we were only ten when it started. We didn't feel responsible for them. When you get into your sixties, if you are a decent person and you live in a democracy, you feel responsible for a lot of things."

But I only felt responsible for Mom. Even the cabin in the Catskills had drifted out of my head. Even the maintenance for my car. The Toyota dealership was only a couple of miles from Mom's house, and I drove past it all the time, but I never stopped and went in for a checkup. It was Davie—young Mr. Observant—who said, one time when I was driving him to his piano lesson because Ava had a dental appointment, "Why do you have to push the brake pedal so hard?"

I glanced at my foot, and it was almost to the floor. As a rule, Toyota brakes work with the least little tap, and I hadn't even noticed. I said, "Gotta check that out," trying not to scare him, and went straight to the dealer after I dropped him off. And I had to stay there. Fortunately, they let me call Ava, and she was able to pick him up, even though her jaw was still numb. Well, fixing up the Tercel cost almost two thousand dollars. But at least it was a Toyota.

BY THE BEGINNING of May, it was evident that Mom was in a lot of pain, but all she would take for it was aspirin, not Tylenol or ibuprofen. When I said, "Can I give you something?" she would say, "A piece of dark chocolate," and I would give her that. I offered chamomile tea, which she drank slowly, and she said that it helped, but I have no idea if it did. She knew what was coming—we all did—and she prepared for that event by ridding herself of as many memories as she could. To Aunt Lily, she said, "When you sent me that snapshot of Brucie, I thought all I wanted was a baby—he was so damn cute. I walked down Hudson Street for an hour in the sleet just pulling that picture out of my pocket and looking at it until it was soaking wet." Then she looked at me, and said, "But I wanted a girl." To Aunt Louise, she said, "I've got to say that I was thinking about when Drew met you. Do you remember that time he brought you home to Grandmother and Grandfather's?"

Aunt Louise said, "Of course I do!"

Mom said, "After you left, Grandfather, Lily, and I sat around the card table, and we played five-card stud. Grandfather had a run of luck—I think he won four of the six games—and every time he raked in his chips, he said, 'This means she's going to accept.' When you did accept, I don't remember how long it was after that game, he made Lily and me pony up his winnings, which was a dollar from each of us."

To Uncle Drew, she said, "It wasn't just the money! Do you remember the time I slit my wrist, but I did it in the wrong direction, so it didn't work, and you saw the cut? We took little Jodie over to Mother and you drove me around the Ozarks for two days, all along the Current River. We stayed in some hotel in Poplar Bluff. Nice spot. And you didn't tell Father or Mother a thing about it." She chuckled, as if this was not an unsettling revelation. Uncle Drew said, quietly, "That was my first car. Hudson Hornet. I was so proud of that car. Green as grass."

Aunt Louise said, "You wooed me with that one."

Mom held out her wrist, and there was a little thread running across it, about an inch and a half long.

The memories she gave me were ones that I knew she wanted me to keep for her. Her favorite was of the dance class she took in Akron, during the summer when she was fourteen. It was a ballroom dance class, and there were ten boys and ten girls. They had to learn every style—swing, waltz, tango, foxtrot, quickstep, and even the polka. One of the boys, who was not as tall as she was and not especially good-looking, could do every step, and Mom watched him no matter who she was dancing with, and did whatever he did. Sometimes, she said, she got to dance with him, and they were like Astaire and Rogers, or, at least, that was what they told each other. At the end of the summer, the teacher sat down at the piano and told the other students to watch while Mom and the boy, Timmy, he was, did every dance. Then he went back to Cleveland. I asked if she ever saw him again, and she said, "No, but I heard he got killed in the war." She said this so calmly. But now she was calm about everything.

One day, she said, "*Annie Get Your Gun*! What a nightmare that was."

I said, "I always thought it was fun."

She said, "Oh, I don't mean the show or the movie. I mean running around trying to get the costumes and the props sorted for the production at the Muni! Last show of the summer, two weeks, and hot as hell. I knew I had to do a good job in order to keep my job, since at that point I was just a temp. It was a fun show, and I liked the actors, but I didn't know a thing about the guns. The woman I was helping said that she would do all that, but then she got the flu on the fifth day of the show, and I had to handle the pistols and the rifles. I mean, I knew that the bullets were blanks, and Annie didn't shoot very much, but there had to be some shots—couldn't be like the '1812 Overture'—all drums. I could hardly get myself to pick one up, just because I thought I might make a mistake. And then the actress—I don't remember who she was anymore, but she was so sweet. She came into the prop room, and set them out, and told me how to bring them to her and take them away. She was from somewhere up north, and she said that she had grown up shooting ducks with her dad, so she wasn't worried. And they did give me a permanent job at the end of the season. What a relief that was."

I didn't ask what her memories of me were, but she started to tell me. She said, "You know, your grandmother came on the train for a visit when you were about two months old. She thought you were darling, of course, and she went on and on about how much you reminded her of me, even though I didn't think that you looked like me, but who knows? The first picture they had of me was taken when I was about eight. She was shocked that I wasn't breastfeeding. But the doctor had given me some newfangled bottles and said that breastfeeding wasn't necessary anymore and that women could easily do without it. I think he told me that his wife had had seven kids in a row, and had breastfed without stopping for almost nine years.

Anyway, Mama took one look at those bottles, which had some sort of hose at the end, and she went straight to Macy's or somewhere like that and brought home some new bottles with red nipples. Oh, you stared at those! Took them like a champ. You must have gained a pound during the week she was there."

One morning, when I was trying to get her to eat something other than chocolate, Mom glanced up at me, then winced. She took a deep breath, and then said, "Oh, you scared the pants off of me." I waited for her to go on, but she kept clenching her fists, and I knew that her condition was getting worse. I said, "Should I . . ."

She said, "No."

But I did turn to go out of the room and call Aunt Louise. She put out her hand, and said, "I was the oldest! I thought that set me up for having a baby, and when I found out I was pregnant, well, you know, in New York, there were plenty of places you could go to get an abortion if you kept it to yourself. But I wanted a baby." She paused. "The beginning was good. I let you sleep with me, and I nursed you. I actually figured out how to change your diapers without passing out." She smiled. "Even in New York, there were these diaper trucks. They brought the diapers and picked up the dirty ones in a hamper. Mama helped me with the bottle. I thought everything was fine, and then you grew, and as you got heavier, my worst fear was that I would drop you. When your dad was around, I made him carry you. I mean, in my little house, there was no way to get up and down the stairs without carrying you—that's what scared me so much—I was afraid of going down without holding a rail. I couldn't carry you with one arm. Some days, I just sat in my room all day, didn't even take you outside." She shook her head, then said, "I was glad you were an early walker. And you didn't mind going down the stairs on your own. You would sit on one step, put your feet on the next one down, and then fold yourself and ease down to that step. Seemed like it took all day, but I thought you were safer doing it yourself."

I said, "How old was I?"

"Oh, eighteen months. By the time we moved to Grandfather

and Grandmother's place, you could go just about anywhere you wanted. That made Mama more nervous than it did me. Even that episode with the cat and the car didn't scare me as much as trying to carry you and stay on my feet."

Another reason, I thought, to be glad that I hadn't had Martin's children. But as soon as I had this thought, I also had an affectionate thought of Martin, and I wondered what he was doing these days.

One afternoon, she was looking out the window, and somewhere nearby, a dog started barking. It was pretty warm, and the window was open. She said, "Close the damn window."

I said, "The sun is shining right through it."

Then she said, "I hated that dog."

"Dizzy?"

She nodded, then said, "She was a mean little bitch. You remember when she bit your hand? You never knew in those days what illness a dog might be carrying, even if she had all her shots. Had to take you to the doctor and then watch you for symptoms—I don't even remember what disease the doctor told me to be looking out for. There was a woman down the street—two doors up from Clayton. She had a big side yard and lots of windows along the south side of the house. Sweet place. She had a couple of Irish setters. I went to her after the bite and asked if she had any ideas about training that dog, and she said she didn't—cockers were very aggressive. Boy, did I get on Drew for bringing you that puppy."

I hadn't closed the window, but the dog had stopped barking. She said, "Do you remember those setters? They were beautiful dogs."

I said that I did, and I did, sort of, but then I said, "I've never wanted another dog. I guess Dizzy taught me a lesson."

She said, "I wonder if the cat did, too."

A few days before Mother's Day, I called around to see if Nancy, Ava, Aunt Louise, Aunt Lily, or Alberta had any ideas about what we might do for Mom, but everyone was out or working, so no answers. We were out of milk and chocolate, which, along with very smooth polenta, were the only things Mom would eat, so I told Mom I was going to get the milk and chocolate. She said, "Go to

Straub's." That was her favorite grocery store, and I thought I might find something there that she would at least try. All the way there, which was about a ten-minute drive, I kept telling myself, "Don't take a walk! Don't take a walk!" because it was that part of Webster that I had such fond memories of. When I was in the bakery area, looking at the Miss Hulling's strawberry layer cake, which Mom had always liked, I saw Alberta. I told her that I thought we ought to do something, and she suggested midafternoon, since it was a Sunday. I said, "I don't think she can take more than an hour, but I know she'd love to see you guys."

Alberta said, "You aren't going to believe this, but my cousin, who was studying French at St. Louis U., got a Fulbright to Grenoble, and he sent me twelve bars of Bonnat chocolate. I've been wanting to give one to your mom. I've got two left, so get it while you can!"

I said, "Way better than Hershey's, right?"

Alberta said, "What's Hershey's?"

We laughed, and Alberta said she would get everyone together.

When I got back to Mom, it had taken me almost an hour to do what I thought would take me half an hour, so I was scared when I heard sounds coming from her room. I didn't even put the milk in the fridge.

As soon as I walked into Mom's room, the sounds stopped, though her hands were still on her completely vanished stomach, pressing.

I didn't dare say, "Are you all right?"

All I said was, "I got the milk. Oh, and Alberta's got some French chocolate for you. Bonnet? Something like that."

Mom winced, and then smiled and said, "Bon-NAH. They make that somewhere around Grenoble. Another spot I wish I'd gone to."

I brought Mom a glass of milk and a slice of the cake, which was sweet and soft. She took a drink and a bite, then said, "So, here's something I never told you. When you were in Winchester, I was so envious that I scraped together a thousand bucks and bought myself a ticket to London. Do you remember that you wrote me when you went to London that you stayed at the Langham? I stayed there, too. I was going to look around and then head down to Winchester and see you. That was my excuse for going. But I chickened out. And besides, there were so many things to do in London that I couldn't make myself leave."

I said, "When did you go? You could have met Martin."

She nodded, then said, "Well, I didn't know anything about Martin at the time. I think it was October—after the Muny season was over, but before the Kiel season picked up."

"What was your favorite thing?"

"Oh, I loved the museums, but the best day was a sunny one at Kew Gardens. Between you and me, I loved getting lost there."

Remembering my own experience, I said, "What about the cars?"

She said, "I was careful."

I said, "Did Uncle Drew know you went?"

"No one knew I went. Just before I left, I called Louise and said I had the flu, so I was going to keep to myself for a week."

I said, "Mom, you are a weirdo."

She said, "Thanks for the compliment!" She meant it.

When I went out of the room to take a pee, I heard her give another little cry, and the thought that I had was that she was a much better actress than those producers in New York had given her credit for being.

The last week of April had been stormy and wet, with plenty of thunder and lightning, but the first few days of May were pleasant—only a little foggy—so I had hopes for our Mother's Day "party." Alberta let me know that everyone was planning to come—Ava was going to pick up everyone except Aunt Louise—and they would show up around two thirty. Uncle Drew was going to bring Aunt Louise and also spend some time with Mom. Then, on Saturday, there was another thunderstorm, and once again, Mom seemed to be in a lot of pain. When I finally made myself mention it, she said, "It will go away when the air pressure rises." But she didn't say any more, or tell me more stories. I sat with her in her room, listening to the thunder and trying to write a song. I titled it "A Long Good-bye" and I knew what I wanted it to mean but I didn't know how to get there. Mom didn't ask me what I was doing.

For Mother's Day, I had bought another of Miss Hulling's cakes—this one chocolate—and around eight in the morning, I checked on Mom, who reached out and squeezed my hand, and then I went to get the cake and a small glass of milk. When I came back, she was lying down, taking deep breaths. I set the cake and the milk on the table and went over to her. She said, "I'm not going to make it."

I said, "Yes, I think . . ."

But she shook her head. I climbed into bed with her and took her in my arms, and I felt her go. Appropriately, her backyard was covered in fog.

WHEN OUR FRIENDS showed up, I didn't want to surprise them, so I met them at the door and told them the news. There were tears, but there was also relief that Mom had gotten away from her pain—I told them a little about the last week, all the wincing and attempts to hide what she could not hide. Uncle Drew led us into Mom's room. He kissed her forehead, her cheeks, her hands, her lips, and said, "Thank you, sis." Then the rest of us each did something to acknowledge our affection for Mom. Aunt Louise stroked her head; Ava put her hand on Mom's heart; Nancy closed her eyes, bent down, and whispered something in Mom's ear; Aunt Lily lifted the blanket, smiled, and tickled Mom's ribs, then kissed her; Alberta put her hand on Mom's forehead and said, "Honey, you are going home." Then she pulled out the chocolate bar and broke it into twelve squares. She handed them around, two for each of us. Then we each put one square on Mom, and ate the other one.

The official funeral and burial were routine. I knew that Mom would have appreciated our unofficial celebration much more.

14

THE RESURRECTION CAME in the summer of 1995—not Mom's, but mine—when I was doing a gig at a festival I had been to several times that was meant to raise money for cleaning up the Hudson River. It was about two hours from the cabin, so after I played my set, I thanked everyone, had a bite to eat, and then drove home during a very pleasant sunset. The next day, I came back from doing a little shopping (and chatting and smiling) to find a voicemail on my phone from a music producer who had been to the festival. He wanted to put out "A Long Good-bye" and "Nobody Told Me." He had actually been at my little concert at the festival (along with maybe a hundred other members of the audience) and he had taken a video with a camera that was so small that I didn't see it from the stage (I later bought one—it was a Ricoh).

In the year since Mom's death, I had returned to practicing my guitar and singing. The things you have to do after a death were a little intimidating at first—selling Mom's house, sorting through her possessions, making sure that the *Post* published an obit that was both true and flattering. Getting back to music was my solace and my rest from all of these details. At one point, I considered keeping Mom's house, because I thought that the interest rates were too high to sell it, but then Alberta called me and asked if it was for sale. It was a house she loved, not far from a park, and nowhere near her relatives, so I sold it to her for what Mom had paid, maybe 20 percent below the going market rate, because I could afford to. When she moved in, I stayed for a few days, and then went back to my cabin. On the way, I picked up Jackie, and I told her that her job, at the cabin, was to listen to me sing and play the guitar—I would watch her and learn from her facial expressions. There would be five categories of facial reviews: "This performance is divine," "This performance reminds me of Mother Maybelle," "This performance could be worse," "Get an instructor," and "Sorry, I'm leaving. This performance is pure hell." Jackie's facial reviews made us laugh a lot, and that relaxed me, so even I liked what I was producing. A lot of musicians have said that making music becomes such a habit that you can come back to it after years and be rather amazed at what your fingers remember, and I felt that, too. But I also thought that being away from it gave me a new sense of what I needed to learn. I was in New York for almost three months, and I tried to go to as many performances as I could, including ones in the city. One thing that I rather liked about those was the three-hour drive back to the cabin—there was something crisp and beautiful about the way the city faded away and the stars appeared, shining and plentiful above the mountains. Once in a while, I stayed with Jackie and contemplated whether I should move back into the apartment, but driving to the cabin and thinking about the concerts (I saw Bonnie Raitt, Aretha, Elton John, Bruce Springsteen, Tom Petty, Janet Jackson, Billy Joel, Mary J. Blige, even the Crash Test Dummies) helped me remember various bits of technique that I thought I could use on my guitar and for singing. When I got home, even though it was usually about one a.m., I would grab my guitar and play for twenty minutes or so, just to stick those bits in my head.

I did not make a plan for what I was going to do at the end of the summer. I thought I could live in the cabin if I had to, at least through October, and anyway, lots of people lived in the Catskills all year round, duh. I imagined putting chains on my tires and driving to the various grocery stores and seeing them preserved in ice. This made me laugh, so I wrote a song called "Ice Palace"—the last bit was what I liked: "No one inside but a giant rat / Standing quietly next to a cat. / They looked around, had the place to themselves, /

Then quietly they went and explored the shelves." I liked the tune I wrote, upbeat and fun, and imagined the music video as a cartoon—maybe this was a kids' song.

I wrote lots of songs that summer—any old thing could inspire me—and that reminded me of something I'd heard about the Traveling Wilburys. One thing I had always liked about their albums was that they were reflective—more about existing than about love or desire (what made me laugh when I listened to "Cool Dry Place" again was a rhythmic sound I hadn't noticed before, a kind of punctuation, that started toward the middle of the song and could have been produced by a kazoo, but sounded like a series of farts). I decided that I had to learn more about sticking to the beat, and I could do that by listening to Bonnie Raitt and Marcia Ball, and also dancing around the room. But, jeez, I thought, I am forty-five now! So I pushed all the furniture in the front room aside and made sure that the rug was smooth before I started dancing around. I would alternate playing, singing, dancing, and writing, all the while listening to what others were composing. One of the most fun things was to figure out what key Bonnie or Marcia or Bruce or Tom was using, and then playing along, as if I were in the backup band. That was perhaps the most enjoyable summer I'd ever spent.

It was when I was going for walks that I thought of Mom. One thing about caring for your mother as she makes her way toward death is that as you are doing it, that pain and trauma become the main thing that you know about her. But I realized over the summer that you don't want that to be a main thing you remember about her, so on my walks, I made myself remember the old days—her putting me to bed when I was small, her whacking Dizzy with the rolled-up newspaper when she pooped in the house, her taking me to the Muny, and even the low sounds of the conversations she was having in the living room on the nights when some of those actors came over and she put me to bed a little early. The best way to mourn, I thought, was to remember and imagine the person you are mourning in as much detail as you can. I tried to write a song about remembering myself at ten, twenty, thirty, and forty, then imagining Mom at the same ages, and having us talk to one another. I must have written down ten different versions, but they didn't work as songs, especially since my first idea was to use different sorts of melodies—jazz, folk, Sinatra pop, rock. I thought it might work as an album, but finally I gave up on the idea, even though I was glad to have written down what I came up with.

September 15 rolled around, and I had to choose whether to stay in the cabin all winter. My apartment in the city was still sublet, and Jackie said that the woman didn't want to move out. I had given up my apartment in St. Louis, as much as I enjoyed it. Because of Uncle Drew and Aunt Louise managing my investments, the question wasn't how to pay for the rental, it was where it should be. One thought that crossed my mind was traveling around the world and staying in hotels—maybe for a week each—and seeing lots of new places. I wrote down a list of a few that I had been curious about over the years—Hawaii, southern Italy, Munich, Istanbul, Stockholm and Oslo, Nova Scotia (which I had seen out my window on my plane back from the UK), Tenerife (just because of the name), Lisbon. But then I thought that I should not go back to the solitary life that was my habit, and decided to move to St. Louis, at least for the winter. I called Uncle Drew and told him my plan, and he offered to put me up, since there was plenty of room in the house, but I thought that I wanted to explore St. Louis a little, too, so I stayed with them for a week. I decided to drive in circles, starting at the botanical garden and then widening my range, sort of the way we had driven Mom around. I didn't get far. There was a pleasant small house for rent on the corner of Bent and Utah, on a little hill and across from a small park. I liked it, I rented it, and then I was a little sorry to have decided so quickly, so I continued my circles, and they became a hunt, or an exploration. One time, I stopped by the side of a small park with a reservoir, and wrote a song using the local street names: Henrietta takes up with Russell, and then, just before they marry and move to Lafayette, she meets someone much more Grand, who woos her by singing "Oh, Shenandoah." He wants to move to Michigan or Nebraska, but then they realize that Russell is after them, and they sneak off to Sidney. It was a mess of a song, but it took me only about seven minutes to write, and it made me laugh. Another time, when it was early October and the leaves were perfect, I walked around Resurrection Cemetery on a cloudy day and wrote a song about the End Times, when all the resurrected souls are sitting on their gravestones, waiting for the Resurrection Bus to arrive. Most of them are happy where they are, and don't want to get on the bus. Then here comes Jesus, in his usual robe, but with a little handbag hanging from his shoulder, and he is there to hand out the bus tickets, which shine through the fog of doom. He seems a little depressed, and every time he passes someone who isn't assigned a ticket, he sighs and apologizes. But no one wants to go. At the end of the song, he stands near the glimmering bus and throws all the tickets in the air, then he goes over and sits down under one of the trees and breathes a sigh of relief. Three-four time. That one made me laugh, too, and after I got home and worked on it for a while, I made a recording of it to be played at my funeral.

In the summer of my resurrection, when I went back to the cabin, and to the music festival, I didn't sing any of those songs—they were all for fun, but I mentioned them to the music producer when I called him after listening to his voicemail. He said, "We'll see," and then said he would call me back. Which he didn't do. I wasn't surprised, but when I got back to St. Louis and into my new house, I called him again, left a voicemail. When he called me, his tone was less brusque. It turned out that he was in Chicago visiting relatives, and he had a few days to spare, so he offered to drive down to see me. I told him my address, and he showed up at nine a.m. the following day—early riser. When I heard the doorbell and looked out the front window, I saw him from the back—he had his hands in his pockets and was staring up Utah Street, apparently wondering how I had fallen so low. When I let him in, he said, "I want you to know that I drove past your place in Roxbury the day after your performance. I couldn't even see the cabin they told me you live in."

I said, "It is back in the woods, but it actually exists."

I could tell by the look on his face that he thought he was being my savior, and I didn't stop him from thinking that. He was younger than I was, and maybe four inches shorter. He was neatly dressed and the car, which he had parked in the driveway behind my Tercel, was a red Subaru. I said, "Did you grow up in Chicago?"

He actually smiled, and said, "Don't tell. Muscatine." Then we both laughed.

It turned out that he was ten years younger than I was, his name was Ernie, and he had first heard my music when he was twelve, because his mother had bought one of my albums and liked to play it.

I said, "My record got to Muscatine?"

He said, "Well, she had to import it from Moline, but she thought it was worth the trip."

I saw that we were going to get along. He was now living in LA, and he worked for Capitol. He had talked them into sending him around to festivals and finding more obscure musicians so that he could expand their customer base. Then he paid me the compliment: "It isn't just your voice, which you know is very appealing. And rich. Very rich. It's the thoughtfulness of your lyrics. It can't be all screaming, and it can't be all 'I love you, why don't you love me, I'm dying here.' " Then he said, "Anyway, boomers are still a big portion of the audience. We can't overlook them, and they like melody and harmony."

I said, "We do."

His proposal was that they would put out a record that mixed the old songs with some new ones—when would I like to give him a taste of the new ones?

I said, "After lunch."

He said, "Where?"

"Gitto's or Schneithorst's."

We ended up going to Schneithorst's for lunch and Gitto's for dinner. Ernie liked both.

I sang for two hours, and Ernie recorded the whole thing on his Ricoh. Fortunately, because the house was small, brick, and neatly made, it had pretty good acoustics. Before he left, after I brought him back from Gitto's, he said that he would get back to me within a week.

The next night, a Wednesday, was our usual biweekly potluck at Alberta's. She had kept some of Mom's furniture and a couple of paintings that Mom had bought in the fifties, but mostly the house did not remind me of Mom, and I liked that. She had also planted a lot of flowers in the backyard, including hydrangeas, which were blooming. They were quite blue, and Alberta said that she sprayed the soil around them with vinegar, which made them go from pink to blue; however, since she also liked the pink ones, she sprayed it here and there. She also put in alyssum and verbena, and she was planning plenty more. I brought the apple pie, Nancy brought the broccoli quiche, Alberta made some baked chicken breasts with paprika and lemon, and Ava brought the wine, the crackers, and the artichoke dip. Aunt Louise and Uncle Drew were in Houston, with Uncle Hank and Brucie.

I waited until I was passing out the pie to tell them about Ernie. They of course congratulated me. Nancy said, "I can't believe there's anyone named Ernie still alive," and Alberta said, "Well, he's from Chicago."

Ava said, "Here's what we are going to do—we're each going to write down a list of our favorite songs of yours and give them to you, and then you can have a plan."

This seemed like a good idea to me, and it got to be a better idea because I didn't hear from Ernie until almost Thanksgiving. By then, Aunt Louise and Uncle Drew had contributed, and so had the other friends I had made in St. Louis. I wrote down my own favorites, too. I decided to write a full list with the number of votes next to each song, and I called that "the long list." I then printed out copies of that and passed them around in order to come up with a "short list." Brucie called and asked if he could play backup, and I said, "Why not?," and he said, "Because my fingers are so arthritic that I can't play for shit anymore."

I said, "That will make you all the more appealing to our audience."

Another person who was interested was Davie. I was still going to Ava's house every so often to help him practice, and he was a lot calmer. He preferred Mozart to all other composers now, but he also liked Chopin and Mussorgsky. Maybe ten days after we had talked about the lists, I went into the living room, and he finished playing one of Chopin's Études that was very lively—and then he glanced at me and played his own rendition of "Oh, There You Are."

Maybe that was the first time I had heard that melody without the lyrics (and Davie had made up the chords), and I was actually moved by it. He finished and threw up his hands, and I went over and gave him a hug. He said, "Mom found the record." Then, "I mean, it's only folk music, so it didn't take me long to figure out the chords." Yes, he sounded like a teenager, but I was flattered all the same.

When Ernie called me, he said that he had set things up, and he wanted me to fly to LA and do the recordings for the single of "A Long Good-bye" and "Nobody Told Me" and for the album, *Rattle Rising*. I asked him what songs he was going to include in the album, and he read me a list—it was the same list that my friends and I had come up with. I thought this was a good sign. I asked if I could add a new one, and he said, "Maybe." The one I wanted to add was the one inspired by the Resurrection Cemetery, so for the next week, I worked on that one, trying to give the tune a sort of soaring melancholy. For the end of the song, I imagined the torn-up tickets turning into stars, and the souls sitting in the cemetery staring up at them. I didn't make that idea explicit in the song, but I wanted to get the listener to feel something that might make him or her imagine what that felt like.

It was a pleasure wandering around in the sunshine in LA while everyone at home was hunkering down. There were four members in the studio band, all of whom were older than Ernie but younger than I was. They called themselves Ceiling Fan Fliers, and they had put out two albums in the eighties. They were a lot like the Freak-Outs—very rhythmic, very enthusiastic, and accepting of their degree of success. Unlike the Freak-Outs, most of them were married, with houses and children. Once again, the one who struck me was the drummer, whose name was Cliff. He was the unmarried one, and also the most easygoing one, unlike the drummer for the Freak-Outs, whose tantrums I remembered very clearly. Cliff had grown up in Detroit and had a lot of Motor City musical talent.

He was the one who smiled a little bit and lifted his eyebrows when Ernie seemed dissatisfied with a take. The other band members put up with it, but it looked like Cliff thought it was amusing, along with lots of other stuff, like the lead guitar player burping very loudly when we were recording "What Dance Was That?" When Ernie told us to start over, Cliff said, "Man, I think we should keep that in there. Adds authenticity."

When we were finished in the studio for the day, I was standing out on the street, looking around (and thinking of Martin), and Cliff, who had just come out, said, "Where are you staying?"

"The Prospect."

He said, "Do you need a ride? I'm parked right over there." He pointed to a silver Lexus.

I said, "It isn't far. I'd rather walk. But thanks."

Cliff said, "Mind if I walk with you?" For a moment I was suspicious, but he had such a bright smile that my suspicions evaporated. I said, "Sure."

After a few steps, he said, "Mostly, I just wanted to tell you how much I appreciate 'A Long Good-bye.' My best friend died of AIDS in '89, and it was such a shock."

I said, "I am so sorry about that. I wrote it about my mom. She died a year and a half ago. But it wasn't like your friend. She was in her seventies, and we knew it was coming, and so did she. I think she was relieved."

Cliff said, "Given what Jim had to go through, I think he was, too. But even though he was sick for a long time, I never got past the first stage of grief."

I said, "Shock."

He nodded, then said, "Now I mostly put it all out of my mind, but playing this song over and over and hearing you sing it actually eased me toward acceptance."

We paused at the corner, and I turned and gave him a hug. He hugged back. We crossed Vine. Then he said, "Are you hungry?" and we both said, "Musso!" I remembered that spot from my previous trip. I hadn't wanted every spot to remind me of Martin, but then I decided that there was something about reliving bits of that affair that would be a real pleasure. When we were seated, Cliff said, "Jim and I loved to go to this place."

Cliff was as easy to talk to as anyone I had ever known. He was funny but also thoughtful and kind. I guessed he was thirty-five, but his skin was so smooth that he looked like he was in his twenties. I thought that I looked like I could pass for his mother, at least in terms of age, and I was therefore very surprised when we got to the Prospect, and he gave me a hug and a real kiss before turning and walking back to his car in the dark. When I got to my room, still enjoying the feeling of the hug, I walked over to the night table and turned on the light, in the process knocking my backpack off the bed. When I started picking everything up, there was my roll of bills, which I hadn't thought of in years—maybe since Grandmother's death. I picked it up and looked at it, and hoped it was a sign that Cliff and I might have an affair.

Which we did. We got into a habit. After a session, I would walk back to the Prospect, and then about six, he would show up and we would walk to Musso and have dinner. I didn't mind going there every night, because the specials were always good. After dinner, he would walk with me back to the Prospect, and we would go to my room, where I would play a few songs and sing, and he would play the rhythm by tapping his shoes on the wooden floor of the room. It was a form of dancing, and I saw that he would have been an excellent dancer. There wasn't enough room for him to jump around, but he went back and forth, swaying his hips and shoulders in time to the music. A half hour of that and we would fall into bed and enjoy ourselves. He always brought a condom. One night, I said,

"You won't believe how old I am." He said, "I know you are seventy, but you don't look like it, so I'm going to choose not to believe it." I scrunched my face into some wrinkles. We had a lot of laughs, and we shared a few things—I told him about Martin and Mom's death, and he told me that he was bisexual and that he liked to switch back and forth. His last affair was with an Australian lawyer who worked in LA and who was out of town at the moment, but was planning to take him to Australia to look around when they both had some time off. I asked if I could go along, and we both laughed, but just the thought of it made me want to see that distant and interesting place. Cliff said, "Pete told me that I have to learn to ride a horse first, because where he lives, that's the only form of transportation." And then, oddly enough, he told me that he knew how to ride a horse, because he had grown up in a neighborhood in LA where kids could learn to ride. He said, "Thing is, I haven't ridden in twenty years, but Pete says it comes back to you as soon as you get on." I didn't ask him if he had named himself after Jimmy Cliff, but I saw a resemblance.

Then he said, "You know, not many people understand how enjoyable it is to be bi. You meet more kinds of people and you learn a lot about how they think and how love works."

I said, "How does love work?"

Cliff said, "Like waves on the beach. Gentle but a little boring, moderate, enjoyable, huge, scary, dangerous. I don't think I'm the only person who enjoys each one and then begins longing for another type. I think everyone is like that, but I'm one of the ones who accepts it."

I said, "What was your parents' marriage like?"

Cliff said, in a very straightforward manner, "I don't really know because my father was shot when I was about five. That's why my mother got me into music, because she thought that would be a comfort. And it was."

I rounded up and said, "You are my twenty-fifth affair."

Cliff said, "Poor you! If you really are seventy, that's less than one every two years since you were a teen. You must be lonely." He exaggerated his look of sympathy and patted me on the shoulder.

I said, "Number, please?"

He said, "One fifty."

I said, "I'm surprised you're still alive!"

He said, "So is my mom."

I said, "Does she . . ."

"Know about all of this?"

I nodded.

Cliff said, "I've been telling her about everything my whole life. She's probably my one true love."

I said, "So—"

And Cliff said, "Freudian!"

We both laughed.

A week later, our recording sessions were over and so was the affair, but when I listen to the album and look at the track list, I can hear in not only the timbre of my voice but also in the accuracy of his drumming a connection and a pleasure in what we were doing behind the scenes, as it were. When I got back to St. Louis, I wrote a song called "Surprised You're Still Alive," not from my point of view, but from his mother's, because I felt a bit like his mother, loving him but letting him go.

How old were you,
My sweet little man,
When your father died
With a gun in his hand?

For years I kept you in the house,
Playing music
My own little mouse
Kind and sweet,
Healthy and neat,

And then you left
With nowhere to go

And made your life
A kind of show.

I love you, child.
Handsome and wild,
Ready to spliff, or
To jump off a cliff,

Your giant smile
Lights up my sky,
Please don't leave again
Without saying good-bye.

THEY DID VIDEOS of two songs, and I think they chose them ("I'm on My Way" and "You Left") because they were cheap. Two guys, a cameraman and a director, showed up in St. Louis. We went to where my former apartment was, and as I walked up the street, carrying my guitar and looking around, they did a voice-over of me singing my song. The only question was what sort of day—a sunny one, a cloudy one, a hot one, a windy one. Ernie couldn't decide whether he wanted the song to be depressing or, as he said, "resigned." We walked up that street six times in two days, and I persuaded the cameraman to follow my gaze and include the trees and the houses. My favorite version was the last one—twilight, the windows of the houses lit up, the clouds still visible. The second video, for "You Left," had to be near the cabin. I chatted up some people around Roxbury to see if anyone would let us make the video at their farm, and one guy said he would, but he would give us only three hours—after lunch and before the kids came home from school. We picked a day, and it turned out to be perfect. It had rained the night before, so all the flowers and plants were brilliant. The wife kept an eye on us, but she didn't mind me standing in the doorway, holding the knob of the door and staring into the distance while I sang. She also stayed out of the way when the cameraman panned toward the misty mountains. The farm was maybe four miles from my place, and subsequently, we stayed in contact, and sometimes had lunch together in Margaretville, where she preferred to shop. She also gave me some lettuce and strawberries from her garden.

After the filming and the recordings, I waited and waited, until, as always with Ernie, I thought, Well, that's that, and then, two days later, he called me and told me when the single and the album would be released, and sent me a list of the festivals he had booked me for. He said, "Jodie, I like the record a lot, but I gotta say don't get your hopes up." I knew he was thinking of my crummy little house on Utah and my future life as a homeless person. All I said was, "Okay." I thought that someday, I would send him a check to repay him for his efforts. As for me, I didn't really know what I wanted. After the call, I went into my room and took the roll of bills out of my drawer and stared at it. Here I was, forty-seven, healthy, with plenty of friends and plenty of money. I didn't need the success. But maybe Cliff and the other members of the Ceiling Fan Fliers did need it.

Everything I knew about the stock market I learned from Aunt Louise, either when I went to have dinner with her and Uncle Drew (and sometimes Allison and Darryl and their kids if they were visiting) or when we saw each other at Alberta's. The news was always good—the stock market was going up and up, and it seemed to like Bill Clinton better than Uncle Drew did. Aunt Louise corrected me—Uncle Drew liked Bill Clinton, and thought he knew what he was doing, but the last thing he ever wanted was for the stock market to go up and up and up. I said, "Why not?"

We were doing the dishes at their place, and she said, "Well, he used to like it, but that was when he could actually keep track of everything. Invest in Ford or Chevy? I remember around the time we were about to get married, one of his favorite strategies was to go to a car dealer and pretend like we were looking for a new car. He'd say that we liked to get a new one each year. So some guy would take us for a test drive, and he'd say that he'd like to have a look under the hood. Then he would say that he would think about it. Then he would make a list of various traits that the cars had. One of the first places he took me was to a Chevy dealer, I think Weber's. He wanted to try an Impala, do you remember those?"

I said, "Were those the ones with back ends like a pair of wings?"

Aunt Louise nodded. "And eyeballs and very angry eyebrows! We drove it around the lot, and I remember him saying, 'This thing isn't put together very well. Do you feel it kind of rattling, like it's going to fall apart?' And then he parallel parked it by some curb and got out and showed me how low the bottom was. Not only didn't we buy it, he never invested in General Motors after that, and one of the first car companies he invested in was Toyota. 'Sixty-five. After he tried a Corona. He loved to sneak around various companies and factories, trying to figure out how they were working. If a factory was a mess, he didn't invest in that company because he knew that whoever was in charge wasn't doing his job. I'm sure they called him by his first name over at McDonnell Douglas. He could always tell when something seemed to be getting out of hand. But he kept his thoughts to himself, smiled like he loved the place. Finance doesn't work like that anymore. You've got to keep up with all sorts of details and watch the ups and downs. A couple of weeks ago he was talking about diamonds, of all things. I have no idea why."

Uncle Drew came into the room and said, "Why what?"

Aunt Louise, who was always straightforward, said, "Why were you talking about diamonds the other day?"

Without missing a beat, Uncle Drew said, "Because you need more of them. A tiara was what I was thinking."

Aunt Louise turned around and put the mixing bowl I had just dried on her head.

We all laughed. Uncle Drew had reached retirement age—or would have, if he wanted to retire, but it was evident to me, Aunt Louise, Allison, and Darryl that he not only didn't want to retire (maybe because his profession had taken him to so many places, and he wanted to see more) but he was also afraid to retire. He told Aunt Louise that he had no fears about their future—their house had been paid off for years, they had sold the little place in the Ozarks that they had bought as a summer house because they only went there twice, and the cars he had were the ones he liked and was familiar with (Aunt Louise said that she never saw him make a mistake on a new car)—but he was afraid of doing it. What he was afraid of was that if Allison, Darryl, and I were in charge of our accounts, we would fail to pay attention and lose our money. So he was our overseer, and he wanted to be one of those responsible, persnickety ones that he had admired when he was investigating businesses as a young man. He also gave plenty to charity, including the botanical garden. He didn't want to stop that either.

One day I did ask Aunt Louise directly if Uncle Drew had any health issues, and she said that he didn't. As with cars and houses and financial planning, he believed in regular maintenance, and yes, he was on several drugs for blood issues, but he took only about six pills a day. She didn't take any. Nevertheless.

However, my worries were overtaken by my responsibilities. Once *Rattler Rising* came out, my job was to go on the road, and the thing I liked best about it was that I went to smaller venues in smaller towns, most of which had older populations.

Kansas City first, then Ames, Iowa, and after that up to St. Paul, over to Milwaukee, down to Indianapolis, and Louisville, Pittsburgh, and Buffalo, then Boston, then to the West Coast. The Ceiling Fan Fliers came along, of course, but we traveled separately. Sometimes I had a chat with Cliff, but we knew we weren't going to rekindle the affair. My favorite stop was in Monterey, where I opened for Lyle Lovett. We were tuning and practicing a little bit in the greenroom, and I heard him hum an old Townes Van Zandt song—"If I Needed You." I said, "I remember that one!" He said, "It's a sweet one." And then, after he finished his set, he glanced toward me, offstage, and said, "Jodie and I are going to sing one together," and he motioned me to come onstage. I didn't know what he was talking about, but I brought my guitar and stood next to him. He sang the first two lines, "If I needed you, would you come to me? / Would you come to me for to ease my pain?" And I sang the next two. He sang two more verses, then we joined on the last two. Lyle was easy to harmonize with, and I thought our voices meshed pretty well, considering we hadn't rehearsed this at all, or even met before. But clearly, he was one of those guys who is always willing to give something a try.

After Monterey, I headed up to Santa Cruz, down to Santa Barbara, and then to Tucson and Austin. Fourteen performances in three weeks, some of them full houses. What was more relaxing was the music festivals. I was sent to six of them, and because they were folk festivals, I went without the Ceiling Fan Fliers, because people who love folk music like to see you play your own guitar (or banjo—some of those guys were so adept that I was tempted to buy a Gibson long neck). The first one, Old Songs, was only an hour's drive up from Roxbury. I alternated my songs with old ones, but no murder ballads, even though I loved them. I stuck with "On Raglan Road," "Farewell to Tarwathie," "Loch Lomond," "John Henry," "Stewball," and "Hobo's Lullaby." I also went to the ones in Lowell, Massachusetts, and North Carolina. Obviously, I went to Newport, and then, after a short break, to the National, which had begun in St. Louis in the thirties and then moved around. When I went, it was in Dayton, and after it was over, I used the opportunity to drive up to Akron and wander around for four days, trying to get a feeling of what it felt like for Mom to grow up there. It was a pleasant town and I enjoyed the art museum, but I was glad to get back to St. Louis, even though when I got back, I discovered that my air-conditioning system was broken. In September, I went to Telluride, where I had never been before. I drove—Telluride is due west of St. Louis, and I stopped in Burlington, Colorado, on the way. I loved the strangeness of the absolutely flat landscape of eastern Colorado suddenly shooting up into the Rockies, so after the festival, I loitered around Denver, Boulder, Colorado Springs, and Fort Collins, spending a night or two in each town. When I drove home, I made a rule that I could stop only in towns with weird names, so that turned into wandering, too—WaKeeney, Broken Bow, Osceola, Tarkio, Moberly.

By the time I got back, I had plenty to do around the house. We had a little party at Alberta's, and my job was to bake the apple pie, but I left it in the oven too long, and had to bake another one, and then we spent such a long time yakking it up that I didn't leave until after midnight, promptly ran over a nail, and got a flat tire, so Aunt Louise had to pick me up, and plenty of this and that, and so I forgot to figure out what I had earned with my record and my tour. It wasn't until Ernie called me in November that I even thought about it. He said that he was sending me a check—$156,934. He sounded disappointed. I put it in my savings account. He never called me back, so no other albums were to be made, but the following year, he sent me another check—$67,345, which I put into the account. I didn't tell Uncle Drew about the money because I thought he, like Ernie, would be disappointed, but I wasn't.

15

IN THE SPRING of 1997, I had nothing else to do, so I decided to buy a house. I'd rented the house near the botanical garden on a whim, and it didn't suit me the way the cabin in Roxbury did. I thought of relocating to the Catskills, but I understood that the Catskills promoted isolation and St. Louis discouraged it, so I thought it would be better to find a house and make a commitment. At first, my house hunt was just an exploration—I drove to Wentzville, where Chuck Berry's place was, and then to the Central West End, where Eliot, Williams, and Burroughs grew up (not John Burroughs, the naturalist and product of Roxbury, whom I revered, but William Burroughs, whom I did not revere, who wrote *Junkie, Queer,* and *Naked Lunch* and also shot his wife). I looked at the house on Skinker, but it was not for sale. Aunt Louise knew where Phyllis Schlafly's house was, so I drove past there—another reason not to choose Ladue. I wondered if maybe Fontella Bass lived in town somewhere, but people said she now lived in Chicago. I also knew that T Bone Burnett was born in St. Louis, but I didn't know where—I had hoped that we might meet at a music festival when I was touring, but that hadn't happened. And I knew that Tina Turner had lived somewhere in St. Louis when she was young, but no one I knew had any idea where—Alberta said it was probably up in the Ville, but she didn't know. So I had to decide on my own. Nancy, Aunt Louise, Alberta, and Uncle Drew of course had suggestions, as did the people from high school that I'd reconnected with. Everyone thought that my failure to find a house must be frustrating, but in fact I enjoyed it, because it gave me a reason to go to a lot of open houses and snoop around. I even wrote a song, called "I Want Your House," about a woman who is obsessed with a house on Hawthorne, in Webster Park, who walks past it every night and then sneaks in and lives secretly in the attic. I saw it as a sort of wicked witch song, with a tune in A minor, and when I was in Roxbury, I enjoyed playing it. I thought Ernie might like it, too, but even when I called him and described it over the phone, he never responded. After I got back to St. Louis in the fall, I sang it a few times around Halloween, and it did get a pretty good response, especially when I put on witchy makeup and messed up my hair. After I finished it, I would slump to the side and then sit up and finish my set with "Ding-Dong! The Witch Is Dead." It was fun.

In the meantime, I did find a house just across the highway from downtown Clayton, and I bought it because it was truly weird. All brick, of course, with a huge front porch that jutted out into the yard that you could get to from both the first floor and the second floor. No backyard. Plenty of cars zipping by on the highway, but the bricks sort of blocked out the noise. It was one of those houses, like the cabin, that you fall in love with, and then you show your friends around and they all say, "You're kidding me, right?" But I liked the fact that I could walk over to Wydown and into Clayton, that the neighborhood, with plenty of trees and idiosyncratic houses, had a sort of private quality. When I showed it to Uncle Drew, he took me to another house down the street that was also for sale, with an actual driveway, but I was already committed. I moved in in mid-October and then discovered that I was lucky again, because in November, when I was walking down the street (which I often did), I saw a lot of trucks outside the house Uncle Drew liked, and when I asked what they were doing, they said that they had to replace the whole heating system, which had broken down just after the new owners moved in. I often imagined Ernie coming for a visit, looking around, and deciding that he had saved me from the poorhouse, but he never did. I still had most of the money I had earned in my savings account, and I had bought the place with money that Aunt Louise and Uncle Drew had earned for me.

It turned into what Mom's house had been when I was young—a place to put up the visitors and the relatives. Brucie and Vicki, his wife, stayed with me, and I came to like Vicki's daughter, Kayla, who eventually decided to go to Washington U. and very much enjoyed meeting Nancy, who steered her away from math and toward astronomy. Aunt Lily moved in for about a year because her place basically collapsed, and she didn't have anywhere else to go, but the house was big enough so that we only chatted or joked around when we happened to see each other. I also gave her my old Tercel, which I had learned to maintain. When I gave it to her, it had 352,000 miles on it and still ran like a dream. It was just big enough for her, and since she was still working at the restaurant, she didn't want to show up in the parking lot in a car that made her boss think that she had enough money to buy a new car. I replaced it with a Prius, small and, I thought, aerodynamic, a hybrid. They later got very popular, but when I bought it, it was because of the pearly light green color and the comfort of the driver's seat, as well as my appreciation of the Tercel (which ended up with 450,000 miles before Aunt Lily put it out of its misery; while she had it, though, I was the one who paid for the maintenance). Aunt Louise and Uncle Drew let me do Thanksgiving and Christmas Eve at my place sometimes—we eventually got to the point where we alternated.

Maybe there was some significance to the fact that not long before the end of the year (or the world), I passed someone standing right next to the sidewalk. I was startled, paused, and turned to look. There was no one. What I had seen was some shadows of a tree limb against the side of a house, shadows that looked like a face—two prominent shining eyeballs, a nose, and a small line under the nose that was the length of a mouth. That line was what gave the shadow-face an expression of thoughtfulness and a little despair—the middle of the line was thin and straight, each end rose and then dipped. Even after I realized that it was just a shadow (the air was still and the tree limbs weren't shaking), I couldn't stop thinking of it as a face, as a mood, as a consciousness. I didn't believe in ghosts, but I did wonder how many times humans had seen something like this and interpreted it as a being, hostile or friendly. When I got to my place, I wrote a song. It went, "You call me God, but I am a shadow / The sun and a tree birthed me, then let me go / I saw you run off with a gleam in your eye as I faded to darkness by and by. / I come and go, day after day / Darkness stretching over the ground / Long then short, round and round. / The sun is my maker, the moon is my friend / My coming and going will never end. / You mean nothing to me, so don't make of me / A being who gives you permission to be / A killer, a thief, a rapist, a chief. / It was you you saw, nothing more / And your feelings now are leading you to war."

When Y2K rolled around, I gave the party—everyone I knew in St. Louis: our group, my relatives, couples, teenagers, a few children, Brucie, Vicki, and Kayla. Nancy and I moved the furniture in the living room into the corners, and I hired a DJ, who brought his own computer, with four speakers, which he set up around the room. He knew that the theme of the party was the end of the world, so he made sure to play a few of those songs. I sang along to "The End of the World," and then to "Redemption Song." I think everyone enjoyed both R.E.M.'s "It's the End of the World as We Know It (And I Feel Fine)" and Soundgarden's "4th of July" the most. The coming apocalypse was my excuse for everything we did at the party—eat dessert first, drink plenty of piña coladas, eat every last bit of two huge roasted turkeys, let the kids stay up past midnight. The last song the DJ played was "Dance Me to the End of Love," and I required everyone to grab a partner and sashay around the room for the whole song, which was a long one because it was Lenny. I also shouted, "Sing along!" and about half of the guests did, or at least hummed and ladada-ed. A few of us were drunk enough to stumble, but no one fell down, though Kayla did a great imitation of swooning into the arms of her boyfriend at the end of the song. The DJ packed up his equipment and left, and then, at one a.m., we went out onto the upper porch and stared up into the sky, looking for evidence of the end (or so we pretended), and it was fun to point out this or that and shout, "There it is!" or "Look at that!" Since I had four bedrooms, I could put up everyone who said he or she was too tipsy to drive, and Brucie drove a few others to their places.

When I went to bed, I stayed awake for a while, thinking about my good luck. I was fifty now, turning fifty-one in less than two months. I remembered when I was in college, and our professors who were fifty were the ones that we tried to ignore. The year I graduated from college, Mom turned fifty. And Grandmother turned fifty the year I turned one. When I was in my teens, I knew I would never turn fifty, because of nukes or the various other apocalypses that someone was always predicting. And here we were, surviving. The great enigma, I thought, was the sense you have, that comes and goes, of who you are, what a self is, how it is physical (when you lift your hand up and stare at your fingers, your palm, your wrist, the back of your hand) and internal (when you sift through your memories, jumping back and forth between the ones that seem to have happened yesterday, even though they happened decades ago—Uncle Drew at Cahokia Downs, handing me the roll of two-dollar bills and putting his finger to his lips while in the background I could hear a sharp male voice announcing the next race—and the ones that happened recently that you can barely remember: the face of the DJ—blue eyes or brown ones, did I give him a piece of cake or not?). I thought of all the songs and books that had been written over the years, of how even the ones that were said to be "trite" or "unoriginal" were actually slightly different from one another, the way twins are slightly different from one another, and so even those songs and books reveal the differences between their creators. That reminded me of my drive around St. Thomas—how each day and even each moment was different, and how maybe capturing those differences is what songwriters or writers or painters and photographers are really after. Then I remembered Leon telling me that as much as he knew that he had to play the music he loved correctly, he was always torn between the various versions he came up with, depending on his mood. Then I thought, Well, if the end of the world is here, perhaps the worst aspect of the destruction will be that no one will know how everyone else has experienced it—for the last moment, we will all be pushed back into our own little selves and that will be it.

Then I wondered, maybe for the first time ever (and I was still staring at my fingers folding and opening, spreading and closing), what it would have been like to have a baby, and watch that little consciousness wake up and expand and become different from my own, as mine had become different from Mom's. I hummed a little bit of "Redemption Song" and also, maybe for the first time, I saw that perhaps the invention of religion had been an attempt to understand this feeling of being alive and aware. I continued humming Bob Marley's song to myself as I fell asleep, and when I woke up, the sun was high. Vicki and Kayla had already whipped up the pancakes and fried the bacon. Around the table, we talked about what a fun party that was, and as I kissed everyone good-bye and watched them leave, I gave thanks to "Whoever" that I had learned how to have friends.

ODDLY ENOUGH, it was thinking about consciousness that got me through the nightmare that was the next twenty years. Uncle Drew was now sixty-nine, and Aunt Louise wanted him to back away from the finance business, especially since Darryl was doing fine and Aunt Louise thought he was fully capable of handling their investments. I actually heard a low-voiced, but intense, argument they were having in the kitchen when I walked into their house one day (doors still unlocked, friends and family still welcome). I backed out of the door and went around to the yard, which was full of jonquils and tulip buds. I made noise closing the gate and shuffled my feet while I was walking. I saw Uncle Drew glance through the window, and I guess that they put their argument aside, because he came to the door and waved me in for a cup of coffee. All they talked about in front of me was whether one of the beech trees in the backyard needed to be pruned, or taken down altogether. The other trees, including the sugar maple, were doing fine. It seemed relaxing to Uncle Drew to talk about trees for twenty minutes, but the next time Aunt Louise came to one of our dinners, she said that she was thinking of completely unplugging his computer, because too much news was making him edgy. By this time I had actually bought a computer, an iBook, key lime. I hadn't had any interest in computers before that one—all I saw were large heavy chunks, sitting on tables and desks, looking dim. After I got the iBook (and internet), I enjoyed opening up various websites and contemplating what the people who were posting on those websites were feeling and thinking. There was a way in which I got to know people without getting out of the house, and I enjoyed it. When I subscribed to the *New York Times,* it was interesting to have the *Post-Dispatch* next to me on the bed and to compare what the editors of the *Times* and the *Post* thought was worth covering, including, of course, who they were talking about in the music section.

In early April, I was reading the *Times,* and in the book section, I came across the long review of a book about horse racing. Of course I paused to read it, thinking of my roll of bills. But it wasn't a book about, say, the history of the Triple Crown, which Uncle Drew might have been interested in, or Epsom, which might have interested Martin or his father. It was about a book that had talking horses as characters. That made me remember reading *Black Beauty* when I saw it at the library not long after Uncle Drew won the money. I remembered enjoying the fact that the horse was telling the story, but also finding it too sad to finish, and in some ways, I had felt the same about watching *National Velvet*. In spite of my winnings, I had more or less lost my interest in horses by the time I was in eighth grade. After I put away the two newspapers and was walking down Hanley into Clayton, I realized that the name of the author of the book that was being reviewed was familiar—the gawky girl. I couldn't believe she was being reviewed in the *New York Times*! But I had other things to do when I got home, so I didn't open the computer, and there was no mention of her in the *Post*. I didn't think about it again until a few days later, when I was having a bite to eat near Left Bank Books, and I walked in and looked around.

The book that had been reviewed in the *Times* was on display. The cover was white, with a sort of nineteenth-century image of a horse galloping, ears back, eyes rolling. The jockey's head was turned. I thought it was an odd picture. I stared at it, then picked up the book and opened it. One of the employees said, "Interesting book."

I said, "I didn't realize she had become a jockey."

The woman laughed and said, "She's way too tall for that, but she did say in some interview that that was her plan when she was in school."

I said, "I went to school with her, and she was about the same size as all of us in seventh grade. Then, as I remember, she was kidnapped, and a beanpole girl was returned to us who did a pretty good job of pretending to be her."

We both laughed.

The woman waved at the shelves and said, "She's been productive."

I glanced at the books and said, "Which one is your favorite?"

She pulled one out. It was called *The All-True Travels and Adventures of Lidie Newton*. She said, "I am quite fond of this one, because it is set around here and over in Kansas, and I like historical novels, but it's hard to choose." She pulled another one out, and said, "She won a Pulitzer for this one." She set it on the table nearby and pulled out another. She said, "This one is funny. Academic novel, if you like those." Then another one. She said, "This one is set in Greenland, in the Middle Ages. It has about four devoted fans, but they are very devoted. I know one guy who has read it seven times, or so he says."

I looked at the books and said, "So, she became a dentist, then time traveled to medieval Greenland, then became a farmer, and now she has fulfilled her dream of becoming a jockey."

The woman smiled and looked around the store. She said, "That's what authors do. Have you read any Ursula Le Guin? She is very fond of visiting other planets, though she's closemouthed about how she gets there."

There was a young man standing by the cash register, so the woman went over to him, and I looked at the novels for a little longer. The one I chose was the funny one, and I did enjoy it, though it took me a while to read. I laughed at some of the adventures of the characters, and I enjoyed the lesbian secretary who was the real boss of the university. Sometimes I lost track of who was who, but there was a list of characters at the beginning that I could refer to. And then there was the hog. Sweet character, sad fate. One thing I liked about it was the way that she jumped around from one consciousness to another, so maybe, since we were about the same age, that was what you thought about when you were in your fifties and worries sort of receded and let you open up to other ideas. After I finished it, I thought of writing a set of songs from different points of view. I was reminded of Lyle Lovett, who was one of the few male singers who did that sort of thing. He had recently come out with "Texas Trilogy," from the point of view of several people going through hard times in Texas. I had enjoyed singing with him that time, but now I also remembered one from the eighties, "She's Hot to Go." At the time it came out, I wondered if there was a single woman in America who didn't hate it for being shallow and mean, but when you get to the end, one of his female backup singers says, idly, "Well, you ugly, too," which always made me laugh and also made me give Lyle the benefit of the doubt (though even if I hadn't, I would have been glad to sing with him).

Out of curiosity, I read a few things about the gawky girl. Apparently she really had been to Greenland, and the Pulitzer novel was based on *King Lear,* which I thought was weird, but I did remember that when we read *King Lear* in senior English, I hadn't liked it. I had always preferred Shakespeare's comedies, especially *As You Like It* and *The Taming of the Shrew*. I remembered listening to some sixteenth- and seventeenth-century songs written by women and played on the lute in one of my music history classes at Penn State.

What had interested me about them was how difficult I thought they were to sing—lots of high notes, arpeggios, and not exactly the sort of resounding rhythm that popular music has today. Leon and I had tried a few, but unless I changed the key, I didn't really have the range. However, thinking about it helped me understand why someone who was addicted to literature rather than music would try to fix *King Lear.* Then, one day, when I was taking a long walk to our school, which I sometimes did, because it was only a little over two miles from my new place, I remembered walking past her in the front hall of the school, maybe a ways down from the front door. She was standing there smiling, her glasses sliding down her nose, and one of the guys in our class, one of the outgoing ones, not one of the math nerds that abounded, stopped and looked at her, and said, "You know, I would date you if you weren't so tall."

She smiled, so I remembered thinking that she thought that was a compliment.

Well, it was interesting. I brought up her name during one of our dinners. Nancy had heard of her, Alberta had heard of the Kansas book, and Aunt Louise had read the farm book—she said she got all the way through it, but it was really depressing. None of them had read the dentist book, and I had lost my copy.

THE REST OF the year was fairly uneventful. Aunt Louise was much more aware than I was of global warming. I'm not sure that people in St. Louis understood global warming as anything other than even more humidity, even more rain, even more floods. It would be bad, but really it would also always be what it had always been. When I made some half-joking dopey comment about this at one of our parties, Nancy set me straight. She said, idly, "Well, it's better to call it climate change, but do you know how many days we had that were over a hundred degrees this summer?"

Alberta said, "It definitely got to a hundred and two in mid-August, because I kept looking at my thermometer and then going back down to the basement. And my relatives stayed with me, because it was hotter uptown."

Aunt Louise said, "What I remember is the temp getting up to a hundred and seven back in '84."

Nancy said, "Well, Jodie, if you live as long as your grandfather, that would be another forty years, right?"

I said, "Almost."

"I'm guessing there will be ten to fifteen days over a hundred degrees, but that doesn't count the flooding and the drought."

I said, "How can you have both flooding and drought?"

"Bigger storms in the fall and spring, then no rain at all during the summer."

Aunt Louise said, "Bigger storms mean more tornadoes."

At the very moment I thought of moving back to New York—no tornadoes—Nancy said, "And worse hurricanes. Worse crops. More bugs and diseases. Believe me, the scientists have worked it all out."

I said, "Why do you sound so resigned? This seems like a big deal."

"Well, the climate guys have been banging on about this for twenty years, and no one is paying a lick of attention. Bush and Cheney are all oil and gas. They are reeking of it. Gore has a plan."

Aunt Louise sighed, then said, "I try to talk to Drew about this, but the only thing he says is that we can help Hank and his family move back to St. Louis if we have to." Then she said, "Drew and I are lucky to be as old as we are. I have no idea how you guys, or Darryl and Allison, are going to deal with this."

I thought our conversation was depressing, and I learned more about it—I read *The End of Nature,* which was ten years old at that point, and I was a little surprised that Bill Clinton hadn't paid a lick of attention to it. He'd gone to Georgetown, Oxford, and Yale. I would have thought that that sort of thing was right up his alley. Or Hillary. She would have paid attention, too.

A couple of days after we had that talk, I walked over to Shaw Park. To get there, I had to cross a bridge over the highway, and as I did, I noticed the river of cars in a different way, and I even sensed the exhaust rising around me. Then, as I walked through Clayton, I looked at all the buildings, so tall and gleaming. By contrast, the park looked spare and ailing. It was the same when I walked back. It was not a happy, distracting walk, like all of the previous ones had been. What Nancy told us had actually changed my consciousness. I knew something now that I couldn't get rid of (though I knew that in the cabin in Roxbury, I could hide out from it). It was seven weeks until the election. What else did I have to do? I donated to Gore, I campaigned for him, I carried leaflets house to house. I didn't have to drive the Prius much, because there were so many walkable neighborhoods. Doing this was what actually perked me up a little bit. In St. Louis, it was the perfect time of year to be exploring neighborhoods, even in the rain. There were some amazing large and beautiful houses near Oak Knoll Park, but even though I loved them, I could not leaflet them every day. However, I could do a multipronged loop that stretched out from that park toward Richmond Heights, our old house on Skinker, Forsythe, Wash U., and Hanley. As the leaves turned, I would start by wandering around the park for ten minutes, do a leafleting loop, then get back to the park and wander again for maybe twenty minutes before returning to my place. It was named appropriately, for the knoll and the many oaks, which were spread across the knoll in a very inviting way. The leaves turned red and orange, lighting up the limbs, and then they fell away as the days passed. Now they crunched under my feet, and the sky appeared, and even though it was usually cloudy, I appreciated that sort of light, too, because there was a privacy about it. Most of the time, I was the only person walking in the park, so in a way, I claimed it—a beautiful estate that I didn't have to maintain.

One day, when I had finished leafleting and was walking back to my place, thinking that Gore would surely win, because whenever he talked about something, he sounded smart and alert, I started humming that song about consciousness. I liked the tune—A minor, strong beat, fading at the end, also short. I had never played it in public, because if and when I got a little gig at a restaurant or a bar, I was expected to play my old songs and also the other songs that people my age enjoyed—"Please Don't Bury Me," by John Prine, "You Can Leave Your Hat On," by Randy Newman, and Lyle Lovett's version of "Texas River Song." I shifted the lyrics around in the last two, beginning the Newman song with "Buddy, take off your coat, / You're old. Real slow. / Buddy, take off your shoes. / I can take off your shoes. / Buddy, hold the rail. It's cold. / You can leave your hat on." My lyrics always got a laugh. All I did with "Texas River Song" was shift the pronouns, to indicate that it was the man who had left, not the woman, and that he left because there were so many girls—"plump and pretty"—by the Sabine and the Sulphur that the singer had too many rivals. Last line, "Never will he walk by the Brazos no more." I thought my lyrics made more sense than the ones that Lyle had recorded, and I enjoyed singing it. I could imagine running into Lyle again and doing a back-and-forth, giving the song more depth.

I enjoyed my gigs, and I also enjoyed the fact that there weren't many of them. I was not a big fan of Sarah McLachlan, but I loved her song "Angel," because it reminded me of the pressures of the music business, and how it turned the thing you loved the most, playing and singing, into a torment for a lot of musicians. Lucky me, I had avoided that. Once in a while, I sang it in a gig, and once in a while, I actually got the tune right, though it stretched my range a bit, the way that song about consciousness had expanded my way of looking at the world.

ALBERTA, AUNT LOUISE, and Nancy were also confident that Gore would win, but Uncle Drew, who did plan to vote for Gore, was not. Aunt Louise said that he made a lot of donations to the campaign, which he had never done before. In general, he didn't like the idea of wealthy people like him paying off politicians. Aunt Louise said that early on, Uncle Drew had been a little torn, because he liked John McCain, and agreed with him that big donations were corrupting. When "the Doofus," as Uncle Drew called him, became the Republican nominee, Uncle Drew recanted his former stance and supported Gore in every way that he could. When Bush took on Cheney as his

VP candidate, Uncle Drew was open about his opinions—he would say, "You know who's the boss, right? It ain't GWB." As far as Uncle Drew was concerned, the real sign of this was Cheney reinstating his citizenship in Wyoming, though he lived in Texas. He had to explain this to me two times before I understood—the candidate for president and the VP candidate could not be from the same state. He had also changed his opinions about the Iran-Contra Affair. I asked Aunt Louise if his worries about government corruption had been the reason for the anxious looks I had seen back when we were dealing with Grandmother, Grandfather, and Mom, and she said that they were. Now, when he looked back, he saw that the Reagan administration had been the beginning of a collapse that he thought was playing out in this election. I said, "A collapse?"

She nodded. She said, "He's much more worried than I am. He keeps telling me that the Republicans are going to look for some issue that they can exploit to divide the nation and keep themselves in power no matter what."

I said, "What do you think?"

She said, "I think they will come around. He did."

Now that I was political, I thought more often of Martin, and I wondered if he had gotten into Parliament. Whatever I read about Tony Blair in the *Guardian* seemed positive, and I suspected that if Martin was in Parliament, he was there as a member of the Labour Party, since he had spent those years disguising his family life and working in that pub. He was my example of someone who could "come around," even more so than Uncle Drew, simply because Uncle Drew had started out as the only son of a man who worked in a tire factory in the 1930s and who knew from the beginning that his father was lucky to have a job. Martin had set out by choice to see what life was like outside the British landed class, and he had liked what he saw. Once in a while, I looked up Martin to see if he was in Parliament, but I couldn't figure out how to do it on my computer, and I didn't ask Nancy, because I was still very secretive about our affair.

Looking back, I would say that 2000 was the last year when I had any illusions about life, but once again, I was lucky. I remembered the feeling I had when I went to Ava's after the 1993 World Trade Center bombing, that maybe St. Louis was safer to live in than New York City, and that feeling expanded after Bush was installed in the White House whether the voters wanted it or not. Things were different in St. Louis. We got a Democratic mayor, and Alberta was especially pleased that Bill Clay replaced his father as a member of Congress. She thought he would be just the sort of congressman to rein in Bush and maybe Cheney. Uncle Drew said, "We'll see." He actually thought everything was fine in St. Louis, but people had seen those times before. He told me that before the Civil War, one of the wealthiest people in St. Louis was a Black woman named Pelagie Rutgers. I mentioned her to Alberta, and she said that everyone in her family knew about her. She also said that some of her younger relatives had hope that the good side of St. Louis was going to take over. I had hope, too. Roxbury was peaceful and beautiful in its eternal way. I enjoyed the annual drive there and the annual drive back, and I did my best to actually do some maintenance on both properties—I will say that the great thing about a log cabin and a brick house is that they require no painting. And if you live in a neighborhood of brick houses, no one buys one as a teardown, because they are hard to tear down. I heard someone talking about it at Gitto's once, and what he described was pushing a chisel into the mortar and taking the bricks out one at a time. When I was driving back to my place, I looked around and said, "St. Louis, you are going to last forever."

Two thousand one was a shocking year. Sometimes, I would talk to Uncle Drew about it. He was as shocked as I was. He said, "I was born in 1931! By the time I had any idea of what was going on, I knew that FDR was going to look after us, if he had to, and that Daddy's job was safe because the tire company meant well. I saw the other kids pushing each other or playing rough, but most of the time we got along, and when we didn't, our folks made us apologize. I meant it when I apologized, and it seemed like the others did, too. When the war came, Uncle Hank joined up, and the stories he told when he came back were of his fellow soldiers being fearless, but also of them helping the people they met in Europe, who were suffering."

Once, when we were talking about the election, I said, "I would have expected you, of all people, to know that these bad guys were out there. You've been investing and working in business for fifty years."

He said, "The one who expected this was Louise. She has more sense than I do. But I also think that if your parents are decent and you come along during good times, then you can't help having a positive view of the world, and when some idiot is picked up and put to use by a ruthless bunch, then it takes you a while to wake up. That's what I think happened to Gore. He just didn't believe they would do something like this."

After we had a few of these discussions, I thought more and more about consciousness, about what it would be like to be, say, twelve different people. I got interested in writing twelve songs. I knew that they couldn't all be from St. Louis, so I wrote one after a short visit with Jackie in New York, another after my first two weeks in Roxbury, another after a gig in Kansas City with a St. Louis band that I sometimes played with, another after I drove past Jefferson Barracks. Each of the twelve characters connects with one of the others, so the twelve songs stretch into different worlds like an imagined road. In a lot of ways, my inspiration was, once again, Lyle—the set of three songs that he wrote about people living in Texas, from different points of view, with different tunes, but held together by a melodious, rhythmic style. One of my first songs was from the point of view of a young woman from Webster Groves (let's say her family now lived in the house my grandparents had lived in) whose boyfriend quits his job and goes off to Iraq.

I wrote the lyrics first, then the music, and I went slowly, walking around and driving around while imagining what it felt like to be each one of my characters. I wanted to do one from the point of view of a child, but that was the hardest. I finally decided that the child was in sixth grade, that his parents didn't want him to worry about, or even know about, the war, so every time he came into the room, they stopped talking and asked him what he had been doing. As the verses go on, he gets more and more worried about what might be happening, and in the last verse, a friend of his tells him that her cousin has been killed in the war. He is ashamed of not knowing anything about it, and so he goes home and quizzes his parents. It was the longest of the songs—four minutes, forty-five seconds—but I liked lowering my voice when I sang it and trying to think and sound like a ten-year-old boy. Each time I came up with a song and a tune, and then practiced it until I liked it, I would sing it at one of our dinners and ask Nancy, Alberta, Ava, and Aunt Louise to critique it. At first they were hesitant, but then I said, "Come on, you guys! I don't have a producer! I need to be told if this is shit or not!" After that, they pitched in. I had expected the strongest critic to be Aunt Louise, or maybe Alberta, since she loved music, or maybe Nancy, since as a mathematician, she was a bit of a perfectionist, but in the end it was Ava, always smiling, but always pointing out the exact places in the song where she stopped paying attention, or didn't understand what was happening. I liked her precision, and it worked, because whatever she said would sort of fascinate me, and I would go home and fiddle with the song until I thought that it dealt with her observations. The last song I came up with, and the one I was most hesitant about, was from the point of view of a woman in Iraq who encounters the young man from Webster—she is older than he is, old enough, say, to be his mother. She is making her way down a road near her village in the countryside, and she sees a caravan of American Humvees go by. One of the soldiers in a Humvee is the boy from Webster. It is hot, and he has taken off his helmet. His hair is fluttering in the wind and he is smiling. He reminds her of her son, who had been killed in the war between Iraq and Iran (which I sort of remembered), and as she walks, she wonders why men can't stop fighting, why even young men as good-natured as this boy and her son would sign up to fight. She looks up at the pale blue hot sky and sees no god there, no reason to fight about religion, and she pulls off her hijab.

If I were still in the music business, I would have been nervous about taking so long to write these songs, but I wasn't, so I could put them together, pull them apart, put them together again. One thing I thought of was putting each song in a different key—if the character's name is Andy, the tune will be in A. I thought I would put the men's songs in major keys and the women's songs in minor keys, Cm, Dm, Em, Fm, Gm, Am. I played around with that for several months, and enjoyed it, but I couldn't actually sing the songs in all of those keys, since my range was smaller than it had been. When I finally came up with the list of songs, these were the titles:

12 songs

1. A young woman in New York City, thinking about the trips her family once made to the Catskills. "Stars over Arkville."
2. An older man in Roxbury, alone in the cabin, remembering Vietnam. "I Never Shot My Gun."
3. A woman in St. Louis, remembering their relationship before he went to Vietnam. "I Told Him Not to Go."
4. Her former priest, listening to a confession at Ste. Genevieve du Bois. "I Have More to Confess Than You Do."
5. A nun that he knows, wondering where the child her priest impregnated her with ended up (she doesn't know if it was a girl or a boy). "Mine or Theirs?"
6. A friend of the nun from high school who has moved to California and wonders where her friend disappeared to. "Vanished."
7. A long-haul trucker who passes the friend outside of Pasadena and notices her car (maybe a flat tire), now in northern Texas, and hot. "I Might Have Stopped."
8. A waitress in a bar in St. Louis, watching the trucker pass out. "Billy, Give Him a Kick."
9. A friend of the waitress, hearing that her boyfriend has joined the army and is heading off to Iraq. "How Long Is the Thread?"

10. The boyfriend, driving past Jefferson Barracks and wondering whether he's made a bad decision. "Hot Here, Hotter There."
11. The woman in Iraq. "No More."
12. George W. Bush, sitting in the White House, going back and forth about whether he should have started this war. "All Tied Up and Left to Rot."

16

OVER THE NEXT ten years or so, you could have said that my friends and I enjoyed living in a little bubble. I wasn't the only lucky one in our group. There were a few dinners in 2005 when Alberta didn't show up, even though she said that she would bring soup or dessert. We worried about her the first time, but then she told Ava that she was seeing a man. He taught history at St. Louis U. and lived in U. City. Since Alberta was our age, we assumed that he had lost his wife somehow, but then it turned out that he was in his thirties. He had bumped into Alberta at a barbecue restaurant, turned and apologized, and then, he said, he was so taken by her smile that he asked her to sit with him when they'd gotten their food. He was from Arkansas, had never been in any city as historically interesting and as complicated as St. Louis, and he loved it, but he was lured away by the University of Virginia, who offered him a tenured position that he couldn't turn down. They remained friends and once in a while Alberta went to Charlottesville to visit him, or he came back to St. Louis to visit her. That was fine with Alberta, who liked her independent life, as I liked mine.

Nancy inherited some money from a distant relative and, in her methodical and thoughtful way, decided to learn how to go rock climbing. Since she needed to get in shape, she started by inviting the rest of us on walks around St. Louis, then driving down to the Ozarks and hiking, then going to the Appalachians and finally the Rockies. She never actually took up rock climbing, but she loved her hikes, and when she visited me in Roxbury, I couldn't begin to keep up with her.

Ava always said that her piece of luck was that her boys continued to behave even when they were teenagers—they got good grades, drove safely, dated girls that Ava liked, and got into their first-choice colleges. As for Davie, he went to Berklee, liked it, got a decent piano career, and actually married Sheila Bancroft, the genius violin player who had lived a few blocks from Ava's house, the very girl that Davie had envied. She also went to Berklee. Now they were living in Washington, DC, where she was second violin in some orchestra and also taught in a local music school.

But there was more to it than that. It seemed to us in St. Louis (and maybe this has always been the case) that scary events were simultaneously nearby and far away. You feel that when, for example, eighty-seven tornadoes zip through Arkansas, Kentucky, and Tennessee, but none of them head for St. Louis, or when the Highway 35 bridge over the Mississippi in Minneapolis collapses, but the Eads Bridge, 134 years old, never has. You could walk past the Islamic centers south of Tower Grove Park and not feel that you were in danger, or that they were in danger. You could stare at the news about places like Virginia Tech or Sandy Hook and realize that the closest mass shooting to St. Louis was in DeKalb, up by Chicago.

Yes, there was crime in St. Louis, but not in the neighborhoods that my friends and I lived in. Alberta's relatives still lived in some of the crime-ridden neighborhoods, but when they got nervous, she took them in, and, she told me, if they brought weapons, she sent them away, so they learned. All of us—Aunt Louise, Alberta, Nancy, Ava, and me—could worry but also feel safe. At one of our dinners (I'm guessing this was around 2010) we even had a conversation about walking around town, day and night, and feeling safer than we had when we were young. Nancy said, "Sure, someone might try to steal something from you, but look at us! We wear plain old jeans and ten-year-old jackets! What would we have worth stealing?" I remembered Mom saying something similar about someone trying to rob the Skinker house—how old was she when she sold the place? Maybe the same age I was now.

There were a lot of people you could help around St. Louis, though maybe not as many as in New York, but it did become an occupation that all of us engaged in. I did what I had done—handed out twenties when I was walking (though there weren't as many buskers in St. Louis as there had been in New York, and that made me sad) and contributed, under a fake name, to both charities and PACs. Nancy helped her students pay for books and computers and kept a few sandwiches in her office in case one of the students who was coming for a meeting hadn't had a chance for lunch. Ava focused on music schools, orchestras, and Save the Children types of organizations. Aunt Louise and Uncle Drew set up a fund and got some of their friends in the finance business to contribute to it. Every year, between Thanksgiving and Christmas, they would send out donations, half of them to charitable organizations around St. Louis—a foster care organization, a veterans organization, an institute specializing in deafness, and an organization that helped homeless people. The ones they supported outside of St. Louis were more political, but not further left than the Roosevelt Institute (in some way, Uncle Drew knew Joseph Stiglitz). I think they dished out about a hundred grand a year. Alberta had enough on her hands with her own relatives, but in honor of her, we all sent money to the NAACP and whatever other organizations she suggested.

I wasn't surprised by this, since we had to do something with our money other than refurbish our houses. What surprised me was some of the conversations we had about menopause, sex, and what we missed or didn't miss. I think the first chat we had happened after Aunt Louise showed up for a dinner at my place with a bottle of icy-cold limoncello, which I had never had, and was, I thought, totally unknown in St. Louis (as far as I knew, the nearest lemon grove was eight hundred miles away). We ate our healthy vegetarian quiche (kale, pine nuts, tofu, Gruyère) and our piles of broccoli, and then Ava, Aunt Louise, and I sipped the glasses of yellow liqueur, and then, bit by bit, we started tossing our heads and grinning and talking about menopause and sex, before and after. Nancy and Alberta pretended to be sloshed, too, and joined in. I was the one who had had no menopausal symptoms, Aunt Louise was the one who had had hot flashes that made her sit up in bed at night (but she was glad to be off the pill), Alberta and Ava were the ones who knew what was coming and were well prepared for it. Nancy, oddly, was the one who had regrets. As she'd gotten closer to menopause, she wanted to have a child, even though she didn't want to get married or have a steady boyfriend. Ava, the most experienced, said, "But why would you . . . I mean, I've always envied your sense of freedom!"

Nancy said, "Well, this is years ago now, but I think I saw it as an experiment that I never got a chance to try. I imagined investigating all of the relatives, figuring out inherited traits versus learned behaviors, keeping daily track of everything I could about my responses, his or her responses. I mean, I know I teach math, but I was always interested in biological sciences . . ." She smiled and we all laughed, then Ava said, "Let me offer you some subjects for further research."

One evening, I asked Ava what she wanted to do now that the kids were taken care of. She said that Dave had come across a book about James Cook. It was called *Farther Than Any Man,* and before they went to sleep at night, they would pass it back and forth and read to each other. Dave didn't allow laptops in the bedroom, because he'd decided they were keeping him awake, so it had to be books and LED lights. The book was about Captain Cook, whom I'd heard of when I was in England, and as they read it, they were planning a few trips. Ava said that Cook was most impressed by Hawaii, but they had been there a number of times. Dave wanted to go to Greenland, Japan, Chile, and South Africa, and Ava wanted to go to Tasmania, Norway, Costa Rica, and the Azores. The questions they tossed back and forth were—one trip or many? What was the most eco-friendly way to travel? Dave said they could paddle a canoe and walk. She said that she wasn't going to try that until they had paddled up the Mississippi to St. Paul. I laughed, and thought that, as always, they seemed to be getting along, sleeping in the same bed, joking around, making plans that included each other. I wondered about their sex life, but didn't ask, of course.

Now that I was living in St. Louis and was getting old, I was no longer terribly impressed by tornadoes, though I did pay attention to the one in the spring of 2011, because it was huge and stayed on the ground awhile, though not as long as I thought it had (sweeping through Maryland Heights, up to the airport, and back around to New Melle). There was plenty of damage, but none of us lived in Maryland Heights, and even Alberta's relatives who lived on the north side were spared. When we had dinner at Aunt Louise's place about a week later, we shared old tornado stories, and then I walked past the Skinker house and saw that it was the same solid chunk that I had relied on in 1959. Not long after that, I tried to figure out how long the tornado that had passed our house on Skinker had been on the ground, from close to Old Orchard to us. About six miles, but then Nancy told me that it had been on the ground for almost twenty-five miles, from Crescent, which was southwest, across the river to Granite City. Straight line.

My big worry was Uncle Drew, because not long after the tornado hit, he turned eighty (and so did Aunt Louise, but she seemed so spry that I didn't worry about her). I wondered if he was getting to be like Mom—doctor resistant—but Aunt Louise said that, as usual, he had gone for a total checkup and even a full-body scan, as his birthday present to her. She glanced at me and said, "No, they didn't find any gold nuggets stored in his liver. But they did tell him that he has to lose maybe thirty pounds, if he can, and walk more."

I said, "So you have to hide the Mars bars?"

She said, "And the fondants and the Violet Crumbles that he orders from the UK."

I said, "I can store those." I thought, One a day, what's the harm?

I ended up going with him for walks, and it was fun. At first he didn't talk much—he had to spend his time breathing—but he did get into better shape, so that even in June, when the weather was pretty hot, we often got to Old Orchard, where Aunt Louise met us for lunch and then took Uncle Drew home. It was about three miles. Once, I even managed to walk from there to my place on Polo, though it was nearly four miles.

I continued playing music, though I didn't take any offers for gigs. The singer I kept my eye on was Marcia Ball, who put out several albums and showed up on YouTube (yes, I managed to discover YouTube). She still belted it out, and it looked like her years of playing the piano like an acrobat had kept her in great shape. At one point, I even wrote a little fan email, asking when she was going to do that backflip over the piano that we all were waiting for. She didn't get back to me.

Alberta suggested that I buy a banjo and try that. She thought it had a sharper and more interesting sound than a guitar, and so I did. I liked it, and sometimes in the summer I would sit on the deck outside my bedroom, on the second floor above the porch, and play it. There was a dog across the street, small but active, who would sit on the lawn and howl in tune. Eventually, all my friends were prodding me to start writing some more songs, because there was plenty to write about. I wrote one of them when Aunt Louise told me about a dream she had that Uncle Drew had died, and when she woke up after the funeral, her bed was in the yard. The house had vanished, and a strong wind was beginning to shake it. I called it "Leave Me Alone Till I Do the Books," three funny verses about a widow arguing with her deceased husband about when she can join him. But Uncle Drew got a little healthier, and right around then, Nancy started talking to me about her regrets that she hadn't traveled much (she also wanted me to write a song based on "No Regrets" called "New Regrets"), and then for the next two years, Nancy and I traveled here and there—Braunschweig, the Cairngorms, but also Naples, Portugal, and even Alaska. She was in such good shape that I had a hard time keeping up with her, but she had plenty of information. It was like having my own tour guide.

That experience made me come up with my own new regrets song—"Watch Your Step"—about spending my whole life being careful. What had I missed?

17

IN THE FALL of 2017, I helped our school put on the fiftieth reunion for our class. I wasn't in charge of anything, but I helped make the list of known addresses for our classmates, and as I did so, I used the Google boy to sneak around the neighborhoods that our classmates lived in, just to see how things had turned out. It was no surprise that several of our classmates declined to supply information. I knew now that we had had an odd class, or rather, a class filled with oddballs. When I looked through the yearbook, it was easy to see who had been nerdy, who had been sociable, who had felt like part of some group, and who had felt sidelined. This is true in all high school classes, but I suspected it was more true of our class than most. The ones I was most curious about were the ones from abroad—a girl from Japan, a boy from the Middle East, and another boy from Egypt—those three were the only ones who had supplied racial diversity, because there were no African American students and no African American faculty. There was also only one Catholic boy in our class, but you would expect that in St. Louis in the 1960s, because there were so many Catholic schools and high schools. Catholic boys from our neighborhood in those days went to Chaminade or Priory, the girls went to Villa or Nerinx Hall—there were something like twenty-five Catholic high schools (there were about fourteen in Manhattan and seventeen or eighteen in Chicago). I would have said that the diversity in our class was a diversity of names: Boesel, Baird, Ozee, Wetzel, Gladders, Latzer, England, Todorovich, Rattler, all of which I had found interesting at the time.

Since I hadn't looked at my old yearbook in at least forty years, what made me laugh was the hairdos. Of the twenty-seven girls in our class, seventeen wore bobs, six wore flips, and four dared to wear their hair below shoulder length. I remembered one of these girls as the most rebellious and outspoken, the most obvious future hippie (as her long hair revealed). The face I looked at the longest belonged to the boy we all had thought was the cutest, and there were plenty of girls who vied for his attention. He had large blue eyes and dark wavy hair. I remembered him making a lot of jokes, but in his picture he looked thoughtful and resigned, worried about something that he wasn't willing to talk about. When I first opened my yearbook, I expected to remember which ones I had liked and which ones I hadn't liked, who had liked me and who had spurned or denigrated me, but I didn't. Mostly, I thought that all of us looked young and weird (maybe because of the haircuts). I did remember that when we showed up at the studio where our senior pictures were to be taken, we had been told to smile for some of the shots and not to smile for others, then, when we saw the pictures, we got to choose the ones we preferred. In some ways, the boys and girls in the pictures did not look like they had as students—for example, the only real athlete in our class, and also a handsome guy, looked like an intellectual in his picture, and the prettiest girl looked serious, her eyes glancing to the left, as if a door was opening and she was suspicious of who might be coming in. Her full lips were turned down, and her hair was perfect, but still . . .

Well, several of them had had misfortunes waiting for them, and so, in some ways, it was sad to be putting together a list of who we could contact, who we couldn't find, who had passed. We had been in the same class for six years (a few had entered later than seventh grade), and there were only sixty-five of us, so we had seen more of one another than high school students do who are in larger classes. Oddly, I think it was this familiarity that drove us apart—when we graduated and got out of town, we were happy to be rid of one another, to meet some new people, and also to have opportunities for anonymity, as I had had at Penn State—the pleasure of not being recognized in a group, and therefore gossiped about or ignored (which was worse?). I wondered if I had been a natural introvert as a child or if high school, for all its musical and educational pleasures, was what had done that to me.

One picture that I hadn't remembered before I opened the yearbook was the informal picture included by the gawky girl. Each page in the senior section of the yearbook had four parts—two formal pictures, one of a boy and one of a girl; a list for each of them of what their extracurricular and athletic activities had been; an informal list of thoughts and characteristics that, as I remembered, had been generated by the editors of the yearbook, and then vetted and added to by each student; and a snapshot that each student supplied that told something or made some joke about themselves—the class beauty who had portrayed the Virgin in the Christmas pageant decked herself out in a black motorcycle jacket and heavy dark eye makeup, and faced the camera in a tough-girl pose. Her picture was labeled "Mary." The gawky girl had stuck her head into a basketball basket, taken hold of the rim, and her caption was "They always have the tall girls guard the basket." Just the sort of girl who would grow up to write that amusing novel I had read, what was it? Umpteen years ago.

The reunion was scheduled for October. As we idled toward it, I thought it was interesting that almost all of us, class of '67, were now sixty-eight. Sixty-seven plus sixty-eight is a hundred thirty-five, and another question I had was not only what life would be like in 2152, but what consciousness would be like. In 1832, Chopin and Mendelssohn were just starting out, still in their early twenties; Wagner was nineteen; Donizetti was thirty-five. I was sure that the ideas just came to them through their eyes and ears and then flowed out through their hands as they put together their operas, mazurkas, overtures, symphonies. Were they thinking about us, 135 years later, as we (or I) sometimes called up a recording of *Lucia di Lammermoor* on my smartphone as I walked down the street, and other times chose a Dolly Parton album, or a few songs by Tom Rush, just to remind me of what I once loved? I was sure that music pervaded the lives of those composers, but in order to have the music, they had to play it or go to where it was played, and now, I had the music following me around wherever I went and whenever I wanted. Chopin lived to be thirty-nine, Mendelssohn lived to be thirty-eight, Donizetti lived to be fifty. Only Wagner lived as long as I had—he got to sixty-nine. I imagined musicians in 2152 putting on a headphone-like object and thinking up some tunes and harmonies, which would then be organized and played back by the object and rethought by the musician. The piano? The guitar? The oboe? How archaic! The best examples would now be stored in museums, and you would take your children to see them and explain how music had once been "composed," and if your child wanted to be a musician, you would supply her with a "compositioner." She would keep that on a shelf next to her "novelizer"—the object she used to imagine stories—and she would go back and forth about which career she wanted to pursue, at the same time watching her best friend power up her hip implant in preparation for running yet another two-minute mile. The big race, in St. Louis, would be the yearly thirteen-minute marathon, which they would run in the dome that had been built over Clayton, between Forsyth, Big Bend, Dale, and Hanley, where the old houses had been preserved for historical reasons, and no one had to live underground, as they did in Ladue or Webster.

These thoughts amused me, but I didn't reveal them to Aunt Louise, Uncle Drew, Alberta, Ava, or Nancy, all of whom were worried about climate change, as well they should have been. I was, too, but I would say that in the last fifteen years, I had passed through the five stages of grief as I watched just about every politician in the US ignore the issue. The one that was shortest for me was denial, because if you live in St. Louis, you can't deny that weather can be destructive and painful. Nor would I say that I had ended up with "acceptance"—that was too positive a word. I had ended up with a kind of harsh sense of retribution—those who thought they could skate around this issue would get what they deserved. At sixty-eight, I thought I would be lucky again. If I didn't escape the destruction, at least, for me, it would be short.

OUR SCHOOL HAD changed over the last fifty years—for one thing, it was now right down the street from a company called Citishred Document and Data Destruction—I imagined us sneaking up there and handing over the mean-girl notes we had passed in math class or the tests that had been returned to us with F's. The school parking lot had gotten huge, as had the soccer, baseball, and football fields, as well as the running track. There were lots of new buildings, but the grounds still had that parklike feel, with hills and dips and trees everywhere. Whenever I drove there, if I happened to pass the Ladue Market on one side (two stories, steep roof, vaguely Tudor style) and the Carmelite monastery on the other side (high fence, acres of green grass, also plenty of trees, hidden buildings), I would think, This is so St. Louis.

I had intended to go to the awards presentation on Thursday—in fact, I had helped arrange it. One of the other arrangers asked me if I was annoyed that they weren't giving me an award, but I wasn't—I said that the only time I had deserved one might have been at our tenth reunion, when I had actually had a career, but no one appreciates such a small blast from the past—"more like a fart," I said, which got a laugh. Then, for some reason I had a lot of aches and pains in the night, and didn't fall asleep until about three a.m., and then was so sound asleep that I didn't hear my alarm. When I got to school an hour late, at nine fifteen, the ceremony was over, and everyone was chatting in what they now called the quad, behind the main building. I joined in the chatting, but I did notice that the gawky girl was wandering around looking at everything. It was a very pleasant day—sunny but rather cool—and the leaves of the trees had progressed perfectly from green almost to red and yellow. I have to say that the fellow alums that I was most interested in were the former nerds—the math guy who went to Harvard was only one of them. What struck me was that two of the nerds had attentive wives, especially the one who was now blind. Some people didn't show up—the girl who had gone to the West Coast and become a hippie, and the most popular girl in our class, who lived not far from where I had grown up. It turned out she had married one of the boys who was kicked out after seventh or eighth grade and who had gone on to become a doctor. Nor did the prettiest girl in our class show up. The outgoing ones did, and they were still outgoing—stepping around the quad in a friendly way, laughing, asking questions. Two or three of them I saw a few times a year, and I enjoyed seeing them again. There was a little bit of gossip about the ones who hadn't shown up—one of them was actually on his deathbed. I overheard the gawky girl say, when she wandered back into the group, that she had been on Facebook maybe a year before the reunion, and noticed that one of our classmates listed his residence as the small village where she lived. She had managed to get him to meet her for a bagel at a local restaurant. She glanced toward the windows of the administrative office and lowered her voice. She said, "It was a sad story." But that seemed to be true of a fairly large cohort of our class, including the woman whose husband (also in our class) had pleaded guilty to robbery and was now in jail—he was not one of the ones I had expected to go in that direction.

I went home after that, and then later went back to school to see the art exhibit they had put up in the gallery (amazing that a high school should have a gallery, but I did remember paintings and other artworks in the hallways when I was a student, and I had enjoyed my painting classes). The painter had graduated ten years ahead of us, and I didn't know a thing about her, but I liked her work—modernist but recognizable, flowers, leaves, shadows. She seemed to have spent her life looking through windows and trying to figure out what was happening among the people (and the objects) she was seeing. I could relate to that, given all the songs I had written about people and events I had witnessed over the years. Another thought about consciousness: you spend your life taking things in and you have to think about them—you can't help it—and you have to make something of it by organizing what you understand. If you are an artist or a songwriter, your way of thinking about it is to produce, and after you do, you understand, not what you saw, but what you felt and thought when you saw (or heard) it. That reminded me of reading *David Copperfield* when we were in ninth grade. At the time, Dickens seemed as dead and buried as Shakespeare, and also as difficult to understand. I had not been ready to read *David Copperfield*. I picked it up with a sigh and started, and I actually understood it, and then, step by step, I started to enjoy it. The thing that didn't seem odd to me at the time, but seemed interesting to me now, was how vividly I pictured what David was seeing as I read it, even though at that point I not only had never been to England, I had never seen a movie set in England. But within a year, I saw *A Hard Day's Night* two times in one week, and I think it was that and *David Copperfield* that set me on the path toward Martin. As I was walking around the gallery, looking at the paintings, I thought I should go back to England and take a bunch of train rides all over the island before I was too old to understand what I was seeing.

The rest of the reunion was a little difficult for me. I thought it was odd that even fifty years on, and possessed of a few friends from our class, I still didn't feel as though I fit in. I went to the events and chatted as best I could, but it wasn't like either having our group dinners or being friendly and chatty with strangers. It was more a case of overhearing what my classmates had done together in school and having no memories of those things, because I hadn't been invited to join them. It was as if I was in a foreign country that I had visited before, and even though I had done my best to learn the language, I still felt excluded. At least the gawky girl had brought her husband along, an older, very sweet-looking guy, but not the tall guy I had seen in Winchester. I could see that even though maybe she felt the same way that I did, she could lift an eyebrow and smile at him, and he would smile lovingly back at her. They even held hands. If I had ever envied a woman who was married, I couldn't remember it, and it was not that I wanted to be married, but I did appreciate that connection she felt in an environment where I should have felt a connection but didn't.

The final dinner was held at the Deer Creek Club, one that I had often wondered about, on that road that I had often wanted to check out—Log Cabin Lane, off Litzsinger. Litzsinger was a long row of fences; handsome brick entryways; scads of trees turning, fluttering in the wind; and the sense that if you were just driving along, then you had no business turning down the private lanes. When we went to our dinner, though, everyone at the club was friendly and welcoming—also a St. Louis tradition—and the food was decent, too. Like all fancy St. Louis establishments, it called up the old days, and when we were in there, it was easy to imagine that it was 1925, and nothing bad was ever going to happen again. Almost everyone I knew in St. Louis had waded or fished in Deer Creek—it ran from Creve Coeur through Frontenac, Ladue, Rock Hill, Brentwood, Webster, and Maplewood, then fed into the River des Peres, which goes into the Mississippi not far from Jefferson Barracks, and so, as I looked out the window down the hill to the creek, I thought of getting a canoe, dragging it down the hill, and then just floating through town, looking here and there, and, no doubt, seeing things that I had never thought of before. Just then the gawky girl stepped on my toe, and I started, which startled her. Fortunately, she didn't fall down. We both said, "Oh! I'm sorry!"

She said, "I hope I didn't hurt you?"

I said, "Not a bit." We smiled, and she went back to her table. One of the women sitting at my table said, "I never thought she would be the one who got ahead."

Then one of the other women said, "In my experience"—she was a doctor—"the late developers have to learn to be observant in order to survive. I'm guessing she was one of those. When she started publishing books, I remembered how she was in class—either laughing, or totally out of it, or looking out the window, or making herself pay attention. I guess it worked."

I didn't say anything about seeing her in England tripping over her feet, but I did say, "When I saw her in England in 1971, her boyfriend, or husband, or whatever, was almost a head taller than she was, and graceful as a bird. Good-looking guy."

The doctor said, "This one is, too."

The woman who had brought up the subject said, "I remember in eighth grade, when we sat in rows, and also in the dining room, she would always take the seat that was between one of us and everyone else."

The doctor said, "She was making sure that she had someone to talk to. I did that, too."

We all laughed.

The next day, I went to the Cheshire to meet Nancy for dinner. The Cheshire wasn't far from Wash U. and since I had such fond memories of the neighborhood, meeting there gave us a reason to take a little walk. I sat at our usual table and looked at my watch. Usually, Nancy was right on time—her last class was over at four thirty. The gawky girl and her handsome husband walked in the door. She didn't see me in the dark—that tradition hadn't changed. I heard them order the risotto. Rick then came over to me, because I had been sitting there for a while, and I saw that I had a text from Nancy, who said that she wasn't able to come because some student had had a crisis, and she had to stay and sort it out. I told Rick that my friend wasn't coming, and ordered the halibut.

Just then, I saw the gawky girl and her husband push their plates away. She said, "There must have been a screwup. This is way too salty."

He said, "Mine, too."

He said, "You want to leave? I have to go to the can first, though."

She nodded.

I sat still for a minute, then I said her name and she looked around. She said, "Jodie! I was hoping to chat with you sometime during the reunion! Hard to believe that you turned up here!"

I said, "I come here a lot. I used to live down the street. My current place is within walking distance, too."

She said, "This is where we're staying. First time for me. It's weirder than I realized. They put us in the George Gissing suite. I love the nineteenth-century horse pictures, though."

Then I told her about seeing her when I was in Winchester, and she said, "How amazing! I enjoyed working on that dig, but I wasn't a good digger. You had to scrape the earth away layer by layer and I was always digging too deep, so they gave me a different job—walking around with a little pouch and a notebook. If someone found something, I went over to them, and they put it in the pouch and I wrote down where they had found it."

Her husband came out of the restroom, and she introduced us. He said, "Let's go back to the room. I want to call Ty and I'm a little too tired to do much else."

She said, "You go ahead, sweetie. I'm going to talk a bit with Jodie."

After he left, she said, "I think this is a fascinating area. I was walking down Skinker the other day, and I couldn't believe the houses. There's one, kind of a pale golden color, with the tile roof and the little balcony? I adore that place. The others—"

I said, "That's where I grew up."

She said, "You're kidding me!"

I said, "I loved it. I always thought I was lucky to live there."

She said, "I felt the same about our street in Ladue. My best memory is of when I would go down the hill and walk along the creek. It wasn't Deer Creek, I don't know the name, but one time, I got all the way to Geyer! I thought that was such a big deal! I never got to where it goes along Marshall, though. I think I thought that was in a whole different world, even though it's something like four miles."

I said, "I think that's Two Mile Creek. It feeds into Deer Creek somewhere around that country club—Old Warson! It's Deer Creek that runs to Marshall. Anyway, that's what I've noticed about St. Louis—two or three miles, and you're in a whole different world."

She said, "So you live here?"

I nodded, then said, "What about you?"

"We live in California, near Monterey. Pure luck that I moved there, but I love it, and that's where I met my husband. Best thing that ever happened to me."

And then we started chatting about luck.

I said, "I remember when my uncle took me to look at colleges, and I didn't like any of them. I was sort of resigned to Wash U., and then we took a wrong turn and there was Penn State, and I couldn't believe how beautiful it was! I don't know that I would have had a musical career if I'd gone somewhere like Berklee. Penn State had a good music department, but there was also a sense of freedom there that you don't have at a music school."

She said, "I enjoyed Vassar, too, especially the Old English classes. Those got me interested in how weird the English language is, and how it differs according to where the invaders came from. I don't even remember the details anymore, but I love those town names, like Yaxham and Scarning. I would love to visit those spots."

I said, "I had a friend who lived in Nether Wallop. That always made me laugh."

She said, "Remember when we read *Oliver Twist* in seventh grade? I think it started there. I couldn't understand a word of the book, but I loved the names—Twist, of course, and Fagin, and Mr. Bumble. There was something about them that was more interesting than the ones in *The Scarlet Letter*."

I said, "I always thought I was lucky when we read those difficult books, too, because they steered me toward music."

We laughed.

She said, "Oh jeez, I took so many piano lessons when I was a kid, and I couldn't get past the first page of 'Für Elise.' But the books kept pulling me in. I always say that eventually you get tired of the Bobbsey Twins."

I said, "I had the same experience! I think I wore out those keys on our piano!" We laughed again. I wondered why we hadn't become friends in school, but then I thought that maybe it was that she was never paying attention and I was always too reserved. I was going to ask her who she remembered as her best friend from school, but she said, "You know, Jodie, I did buy your records. I always wanted to go to a performance, but as far as I know, you never came to Iowa."

I said, "I went to Ames, once, that stop . . ."

"Off 35 and 80, on the way from Minneapolis to KC! I can't believe I missed that. When were you there?"

"'Ninety-seven."

"Ah. We had already moved to California at that point."

"We?"

"My ex. He grew up in Clinton, and said the last thing he wanted to do was die in Iowa. We looked around and ended up in Carmel Valley."

"Didn't you say you met your husband in California?"

She raised her hand, her four fingers spread. She said, "Number four. The one who took me there was number three. He dumped me for his dental hygienist. Best thing that ever happened to me. And I got to tell him that when he was at our place for dinner a few years ago." She grinned.

There was a long pause, and I said, "I never got around to getting married. I think that was my piece of luck, too."

She said, "I remember how the boys looked at you in school. Not actually the boys in our class. They were too nerdy, but what I remember is when we were in tenth grade, and some of the seniors used to keep an eye on you when we were eating in the dining room. There were so many cute guys in that class. Did you ever date any of them?"

I said, "Not a one. I think by tenth grade, I was so obsessed with music that I hardly noticed anything. Except for the fact that you were taller than all the boys." I did not tell her about Mom's difficulties during those years. I did say, though, "I seem to remember that you had a stepdad? My mom worked at the Muny for years, and he was connected to the Muny somehow?"

She said, "Well, what he always said was that he worked there in '31 as Cary Grant's understudy when Grant was still named Archie Leach."

I said, "I wonder if Mom knew that."

She said, "That was a spot of luck, Mom marrying Uncle Bill when I was eleven. Such a kind man. Just the sort of guy who gives you just about everything you want, even if it's a horse. He was very sweet to my mom. One night, I happened to get up for a drink of water, and I saw him guiding her through the living room. She was so obviously smashed. I always thought that was a World War II problem. But he died when they'd been married only about eight years." She sighed.

I said, "My mom had a drinking problem, too, but she actually gave it up a year or two before she died."

The gawky girl shook her head and said, "That was lucky. My mom was still at it until she died last spring, and she was pretty much totally off her rocker. My sister dealt with her much better than I did. The last thing I want is to live to be ninety-six."

I said, "I'm sorry about your stepdad. I think I remember you bringing him to some event. I also think I remember thinking that you didn't look like him at all."

She said, "My parents split when I was a year old. He was schizophrenic, or had bipolar disorder, or something. The diagnoses keep changing. I only saw him twice after the split, and even though he was very handsome, and from a wealthy family, Mom and I were both lucky to get him out of our lives. My opinion is that there was an obsessive streak and a dominating streak, and he would have been hard to handle and hard to escape."

All I said was, "My dad was out of my life when I was about two. He lived in New York. Mom never remarried, though."

We let this subject pass, and then she said, "My mom was about your height. She would have said that it's the best height, but I love being this tall. You can't imagine the number of assholes I've stared down at and then walked away from." We both laughed again.

I said, "I like my height, too. I think there were some boyfriends that I really enjoyed who would have stayed away from me if I'd been six inches taller than they were." She knew I meant lovers, but she said, "How many boyfriends have you had?"

I said, "Twenty-five."

She dipped her head and said, "I applaud you!"

I said, "Can I count the songs I wrote about them as literature?"

She said, "Only if I can count all the lyrics I've tried to sing without being able to remember them as music." Then she said, "Okay, I'll admit it. One of the things I did when your early records came out was sing along. I tried harmonizing with you and had this fantasy that we could sing together." She squeaked out a few notes, and we laughed again, then she said, "I do love music. One of my exes was a folk musician—the one who dumped me for the dental hygienist—and another one was an expert. Do you remember in the seventies when a guy on the radio would play the first bits of a song, and then get listeners to call in and guess the song?"

I nodded.

"That husband called in and was right so many times that the DJ started hanging up on him as soon as he heard his voice." Then she said, "They all had their good points, but the first one was also my first boyfriend, and being with him was like being married to your brother. I think he would have left me if I hadn't left him. The musician was funny and handsome, but he could never figure out what to do with himself, so I think the dental hygienist perked him up. She was a lot younger. He's married to a musician now, and they have a little band. The rock and roll savant—well, we had to get married, so we did, but now he's with his college girlfriend. When we all met at my daughter's wedding, I said, 'Here's a toast to the fact that we all found true love!'" After a moment, she said, "You know what I love about music? The repetitive quality that carries you along, gets you bobbing your head or tapping your feet. I think that's what is soothing. Novels? You have to make sure that sometimes you remind the reader what's already happened, but you have to also keep making it new. Plot twists, fresh scenes, that sort of thing."

I nodded, then said, "I am an avid reader."

It was just then that the waiter finally brought my dinner. I said, "Are you sure you don't want anything? It didn't look like you ate much of what you had."

She said, "I would love some gelato."

The waiter brought two scoops, vanilla and chocolate. She ate them bit by bit, while I finished my halibut.

She said, "Did you have a favorite of the twenty-five?"

I didn't say anything about Martin. I thought for a moment, then said, "One of the ones in New York was dying to get onstage. I think we were together for maybe two weeks. Every time he came to my place, he acted out a different role, and he was good at it. One night, he gelled his hair and combed it into a quiff, you know, like James Dean." I didn't actually remember if he had, but I did remember his face, and that would have been a good style for him. He had the jawline. I said, "We had a lot of fun. The most recent one was a drummer who worked with the band on a record I made maybe fifteen years ago. His name was Cliff, and he did look like Jimmy Cliff. He was sweet. I loved the fact that he was younger and still willing to take me on."

She said, "You know you still look great, don't you?"

I said, "I try not to care, but you don't look bad yourself."

She said, "Well, here we are, sixty-eight! But I don't think, most of the time, that we actually notice. My big piece of luck, apart from my husband, is that I don't have any illnesses or aches and pains, and I don't drink. I remember when I first got to Vassar and the drinking age was eighteen, and I went to some local bar and drank enough to feel drunk. Went back to the dorm, threw up, and that was that. My roommate said I'd had two drinks. Sometime later, I read that if you are sensitive to alcohol, you're much less likely to go down that path. Anyway, sometimes when I am walking along or driving, I see my finger touch the brim of my cap, or I look down at my feet . . ."

I thought, As you always have.

". . . and I wonder if we ever see ourselves the way others see us. I think we just go on being that person we've always been, accumulating memories and feelings, sensing the light and the sounds, forgetting about time. One thing I love about writing novels is that the thoughts and feelings have a way of getting out of your head, onto the page, and you can leave them there. My husband, he had a real crisis in the eighties, when some guy fleeced him out of everything. Once we made a novel about it, he could finally stop thinking about it."

I said, "What was that one?"

"*Good Faith.* Anyway, breathe in, breathe out, look around, let the thoughts come and go. Consciousness."

I said, "I've sort of become obsessed with consciousness, too. Maybe it's an old lady thing."

She nodded.

I said, "I do know what you mean. I wrote twelve songs about interrelated consciousnesses during the Iraq war. One was from the point of view of a female bartender who watches a long-haul trucker pass out in front of the bar. I called it 'Billy, Give Him a Kick.' And the one from George Bush's point of view was called 'All Tied Up and Left to Rot.' "

She said, "I would LOVE to hear those! You could win a Nobel Prize! Dylan did!"

I said, "Well, if I did, I would give that money away to war victims, since that guy invented dynamite."

She nodded, then she said, "What intrigues me about writing novels is the effort to get inside the consciousnesses of the characters. In plays, the actors do it, and when we see them moving and talking, we follow along. In novels, the writer has to imagine the consciousness of the character, and then display it so that the reader can understand it. I think that's why Sherlock Holmes is so popular, and Agatha Christie. Most people would never think of committing a murder, but we know it happens, and we want to know who did it and why they did it. Sherlock and Poirot guide us toward that, and Watson is a sort of intermediary, the friend, you might say, that links us."

I said, "My friend Nancy is a mathematician. She loves those books. She says that when a physicist or an astronomer comes up with a theory, he depends on a mathematician to sort out the details and tell him if it's true, or at least plausible. The scientist is Dr. Watson and the mathematician is Sherlock Holmes."

She said, "That's interesting. To be honest, in order to be a writer, you have to be an avid spy, so that you can see and hear how other people are expressing their consciousness, and then you can invent a system that makes that consciousness both believable and interesting. And, then, well, I don't know what it's like for you, but I think that the reason I just keep writing is that at some point, I figured out how to make the best of things, just to look at what was on the table, or in the manuscript, and do the best I could to sort it out, and then be satisfied with that. A lot of writers are perfectionists, and that is the last thing you should be."

I nodded and said, "There are so many ups and downs in the music business, so I know what you mean."

She said, "Did you have any particular ups and downs?"

I didn't tell her about Uncle Drew, or the money, but I did say, "I was a good girl. I knew how to stay out of trouble."

She laughed and said, "Yes, me too! We should have been friends in school!"

I said, "I don't know if you did this, but I used to sit in the can, totally quiet, listening to the other girls. At first, I was listening to see if they were saying anything snotty about me, but then I just listened so I could figure out a way to stay out of their conversations."

She said, "Do you think they were especially mean?"

I shook my head. I said, "I think they were teenage girls. Maybe if I'd had a couple of sisters, I would have understood things better."

She nodded, then said, "Well, we survived!"

I said, "Judging by what I saw during the reunion, I don't think that when we were in school, we had even a notion about who would be the lucky ones. The popular girls seemed to know what they were doing all the time, and so did the ones who were getting straight A's. Some of the boys were so cute and some of the boys were so dorky."

She said, "Turns out that the limelight isn't very good for you."

I said, "That's my experience."

Rick caught my eye, and I saw that he wanted us to pay up and get out of the restaurant. I gestured to him, and said, "Well, I guess it's time to leave. What time is it?"

She looked at her Timex and said, "Eight thirty-six."

She handed me a five for the gelato (it was actually $7, but I didn't say anything) and we walked out into the parking lot. She gestured toward the Hi-Pointe Theatre, and said, "Last night, we went there and watched the new *Blade Runner* movie. Scared the pants off me."

I said, "I don't watch sci-fi, though I did see *WALL-E* . . ."

She said, "I saw that one, too! I wish . . . Oh, I don't know. I'm ashamed at the mess we are leaving the kids. My granddaughter is two and a half. Every time I see her, I want to apologize. My daughter and her husband are vegan and only take public transportation and are giving her very good habits, but I'm not sure it will be a good thing to survive this mess we are leaving them."

I lifted my eyebrow. I didn't mean to say that I was glad I hadn't produced any kids, but she knew what I was thinking, and nodded. Then she said, "Don't tell the kids!" and we smiled again, shook hands. We didn't say anything about staying in touch, but the information concerning the reunion contained addresses for the students who were still alive, even if they hadn't shown up. She walked across the parking lot and into the hotel. It was dark, but I strolled down Clayton to Skinker, crossed at the light, and then headed down Skinker to Lindell. The lights were on in our old house, but I didn't see a car in the driveway or anyone through the windows. I knew the gawky girl had gone up to her room to be with her husband, and I knew that I would walk back to my car, that the walk would take me maybe twenty-five minutes. I didn't feel unsafe. What I felt was a kind of loneliness that I had spent years rejecting—no one to open the door, no one to welcome me, no one to take me in his arms and give me a kiss, no one to make a joke with. I wondered if I had made a mistake that I finally understood.

Epilogue, 203——

THIS IS COMPLICATED for me to write, and undoubtedly will not be seen by anyone, but I have to put it on the page anyway. I am Jodie Rattler, but actually, I'm not—my name is Jamie Ring. I no longer live in St. Louis.

A few years ago, when I was still at my old house, which I loved, in Clayton, Missouri, I received a package in the mail. It contained a hardback copy of a book. On the cover was a Gibson acoustic guitar resting on a stand in a lovely wood-paneled room. The book was entitled *Lucky,* and it was by the gawky girl. Since I had a chat with her in October of 2017, I had corresponded with her from time to time. I thought we were on good terms, and I sent her a couple of recordings that I did on my own of the songs I had written about consciousness. She responded positively, and I began to think of trying to find a studio where I could put together my own disc, just for the record. I asked her about things like fires and floods in California, that we had heard about in the news, and I had also bought copies of two of her books, a used copy of *The Greenlanders* and a new copy of *Perestroika in Paris*. It took me a long time to get through the one about Greenland in the Middle Ages, but I thought that it did what a book is supposed to do, which is to pull you into a world that you had never even thought of before, and get you to think that you could picture it and understand it. I won't say that I loved it, but when I looked on Amazon at the reviews, I found that there were a lot of five-star ones. One that I agreed with was, "Believe it or not I found it hard to put down and I am sad that it's finished but it's hard to recommend it." I could easily picture the book set in Paris, not because I had been there, but because I could pull up Google Maps and have the Google boy walk around the Eiffel Tower and the west side of the Seine. I liked it (everyone seemed to), and eventually I saw the animated movie on Hulu. I gave it to a friend who liked it, too, and she told me she had a little fund she called "the Paris Fund"—she wanted to go to Paris and to Vienna. We talked about going together.

We all know what happened not long after that. I am not going to go into it, except to say that my friends and I were not surprised as much as we were outraged, and we took part in various women's rights rallies—as many as we could at our age—as well as the Pride-Fest not far from the arch and the courthouse. One friend of mine was particularly worried that the right of women to vote would be "rescinded," as she said. At the time we didn't believe her.

It took me a while to comprehend what the gawky girl had done. I didn't take the hint from the cover photo, even though I appreciated it. An acoustic Gibson didn't have anything to do with me. I thought it was amusing that she set the beginning of her book in our old house on Skinker, but I didn't think much about it—it's an interesting house and a good one for a writer to choose if she wants to keep her imagination going, or so I thought. I also remembered someone saying that Jane Austen had based Pemberley on Chatsworth House, and why not? I had based plenty of my songs on things I only heard or saw. When I was reading the opening part, I thought the characters she had made up were interesting enough. I didn't like the dog. I never liked dogs. When I was a girl in that house, we had three cats, Winnie, Poo, and Robin (the male). All three were Siamese cats, and Robin was almost gold. He was my favorite. I thought it was interesting that Jodie's uncle had taken her to Cahokia Downs. I'd never gone there, though my grandfather liked to explore Cahokia Mounds because he was, he said, an amateur historian. So, no uncle, no winnings, no superstition about a roll of two-dollar bills.

I think the first time I had an inkling that the book was about me was when she put in the parts about Jodie singing in the school Christmas pageant and some other concerts. I was surprised that she remembered that sort of detail, but I didn't think much of it until she sent Jodie to Penn State. One incident that I appreciated in a sort of odd way was when Jodie's mom drives down Brentwood Boulevard on the wrong side of the road. My mother never did that, but when I was in eighth grade, one night in January, I did get up from bed to go to the bathroom, and on my way back to my room, I thought I might get into bed with Mom, because it was a cold night. I opened the door, went into her room, and she wasn't there. I saw that the door to the balcony was slightly open, and I went to it. Mom was standing on the railing, holding one of the posts. I was old enough to know what not to do. I thought if I spoke, I would startle her and she would fall, but I also thought that if I didn't say anything, she would jump. The only thing I could think of was to go over to her bed and turn on the light, which I did. With the light on, I couldn't see her as well, but I did see that she didn't fall, that she hopped down onto the floor of the balcony (she was very agile, and only thirty-three at the time, because I was born when she was twenty). I never asked her and I still don't know what she was doing on the railing. She came over and kissed me, and said, "You all right, sweetie? Any nightmares?"

All I said was, "I had to go to the potty."

She took me back to bed.

So maybe there was something about Mom that the gawky girl noticed in those days that reminded her of a woman who did drive down Brentwood on the wrong side of the road. As I remember, the story was in the papers, and some people talked about it.

I think that she also remembered my cousin. She named him "Brucie" in the novel (maybe after Bruce Springsteen?). My cousin was named Brad, and he was a handsome guy. His father was my mother's older brother, old enough to fight in the Second World War, and prosperous enough to send Brad to our school until he flunked out in ninth grade and went to Webster. My mother had another brother, too, but he died in the 1930s, when he was twelve, of scarlet fever. Our family has lived in St. Louis since the nineteenth century. My grandparents did live in Webster Groves, but not on the street she described, which might have been Clark or Atalanta. They lived in Webster Park, on Hawthorne, and the money my mother and I had did not come from luck, it came from them. The list goes on, including the way she inflated "Jodie's" earnings from the songs she wrote. That made me laugh. But there were some things that were at least sort of true—Mom's drinking problem, the fact that my dad lived in New York and was out of my life by the time I was two, and the fact that I didn't really need to make money with my music, and so I was free to do as I pleased. Also, the twenty-five lovers. Maybe she remembered that number because it's an interesting number. That was what really clued me in that the novel was about me.

Once I realized this, the more I read, the angrier I got. One thing that was correct was our conversation at the Cheshire. I did tell her about the place in Roxbury and some other things. And she must have noticed that I admired her husband, because I did. And I do live in Clayton—she would have gotten that address from the list of addresses we received around the time of the reunion. Hers wasn't on it—it was a PO box.

I finished reading *Lucky* late one night, I went to bed, tossed and turned, and then got up at about four a.m. and sent her an email. It is still in my "sent" box. It read, "My name is Jamie, I never played the guitar, only the piano and the autoharp, I didn't write the lyrics you said I did, and I do not appreciate you going into any detail about the twenty-five lovers that I had. I feel like I have been invaded and then exposed. I would have said something about this when I saw that *NYT* review, but there wasn't a comment section. Thanks for nothing."

I did not mention this to any of my friends, but I did go to Left Bank Books and the Novel Neighbor and buy up all the copies, then I stored them in my basement. I didn't hear back from the gawky girl.

I think I finished reading it around Halloween. After I got it out of my system, there was plenty to do and think about during the holiday season. At the time, in St. Louis, every woman I knew was protesting, writing letters to the legislature, going house to house. Yes, there had been the Dred Scott decision, but that was in reaction to a previous decision, also originating in St. Louis, in which a Black woman was allowed to claim freedom because she had lived in a free state. She won her case in 1824. After that, several hundred slaves won their freedom in Missouri using her case as precedent. St. Louis has a long history of NOT agreeing with what a lot of other places in Missouri want, including slavery. A lot of us were taking women to Illinois for medical procedures, and when we brought them back, officials in St. Louis and St. Louis County turned a blind eye, as we knew they would. The winter was warm and rainy, and after New Year's there was a flood a ways down on the Mississippi. When things settled again (briefly), I saw *Lucky* on my shelf and picked it up. I reread it.

This time, there were no surprises, but there were things that I noticed. One of them was that she made me a thoughtful young woman with ideas and determination, and I liked that—I would say that that was the sort of young woman I had been. Another one was that she made some of my songs funny, which I had done (and she did say that she had loved to sing along, so she knew at least several of the songs I had written). One thing I hadn't noticed the first time was the remark that she gave Jodie on the Jay and the Americans song "Come a Little Bit Closer," where she said that I thought that when the woman in the bar said that her nasty boyfriend was her kind of man, she did it because she had to suck up to him to avoid getting abused. And maybe she said it to the narrator because she wanted to escape the abusive boyfriend. I had always thought that, and I wondered if the gawky girl had, too. At any rate, this time, I found the novel amusing and worth reading (one Amazon reviewer wrote, "Too somber for me," and another wrote, "This was okay, but I preferred *The Greenlanders*").

I had to put it down because of two more downpours that flooded the old railroad line that ran behind my house (and also my basement), but I finished it, and I wrote another email, apologizing for the first one. I said, "I am not going to thank you for using my material, but on my second read, I enjoyed it, and I realized that it is FICTION rather than invasion. Thank you for making me a well-meaning and thoughtful woman, also independent and a decent musician. We should get together again if we possibly can. I am sorry about what is happening in California. I remember you saying that your place is in something of a bubble because of the orientation of the mountains, and I hope that's still true. Anyway, if you wrote a sequel after my email, and put me in as a stupid bitch, I forgive you for that, too. Hope I hear from you, Yours, Jamie."

This time, I didn't hear back, either, so I assumed she had blocked me. I would have checked Meta, but that was gone, so I wrote the letter on paper and sent it to her publisher in New York. I didn't hear back from them, either, but there was also chaos in New York because of what was happening with the Arctic ice shelf.

Later that spring, one of our classmates from high school told me the gawky girl had died, but she didn't know how. Because of the demise of the internet, I couldn't look it up, but what I imagined was her falling down the stairs. Let's say, I thought, she was researching a sequel to *Perestroika in Paris,* and she went to Montmartre and fell down the stairs there. I imagined her rolling, bumping her head, passing out, doing it at night, and so being left to die because it was dark. Then, knowing what was happening all around me, I thought maybe she was the lucky one.

AROUND THAT TIME, many of my friends and relatives were talking about where to go. Brad was almost eighty and he lived in the house on Hawthorne that his family had owned since it was built. All of his three children wanted to get out of the US, but they didn't agree on where. Daphne, who was thirty-five, wanted to escape to Iceland, because she said that women there had equal rights, and she also suspected that climate change would favor Iceland, as it had, she said, during what she called "the Medieval Warm Period." Brady, as he was called, rather than Brad Jr., was almost forty. He did a lot of business in Germany, spoke German, and said that he loved Frankfurt. Mary and her husband, Ethan, who had three-year-old twins, had set their hearts on Norway, north of Oslo, in a lovely mountainous area. They were all convinced that Europe would handle the multiple crises we were going through better than the US. Brad didn't want to leave his house, though it was a big house and he could no longer afford to air-condition the whole place for six or eight months. The kids left, and he was alone in that giant house. He moved from room to room, taking his portable air cooler with him, but when the electricity started going out on a regular basis, he had to move to the basement.

The other problem was Russia. Everyone expected the Ukraine war to be over in a few months, but it lasted for years, and then everyone expected Putin to be assassinated or tossed out by his own people, but he hung on. I remember that we had all worried about nuclear war when the conflict in Ukraine had begun, and then we had put away those fears, thinking that no one would be that stupid. And the Ukraine war did end in a truce—Russia hung on to the eastern part, but they retreated from Odesa and Lviv. Then, a few years later, he decided that he wanted, or, I should say, was going to take over, Estonia, Latvia, and Lithuania. Everyone thought this was ridiculous, but that didn't mean there wouldn't be another war.

As for US politics, everyone who might conceivably read this knows what happened. Nothing was sufficient to challenge the loyalty of a good part of our population to a criminal, and when he wasn't elected, they went to war, even though a week after that election, he had a heart attack and died. His vice presidential candidate insisted on being made president, and his followers drove their SUVs and took their AR15s everywhere. In a lot of ways, a fatal fall down stairs in Paris was better than that.

Brad and I both still had some money, though, so about a year after his kids left for Iceland, Germany, and Norway, we bought tickets, or, I should say, I bought the tickets and I slowly prodded Brad into accepting the fact that we were leaving St. Louis. It was evident that he was losing it, because he would ask me where

Daphne was, and I would say, "Hella, Iceland," and then he would repeat that to himself a couple of times. Once in a while, maybe an hour later, he said, "Did you say Daphne has gone to hell?" And I would explain again—"Daphne moved to a town called Hella. She said it refers to rain, but it's actually a sweet place and not very rainy." He would nod. He remembered that Brady was in Germany better than he remembered that Mary and Ethan were in Norway. After I bought the tickets, he asked me several times if they were for a flight to Norway. They weren't.

Sometimes we would sit in the basement of his house or my house in our underwear and remember times that we thought were hot when we were young—how impressed we were if it got to be a hundred, or even close to a hundred, how we would go to Algonquin, a country club that his father belonged to, and stay all day, jumping in and out of the pool. In his neighborhood, some people had installed their own pools, but his parents didn't want to do that, and why would they? St. Louis County was full of country clubs. That summer—it was five years after the Supreme Court outlawed any sort of governmental climate restrictions—it got so hot that it wasn't possible to sleep even in the basement of his house. Over and over, I said, "We have got to get out of here."

What convinced him were two incidents that happened in the fall—a group of "crusaders," as they called themselves, exploded a car bomb outside of a doctor's office in Sappington, which was maybe ten miles from an abortion provider in Illinois. The doctors in the office were not gynecologists, they specialized in ENT, ophthalmology, and spinal rehab, but the two guys who drove the car to the office (and then ran) were convinced that those doctors were secretly shipping girls over to Illinois for abortions that the girls themselves didn't want. When they were caught, they claimed that they were "saviors," and as the police closed in, they shot themselves. And then, even though they were protected by security, the mayor, the first male mayor in years, and his wife and two children, were shot and killed in Forest Park.

Two weeks later, the day after Thanksgiving, Brad and I got on a plane, and now we are here.

When we first arrived, we were required to hand over our passports and our laptops and we were sent to a camp outside of Whitianga. We lived there for three months, and were interviewed by officials concerning our plans and our reasons for moving. Given what had happened in the US, the government was very suspicious of anyone who might have dedicated himself or herself to bringing American fascism to other countries. I would have thought that we were too old to be suspect, but I also thought that their concerns were realistic, since there was evidence that the US government had put pressure on Britain and the EU to suspend women's rights and restrictions on emissions. The place where they put us wasn't bad—two rooms and a small kitchen, with access to the local library and the local grocery store. There was a beach nearby that Brad and I often walked to, where James Cook had actually stopped for a while when he was sailing around the world.

The simpler life that we led here seemed to calm Brad, and his condition, whatever it was, steadied. Now we live in a small, spare house in a pleasant town with a lovely botanical garden. This may be the only spot in the entire world that remains similar to the world we grew up in—electricity, cars (all electric, though), affordable groceries, flowers, trees, vegetables, the last habitable place in a world bombed out and covered with radiation. I haven't told Brad that his children were killed in the war, that St. Louis (my favorite place) and Rome (his favorite) are gone. I know he doesn't have long to live, so I take out pieces of paper and read letters from the kids that I wrote myself, saying how much they are enjoying Iceland, Oslo, and Germany, promising to come for a visit sometime, "when things cool down." He always says, "They'll like it here. Maybe we can talk them into moving."

I know that I will outlive him, as I have outlived everyone I ever knew. If anyone ever reads what I have written here, what I want them to know is that that is not a piece of luck.

A NOTE ABOUT THE AUTHOR

JANE SMILEY is the author of numerous novels, including *A Thousand Acres,* which was awarded the Pulitzer Prize, and the Last Hundred Years Trilogy: *Some Luck, Early Warning,* and *Golden Age*. She is the author as well of several works of nonfiction and books for young adults. A member of the American Academy of Arts and Letters, she has also received the PEN Center USA Lifetime Achievement Award for Literature. She lives in Northern California.

A NOTE ON THE TYPE

This book was set in Granjon, a type named in compliment to Robert Granjon, a type cutter and printer active in Antwerp, Lyons, Rome, and Paris from 1523 to 1590. Granjon, the boldest and most original designer of his time, was one of the first to practice the trade of typefounder apart from that of printer.

Linotype Granjon was designed by George W. Jones, who based his drawings on a face used by Claude Garamond (ca. 1480–1561) in his beautiful French books. Granjon more closely resembles Garamond's own type than do any of the various modern faces that bear his name.

Composed by North Market Street Graphics,
Lancaster, Pennsylvania

Printed and bound by Berryville Graphics,
Berryville, Virginia

Designed by Cassandra J. Pappas